I0742235

YESTERDAY'S SAVIOR

Keith Bliss

EDGE SCIENCE FICTION AND FANTASY PUBLISHING
An Imprint of HADES PUBLICATIONS, INC.
CALGARY

Yesterday's Savior

Copyright © 2017 by Keith Bliss

EDGE SCIENCE FICTION AND FANTASY PUBLISHING
An Imprint of HADES PUBLICATIONS, INC.
P.O. Box 1714, Calgary, Alberta, T2P 2L7, Canada

The EDGE Team:
Producer: Brian Hades
Acquisitions Editor: Ella Beaumont
Edited by: Michelle Heumann
Editorial Consultant: Sharon Sheffield
Cover Design: Ella Beaumont
Cover Art Elements: Nupean Pruprong, Eliane Haykal, Vlastimil Šesták
Book Design: Mark Steele
Publicist: Janice Shoults

ISBN: 9781770531611

EDGE Science Fiction and Fantasy Publishing and Hades Publications, Inc. acknowledges the ongoing support of the Alberta Foundation for the Arts and the Canada Council for the Arts for our publishing programme.

Library and Archives Canada Cataloguing in Publication
CIP Data on file with the National Library of Canada
ISBN: 9781770531611
(e-Book ISBN: 9781770531451)

FIRST EDITION
(20170911)
Printed in USA
www.edgewebsite.com

Publisher's Note:

Thank you for purchasing this book. It began as an idea, was shaped by the creativity of its talented author, and was subsequently molded into the book you have before you by a team of editors and designers.

Like all EDGE books, this book is the result of the creative talents of a dedicated team of individuals who all believe that books (whether in print or pixels) have the magical ability to take you on an adventure to new and wondrous places powered by the author's imagination.

As EDGE's publisher, I hope that you enjoy this book. It is a part of our ongoing quest to discover talented authors and to make their creative writing available to you.

We also hope that you will share your discovery and enjoyment of this novel on social media through Facebook, Twitter, Goodreads, Pinterest, etc., and by posting your opinions and/or reviews on Amazon and other review sites and blogs. By doing so, others will be able to share your discovery and passion for this book.

Brian Hades, publisher

Acknowledgement

Thank you to Georgie Preuschoff for her invaluable feedback on the first draft, to Katharina Camp for her support, ideas, and encouragement, and to my parents for everything.

"I cannot and I will not recant anything, since it is neither safe nor right to go against conscience. May God help me. Amen."

(Martin Luther — *Reply to the Diet of Worms*, April 18, 1521)

PROLOGUE

London, 2037

The old redbrick building had somehow managed to survive World War II, but it had been razed to the ground by the fire that had gutted the entire row just two days ago. Now, after the blaze had been extinguished, hardly one brick was left standing on another. Swirls of wispy, acrid smoke rose unhurriedly from parts of the rubble that had not been as thoroughly doused with water from the fire hoses. A surly-looking workman in his late fifties, his shabby blue overalls blackened by soot, carefully led the way through the wreckage of the building to a place where an ancient-looking stone staircase in the foundation had been half-heartedly cleared of debris. Stumbling awkwardly after him over the hazardous terrain, three young men in their mid to late twenties wearing dark overalls and white priest's collars eventually caught up and peered curiously down the staircase into the darkness below. The fire inspector had previously given them the permission to enter the wreckage, having deemed it safe, but the priests still looked rather skeptical.

"Dahn there," the workman said in a bored voice, as if he had already shown hundreds of people the same uninteresting site a dozen times. He waved a fat, grubby finger in the general direction of the stairs. After a lung-filling drag on a homemade cigarette stuffed with highly illegal tobacco, the man coughed and spluttered for a moment before he was able to speak again. The stench of sweat and illicit smoke surrounding him was almost unbearable to the three priests. He added in his thick Cockney accent, "Dunno wot all the fuss is abaht if yer ask me. Coupla old papers in rusty metal boxes. So bloody wot, eh?" He turned on his heel and stalked off, muttering incessantly as if disgusted by this imposition on his valuable time.

The three younger men looked at each other, suppressing snickers, then back at the blackness at the bottom of the stairs. A few seconds later one of them, unable to stifle a smile, raised his eyebrows at the tallest of the group.

"Well, the boss put you in charge, Brian. Down you go!" he said jovially.

Shrugging, Brian clicked on a flashlight, pointed its extremely powerful bluish-white beam down the steps, and proceeded to follow it into the cellar of the burnt-out building. Halfway down he paused, realizing he was alone. He turned and admonished his companions, "Come on, then, I'm not going on my own!"

The other two grinned and followed him down. The beams of their flashlights stabbed through the darkness and illuminated a small space that was flooded with about ten centimeters of water. At this point, the joviality ceased.

"Oh, you're joking!" complained one of the men. "I've got my good shoes on!"

Dmitri was new at this, and had not been prepared for such eventualities. When he had joined the Church's historical department, he had thought it would involve a desk job in a warm, comfortable office — not splashing around up to his ankles in filthy water in derelict buildings! None of them was particularly thrilled about the idea of getting their feet wet, but with various groaning sounds and sighs of resignation, all three tentatively stepped in, shivering at the unpleasant sensation of cold, dirty water flooding into their shoes. Not knowing if there was broken glass or perhaps jagged, rusty metal in the murky water, they felt it best to keep their shoes on rather than risk impaling their feet on something lurking beneath the surface.

The room was about three meters by five, and the low ceiling meant that Brian was forced to stoop a little to avoid banging his head. The walls were covered from floor to ceiling with shelves bearing metal boxes about thirty centimeters long, twenty-five centimeters wide, and fifteen centimeters high, each with a tightly fitting lid. Despite the rusty, dilapidated look of the boxes, closer inspection revealed that the lids came off easily enough and that each box was filled with old, yellowing papers.

"Hmm. Doesn't look like anything spectacular," Chris remarked. "Late nineteenth-, early twentieth-century government archives. Still, pretty well preserved, considering. Must've been sealed up down here the whole time."

"Oh, well," Dmitri chimed in, "every bit helps."

"OK," Brian said, with an air of finality, "let's get the stuff out and take it home."

They started removing the metal boxes from the flooded cellar and carrying them up into the daylight, which they hadn't been exposed to for well over a hundred years. About half an hour later, all the boxes were laid out on the well-kept lawn in front of the burnt-out building. Fifteen minutes after that they were loaded into the immaculately clean Church-owned electric van in which the three men had arrived. As was the case with all property belonging to the Church, the van bore the symbol of the Second Coming on its sides.

"So, same procedure as last time, then?" Chris asked as they drove away. "Split the loot three ways?"

"Sure," Dmitri said, smiling. "You can have my share of the 'loot', too, if you want. It's going to take ages to sort that lot."

"Come on," Brian said, attempting to adopt a more serious tone. "These might be important historical documents. Anything that can shed a little more light on the past should be taken seriously. Who knows, we may even turn up something sensational in this little treasure trove."

"Always the optimist, eh, Brian?" Chris replied. "You'll make cardinal one day!"

They all laughed. Although Brian was the most serious and responsible of the three, none of them could imagine one of their own becoming a *cardinal*. Not even Brian.

Roughly an hour later, they had returned to their headquarters just outside London and began unloading the boxes immediately, carrying their cargo into a relatively new two-story building. Once inside, they walked down a long corridor and into a medium-sized room with high windows. As it was starting to get dark outside, bright LED lights sprang to life automatically as they entered, and they began placing their boxed documents on the thick wooden workbenches that lined three of the walls. The fourth wall was reserved for large metal filing cabinets with cryptic-looking labels denoting the historical and chronological data of their contents. Above the filing cabinets, a life-sized picture of Jesus Christ, the Lamb of God, adorned the wall. In the past, such iconic pictures had been oil paintings, reproductions of oil paintings, even pop art. The picture on this wall, however, was an actual color photograph. In fact, most homes and workplaces in the Christian world had an actual color photograph of Christ on the wall, a testament to the belief in the Second Coming.

"All right, then," said Brian, once they had placed all their boxes on the workbenches. "I'll go make the tea and you two can get started."

The other two young men donned thin, white cotton gloves and opened one box each, removing its contents with tweezers and carefully spreading the yellowing papers over their respective workbenches. Both of them knew, judging by the amount of material that made up this haul, that they would be here for all the working hours of the next few weeks, sifting through the past that these papers represented, sorting information, gleaning facts, some of which might be useful or interesting to historians. The historians, who would work with the data collected by Brian's small team, were better-qualified priests: colleagues who held master's degrees and doctorates in history, anthropology, theology, or archaeology.

Brian returned with three steaming mugs of tea and some biscuits on a tray. "And? Found anything interesting?"

Chris and Dmitri merely grumbled, shaking their heads and reaching gratefully for the tea. Brian understood their lack of enthusiasm, but he really did believe he was doing an important and necessary job. He was absolutely convinced that one day he would find something sensational for his Church. As the burnt-out building in which these archives had been found was an old government building, though, they knew that most of what they had would most likely be horribly boring statistics: facts and figures from long defunct government departments whose documentation, for one reason or another, had not been digitized. In the twentieth century most important documents had been stored on electronic media, so presumably these papers had been overlooked when all useless data had been destroyed.

For the next few hours, the men worked diligently, the silence only broken occasionally by a quiet grunt, a pensive "Hmm", or a sarcastically mumbled "Fascinating!" But just before they were due to finish for the day, Chris muttered, "That's odd!" This in itself was not all that remarkable, but the way he said it made the other two turn toward him.

"What's odd?" Dmitri enquired.

"Well, up to now, all the documents I've had the immense pleasure of perusing had something to do with nineteenth-century acquisitions of ink and paper, and other such enthralling treasures of that peculiar age," he replied, with the humor of a man attempting to make light of a particularly mind-numbing situation. "But I've just picked out two sheets of paper that have nothing whatsoever to do with any of that. In fact, they don't look like they belong in this box at all. They appear to be pages from some kind of diary."

Dmitri sighed. "Probably someone just chucked everything he could find into a pile, no matter what it was."

"Yeah, but this looks different."

"I don't know about you two, but I've really had enough for one day," Brian said, rubbing his tired eyes. A quick glance at his watch confirmed his suspicions. It was late. "Tell you what; it's Friday evening and I reckon we're all ready for a nice quiet weekend. Leave everything on the tables and we'll deal with it first thing Monday morning."

"Oh, thank the Lamb!" Dmitri exclaimed.

Undecided, Chris glanced once more at the sheet of paper he was still holding with his tweezers. Looking at his colleagues' expectant faces, though, he made up his mind and placed the paper carefully on the workbench. "You're right. These things have been lying around for a hundred years at least. They can wait a few more days."

With that, they left everything as it was and locked the door behind them.

CHAPTER 1

Liverpool, England, December 17, 2060

Before the Second Coming of Our Savior, the Lamb of God, most people lived in fear of war, poverty, famine, natural disasters, unemployment, and hundreds of other things over which they had no control. This all changed when the Lamb of God returned to Earth. The Signs had been prophesied for thousands of years, but people had not taken them seriously or fully comprehended them. So when the Lamb suddenly appeared, they found it difficult to believe what they were seeing. It didn't fit with the Bible, either. According to St. John in Revelation, the Second Coming of Christ would herald the end of the world. Mankind would be judged, and life as we know it would cease to exist. So how is it possible that the Lamb returned and we are all still here? There is a simple answer: the Lamb in His eternal mercy has once again saved humanity by intervening with His Father, the Lord our God, on our behalf. He has given us, for reasons known only to Himself, a second chance! What love! What empathy!

No one today seems to want to remember much about the time before the Second Coming. Things looked pretty grim in those days, one thing on which almost all experts agree. In every country of the world there was war, greed, famine, or a combination of all three. Some people were ridiculously rich; some had to kill in order to remain alive for just one more pitiful, miserable day. Luckily I was not yet born in those unhappy days, so I will have nothing to explain to the Lamb when the time comes to join Him in Paradise.

It began exactly fifty years ago today. The Second Coming of the Lamb was in a now defunct institution called the "United Nations General Assembly." The speaker at the time of the Initial Appearance was the ambassador for the Central African Republic. The government of this troubled country was not popular with other UN members, as they had continued to purchase weapons with the money granted by the UN instead of feeding their starving population. The speaker noticed that something uncharacteristically interesting for a UN meeting was happening when looks of stunned amazement crossed the faces of the delegates before him. He must have believed that the interpreters had misinterpreted something he had said. If he looked behind him, he would then have seen the "Apparition," as the Lamb was called in those unenlightened days.

He appeared to them as a tall man with the olive skin of someone from the Middle East, a full black beard, and shoulder-length black hair, wearing simple white robes and primitive sandals. In fact, Our Savior materialized before the UN precisely as He has been depicted in paintings over the last two millennia. Surely this was done for the benefit of those who would otherwise have doubted Him. The only real surprise was the color of his eyes. Instead of the dark brown of the majority of people from the Middle East, the Lamb's eyes were a piercing light blue which seemed to mesmerize anyone who gazed into them. Today we can only smile knowingly and think, "Well of course. He is the Savior, after all!"

> *David Dyson, Seventh Grade, School of the Second Coming No. 21,*
>
> *District 12, Liverpool, England, December 17, 2060 Inter-Schools essay-writing competition.*

CHAPTER 2

Archives of the Holy Church of the Second Coming
New York City, 2075

David Dyson's whole life had been leading up to this moment. He felt a warm glow, remembering the faces of his proud, aging parents — flown in from England especially for the occasion — as he was awarded his doctorate diploma by the president of the University of the Holy Church of the Second Coming of the Lamb, New York. He had always been somewhat of a prodigy, never having to actually sit down and learn. He had simply soaked up knowledge and stored it with wide-eyed enthusiasm as his teachers had imparted it to him, excelling at every subject in the Church's theological schools in his English homeland. Whenever anyone had asked him, even at a very early age, what he wanted to do when he grew up, he would invariably reply, "Serve the Holy Church of the Lamb!" The Church — *his* Church — had educated him, had put him through college studying theology, history, and archaeology, culminating most recently in his doctorate in history.

Yes, he had been a shining example, a high flyer. His parents had eagerly leaped at the opportunity for their precious only child to be educated at the prestigious Church schools after winning a scholarship at the tender age of ten. They had been delighted when letters full of praise for their son's academic abilities and strength of character arrived at their tiny flat in Liverpool, England; letters signed by an actual cardinal, no less! And when their son had graduated from high school with honors as the student of the year, the pride felt by Mr. and Mrs. Dyson had known no bounds.

Things had turned somewhat sour, however, when David had announced to his parents that he intended to become a priest. Somehow, all three of them had always known deep within their hearts that he was going to take up this career. Given his education, his daily indoctrination by the priests and nuns — outstandingly well-qualified and highly trained priests and nuns who were even respected in their fields by the academic community outside the Church — it had seemed inevitable that David would one day choose this path. Nevertheless, his parents had attempted to avert the inevitable. "You're so bright," they would say. "Don't throw it all away, son! You can be anything you want to be!"

"But this *is* what I want to be!" he would invariably reply. And invariably, frustration would rise in his voice as he saw that his parents simply did not understand. "I want to give my life to the Church!"

If young David had been a little older at the time, he might have realized that there were ulterior motives in his parents' arguments. Despite all the evidence of the Second Coming — the video footage, the eyewitness reports, etcetera — his father remained an agnostic. Well, at least this was better than being an atheist, but it was nevertheless a far cry from actual faith. Nothing David or his mother could say or do could convince John Dyson that Jesus Christ had actually returned in the Second Coming promised in the Bible. Mary Dyson had given up attempting to convince him, but David saw it as his duty to continue trying, in order to save his father's immortal soul from eternal damnation.

His mother, however, had a completely different agenda for wanting to prevent her only child from joining the priesthood. She wanted a pair of grandchildren: one boy, one girl. Her heart ached at the thought of her wonderful child never falling in love with a beautiful, intelligent young woman and eventually giving her two beautiful, intelligent grandchildren whom she would spoil in a way that only a grandmother can. She silently wept herself to sleep many a night thinking about the loss, not only for herself and the never-to-be-born grandchildren, but also for her beloved son who would never experience the joys of being in love and of fatherhood. He would be missing so much!

Intense pleading, partly accompanied by sobbing, on the part of Dyson's mother, and the usually calm but sometimes heated theological debates with his father had not been as strong an influence on him as his calling. In the end, he had left England to study at the Church's most prestigious university in New York City, becoming, at the age of twenty-four, what he knew in his heart of hearts he had always wanted to be: a priest of the Church of the Second Coming, humbly serving the Lamb of God. His faith was blind, unquestioning. Even back then, his teachers knew he would go far. David Dyson was indeed a rare breed: an excellent scientist whose faith in the Church was rock-solid.

The Church of the Second Coming had been good to him — better than he could ever have imagined. He had always been interested in history and archaeology, and the Church had noticed, supporting his interests, financing his studies, deploying him on archaeological digs in the Holy Land. He had continued his studies, receiving master's degrees in history and archaeology, until it had one day all culminated in this: his doctorate and his subsequent promotion, at the age of twenty-six, to the position of Keeper of the Sacred Archives of the Holy Church of the Second Coming of the Lamb in New York City. This was the home of the Church's central database for archaeological and historical information gathered over the past two millennia. The Archives contained not only the full contents of the old Vatican library in digital form, but also most books on the subjects of history, theology, ancient languages, and archaeology ever printed in the western world. The Archives building was the workplace of thousands of historical and archaeological researchers responsible for gathering new information and processing it together with all the information that had been gathered in the past.

Although it was Saturday, and he was not officially meant to start work until Monday, Dyson was as impatient as a small child on Christmas Eve, unable to wait to see his new office. If he had any fault at all, it was his all-consuming passion to succeed in everything he did. Standing outside the enormous building that housed his new place of work, the most accurate word to describe what he felt would be awe. He looked up at a tall, rounded skyscraper made of brushed stainless steel and blue-tinted glass. Almost at the top of the north side of the building, a colossal, dark blue holographic crucifix, superimposed with the number two in a circle, hovered about two meters away from the wall. He felt proud to be a part of the Church of the Second Coming. For David Dyson was not merely one of the flock; he was a shepherd, working to advance the knowledge of mankind. Thus, as far as he was concerned, he was working for the good of mankind as a whole.

Two grim-looking, extremely muscular, and heavily armed security guards — Salvation Army, Dyson noticed, judging by their black uniforms and silver Church insignia — stood before the glass doors leading into the building. The chiseled jaws, steely, emotionless eyes, and menacing machine pistols left no room for doubt: if you were not supposed to enter this place, you wouldn't. One of them regarded Dyson's face, then the silver cross dangling from the chain around his neck. Not knowing the priest personally, the guard addressed him gruffly but nevertheless politely. People were never rude to priests; you never knew how powerful they were or what connections they had.

"How can I help you, Father?"

Dyson held out his left arm, his palm facing up, toward the guard.

"Father David Dyson. I'm the new Keeper of the Archives here," he replied, nodding up at the skyscraper. With a swift, fluid movement, the guard whipped out a laser scanner from a pouch strapped to his belt and scanned the tiny silicon chip embedded in Dyson's arm. He then shot a glance at his partner, who briefly consulted a small, flexible screen built into the left sleeve of his uniform. The second guard looked up and nodded wordlessly to the first black-clad man, who motioned Dyson to enter the building: "Proceed, Father. Have a blessed day."

Dyson traced a number two in the air with his forefinger and middle finger before the two guards and smiled at them.

"Thank you, my son. May the Lamb be with you both."

The guards bowed briefly but politely to the priest and moved aside to allow him to enter the building.

Dyson had thought the *exterior* of the skyscraper was impressive, but when he saw the *interior*, his eyes widened involuntarily and he could not keep himself from letting out an audible gasp of surprise. The floors and ceilings were made of white marble infused with light-gray to black veins. Fine, extremely intricate detailing depicting floral patterns and verses from the Bible was picked out in gold on the floor, so that everyone entering the building unconsciously read Bible verses as they followed the marble path to the front desk. The windows, which appeared silvery blue and opaque from the outside, allowed the occupants of the building to look out as if there was no glass at all. This was rather disconcerting at first, but Dyson was sure he would get used to it eventually.

The lobby was vast, reaching up at least four stories. Dyson had not expected to find anyone here on a Saturday, but dozens of priests and even a few bishops, along with some civilian staff, were busily traversing the huge space, circumnavigating the fountain that formed the colossal centerpiece. At the heart of the fountain, which was about two stories high, stood a statue of Christ the Redeemer with arms outstretched at ninety-degree angles to the body. The base upon which the Christ figure stood was adorned with larger-than-life-sized cherubs chiseled out of pink marble. From the stone vases they carried, water poured into the marble circle that formed the base of the fountain. Solidly padded leather sofas and armchairs were grouped around the transparent walls, presumably for visitors to make themselves comfortable while they waited for a member of the staff to fetch them for an appointment. Real palm trees appeared to be growing, somewhat incongruously, out of the marble floor. The walls were adorned with gigantic semi-circular marble vases from which hung all manner of vines, reminiscent of the fabled Hanging Gardens of Babylon. This building had clearly been designed by an architect who had no budget restrictions whatsoever.

From the corner of his eye Dyson spotted a black-uniformed guard peering at him suspiciously from beneath the peak of his cap, a machine pistol nestled in the crook of his arm. *Uh-oh*, thought Dyson. *Can't just loiter here!* He quickly made his way to the reception desk before the guard had an opportunity to come over and question him.

"First time here, Father?" enquired a middle-aged receptionist, smiling kindly. She was used to the awe when people entered the Archives building for the first time. She was good at her job: the calming tone of her voice and her welcoming smile had been practiced over the years to allay the fears of those summoned here for some kind of dressing down, or of those who were here to begin a career on the Church's ladder to the top.

"Err, yes, I'm new here," replied Dyson.

"That's all right, Father. If you wouldn't mind…" The woman waved her hand at a palm-sized rectangle of clear yellow plastic mounted on a miniature tripod on the counter next to her. Dyson knew what she wanted and positioned his face in front of the scanner. A second later the receptionist's face lit up as Dyson was recognized by her computer.

"Oh, good morning, Father Dyson! We weren't expecting you today."

"Well, I hope it's no trouble, but I'd quite like to see my office."

"No trouble at all, Father. Just a moment, let's organize your key."

Without thinking about it, Dyson stretched out his left forearm and placed it in a molded depression in the desktop. A green laser scanned his chip, then an audible *beep* told him that the scanning process was over and he lifted his arm from the desk.

"There you go, Father Dyson. Your chip is now programmed to open your office door. Welcome to the Archives."

"Thank you very much," he replied, and enquired as to the whereabouts of his office.

After taking the elevator to the floor of his new workplace, he stood before the heavy wooden doors of the room that had been assigned to him, pensively fingering the symbol of his faith on the silver chain around his neck. Taking a deep breath, he pulled back the left sleeve of his cassock. Glancing up at the security camera, he suppressed an unseemly grin of pure, unadulterated joy, and held the chip embedded in his arm to the small white box on the wall. A discreet beep issued from the box, and a tiny orange light turned green for a second. Almost simultaneously, the double doors swung silently and invitingly open, pointing the way into Dyson's new office.

Despite the air conditioning that maintained the temperature at a constant twenty degrees Celsius, the air in the room seemed somehow stale. This had nothing to do with the contents of the room, but because the room had been sealed for several weeks since the death of his predecessor, the last Keeper, and pending Dyson's own appointment to the coveted position.

There was a definite spring in Dyson's step as he strode happily into his new domain. If all went as planned, this would be his home from home for the rest of his working life. Here he would have assistants, resources, and centuries of digitized knowledge at his fingertips, to aid him in his lifelong passion: unraveling the mysteries of the past. David Dyson's goal was to play a major role in painting a complete historical picture of the development of the human race from its primitive beginnings all the way to the present day; to fill the myriad gaps which, even in the twenty-first century, did not permit a complete understanding of the history of humanity. This would be his life's work: finding the truth as proof of his devotion to the Lamb, forsaking all others before his Savior, as was required of him by the Bible.

Enjoying the quiet moment alone in his new domain, Dyson took in his surroundings. Considering this room provided just one workplace, it was large, *very large*: about fifteen by fifteen meters, with a four-meter ceiling. A glittering, ancient-looking crystal chandelier dangled ostentatiously from the center of the ceiling, more decoration than of practical use, hence the numerous modern wall lamps strategically positioned around the room. The luminescent tubes were concealed within decorative chrome-plated orbs that caused the light to illuminate the walls and ceiling without dazzling the occupants. The invisible glass of the wall to the left of the doors offered a breathtaking 175th-floor view across the city of New York. At the far end of the office stood an enormous solid mahogany desk. A virtual keyboard was projected from inside the bulky piece of furniture onto a thick plate of crystal-clear plastic set into the desktop, ready to call up a 3D virtual monitor cube above the desk. Three short, narrow slits set into the desktop next to the keyboard indicated that the computer system could simultaneously process three mem-tabs, a medium for storing vast amounts of data on a seemingly featureless, wafer-thin but exceptionally durable strip of plastic. Behind the desk stood a sumptuously padded, old-fashioned, dark brown leather armchair on five rollers. In front of the desk there were two rather less luxurious leather armchairs on four stainless steel feet. In the center of the room stood a long conference table with solid-looking padded leather chairs for twenty people. Around the three walls that were not the glass outer wall of the building were various shelves and workbenches for storing and examining original documents and artifacts.

After a brief glimpse through the windows, Dyson walked to the leather armchair behind the desk and dropped heavily into its thick, sturdy padding. He was delighted to discover that the chair was equipped with a spring mechanism, allowing him to recline at a satisfyingly relaxing angle. In his exuberance, Dyson irreverently pushed at the desk with his feet and propelled himself gently backward, giving his legs room to stretch out beneath the desk. The last few days had been extremely hectic, what with the doctorate ceremony, his promotion to the Archives, playing the tour guide for his parents' visit to New York, and finally accompanying them to the airport and saying goodbye.

This was at last a long-awaited moment of peace and tranquility. Placing both hands behind his head and locking his fingers, he closed his eyes and finally allowed the long-suppressed grin to creep across his face. Modesty forbade him from admitting it to a single living soul, but there was one thing he knew for certain: he was born to do this job. He was the only one who could utilize the resources now at his disposal to glean the maximum degree of knowledge from the available data. Hopefully, he would even be able to combine known facts with new knowledge and take one more step toward discovering the ultimate truth from the relatively sparse information other historians had laboriously pieced together in the centuries before him. Consciously inhaling as deep a breath as his lungs would allow, he intended to release a *very* long sigh that would simultaneously express the satisfaction of his achievement, the relief that the stressful past few days were now over, and the pleasure of having absolutely nothing at all to do until Monday, when his new post officially began.

"Father Dyson?"

The sharp tone of the voice, obviously no stranger to issuing commands, shook Dyson from his reveries. His now wide-open green eyes darted to the double doors from where the strong baritone voice had come. As it was Saturday, and this floor of the building had seemed deserted, Dyson had neglected to close the doors.

Oh, Holy Lamb! he thought, sitting bolt upright in the armchair as if electrocuted. For there, in the doorway, stood a cardinal; instantly recognizable by the scarlet piping of his black simar and the scarlet zucchetto on his head — the color originally chosen by the old Roman Catholic church to denote the cardinal's willingness to shed his blood for the faith. This interpretation of the cardinal's red uniform had been another feature that had been all but forgotten toward the end of the Roman Catholic Church era. The Church of the Second Coming, however, with its dedicated — some might say fanatical — clergy, was determined to revive such symbolism. The man appeared to be in his mid-sixties, but nevertheless made a much younger impression with his confident, upright stance. His arms were crossed and there was a smile on his face. Something about the smile, though, seemed insincere. Dyson could not quite put his finger on what it was, but something was definitely not right.

Gathering his decorum, he realized that he, a mere priest, was still sitting in the presence of a cardinal.

"Your Eminence!" The words left his mouth with more energy than he had intended; almost a shout.

In his rush to stand and walk toward his superior, he pushed the heavy leather chair backward with too much force, causing it to crash loudly into the wall behind him. With a burning face and ears now as scarlet as the cardinal's zucchetto, Dyson marched briskly toward the doorway and dutifully went down on one knee before the older man, who stretched out his hand, palm facing down, fingers spread, so that Dyson could kiss his ring. Having performed this centuries-old ritual, Dyson stood uncomfortably before the cardinal, unable to look for long into his cold, steel-gray eyes.

"I do apologize for startling you like that, my son," the cardinal began, his mouth, but not his eyes, still smiling. There was an oily, condescending tone in his voice. "I have merely come to congratulate our new colleague on his doctorate and his appointment to the Archives."

Dyson was still embarrassed about his superior finding him as he had done, but managed to reply, "Thank you, Eminence," in a relatively steady voice.

The silence that followed was exceedingly uncomfortable for Dyson, but the cardinal did nothing to relieve it. In fact, he seemed to be relishing Dyson's discomfort. Finally Dyson felt he had to say something.

"I'm afraid you have the advantage, Eminence," he managed to say.

"Hmm? Oh, I see what you mean! I do apologize, Father!" the cardinal declared in a voice that was anything but apologetic. "I am Cardinal Goodfellowe. I am the administrator of this facility. Your *boss*, so to speak."

He stressed the word "boss" as if it were distasteful to him. Again Dyson had the impression that the man was insincere, even sneering at him. *But why would he want to do that?* Dyson put it down to nerves and dismissed the notion.

"It is an honor to meet you, Eminence," he replied.

Once again there was an uncomfortable silence, which Dyson felt obliged to fill. "Of course I will do my best to serve the Holy Church with my work."

"Yes, I'm *sure* you will," Cardinal Goodfellowe acquiesced, his humorless smile not faltering. "Father, let me say just one thing before I leave you to relax in your comfortable chair."

Ouch! Dyson thought, the blood of embarrassment once again rising to his cheeks.

"One thing I hope you will remember as long as you are serving the Church under my administration is this: there is apparent truth and there is genuine truth. One type of truth is acceptable, the other is not. Your task is to find whatever you might find, and present your findings to me. You, Father Dyson, do not decide on the acceptability or the quality of truth. That is a matter for His Holiness the Arch-Cardinal to decide, once I have presented all the facts to him. If you observe this rule, Father, we shall get along famously. If you do not, however, then I am afraid we shall be looking for a new Keeper of the Archives in the very near future."

Dyson's mind reeled. *"Apparent truth" and "genuine truth"? How can there be more than one truth? Surely there is only one God-given truth acceptable to the Lamb! The cardinal gathers facts and presents them to the Holy Father? The Holy Father decides which "truth" is the "genuine truth"? What could that mean? Did he just threaten to fire me?*

Dyson had barely finished this train of thought when the cardinal said, "Well, Father Dyson, I hope we've now clearly established a basis for a good working relationship. All that remains is for me to wish you all the best in your new position, and to say that I look forward to working with you for many years to come. Good day to you. And may the Lamb be with you."

With that the cardinal turned slowly on his heel and, without waiting for a reply, left the room. As he walked away, Dyson noticed that the cardinal's left leg seemed to be somehow lame: the man had a pronounced limp.

Still a little shaken, shocked even, by the encounter, Dyson quietly closed the doors to the office before returning to his leather armchair. Realizing that his brow was covered in sweat, he wiped it unceremoniously with a sleeve of his cassock.

What in the Lamb's name was all that about? After he had managed to calm down, two more questions occurred to him: *Why was the cardinal here on a Saturday, and how did he know I was here?* The first question seemed relatively easy to answer. The lobby had been a hive of activity; and, after all, this *was* New York City. Presumably most people at Church Headquarters worked on Saturdays. The other question was rather more troubling, though. Were there spies here…reporting every little thing directly to the Cardinal? *No*, he thought after a while. *There are thousands of people working in Church Headquarters. Cardinal Goodfellowe couldn't possibly keep tabs on everyone. Could he*? Dyson shook his head to clear away such nonsense. He had merely been embarrassed and shaken by the unexpected meeting.

Dyson remained in his office for another two hours, testing the computer's instantaneous access to the vast amount of data stored on the Church's database, and marveling at his hitherto unprecedented access. It took him some time to put the unpleasant encounter with Cardinal Goodfellowe out of his mind.

— «» —

On his first official day of work at the Archives, as Dyson was walking toward the elevators in the magnificent foyer, two priests approached him. The older of the two wore a long black cassock like Dyson's own. He was about fifty, quite short, with stubbly, graying hair. The other man was dressed in a dark gray suit with a white clerical collar, and looked remarkably similar to Dyson: roughly one metre eighty tall, medium build, short brown hair, late twenties. The older man was the first to speak, offering a handshake and smiling warmly.

"Father Dyson, on behalf of the Department of Archives, we'd like to congratulate you on your promotion and welcome you to your new position. My name is Tom O'Rourke and I'll be your personal assistant."

Dyson shook the man's hand firmly and returned the smile.

"This is Simon Evans," O'Rourke continued, before Dyson could speak. "As I'm also the liaison officer between this office and several other departments, I'll be away on missions for the Archives rather a lot, so Father Evans will act as your executive assistant; a kind of liaison between you and me, so to speak."

Evans beamed and also offered Dyson a hand.

"Pleased to meet you, Father," he said, shaking Dyson's hand with a firm, sincere grip. "We've heard so much about you."

"Please," said Dyson, smiling at both of them, "just call me David."

O'Rourke seemed delighted.

"Tom," he said buoyantly.

"Simon," Father Evans added.

O'Rourke pointed at the row of elevators along one wall of the lobby.

"Shall we go up to your office?" he asked.

"Let's go," Dyson replied affably, indicating with an open-palmed gesture that his new colleagues should lead the way.

While they were waiting for the enormous stainless steel doors to open, Dyson realized that although he had a good idea what was expected of him in his new post, and an even better idea of how he was going to fulfill these expectations, he knew practically nothing about the day-to-day running of the Archives Department and what went on behind the scenes. So he asked O'Rourke and Evans who was responsible for what, who reported to whom and when, and so on.

"Well, David," O'Rourke replied, obviously having been waiting to deliver a prepared speech on the topic, "as you already know, the Archives Department is the heart of the Church information system. Any information on anything to do with history, religion, archaeology, anthropology, philosophy, philology, or paleontology from anywhere on the planet and from any period in time is stored here. In fact, we have, on more than one occasion, been compared to the Great Library of Alexandria. From time to time, we receive enquiries from institutions and governments from all over the globe. Sometimes someone is asking for historical information; occasionally some religious dispute has to be settled.

"As the new Keeper of Archives, you will not be troubled with the petty details of it all, however. Such mundane matters are left to the hundreds of clerks working here for that specific purpose. No, David, you and I have, by the grace of God, a much greater purpose. You now have a wide range of unbelievably powerful resources at your disposal and can deploy them as you see fit. There are ongoing archaeological digs around the globe, and there are researchers working on documents, some of which are thousands of years old. Your principal task is to coordinate all of these and put together the information in a coherent form for the cardinals, even for the Arch-Cardinal himself. You are now responsible for collating this information and deploying the staff in this department. You can decide who does what among your staff, and when they should do it. You can even request different staff."

"Whoa, wait a minute!" Dyson interrupted, raising both hands. "Don't get me wrong; I was merely trying to learn the ropes. I don't want to start off by throwing a wrench into the works, and I certainly wouldn't want to change a winning team. For now I'll be quite happy if you and Simon would help me to find my way around this place. Think of me as the passenger on your guided tour, at least until I get a feel for the job."

"Very wise!" O'Rourke answered with a broad smile and a friendly wink. "All right, then, let's bring you up to speed. You have a staff of ten, including Simon and myself. Simon will be at your side most of the time, doing any necessary secretarial work here in the building. You know, organizing your schedule, arranging meetings, press statements, and so on. Simon is also an excellent historian and researcher, by the way. He was even awarded the Arch-Cardinal's Medal of Honor for Service to the Church a couple of years ago."

Evans smiled modestly and looked at the ground.

"And I'm responsible," continued O'Rourke, "for the liaison side of things; contacts with other departments, international branches of the Church, universities, etcetera.

I will be away on Archives business quite a lot, meeting with external departments and such, but you can deploy the other eight priests to carry out your orders as you see fit. They are all experienced researchers with master's degrees or doctorates in history or archaeology, so you can set them practically any task in their fields just about anywhere in the world. As far as I remember, one of them, Victor N'Komo, is still on leave in Africa, but he'll be back next week. And two others are on an archaeological dig in Israel. They're due back at the end of this week, if memory serves. The others will be upstairs in their offices."

The elevator arrived and the three men stepped in. Dyson pressed the button for the 175th floor.

"Oh, I see you've done your homework," Evans said, with a polite smile.

"What? Oh, yes!" Dyson replied, realizing that his new colleagues did not know he had already been to his office. "Actually," he added, "I must confess that I was a little over-eager. I was here the other day, in fact. Had a look at my new office."

"Well, there's no harm in getting a head start," O'Rourke said. "Must've been pretty dead on your floor, though. Most of the staff have been taking the weekends off until the new Keeper arrived."

Dyson's mood darkened visibly as he remembered what had happened.

"Hmm. Well I *did* meet one person," he admitted. "Cardinal Goodfellowe."

The brief but meaningful glance his companions exchanged did not escape Dyson's attention.

"Explain," he said simply.

"I beg your pardon?" O'Rourke enquired in a voice dripping with feigned innocence.

Evans merely shrugged, but he looked for all the world like a guilty, overgrown schoolboy who had just been caught cheating on a test.

"Oh, come on! I just saw the way you two looked at each other. Tell me about Cardinal Goodfellowe. I mean, I'm new here. You two have probably been here for years. You know what's going on. So *tell* me! I don't want to get caught out again through my ignorance of the way things work around here."

Once again, O'Rourke and Evans glanced briefly but meaningfully at each other. Evans suddenly found his shoes so fascinating he seemed unable to tear his eyes away from them. O'Rourke fixed his gaze on the ceiling of the elevator for a second, as if seeking divine guidance. He took hold of the cross hanging from a chain around his neck, identical to the one Dyson was wearing, and began concentrating on it, as if he found it uncomfortable to make eye contact with Dyson while discussing the subject. When he spoke, his voice was hushed, as if he were afraid of being overheard, even in the cramped confines of the elevator.

"Well, David, if you insist. I suppose it's only fair to give you a heads up. As much as it shames me to speak badly about another human being, let alone a cardinal of the Holy Church, I'm afraid it must be said that Cardinal Goodfellowe is not the easiest of men to get along with. But I'm sure it's because of the heavy burden of responsibility he bears. He is not only the head of this entire institute, he is the second most powerful representative of the Church in the USA, second only to Cardinal di Galassini, and he takes his job very seriously indeed. One might say he runs a tight ship."

At this point Evans muttered something under his breath that sounded suspiciously like "Captain Bligh," which earned him a severe, tight-lipped, narrow-eyed glare from O'Rourke, but Dyson did not press him on the matter.

"Hmm," Dyson said. "That's kind of the impression I got," leaving it up to the other two to figure out whether he thought Goodfellowe ran a tight ship or resembled Captain Bligh. When they finally arrived at Dyson's office, the other two men made way for Dyson to hold the chip in his forearm to the box next to the door.

"Can't either of you open this door with your chips?" Dyson wondered aloud.

"Well, not at the moment," Evans answered. "We all have access to this building, of course, but our chips are only coded to open certain doors. When there's a change of occupant, the codes on our chips are electronically wiped by the administration until the new occupant applies for them to be recoded. That way, you can decide who can open your office door."

"And were you both able to open this door under my predecessor?" Dyson enquired.

"Well, yes," Evans replied hesitantly. "Both Tom and I will need to pick things up from your office from time to time even when you're not there, so it's really a matter of convenience. But it's up to you, of course. We could always make arrangements to have the departmental assistant open the door for us when we need to get in."

"Oh, no, I won't hear of it! I don't have a problem with you coming into my office. So how would I go about getting both your chips fixed so they open my office door?"

"Ah, now that would be my job." O'Rourke tentatively raised a finger and smiled. "You just make a list of who you want to be able to open which doors in *your* department and I'll set the wheels in motion with building administration."

The way O'Rourke stressed the word *your* did not escape Dyson, and for a moment he was both surprised and flattered.

"Hmm, but I don't know anyone here yet. Apart from you two, of course. Err, tell you what, Tom. Is there still a record of who could open which doors under the last Keeper?"

"Of course. We keep records of *everything* around here."

"Well then, couldn't you just get all the same codes to work on all the same doors for all the same people? Would that be a problem?"

O'Rourke smiled warmly. "Not at all, David. I can see it's going to be a great pleasure working with you. And talking of pleasure, there is one duty I am particularly pleased to perform today."

He reached into the brown leather satchel he was carrying and removed a small, black, unmarked box. Opening it, he showed Dyson the contents: an antique-looking silver wristwatch with a metal strap. The black face behind the chrome hands bore an ornate cross with the number two in a circle at its center. It was actually quite beautiful: a real work of art.

"This is not only a beautifully crafted symbol of our faith, David; it's also an extremely accurate timepiece," O'Rourke said with a nod of affirmation. "It's radio-linked to an atomic clock right here in New York, which means the time is corrected to the millisecond every day. And, even if you travel abroad, the watch automatically adjusts itself to the nearest atomic clock in the country you're in. It should come in very handy when you're off on a dig somewhere in the world."

Evans smiled. "We all have one," he said, lifting a sleeve to show Dyson his own identical watch.

"Well, thank you very much," Dyson said. The other two were looking at him so eagerly that Dyson somehow felt obliged to take off his old, and admittedly cheap, watch and put on his present.

"Oh, while we're exchanging pleasantries," he said.

Reaching into a pocket of his cassock he pulled out his comPod, a palm-sized, rectangular device made of a light metal alloy. There were no obvious controls on the device, almost all of its upper surface taking the form of a display screen. "Janet," he said. "Store a number, please."

"Certainly, David," the device replied, its computer voice perfectly imitating that of a young woman. Holding his comPod up to O'Rourke's face, Dyson merely raised his eyebrows. O'Rourke knew what was expected and obliged.

"O'Rourke, Tom," he said, pronouncing the words clearly. He then dictated his own comPod's identification number. When he had finished, Dyson spoke to his comPod once again, "Thank you, Janet."

"You're welcome, David," the woman's voice replied.

The procedure was repeated with Evans, then he and O'Rourke stored Dyson's details on their own devices. The ubiquitous electronic personal assistants were the great-grandchildren of the mobile phones that had spread to the four corners of the globe at the end of the previous century. Although the name "comPod" was actually a registered trademark of the JNT Corporation of Japan, similar devices manufactured by other companies were also dubbed, albeit erroneously, comPods by the public at large. When Dyson had bought his device two years earlier, he had diligently read the accompanying Japanese Neural Technologies instruction manual, which referred to the product as "your JNT comPod." For want of a better name, Dyson had taken the acronym "JNT" and added the vowels "a" and "e" to make "JaNeT." Not particularly creative, as Dyson himself would have been the first to admit; but the comPods were equipped with artificial intelligence, and it seemed only natural to address them as if they were human personalities. This also included saying please and thank you, and giving them human names.

They were still standing in the middle of the Keeper's office when it suddenly occurred to Dyson that he knew nothing at all about his predecessor.

"So tell me about the last Keeper."

"Oh, Father Tim Nelson was an excellent Keeper of the Archives," O'Rourke offered.

"A very nice man, too," Evans put in.

O'Rourke continued: "Actually, Tim Nelson's background was a lot like your own, David. When he started here, he was also a young prodigy who was supported by the Church from an early age."

Hmm, Dyson thought, *you've done your homework on me, too.*

"Tim was the Keeper for over twenty years," O'Rourke went on, "and he was very popular with all his staff. Unfortunately, he had a heart condition which he failed to have treated, for some reason. Perhaps he wasn't aware of it himself, who knows? I'm afraid we only found out about it after the autopsy."

"Autopsy?" Dyson asked, surprised.

"Hmm, yes," O'Rourke continued in a more subdued, thoughtful voice. "Tim was found dead in this very office. He was actually slumped over the desk there," he said calmly, indicating Dyson's new workstation.

"Holy Lamb!" Dyson exclaimed.

"As you know, the Church runs its own hospitals and has its own medical staff, including medical examiners. Cardinal Goodfellowe had the body removed by the DFP and the autopsy was performed internally."

Dyson was unable to conceal his astonishment. The DFP, the Doctrine of the Faith Police, were supposed to be a supplementary branch assisting the official local police force in all matters in which the Church was involved. The roots of the DFP were founded in the Congregation of the Doctrine of the Faith, an organization of the former Roman Catholic Church, which had, in earlier times, been called the Supreme Sacred Congregation of the Roman and Universal Inquisition. This had been the infamous institution of Roman Catholicism that had, for centuries, terrorized non-conformists in Europe with torture and execution. The modern-day DFP were called in, for example, in cases entailing blasphemy, slander of the Church, libelous statements about the Church, and the like. They were not usually called upon to investigate deaths presumably caused by heart attacks.

"You mean there was a sudden death in this office and you didn't inform the authorities? The state ones, I mean. Like the coroner, for example."

"David, this is New York, the seat of the United States headquarters of the Holy Church of the Second Coming. When you've been here a little longer, you'll realize that *we are* the authorities."

Dyson had heard rumors about his Church's absolute power. Well, actually, they were more than just rumors; he was not *that* naïve. Over the last couple of decades, the Church of the Second Coming of the Lamb had become a major influence on governments all over the world. After varying degrees of skepticism, sometimes resulting in civil disobedience, demonstrations, and, in one or two cases, in civil war, most of the predominantly Christian nations had gradually accepted the fact that their Savior had indeed returned and had given mankind a second chance for redemption before the world was destroyed. It had been a violent and troubled couple of decades, but eventually the vast majority of people in these nations had turned their backs on the divisive views of the old Catholic and Protestant churches and joined together in the unified Church of the Second Coming.

So many influential people now had leading positions in the secular wing of the Church that it was run like a business; an extremely large, wealthy, and powerful business. For a man as upright as Dyson, it was difficult to accept the stories of corruption in high places. There were even stories of DFP officers taking people into custody without charge and actually torturing them. That was absurd, though. Such rumors were often spread by malcontents in any society, and because the Church of the Second Coming was constantly pursuing a vigorous campaign against blasphemers and other subversives, it had practically set itself up as target number one for any kind of defamation.

CHAPTER 3

**Archives of the Holy Church of the Second Coming
New York City, 2077**

Dyson blossomed in the Archives. He had never been so contented before in his entire life. Over the past two years as Keeper of the Archives, he had managed to piece together bits of history like a detective reconstructing a crime scene. Sometimes he was given specific tasks by a cardinal, and these tasks obviously took priority, but much of the time he was left to his own devices to pursue any research as he saw fit. This research, of course, had to be within certain rigid parameters set by the Church, and before any of it could be published, it needed to be sent to his superiors for approval. Nevertheless, Dyson never had the feeling he was restricted in any way, and most of his findings were indeed published as articles in scientific journals, earning him an international reputation as an outstanding researcher and scholar.

Funding seemed to be no object, either. Whenever Dyson needed to send a member of staff on a mission, he filled in a brief application describing who he wanted to send where, and why, and sent this to Tom O'Rourke. The matter was thereupon clarified with the finance department, and, usually within forty-eight hours, an electronic response was sent to Dyson's computer, informing him that he could deploy his staff as per his application; funding would be forthcoming as required. Over the last two years, Dyson had sent his staff out on numerous missions and had even been on a few himself. In all that time, no request he made for funding had ever been refused — no matter how bizarre even

Dyson himself believed it might sound to those responsible for the Church's financial affairs, and no matter how much money he applied for. It seemed that Keeper of the Archives was truly the coveted job he had always believed it was. There appeared to be no end to his resources, both financial and human.

This was one major reason why he loved his job so much: he could get on with his research without having to consider more mundane matters, such as budgeting. He compared it with the sumptuously designed foyer of the Archives building, which he admired anew every morning. If the architect who had designed the awe-inspiring entrance hall had been forced to adhere to a strict budget, then, in all likelihood, the impressive foyer that Dyson knew and admired would probably not exist in its present form. Indeed, if there had been stringent budget restrictions at the time the building was designed, the foyer might have turned out to be an unimaginatively empty and probably much smaller space with no character whatsoever. Similarly, if Dyson's research budget had been restricted in any way, he would have had to limit his curiosity, his creativity. For Dyson, this would in itself have been a contradiction in terms, for how can creativity be limited and still be called creativity?

Despite the somewhat shaky start Dyson had with Cardinal Goodfellowe, things had turned out all right on that front, too. Dyson seldom saw the cardinal, in fact, and on the rare occasions he did, it was a chance meeting in the foyer or the corridor, which usually involved a curt nod of the head and a grunt from the cardinal and an uncomfortably mumbled "Good day, Eminence," from Dyson. Cardinal Goodfellowe apparently did not engage in small talk, the feeling around the Archives being that this was not necessarily a bad thing. To date there had been no sign of the cardinal having had a problem deciding which kind of "truth" Dyson had discovered, so it was not that difficult just to stay out of the unpleasant man's way.

The staff he had at his disposal proved to be an invaluable, thoroughly competent team of experts, each working diligently and loyally in their relevant fields.

Whenever Dyson had a hunch about something, he would send his people out to follow up on his train of thought on site, no matter where in the world that might be. He found them to be willing and able men who not only followed his instructions to the letter, but who also took the initiative and often went one step further, usually bringing back even more than he had required or even expected.

One very unusual encounter he'd had in his first week at the Archives had been his meeting with Bjørn Svensson, one of his researchers. O'Rourke had attempted, in his uniquely politically correct manner, to prepare Dyson for the encounter:

"Well, David, you know of course that the Church is an equal-opportunity employer. That is, we do not discriminate against any man who might be academically suitable for a position in the organization, no matter what his physical status might be."

Dyson's imagination had immediately conjured up someone in a motorized wheelchair. *Well, I certainly have no problem with that*, he had thought. *If the man can do the job, I don't care what his "physical status" might be! What on earth is Tom thinking?*

However, when Dyson eventually met Bjørn Svensson, a wheelchair would have appeared downright dull by comparison. Svensson was, in fact, an SCE: a Shahani Cube Entity. Dyson had, of course, heard of these people before; they had, after all, been all over the news for the last five years at least. But it was the first time he had ever met one of them.

When Tom, with Dyson in tow, politely knocked at an office door on the sixtieth floor, they had been greeted by the youthful-sounding voice of a man in his twenties, inviting them to come in. Once inside, Tom announced,

"David, I'd like to introduce Bjørn Svensson; Bjørn, this is our new Keeper, Dr. David Dyson."

Dyson was confused, for apart from Tom and himself, the room appeared deserted. Suddenly, the youthful voice spoke from nowhere in particular:

"I'm very pleased to meet you, Dr. Dyson. And I'm looking forward to working with you."

Dyson's eyes widened as he scanned the room in vain, searching for the source of the voice. The first thing he thought was that they were playing some kind of immature trick on him. But then he remembered a documentary he had seen about the SCEs. Instead of a computer monitor on the desk, there was a fist-sized black cube. It was completely featureless, but Dyson realized with a start that this simple object contained the life essence of Bjørn Svensson.

The Shahani Cubes were named after a scientist who had first discovered a method of storing in electronic form every memory, every feeling, and every thought an individual had experienced in his or her life. When they were gradually approaching death after having enjoyed a full life — or even long before that in cases where terminal illness had been diagnosed, for example — individuals could have their data, which some people still insisted on calling the "soul," uploaded and stored in one of the many Shahani servers strategically placed around the globe. These servers were backed up by the most elaborate safety mechanisms the world had ever seen as far as computer technology went, in order to prevent tampering or hacking or even inadvertent deletion.

The cubes were merely interfaces that enabled the "souls" to interact with their surroundings, remotely from their server. The advantage of this was that if anything happened to a cube, the mind of the entity could be downloaded from the servers to another cube almost immediately. Backups automatically stored at short, regular intervals throughout the day ensured that all new experiences the entity made through the cube were also stored on the servers, just as "real" memories were stored organically in the human brain.

There had been initial teething problems when customers paying a fortune for the process to be carried out on them believed they could dictate to the scientists exactly how the latter should do their job. Some of these tycoon-types, not used to being told "No, that's just not possible," demanded that their essence be downloaded into several cubes simultaneously. That way, they believed, they could keep a watchful eye over their entire multi-billion-dollar enterprises. Needing the customers' money for further research, the scientists had complied, albeit reluctantly. Soon after the first entities had been downloaded into multiple cubes simultaneously, though, it was realized that even in electronic form, the human mind could not cope with being in several places at the same time. Attempts to consolidate the memories from several copies of the entity back into one single entity on the servers resulted in what could only be referred to as mental illness.

Initially it had been so expensive to undergo the upload and storage treatment that only the fabulously rich were able to afford it. Also, it must be admitted that those who pioneered the treatment in its infancy were lost forever when the science simply failed. Naturally, this was off-putting to those who could afford the treatment, so the numbers of paying customers dwindled, meaning that the jobs of subsequent generations were not endangered. And in any case, the fabulously rich who could afford the treatment were not likely to be desirous of taking those jobs performed by those who were not able to afford such treatment. As far as the psychologists' qualms about locked-in syndrome were concerned, Shahani's cubes were able to dispel these, too. The cubes that developed several years after the prototypes acted as an interface to modern, late-twenty-first century computers. This meant that the minds contained in the cubes were able to interact with their environment almost as well as their flesh-and-blood counterparts, and in some cases even better. In certain environments, for example, the frail human body is unable to function well, if at all. However, it was no problem whatsoever for an SCE to be sent to polar regions or to the deepest depths of the ocean for research purposes.

Svensson had been born in 1979, making him ninety-six years old now. Dyson was at a loss about how to act. This being, this "man," was old enough to be his great-grandfather, but sounded younger than Dyson. *That's just the computer software,* he told himself. *Just follow Tom's lead and pretend there's nothing out of the ordinary about this.*

"So, Bjørn, well, I'm, err…pleased to meet you."

Pleasant, musical laughter filled the room. Dyson, of course, realized that the sound was computer-generated, but for all intents and purposes it sounded real. Svensson replied, "I can hear from the timbre of your voice that you're totally creeped out right now. It's all right. It takes a bit of getting used to at first, I know that."

"Oh, I'm so sorry… I didn't mean…"

"No, no, really. It's OK. I'm used to it." Dyson was treated to another pleasant computer-generated laugh. "And if our positions were reversed, I would have reacted in much the same way, believe me."

Still rather embarrassed, Dyson attempted to carry on as if nothing out of the ordinary had happened, until Tom intervened.

"Well, Bjørn, I have to take David to meet other people, so we'll leave you to get on with your work."

"All right. It was a pleasure meeting you, David."

"The pleasure's all mine," Dyson replied politely.

Once they were in the corridor, Dyson tried to figure out how he was ever going to work with a disembodied entity.

"But I can't send him anywhere. How can he physically take part in excavations?" he whispered, afraid that Svensson's cube might have detectors outside his office. After tut-tutting and shaking his head sadly for a second, O'Rourke was able to belay Dyson's misgivings.

"Think about it, David. Bjørn is practically a computer with a human personality. His server connection is actually directly linked to the main Archives computer. Ask him to find anything at all in the vast stores of data we have on that computer and he'll be able to give you an answer faster than you could even formulate the next question for him. Remember, David, we all have our own particular skills around here. If you deploy your staff with that in mind, you will be maximizing their usefulness. Not only that; you will be serving the Holy Church to the best of your ability. Use Bjørn's particular talents for data storage and retrieval. Of course, you can send him anywhere you want! His cube is in constant contact with us through the worldwide net. In fact, you could drop him into the ocean or send him into space safe in the knowledge that you are in no way endangering his life. If anything happens to his cube, another will be placed on his desk within hours, and you'll be talking to the very same person."

Dyson mulled this over for a few seconds, but he had to admit that O'Rourke's advice was flawless. He would simply have to get used to treating a small black cube as respectfully as he would treat a "normal" human being.

— «» —

One morning, Dyson was thoroughly absorbed in the contents of the three-dimensional diagram projected above his desk. It was a representation of one of the Nag Hammadi codices; one that had never been released from the old Vatican vaults, as its contents did not seem to be at all compatible with the doctrines of the Church. It was in fact an unpublished part of the Gospel of Mary Magdalene. A translation of some chapters of Mary's Gospel had been found in Egypt in the late nineteenth century, but had not been published until 1955. For the then Roman Catholic church, this document had been disturbing enough, as it seemed to portray Mary Magdalene not as a prostitute, but as Christ's most favored disciple. The Vatican had downplayed this, however, initially publicly doubting the authenticity of the document. When the evidence became overwhelming, the church officially apologized in 1969 for its claim that Mary had been a prostitute, blaming the error on Pope Gregory the Great, who, in 591 AD, had confused Mary Magdalene with a different character in the Bible, also called Mary. For the Vatican it was bad enough that the document proved that Jesus of Nazareth had treated women not only as equals, but had also favored one of them in particular, even entrusting her with words of insight he did not impart to his closest male disciples.

It was clear to Dyson why the church had suppressed the part of Mary Magdalene's gospel he was currently reading; it not only portrayed her as Jesus' close friend and ally, it actually quoted Jesus as saying that churches — or in the original Coptic text he was reading, "temples" — were not only superfluous, they were places of evil where sinful men exercised their will over the innocent for immoral purposes. In the Gospel of Mary Magdalene, a woman who was probably closer to the historical Jesus than any of his other followers actually advocated the abolition of all churches. Instead, people should seek God within themselves, she wrote, quoting "Jesus the Messiah." For fifteen hundred years, the Vatican had hidden this knowledge from the faithful for obvious reasons. Although Dyson understood perfectly well why this information had been kept from the public at large in the past, he nevertheless found himself faced with a dilemma.

Of course, the old Vatican had for centuries known it was necessary for their survival to continue propagating the lie that Mary Magdalene was a prostitute, because it was feared the knowledge of what she had written would damage them. But even after the Vatican's admission, they still did not publish the Gospel of Mary, claiming that it was too fragmented to provide a complete translation. Dyson's dilemma was that he was currently reading a document that seemed complete in every way. So why was his church still refusing to publish it?

Christ said that temples were unnecessary. Can we really take that at face value? He often spoke in parables. Has this one been transcribed correctly? Yes, people should seek God within themselves; of course they should. But some people need help before they can find God, and that's where the Church comes in. But the Savior says we don't need the Church. His word is divine! On the other hand, the church has been doing so much good for the last two thousand years. Surely that counts for something. But would people understand if they found out what Jesus of Nazareth said to Mary Magdalene? They might turn their backs on the Church forever! But is it right for the Church to conceal this document? Couldn't we release it and let people decide for themselves? Christ now appears all over the world, ensuring we all know he is still there, watching over us. Wouldn't he have let us know if we were doing something wrong?

Dyson's work often called into question the Church's role in such matters. His reveries, which he could never have revealed to a living soul, were interrupted when there was a familiar sharp double-rap at the door.

"Come in, Simon," he called, without raising his head. His voice sounded distracted, concentrating as he was on the conundrum displayed before him. It was indeed Evans, but there was another priest standing behind him, looking eagerly and curiously over Evans' shoulder into Dyson's office. As soon as Dyson saw the shock of red hair, his eyebrows shot up and a broad grin crossed his face. Leaving his desk, he walked toward his visitor, arms outstretched.

"Pete!" he called, genuinely pleased. "I don't believe it! What are you doing in New York?"

The red-haired priest pushed roughly past Evans, charged into the room, and proceeded to wrap his arms around Dyson in a tight bear hug. The two men patted each other heartily on the back, *obviously old friends*, thought Evans. The red-haired priest appeared to be about the same age as Dyson, but did not have Dyson's studious look. Actually, apart from his priest's cassock, the visitor rather reminded Evans of a huge twelve-year-old.

After the initial zeal of their reunion had died down somewhat, Dyson attempted to free himself from the embrace, but his friend held on, rather too tightly, Dyson thought, for a moment longer. When he was finally released, Dyson was gasping for breath, but grinning with the pleasure of the unexpected reunion. Pete withdrew a little, but held tightly onto Dyson's shoulders, his arms outstretched.

"Dave, I'm so happy to see you again," the red-haired priest said.

That brings back memories, thought Dyson, who had not been called Dave since his schooldays. Something in Pete's voice told both Dyson and the discreetly waiting Evans that this greeting was no meaningless phrase, but was based on sincere, heartfelt emotion.

"Same here, old mate," Dyson replied, somewhat taken aback. "Hey, what happened to your face?" he asked, registering for the first time the bruising around his friend's right eye and a cut on his bottom lip. Pete shot a quick sideways glance at Evans, who was now standing next to the two friends, apparently awaiting further instructions from Dyson. Pete's expression turned suddenly serious, and when he turned his eyes back to Dyson, he muttered, "Dave, do you think I could talk to you alone for a minute?"

A little perplexed by his friend's sudden mood swing, Dyson addressed his assistant. "Thanks, Simon. I'll call you when I need you again."

Evans shrugged and left the room without comment, closing the door quietly behind him. Once he had gone, Dyson motioned for his old friend to take a seat in one of the leather armchairs and then sat down behind his desk.

"Can I get you anything, Pete?"

"No, I'm good, thanks."

As teenagers at school in Liverpool, they had been inseparable. For years they had done everything together — including some pretty stupid things — until one day the time had come for David to leave for university to embark on what would subsequently turn out to be an illustrious career. Dyson had gone on to do great things academically, whereas Pete had seemed to become stuck in the proverbial rut. Far from being blessed with promotion and recognition like his old school friend, Pete had remained in his humdrum job as a field researcher, gathering historical and archaeological data to be subsequently processed and interpreted by better-qualified people like David Dyson.

Sitting down in one of the sturdy leather chairs in front of Dyson's desk, Pete was clearly unable to relax. He sat nervously on the edge of the seat, his hands resting on the desk, fingers clasped but wriggling against the backs of his hands, both feet audibly tapping on the floor. His eyes were downcast, staring blankly. A single bead of sweat trickled from his temple down the side of his face, but he did not bother to wipe it away. In fact, he seemed so preoccupied that it went wholly unnoticed.

"Pete, what's wrong?" Dyson enquired, worried. "I've never seen you like this before."

"Dave, I honestly have no idea what's really happening. But it's something dangerous, I know that much."

It was only now that Dyson realized that, apart from the bruising, his friend also looked unusually pale.

"I need to talk to you," Pete went on.

"I'm listening."

"No! Not here!" Pete sounded agitated, his voice raised. He abruptly turned his head to look nervously over his shoulder at the closed door behind him, seemingly afraid that someone might come in to see what the commotion was about.

"Where then?" Dyson asked softly, hoping that a more gentle tone would calm his friend.

"Meet me at the statue of the Lamb in Central Park. The one at the back of the Museum of Modern Art. Tomorrow morning. Eight o'clock."

Dyson was suddenly concerned about getting in to work on time. "But, Pete," he began, "I can't just…"

"Dave, I'm begging you. Please! Don't ask me to say anything more right now. Just trust me!"

With that he stood up and hurried to the doors of Dyson's office as if he could stand sitting no longer. Tearing the doors open, he stuck his head cautiously through them and looked up and down the corridor before heading toward the elevator almost at a run, leaving the heavy office doors open behind him.

About an hour later Evans returned, bringing coffee for Dyson and himself. Working closely over the last two years had resulted in the two men becoming quite good friends. Neither of them had any family in New York and neither of them dropped everything and shot off home when their working day officially finished at five o'clock, so they had often found themselves leaving the building together around six or even seven in the evening on quite a number of occasions.

"Thanks, Simon," Dyson said, gratefully accepting the steaming coffee in a stainless steel mug.

"So what was all that about then?" Evans enquired.

"Huh? Oh, you mean Pete. Hmm, just an old friend who appears to be having a few issues. I'm meeting him tomorrow before work. Hope I can help."

"Any idea what the problem might be?"

"No, actually, I don't. To be honest, I'm afraid Pete might be having some kind of psychological problem. I've never seen him like that before. That is definitely not the happy-go-lucky guy I used to know."

"Well, if you need any help, you know where to find me."

"I know I can always count on you. Thanks, Simon, but I'm sure I can deal with this myself."

— «» —

That night, as Dyson was lying in his bed in the small apartment the Church had organized for him in the leafy Brooklyn suburb of Carroll Gardens, he ran through the meeting with Pete in his mind. What could possibly be troubling his old friend so much that he would turn up out of the blue like that, acting weird and with marks on his face that looked like someone had given him a beating?

Just then, Janet addressed him.

"David, there's an incoming message for you. It is a recording, audio only, no video. Would you like to hear it?"

A quick glance at the faintly glowing clock on his bedside table told him it was almost one thirty in the morning. Dyson wasn't one to sleep very much under normal circumstances, but this matter with his old friend seemed to be depriving him of even the little sleep he normally had.

"Who is it from, Janet?"

"I'm sorry, David, I'm afraid the sender has blocked that information. How would you like me to proceed?"

"All right," Dyson sighed, "play it for me. It might be important."

At first there was silence, after that came the sound of loud, heavy breathing.

You've got to be kidding me! Dyson thought.

Then someone cleared their throat and spoke. It was Pete.

"Dave, listen. I can't meet you tomorrow. They're on to me. It's too dangerous. For both of us."

His friend's voice sounded desperate, in panic.

"Come to Carly's Diner on Madison, at noon this Friday. I can't say any more. Please, Dave, you really have to just trust me on this one. I need your help. Please!"

"End of message," Janet proclaimed pleasantly.

"Janet, trace the message, please."

"I'm sorry, David, the caller blocked that information, too."

Dyson hardly slept at all after that. He tossed and turned with all manner of horrible scenarios running through his mind. His usual nightly battle with insomnia became a long, drawn-out war of attrition. The last thought he had before finally defeating the plague of sleeplessness was that he would have to wait two days to find out what was going on.

— «» —

Friday arrived at last, and Dyson left work early to be at the appointed place at twelve o'clock. But Pete was nowhere to be seen. Dyson ordered a steaming hot coffee at the counter and took it to a dilapidated seat at a red Formica table in a strategic corner from where he could observe all the comings and goings through the only door in the place. It was not too busy, so Dyson was sure he would see Pete as soon as he entered the establishment. When, at 12:45, there was still no sign of his friend, Dyson addressed the bored-looking young waitress who was listlessly wiping the grubby plastic-coated tables.

"Excuse me, miss. I'm Father David Dyson. Has anyone left a message for me? Another priest, perhaps?"

The waitress shot him a brief glance, registering his priest's collar.

"Not that I know of, Father." Despite her air of abject disinterest, the waitress was still careful to be respectful. *You never knew how well-connected these bastards were,* she thought. *They could have you hauled away by the DFP in an instant on some trumped-up blasphemy charge.*

"Thank you," Dyson said, disappointed.

After finishing his third coffee, he glanced at a clock on the wall. It was now 1:15. As he still had to finish up a report he was writing for Cardinal Goodfellowe, he paid and left.

Can't have been that important after all, he told himself.

— «» —

The following Monday began as usual with a Church service in the chapel on the first floor of the Archives. The service was usually led by various bishops taking it in turn to perform the unpopular duty. Dyson did not have to worry about having to hold such a service himself. He'd had no practice at all in this regard since his seminary years, but as the Keeper of the Archives he held a special position and would not have been expected to hold services anyway.

When he had first come to the Archives, Dyson had been surprised at the comparatively low number of people attending the regular services in the building's chapel. The chapel was built to hold around three hundred worshippers, but there were never more than a hundred at any given service. In fact, sometimes the numbers even dwindled to below fifty. Upon enquiring about this, he had been told by a smiling O'Rourke that most people on the payroll of the Church preferred to worship the Lord through their work, so instead of coming to chapel, they simply started work earlier. After all, O'Rourke had added, it *was* like preaching to the choir, wasn't it? At the time, this attitude had surprised Dyson greatly, as he had always been taught that every member of the clergy — from the novice nun to the Holy Father — was expected to set a good example and worship in public.

On this particular Monday, Bishop Marat, a stocky, intense-looking man in his mid-fifties, was doing the honors, standing before the altar addressing a mere seventy or so members of the congregation, all of whom worked in the building. A quick look confirmed to Dyson that not one other colleague from his own team was present; a fact which rather irritated him. Of course, as the head of the Archives department, Dyson could have insisted on his colleagues' attendance, but he would never have entertained pulling rank on them in such a manner.

— ⟨⟩ —

The service began with the bishop welcoming his flock in his peculiar French accent, which was still quite pronounced despite living in New York for over thirty years.

"May the Lamb of God be with you, my children."

"And with you, blessed Father," the Church administration staff replied in a subdued, ninety-five-per-cent-male monotone.

"The subject of this morning's sermon is faith. We all know that we, in the late twenty-first century, are in a far more fortunate position than any other generation before us. We are blessed with the ability to physically perceive the Lamb of God."

At this point, a life-sized hologram of the Lamb appeared in a bright flash of light, standing on the altar behind Marat. The figure was, of course, in the traditional pose: hands clasped before him, head slightly bowed. His long white gown flowed dramatically in a non-existent breeze; an effect Dyson had never noticed in any of the footage of the Lamb he had previously seen. Artistic license, he assumed.

"Of course, my children, we are indeed blessed. There is no doubt about that. But there is a downside to this. Our ancestors had only blind faith to go on. They had no actual proof of the Lamb's physical materialization as we have today. That is why those of our forefathers who believed blindly in the Lamb are to be envied, for surely this simple, childlike faith will be rewarded when those believers are admitted to the Kingdom of Heaven!"

Marat's voice had begun to increase in both pitch and intensity. The man was known for his fiery, sometimes even intimidating sermons, in which he not only blessed believers, but had also been known to actually *curse* those who did not accept the faith of the Church without question.

"So, my children, I have been thinking about our faith today. Some of you believe, perhaps, that it is easy for us, as we see the Lamb before us. Behold!"

The brightness of the hologram on the altar increased so suddenly that Dyson still saw the image of it when he instinctively closed his eyes.

"Yes, there he is in all his glory. *Ecce homo!* Behold the Man! Behold the Lamb of God!"

Dyson blinked a couple of times and cautiously reopened his eyes when the figure of the Lamb had dimmed somewhat.

"I have been thinking," Marat mused, "and I have come to a conclusion. When the Lord our God demands faith from us with no hard evidence, He rewards us richly for believing in Him. But when He sends us His Son for all to see, then surely He expects more than a mere nodding acceptance of His power and His glory. Surely He wants more than just lip service in a once-weekly visit to the chapel!"

The bishop was now positively roaring at the people sitting in the pews. Dyson noticed a vein throbbing on the man's temple and could not keep himself from briefly wondering what would happen if it burst.

"Then imagine this!" Marat bellowed. There was a pause in which a dropped pin would have sounded like an explosion. When the bishop resumed his sermon after a few seconds of intense silence, his words were like acid, etching away at the minds of his listeners.

"To the non-ordained among you this morning: I would like to crave your indulgence, as I shall be addressing the priesthood first and foremost."

There was an almost audible sigh of relief from the non-ordained secretarial staff and assorted janitors as they realized the bishop's wrath today was directed at the priesthood and not them. Marat glared at his audience as if trying to find some party among them who was guilty of...well, *anything,* actually. Most people sitting in the pews, even those who had a clear conscience, began to squirm uncomfortably. The bishop seemed to have this effect on most people.

"Well, then," Marat continued, in his poisonous, spitting voice. "Just imagine what the Lord thinks of someone who has experienced the manifestation of his Holy Son, and who then sees fit to ignore this. That, my children, is bad enough! Surely such a person will find no forgiveness, even in God's boundless mercy. Now just imagine that this person is not a scientist or a philosopher, or some other such unfortunate person whose job it is to question the validity of the patently obvious. No, let us imagine that this person is a priest of the Holy Church! How far will such a person fall! A priest of the Holy Church who not only turns his back on the Church, but actually betrays it willfully! My children, there is no pit in hell deep enough or filled with tortures painful enough for such a priest. This man will not only be damned for all eternity, but his damnation will be far worse than the damnation of a layman!"

Although Dyson could follow the bishop's argument, it seemed to him that a God of mercy, as described in the New Testament, must surely be willing to forgive even the most recalcitrant sinner. *We just need to get the sinner to voluntarily accept his sins and to turn to the Church for help and forgiveness*, he thought. *Surely that's the message the Lamb of God has been trying to preach for two thousand years!*

— «» —

He had only been sitting at his desk for about ten minutes when Evans knocked on the door with his familiar, loud double-rap and, without waiting for a response, walked in.

"David, I'm so sorry," he said, his voice unusually subdued.

"Huh? What about?" Dyson asked.

"About your friend, Pete, of course."

Dyson had no idea what Evans was talking about, but a sinking feeling suddenly took hold of his stomach.

Evans' eyebrows raised in surprise. "Haven't you heard the news?"

"Err, I locked myself away in my flat all weekend trying to put together pieces of a three thousand-year-old scroll with a magnifying glass and a pair of tweezers."

"Oh, my goodness," Evans said. "David, I'm sorry to be the one to have to tell you this: I'm afraid your friend Pete was involved in a car accident on Friday. He was rushed to hospital immediately, but his injuries were serious." Evans gulped and drew a deep breath. "He didn't make it, David. I'm so sorry."

Dyson felt the blood draining from his face as the realization of what Evans had just said sank in. While he had been waiting impatiently at the diner on Friday, gradually becoming annoyed at Pete's usual disregard for the etiquette of punctuality, his friend had been fighting for his life in a hospital. Without another word to Evans, Dyson switched on his computer and snapped a few verbal commands at it, instructing it to find the *New York Times* netsite. It took him only a few seconds to find what he was looking for in the Saturday edition:

Priest Killed In NYC Accident

A priest of the Church of the Second Coming of the Lamb was involved in a serious road accident yesterday. Father Peter MacKenzie (28) of Liverpool, England, was in New York on Church business, according to colleagues. While crossing 7th Avenue at the corner of 17th Street, Father MacKenzie was knocked to the ground by a speeding black car that failed to stop after the collision. The priest was taken to NYC Church Hospital No. 3, but later died of the severe injuries he had sustained in the accident.

The DFP are investigating, though results are not expected anytime soon, as eyewitnesses were unable to provide detailed information about the hit-and-run vehicle. Coincidentally, due to a computer malfunction, the TraffiCams at this very junction went offline just moments before the accident, which will make the authorities' investigations even more difficult, if not impossible.

— «» —

Dyson was devastated. The joy at seeing his friend again after so many years had been brutally curtailed by a stupid, pointless accident. He was angry; no, furious would be a better word. How could this be allowed to happen? He slammed his fist onto the mahogany desktop in a fit of helpless rage. Feeling tears well up, he realized that Evans was still standing in the doorway.

"Simon, I'm sorry. Could you give me a minute alone, please?"

"Sure, David. Just let me know if there's anything I can do. You know…" replied Evans softly.

"Yes, thanks, Simon."

Evans left, closing the door quietly behind him.

After a few minutes and a few deep breaths, Dyson managed to calm down and start thinking clearly again. *Someone will have to inform Pete's parents. And they'll want his body flown back to England.*

He said "Church Hospital No. 3, NYC, USA," and the 3D virtual monitor floating above his desk instantly lit up with the contact details of various departments and representatives of the establishment in question. Poking his finger at the icon for "Reception — Patient Inquiries," a sub-cube opened, showing the smiling face of a friendly-looking woman in her mid-fifties.

"Good morning, sir… err, Father," she corrected herself, noticing Dyson's collar. "How may I help you today?" she chirped. Dyson, who was something of an accent buff, and had been studying US accents in particular for the past two years, noticed the twang in her intonation, and believed the woman had probably grown up in Texas.

"Good morning. My name is Father David Dyson. I'm enquiring about a Father Peter MacKenzie who died in your hospital on Friday."

"Are you family; next of kin, Father?"

"No, I'm just a friend."

"Well, I'm very sorry then, Father, but I'm not permitted to discuss the patient's details with you," she replied, her whole demeanor one of somber sympathy, but detached professionalism.

"But he's *dead*!" Dyson hissed, trying to remain calm.

"Yes, so you said, Father," the woman replied, with an appropriately solemn face. "But if you are not a relative, then I'm afraid I cannot help you," she said, trying to sound fair and reasonable.

"Listen to me." Dyson was struggling to remain civil, summoning up as much patience as he could. "Peter MacKenzie was my friend. He was here in New York for the sole purpose of visiting me. He was not married, had no children, and his only relatives are his parents, who live on the other side of the Atlantic Ocean, and are pensioners in their seventies. They are probably as yet unaware that their only son has been killed here in the city. Now *if you wouldn't mind*, I would like to settle his affairs over here and make sure that his parents at least receive their son's body so that they can give him a decent Christian burial."

It was clear to the hospital worker that Dyson was becoming very angry indeed. She paused for a second and took a deep breath before replying.

"One moment please, Father. I'll look him up," she said. The attitude of fairness and sympathy she had allowed to creep into her voice had now given way to professional detachment. Dyson watched his monitor with interest, observing the woman's expression as her eyes were focused on another corner of her own monitor. At first her eyebrows knit together in a frown of concentration. Then she raised one eyebrow quite slowly in an expression of interest or confusion. Several seconds later, the other eyebrow shot up to join its companion, indicating that the woman had discovered something completely unexpected.

"Err, I'm sorry, Father." Her voice was now hushed, as though she wanted nobody to overhear her. She even glanced over her shoulder to make sure no one was standing behind her. "Somebody has already collected Father MacKenzie's body."

"What? Who?"

"It was the, err… the DFP, Father."

Muttering a brief "thank you," Dyson broke the connection and buried his face in his hands with a groan. *The DFP! What do **they** want with Pete's body?*

A quick wave of the hand over a motion-sensitive part of his desk caused Evans' virtual head to float before him.

"Hi, David, you OK?"

"I'll be all right, thanks. Simon, do you know anyone in the DFP?"

Evans' eyes involuntarily widened. He looked taken aback.

"Erm, no, can't say I do, actually. Why?"

"They took Pete's body and I want to know what's going on."

"They *what*?" Evans was apparently as astonished as Dyson. "Any idea why?"

"No," replied Dyson, "but I'm going to find out. What about Tom? Do you think he'll be able to help?"

"You'll have to ask him about that. His job as liaison officer between this department and others, including the office of His Holiness, means he has a lot of contacts, but I'm really not sure about the DFP. People generally tend to avoid any contact with them if possible, if you know what I mean."

"Hmm," Dyson replied noncommittally, although he knew exactly what Evans meant. "Is Tom around today, do you know?"

"I have a meeting with him penciled in for eleven o'clock this morning, so it's pretty certain he'll be around then."

Dyson contemplated for a moment, then said, "Could you find him for me, Simon, and put him through to my office? Thanks."

— «» —

About fifteen minutes later O'Rourke appeared on Dyson's monitor. His voice was low and somber. "Good morning, David. Simon told me about your friend. I'm really very sorry. Is there anything I can do to help?"

Dyson told O'Rourke about the DFP taking Pete's body and asked his advice.

"Well," O'Rourke answered carefully after a moment's reflection, "I can't imagine what the DFP want with the body, either, unless they think their forensics department can find something out about the hit-and-run driver."

"But why the DFP and not the NYPD?"

"Your friend was a priest. Perhaps the DFP feel the case should be treated as an internal matter."

"But this was a hit-and-run! It has nothing to do with the Doctrine of the Faith!" As soon as the words had left his mouth, doubt crept into Dyson's mind. Pete had been extremely upset about something. He believed he had some kind of knowledge that was dangerous, both to himself and Dyson. What could be more dangerous than a matter that might be of interest to the Doctrine of the Faith? Quickly attempting to cover this lapse in his train of thought, Dyson returned to O'Rourke's statement. "So who would make that decision? I mean, who decides if it's an internal matter or not?"

"Well, here in New York City that would be a matter for Cardinal Goodfellowe to decide."

At the mention of Goodfellowe's name, Dyson's fury involuntarily rose again.

"It's another bloody cover-up!" he shouted. "Another suspicious death, like my predecessor's apparent heart attack, that the authorities will have no chance of investigating because Goodfellowe wants something hushed up!"

"David, I can see you're upset, but I hardly think …"

"No, Tom! I mean yes, I am upset! But this is ridiculous. Who does he think he is?"

O'Rourke's expression became rather stern.

"Listen to me, David. Listen very carefully to what I am about to say. I consider you a friend, so I want to give you some advice before you get yourself into the kind of trouble even I can't get you out of. No matter what you or anyone else might think of him personally, Cardinal Goodfellowe is the head of this institute and a representative of His Holiness. As such, he is to be respected. Cardinal Goodfellowe's authority is wide-ranging and practically limitless. And apart from anything else, it is usually wise to have as little to do with the DFP as possible. I hope I'm making myself very clear on this point, David."

There was no mistaking the warning in O'Rourke's voice. The somber yet friendly timbre had vanished; he was almost imploring Dyson to be careful of what he said, it seemed. The path Dyson had started along was indeed a dangerous one, and it looked as though O'Rourke was attempting to bring him back to reality before he went too far. Dyson thought about his colleague's words for a second, and gradually common sense, supported by a healthy survival instinct, prevailed.

"But it's not right, Tom. It's not right of them to take Pete's body like that."

"No, David, it's probably not." O'Rourke's voice had once again taken on a much kinder tone. "Leave them to do their job, though. We have our job, they have theirs. Take some time off to mourn your friend, but don't get involved with the DFP. That really would not be advisable."

— «» —

Dyson slept on it and chose not to act, although it went against every principle he held dear. He was sure his enquiries would lead nowhere and did not want to risk endangering his position at the Archives. Any suspicion cast on his loyalty to the Church and its affiliated organizations might jeopardize his standing with the administration and ultimately the job he loved so much. Although the pain he felt at dropping the matter was almost physical in its intensity, he weighed up the pros and cons, and decided that there were definitely more disadvantages than advantages to acting on his gut feeling. Why was he even questioning this? He had worked so hard to get where he was today, and there was actually no proof of foul play of any kind. Perhaps it was as Tom said: the DFP believed they could find the hit-and-run driver using the extensive forensic means available to them. He felt foolish for being so paranoid.

CHAPTER 4

**Archives of the Holy Church of the Second Coming
New York City, 2077**

Dyson was working at his computer one morning two weeks after Pete's death when a small virtual cube appeared in the top right-hand corner of his 3D monitor. Evans' face, looking unusually perturbed, frowning, brow furrowed, filled the three-dimensional space.

"Sorry to disturb you, David." His voice did not come from any particular point of Dyson's computer system, but resonated through the image floating over his desk, making it seem as if the sound was emanating from somewhere in the center of the picture. Dyson rubbed his eyes wearily and pushed a virtual data cube within the monitor's image to one side, causing the image of Evans to expand automatically. He hated to be interrupted while he was working, but he tried to make his voice as friendly as possible when he replied.

"It's all right, Simon. What is it?"

"Well," Evans answered, "there's, em, a young lady here to see you."

Odd, Dyson thought, *I don't know any women here in New York*. Looking at Evans' image on his monitor he said, "I'm not expecting anyone. Did she say what she wants?"

"Not exactly. Just said she was a reporter and wanted to get some background information on a story she was writing. She says she wants to speak to you. Personally."

Dyson groaned quietly. "Surely there are enough priests in this place who can answer reporters' questions. In fact, haven't we got a whole press office full of staff to do just that? Tell her I'm very sorry, but I have a lot of work to do and..."

"Please excuse me, Father Dyson," a woman's voice said, "but I've spent half the morning negotiating with armed security gorillas at the entrance to let me into the building, cajoling people at the reception desk to tell me where I could find your office, and then trying to persuade your buddy here to let me see you personally."

Suddenly the face of a woman in her early thirties materialized on Dyson's monitor, hovering over Evans' right shoulder, causing poor Evans to flinch away in embarrassment at the close proximity of this rather forward young woman. The woman's face then beamed at Dyson with such a disarming smile that it was all he could do to prevent himself from beaming back at her.

"I beg your pardon!" Evans exclaimed, jumping up from his chair.

"Oh no, I beg *yours*, Father," the woman replied pleasantly. Evans had never been treated like this by a member of the public before. Depending on the rank of the clergy, the public either displayed polite respect or open fear toward men of the cloth. This woman was different, though. She seemed not to fear the priests at all, and the way she was apparently enjoying torturing the unfortunate Evans was anything but respectful. Partly in order to avoid an escalation of the rather embarrassing situation, and partly because he was quite intrigued by their visitor, Dyson called, "It's OK, Simon. Show her in!"

"But..." Evans started to protest.

"Simon. Please. It's all right, I'll see her."

The image of Evans and the woman on Dyson's monitor disappeared without further comment, and a few seconds later Evans rapped at his office door with the familiar double-knock.

"Come in, Simon," Dyson called.

The twin doors opened and in stepped Evans with the mysterious young woman in tow.

"David, may I introduce..." Evans began. "Erm, I'm sorry, I didn't quite catch your name," he said, looking doubtfully at the woman reporter. It was quite obvious that Evans was out of his league dealing with this female visitor. The woman then reproduced the same beaming smile that Dyson had admired on his monitor. *She lights up the room*, he thought. Her presence aroused feelings in him that he had believed long since extinguished through lack of use. His heart was fluttering in a most unseemly manner for a priest. Before he was able to focus his mind, she was advancing on him, arm extended, offering a handshake. He took her soft hand and it felt as if the warmth from it was gradually radiating throughout his body. He would never have admitted to a living soul that he actually felt physically weak at the knees.

"Rachel," she announced. "Rachel Watson, *New York Gazette*."

"M… my pleasure, Ms. Watson," Dyson managed to stammer. He was fascinated. She was so *alive*! She was not really a classic beauty in the sense that she would have been portrayed on the covers of e-zines, but she was so vivacious, positively radiating warmth; she was irresistible. Her shoulder-length reddish-brown hair threatened to partly cover her face, so she thrust it behind a slightly pointed, pixie-like ear with a practiced hand. This drew his attention to her large, almond-shaped blue eyes made even more startling by black eyeliner. Her eyes were accentuated by eyebrows that tapered upward at a seemingly impossible angle and then down at the ends. Full red lips framed small, perfectly white teeth that were currently treating him to the most beautiful smile he had ever seen. *Holy Lamb, what's happening to me?* he wondered. *Pull yourself together, man!*

"If I can have my hand back, I'll give you my card," the reporter said, one eyebrow raised and the corner of her mouth turned up in a playful smile.

Blushing like an embarrassed schoolboy, Dyson realized he was still clutching her hand, smiling foolishly and absent-mindedly at her. Releasing it, he stammered, "Oh, I'm s… so… sorry. Please, sit down, Ms. Rachel."

"Actually it's Watson, but Rachel will do fine," she said, taking the seat he had offered her in front of the desk.

Realizing Evans was still standing there looking rather lost, Dyson mumbled distractedly, "Thanks, Simon, I'll deal with this." An expression of relief briefly crossed Evans' face as he left the room with no further comment.

While Dyson was walking to his own seat, he took the opportunity, with his back turned to her, to quietly take a deep breath to calm himself. Sitting down and trying to make himself comfortable, he now enquired, "So, Ms., err… Rachel. How can I help you?"

"Well, Father Dyson, the question, actually, is how can *I* help *you*?"

"What do you mean? I don't even know you."

"Well, that's right," she agreed, "but we have, or rather had, a common acquaintance: Father Peter MacKenzie."

Dyson was intrigued. In an effort to maintain his composure he merely uttered, "Go on."

Rachel obliged. "Father MacKenzie came to my office at the *Gazette* when he arrived in New York last month. He had apparently asked around trying to find a reporter with a reputation for revealing the truth and writing the facts, no matter whose toes got trodden on. Even if they were ordained toes. Basically he was looking for someone with balls, and sooner or later, my name came up."

Rachel waited for Dyson's reaction to her little joke, but he was so nonplussed by her vocabulary that he said nothing, so she continued.

"Father MacKenzie seemed to have a problem with some knowledge that had come into his possession during the course of his work. He was quite worried about it. In fact, I won't beat around the bush with you, Father; he seemed positively terrified. I recorded our initial conversation. Would you like to hear it?"

When Dyson gravely nodded his agreement, Rachel pulled a mem-tab from her handbag and offered it to him.

"It's only audio, but that doesn't matter," she told him as he inserted the featureless piece of plastic, as small as the nail on his little finger, into a slot in his desktop.

Rachel leaned toward Dyson's virtual monitor and spoke in a clear voice: "MacKenzie recording." The tab started playing the audio file through the monitor, and an eerie feeling swept over Dyson as he listened to his friend's voice, as if from beyond the grave, talking to this female reporter, Rachel Watson, now sitting in his office:

"Something's going on. Something weird. We were processing some historical documents at the repository in Lambeth. They were found in some cellar somewhere near London in a house that was due for demolition. The last owner had died without an heir, so everything was deemed to have been legally bequeathed to the Church, of course. The documents were pretty old, but not *that* old: nineteenth century. My mate Philip was going through a batch of papers in a box and found something funny. It was something about the crucifixion of Christ. Philip said it was strange because it sounded like whoever wrote the document actually wanted to *see* the crucifixion. Kind of like he thought it was really still possible somehow. Well, Steve and I just thought there was some nineteenth-century nutcase with delusions of being the Savior. You know the sort: hears divine voices telling him to absolve people of their sins and so on. So the three of us got on with our sorting and for a couple of hours nothing out of the ordinary happened.

"Then Philip found another document written by this oddball and made some flippant remark about his 'loony' changing the date of Christmas to April or some such rubbish. We didn't think anything of it at the time, of course, that's why I'm not really sure any more exactly what it was Philip said."

Dyson had listened patiently up until now, but was gradually finding it more and more difficult to see why these rather banal details should have had such an effect on his friend and indeed where the whole tale was leading. Rachel perceived that Dyson was slowly losing interest and held up a hand as a signal for him to be patient.

"So far so good, Father," Rachel's voice interrupted gently from the recording, "Now, if you'd mind telling me why you came to *me* with this... As far as I understand it, some schizophrenic thinks he's the Lamb of God and wants to celebrate Christmas in April? Well, OK, Father, that's weird, but more the sort of story a less reputable paper than the *Gazette* would want to print."

"It's more than that, Ms. Watson. My mate Philip was killed in a car crash two days after this happened."

"Hmm, well, look, Father, I'm truly sorry about your friend, but I still fail to see the relevance of all this. There must be dozens of people killed in road accidents every day all over the world. It's tragic but it's a fact of life!"

Pete's voice turned into a hushed whisper. "I haven't finished yet," he hissed. "There's more."

A shiver ran down Dyson's spine. It was as if he were listening to a stranger. It was not only the promise of finding out about some nefarious secret that chilled him; it was the eerie sound of his friend's voice. Something had happened to Pete since Dyson had last seen him in England. Something awful. What was it?

Rachel also seemed to have been enthralled at the time the recording was made. She encouraged Pete to continue.

"Philip lived in the room next to mine at the priests' hostel, so we saw quite a lot of each other. On the day he died, two cars arrived at our building. It was the DFP."

At this, Dyson stirred uncomfortably in his chair. Risking a quick glance at the journalist, he noticed that she was watching him intently, as if to gauge his reactions.

"They cleared everything out of Philip's flat. And I *mean* everything. Philip didn't have a lot of stuff but it took them ages. They were thorough, I'll give them that.

"While four or five of them were doing that, two of them hammered on my door and said they wanted to ask me a few questions. When I asked them why they were taking all Philip's stuff, they shoved me around a bit and warned me to mind my own business. Then they started asking me funny questions about the documents Philip had found written by that loony. They seemed to be taking the matter extremely seriously. I told them I knew nothing, but they didn't believe me. At first they considered taking me in for questioning, but then they decided to do it there and then, in my flat. They seemed to need a result, and fast. One of them held me down while the other hit me. About half an hour later I'd told them again and again what I've just told you. They seemed to be satisfied that I knew nothing else but told me they'd be back if they had any more questions."

There was silence for a few seconds before Rachel spoke on the recording again.

"All right then, Father. So what do you want me to do now?"

"After the DFP had left, I emptied my post box just inside the front door of our building," Pete said conspiratorially. "I found a brown envelope in it with no stamp or postmark. Someone must have dropped it in there personally. When I looked inside and saw what was in it, I knew it must have been Philip. Don't ask me why he would have done that, I don't know. Perhaps he suspected that he'd found something dangerous.

"A friend of mine works for the Church Archives here in New York. I want to ask him about this, but if the DFP catch me with it, which is quite likely if I take it into the Church Headquarters building, it'll all be hushed up and the truth will never be told. And I'm afraid I'll end up like poor Philip. Accidental death, no one to blame, no trial, nothing."

"Father MacKenzie, look at this from my point of view. You come in here and tell me that a friend of yours read some old papers written by someone you yourself have called a 'loony' and an 'oddball.' Then you imply to me that the DFP have killed your friend who left you a brown envelope. Why would the DFP be interested? And, quite frankly, Father MacKenzie, the most important question for me right now is why should I be interested?"

"Because it's happened before," Pete's hissed voice from the tab. "It's rumored that about forty years ago similar documents were uncovered in London. They were also confiscated by the Church because of the dangerous content."

"Rumors?" Rachel put in skeptically.

"Rumors, myths, legends, whatever!" Pete snapped. "It is generally well known and believed by many experts in certain circles that these papers exist. I'm not sure why they should be so dangerous, but people who have come into contact with them have died!"

"OK," Rachel said on the recording. "Let's say I play along. You still haven't answered my question: what do you want me to do?"

"I want you to keep the envelope safe for me in case anything happens to me. Here."

There was a rustling sound on the recording, then Pete went on.

"This is the paper I found in my post box. I want you to keep it for me. If you don't hear from me by the end of the month, contact my friend, David Dyson, at the Church Headquarters building, Archives Department."

The recording ended at this point, but Dyson and Rachel remained silent for a few moments longer, both seemingly lost in their own thoughts. Dyson was about to ask about the mysterious document Pete had given her but when he looked up, he realized Rachel was already holding out a sheet of paper for him. The document he took from her was indeed old, probably two hundred years or more. The yellowed paper was extremely dry and quite brittle. Normally it would have been unthinkable for him to handle such a treasure with his bare hands for fear of the oils in his skin destroying the precious document. These were exceptional circumstances, though, calling for exceptional measures.

The document was handwritten in an elegant, extravagant script. Unlike many documents of the same era, the handwriting of this one was extremely neat and therefore easy to read. Part of the first sentence was missing. Dyson read the document aloud:

…Hebrew month of Nisan corresponds to March — April in our calendar reckoning. On the other hand, some informed me that the synoptic account tallies with the account in John. Allowing for the period of Pontius Pilate's time as procurator and the dates of the Passover at that time, Jesus' death is most likely to have been on April, 7, AD 30. As surprising as all this new information would appear to be, it has nonetheless given me a starting point at least, from which I shall, if fortune smiles upon me, be in a position to embark

upon more accurate research with a view to pinpointing the exact date of the event.

Based on this information, I now intend once again to visit every day in April, but this time proceeding from the year AD 30. However, this will be such a time-consuming exercise that I have decided to rest for a few days before embarking upon this renewed mission. My efforts have once again been consuming me, both physically and mentally, over the past several months, so that I am finding it increasingly difficult to concentrate on the task at hand. I feel that it would be a waste of time and effort if my experiments were to fail simply because I was too fatigued to calibrate my instruments properly.

"This is the paper Pete gave you?" Dyson asked.

"Yes."

"Any idea what it could mean?"

"I was hoping you'd be able to tell me."

Dyson read the sheet of paper again, silently this time. When he had finished he heaved a sigh.

"Well, as far as the time of the crucifixion is concerned, the author's reasoning is correct."

The reporter stared at him. "Err, isn't that some kind of heresy?"

Dyson looked puzzled. "No, why should it be?"

"Well, if Jesus was crucified in AD 30, he wasn't thirty-three like it says in the Bible. Aren't you contradicting your holy book?"

"Well for one thing, it doesn't say anywhere in the Bible that Our Lord was thirty-three when he died. And for another thing, the year of his birth was miscalculated."

"What?!"

"Oh yes, most experts agree he was born several years before the date commonly publicized."

"But...don't you think people, I mean the public at large, should know about this? Surely it changes everything. It would mean this isn't even 2077!"

"Well, no, you're right. But quite frankly I don't see the problem. We believe that Our Lord and Savior Jesus Christ, the Lamb of God, was born, lived for roughly thirty years or so as a man, was crucified by the Romans and then rose from the dead on the third day. Who cares in what year he was born on Earth or in what year he left? The fact is, he ascended into heaven to watch over us until the end of days and has been appearing to us around the world to remind us that he is still there."

Rachel shook her head in disbelief; partly at this nonchalant attitude of a priest confronted with facts that evidently didn't agree with what his organization was allowing people to believe, and partly at the uncritical parrot-like recital of the man's faith. It looked like his church had done a pretty good job of brainwashing him. She tried a different tack:

"So what about the cover-up regarding the papers? Why is the Church concealing the truth?"

"OK, look, I too have heard rumors about mysterious papers which the Church is supposedly keeping under wraps. After all, I do live in the real world despite the white collar, Ms. Watson. That's just nonsense, though: just your typical conspiracy theory that arises when the man in the street feels powerless in the face of the inexplicable. I'm sure if there really was such a thing going on, then I would have found at least some small clue in the Archives. Quite apart from all that, this person supposedly wanted to 'visit' the year AD 30! No wonder Pete said he was an oddball."

But Rachel was not laughing. She thought for a little while longer and when she spoke, her voice was serious.

"Father Dyson, for decades, books and television shows made a lot of money for a lot of people discussing the existence of so-called inexplicable apparitions and occurrences; the Bermuda Triangle, spontaneous human combustion, the Loch Ness Monster, UFOs, to name just a few. In the past, people argued about the existence or non-existence of these phenomena. Today we know that there was indeed some manifestation of each of these things, the difference being that we now know the cause of each of them. They have been scientifically proven: explained as natural occurrences or as coincidences completely unrelated to one another and therefore eventually discounted as linked phenomena at all.

What they all have in common, however, is the fact that they were once *rumors*; then they developed into something akin to urban legends, before subsequently either being proven or explained away by science. Let's now suppose that there are indeed rumors of something similar happening forty years ago. I mean about secret papers being confiscated and about a cover-up. There is usually a grain of truth in myths, legends, and rumors, as I've just said; that's what I've learned in my job, anyway. 'There's no smoke without fire,' as they say."

"All right," Dyson agreed, "but..."

Rachel cut him off with an index finger raised to her lips, requesting silence. Intrigued, Dyson obeyed.

"Let's assume that the two cases are related; that the paper you hold in your hand is actually one of a set of documents written by the same person in the nineteenth century.

"All right?" she added when Dyson remained silent.

"All right."

"We both know that a man from the nineteenth century cannot visit the year AD 30."

She raised her eyebrows, waiting for a response, and Dyson nodded.

"How unusual is it for the DFP to confiscate the body of a hit-and-run victim?"

Understanding that Rachel was trying to piece the story together in logical steps, he did not wish to disturb the flow, so he merely said, "Very."

"So there must be something in these papers to get them involved. Your friend was genuinely frightened when he came to see me. He claimed people had already died and he was afraid for his own life, and that's why he came here to the States. He knew the British branch of the DFP was interested in him, but he didn't think they would make it an international matter. Not at the time anyway. Father Dyson, we need to get our hands on more of these papers."

After a moment's silence Dyson realized she was again waiting for a reaction.

"And just how do you intend to do that?" he enquired. *Well, that was pretty feeble*, he thought as soon as the words had left his mouth.

That delightful smile spread across her face once again, causing Dyson's eyes to involuntarily light up in response.

"Well, Father, correct me if I'm wrong, but I seem to remember that I'm an investigative journalist and you are a trained historian and archaeologist with the largest, most powerful historical database in the world at his fingertips."

Dyson smiled back, rather nervously. "And the DFP?"

"Nobody said it would be easy." Her coyly raised eyebrow and her crooked, ironic smile temporarily caught him off his guard, leaving him in speechless wonder for a second before he came to his senses.

"Wait a minute, though. Do you seriously expect me to believe that my Church — *our* Church — could be responsible for a cover-up of such magnitude that they would be willing to commit the ultimate sin of murder to protect their secret? I'm afraid I can't even begin to entertain such a thought! That's not only heresy; it's simply madness."

"Father Dyson, quite frankly I don't even know what to believe myself. But something smells rotten here, that's one thing I *do* know from my years of experience in my job. Perhaps even your Church leaders don't know what's going on, but I'll bet you anything you like that the DFP wouldn't be squeamish about murder if it served their interests."

Dyson was honestly shocked by her openness. This kind of talk got people into very serious trouble indeed, and here she was saying things like this to a priest!

"What makes you think I won't have you arrested?" he asked out of interest. "After all, I am a loyal servant of the Church with nothing to gain and everything to lose by even listening to your heresy. You come in here making wild allegations about one of the Holy Church's departments, and you seem to expect complete cooperation on my part. How do you know you can trust me?"

"Well, for one thing, Peter MacKenzie trusted you with his life. He wanted to inform you about what's going on here and he wasn't afraid you'd turn him in to the DFP over it, so I'm gambling that you're not the kind of man to shoot first and ask questions later."

Dyson was about to stutter something unintelligible, but thought better of it.

Rachel went on, "Another thing is that I'm quite sure you are a professionally curious man; otherwise you wouldn't have gotten the job as Keeper of the Archives. That's another reason why I'd bet you want to get to the bottom of this."

Dyson acquiesced. She had read him like a book, seeming to fully understand his motivation. He was indeed burning to discover what was going on, so there was obviously no point in denying the truth of anything she had just said. It would probably also be useful to have someone outside the Church working with him, especially an experienced journalist. He nodded his silent agreement.

Rachel's blue eyes seemed to flash at him for a second, but she continued with a deadpan expression on her pretty face. "Apart from that, didn't I tell you I have big balls?"

This time Dyson was able to smile at her humor and even found himself admiring her courage, too. In fact, he was completely enchanted by the young woman's irresistible charm.

"All right, let's say I'll help you. Where do we start?"

"Well, what about forty years ago?"

"But they were just rumors. And anyway, 'about' forty years ago, which is what Pete said, could mean a span of *at least* five years on either side, maybe more. We might have to cover a ten to fifteen-year period."

"All right, but that's still a starting point. It's better than nothing; in this business you have to take what you can get. Your friend Peter MacKenzie said someone died back then. Let's assume, just for the sake of argument, that that's true. Once again, we have to start somewhere, so we take an assumption as a truth — a thesis, if you will — until it can be disproved. In a way, it's similar to scientific method. So, who would have had access to these papers in the first place?"

"If there was a definite case of someone dying, or being murdered, as Pete claimed, because of these papers, then it could have been the person who found them." Dyson still could not believe he was allowing himself to be drawn into this... this conspiracy theory, but he seemed to be helpless in the face of Rachel's logic. Or was it her femininity that he found so irresistible? No, he wouldn't allow himself to go down that path.

"But if that person had just been Joe Public, wouldn't he have gone to the press with it? Wouldn't the content of the papers now be common knowledge already?"

"Hmm, obviously it hasn't been leaked to the world at large," Dyson contemplated, "otherwise there would have been no element of danger. Then I suppose it was probably someone from the Church."

As soon as he said it, Dyson felt very uncomfortable. Years of devotion to his faith, as well as his long training — some, like his father, might even say brainwashing — in Church institutions, had left their indelible mark on him. He felt like a traitor for merely contemplating that something might not be as he had believed it was. Nevertheless, he pressed on. Always the pragmatist, he knew he could never rest until this particular mystery had been solved, no matter what the outcome might be. He took a deep breath and tried to convince himself that becoming involved with the pretty woman with whom he was currently plotting was not going to lead to him doubt his faith.

"Pete said it had happened before. Maybe it really was an identical occurrence. Maybe it was a field researcher who was sorting the papers back then."

"So we're looking for a suspicious or accidental death of a field researcher around forty years ago. MacKenzie said the papers were found in London. By the way, are all Church field researchers priests?" Rachel was now visibly warming to her subject, her whole demeanor becoming more intense and concentrated.

"Yes," Dyson replied without hesitation. "The Holy Church considers the history of the faith to be sacred, so that it may only be kept and researched, officially at least, by the ordained."

"That makes it a little easier, then. It reduces the search to priests who were also historical field researchers. What do you think?" The reporter was now visibly excited. She was apparently moving in for the kill.

"I suppose I could do a database search based on that, but it's still not an awful lot to go on considering the time span we're dealing with. I could get some of the team to help me." *Am I seriously offering an outsider that I will use Church resources to perform illicit research into Church business?*

"No!" she almost shouted at him. Then her voice softened again: "Listen, Father, we're dealing with something that has already cost lives here. We have to be careful. I've been in this business for quite a number of years already, so I'm kinda used to it. But you..." She trailed off, but Dyson fully understood what she was carefully trying to avoid saying.

"Hey, look, I may be a novice at the cloak and dagger stuff, but my friend has probably died because of this and I want to know why."

"I completely understand, but until we're sure what's going on here and who's involved, you should speak to no one. Trust nobody. Absolutely nobody."

"What about Simon?"

"Simon?"

"The priest who showed you to my office."

Rachel shook her head slowly. "Uh-uh. Not even Simon. Even if he's not involved..."

"Which he most certainly isn't!" Dyson said indignantly, with rather more force than he had intended to use.

"Even if he's not involved," Rachel continued as if Dyson hadn't spoken, "a careless word from him to someone who *is* involved could be disastrous. Agreed?"

Dyson had only just met this woman, but he had known and worked closely with Evans for two years. It was therefore with a heavy heart that he actually forced himself to think about what this stranger was expecting of him. Simon was his friend. Over the last two years they had talked together about all manner of work-related as well as private matters. Simon certainly knew him better than anyone else at work. Upon further reflection, he had to admit that Rachel was right. He would have trusted Simon with his life, but agreed, for the moment, not to confide in him. Dyson realized he couldn't drag his friend into a potentially dangerous scenario. He was planning to use the Church databases for private research.

This in itself was bad enough, but they were going one step further: they intended to investigate the Church itself. A slip of the tongue in the wrong place to the wrong person could mean the end of his career, or worse.

"All right then, Father. I suggest we meet again in a couple of days when we've both had time to do a little research. Where do you want to keep the document? I mean it's not the kind of thing you want someone to find in your office. Especially not here," Rachel said, motioning with her arm to indicate the whole building.

"Have you got somewhere *you* could keep it?" Dyson asked, offering to give her back the paper.

"Sure, I have a safe at home," she said, replacing the paper in its envelope and storing it in her bag again. "So how does Friday sound to you? We could get together and discuss what we'll hopefully have found by then."

"Hmm, three days. Friday sounds OK, but I don't think it's a good idea for you to come here again. It's awkward enough that the people in reception know that a female journalist was here to see me. If anyone asks, I'll tell them you were enquiring about a childhood friend of mine, which is true. But if they notice you coming here to see me again, I'll have quite a lot of very unwelcome explaining to do."

"OK, your place or mine?" She flashed him that one-eyebrow-raised, coy blue-eyed smile again.

Dyson blushed. "Well, err, what about somewhere more neutral? Say, the Church Library on 4th Avenue? Archaeology section?"

Rachel smiled. "All right, Father, if it will make you feel more comfortable."

"It would. Oh, and Rachel?"

"Yes?"

"Under the circumstances I think it would be all right for you to call me David."

"David it is. See you on Friday. Two p.m. OK?"

"Fine. I'll show you out."

Returning to his desk after guiding Rachel back to the elevator, Dyson sat motionless for a few minutes, gathering his thoughts. The idea that Pete had been murdered in cold blood was upsetting enough. The idea that the DFP, an arm of the Holy Church — *his* Church — was supposedly behind it, was, quite frankly, shocking to him.

The DFP had a reputation for carrying out the unpleasant but necessary tasks required by the Church; things an ordinary man of the cloth could not be expected to do. Until now Dyson had known these tasks involved collecting Church Tax from late payers and handing out on-the-spot fines to people who publicly — or sometimes even privately — criticized the Church. They also investigated people suspected of subversive activities against the Church and interrogated them. He knew their methods were occasionally controversial, but a tough job required tough methods. It was not the kind of thing you thought about normally, and it was especially not the kind of thing people *talked* about, particularly in public. As a Church-going, law-abiding citizen, you had nothing to fear from the DFP and would usually never have the misfortune to come into contact with them. But something at the back of Dyson's mind was nagging at him. Something wasn't right. Should people actually have to *fear* an arm of the Holy Church?

There was a rap at the door.

"Come in!"

"Hi, David." It was Victor N'Komo, his Congolese colleague. "Bjørn asked me to pick up the package of fourteenth-century contracts you have for him."

Distracted by his thoughts, Dyson pointed at a corner of the desk without looking. "Sure, Victor, there they are."

"Thanks. And bye!"

As the door closed behind the heavy-set African, Dyson suddenly realized he had been talking to Rachel Watson for so long that he had very little time left to finish a report he needed to submit to Cardinal Goodfellowe that afternoon. Temporarily putting aside everything apart from the job he was actually being paid to do, Dyson called up his half-finished report on the monitor and carried on with it, leaving the other matter until the next day.

CHAPTER 5

**Archives of the Holy Church of the Second Coming
New York City, 2077**

When Dyson arrived for work the next morning, he discovered Artur Meltz in his office. This was nothing at all out of the ordinary, as Artur was a member of his team of researchers and had access to Dyson's office via the chip embedded in his arm.

"Morning, David," he said jovially. "I've just brought you those Gnostic scrolls you sent to the lab last week. You were right about their age, by the way: carbon dating puts them around AD 30, as you suspected." Meltz gently laid a light blue plastic box, about thirty centimetres square and ten centimetres high, onto Dyson's desk.

"Oh, thanks, Artur, I'll look forward to translating these now that the date has been verified."

"OK, well you have fun doing that, and I'll see you in a couple of weeks then." Artur was grinning from ear to ear.

Dyson looked at his colleague quizzically, but then remembered that he had instructed Meltz to join a party of researchers who were leaving for Hawaii that same day to investigate and report on a purported appearance of the Lamb there.

"You lucky dog," Dyson said, smiling wryly.

"You know, it's at times like this I'm glad I'm just a humble researcher and not the boss who has to stay here and manage everything!"

"Get out of here!" Dyson called in mock anger.

With his back already turned, Meltz waved a cheery goodbye and left Dyson's office.

As soon as he was alone, Dyson pulled a flat piece of aluminum the length of his index finger from a drawer of his desk and pointed it at each of the box's four plastic seals bearing the emblem of the Church. Each time he aimed at a seal, he pressed a tiny button in the middle of the device, and each time there was an audible beep from the microcircuits embedded in the seals securing the lid onto the blue box.

Whenever the Church needed to dispatch physical documents from one place to another, these blue boxes with electronic seals were used to ensure that only the intended recipient was able to open them. Dyson's electronic key decoded the signals emitted by the seals — which were especially coded for his key — and sent an electronic command to disarm them. Any attempt to force the lid or to cut through the box would have resulted in the box and its contents being engulfed in a chemical blaze that would not only consume the box and its contents, but also seriously injure whoever was trying to open it illegally. Of course, the Church made copies of everything that was dispatched in such boxes so no information was lost, but it was nevertheless a loss for humanity when genuine documents were destroyed by people meddling in the affairs of the Church. This almost never happened, of course, as it was common knowledge that the Church's boxes could not be opened by anyone other than the intended recipient.

Once the seals had been disarmed, Dyson used a sharp knife to cut through the now harmless plastic stickers. It saddened Dyson that such measures were necessary, but wherever important Church documents were concerned, there was always a danger of terrorists accessing them and using them for their own nefarious purposes, such as publicly attacking the Church's interpretations of the scriptures. Once he had removed the lid, Dyson donned a fresh pair of white cotton gloves and unwrapped a sterile pair of tweezers to lift the scrolls from the box. The tweezers were just about to make contact with the precious freight when a gong sounded, breaking the total silence in the office, and almost causing Dyson to stab the scrolls with the tweezers. Annoyed, he turned to look at his monitor, which had been the source of the noise. There was now an e-note floating serenely above his desk, tracing an apparently random path within the almost invisible confines of the 3D monitor. It read:

"Father Dyson, please come to my office as soon as you read this. Goodfellowe."

"Oh, no!" Dyson groaned. "What now?"

Although he had written several reports for the cardinal over the last two years, he had always submitted these electronically, thus avoiding any personal contact with his boss. Even at the annual Christmas and Easter celebrations, Goodfellowe had put in a brief obligatory appearance and had then discreetly vanished without mingling with the minions. Dyson had never been summoned to the head of the facility like this before, so he had never seen the inside of the cardinal's office. With a sigh of resignation, he left his own office and walked down the corridor to take the elevator to the 192nd floor, the penthouse. On his way there, he met O'Rourke coming the other way.

"Good morning, David, and where might you be off to then?" O'Rourke enquired cheerfully.

Dyson answered glumly, but carried on walking. "Have to see Cardinal Goodfellowe about something."

O'Rourke's expression became more serious. "Oh, nothing wrong, I hope?"

"We'll see," Dyson said, shrugging noncommittally.

O'Rourke raised his right hand in the air as they passed each other, as if to wish his colleague good luck.

On the 192nd floor, Dyson stood for a few seconds in front of the cardinal's ornate office door. Scenes from the New Testament were carved in relief, adorning the door in exquisite detail: the Sermon on the Mount, the Last Supper, the Resurrection. He smoothed down his cassock, brushed back his hair, took a deep breath, and knocked on the door with what he hoped sounded like a confident rap.

Two seconds later the door swung open and Dyson gazed into what looked like a room for entertaining heads of state in a sumptuously decorated palace. For a moment he was so stunned, he merely stood there and goggled. The room itself was enormous. *It must take up half the floor*, he thought. Crystal chandeliers dangled heavily from the ceiling; thick Persian carpets adorned the floor. The ubiquitous, almost invisible glass that constituted three of the four walls of the office offered the occupants a bird's-eye view of the city where they weren't festooned with rich tapestries depicting scenes from the Old and New Testaments. Here and there, oil paintings had been hung between the tapestries. Dyson recognized works by Botticelli and Rubens. *Surely not originals*, he mused, but he was not at all certain. Strategically placed around the walls were gilded chaises longue upholstered in pleasant pastel shades. In the center of the room stood a gigantic, solid oak conference table with equally solid wooden armchairs for fifty people around it. The chair at the head of the table resembled a throne with its high, ornate, padded back, onto which the symbol of the Church of the Second Coming was embroidered in spun gold.

"If you'd like to come in now, Father Dyson..."

Dyson realized with a start that the cardinal was sitting at a colossal wooden desk at the far end of the room, still waiting for him to enter.

"I, err, beg your pardon, Your Eminence," he stuttered, and finally walked through the door. Turning to close it behind him, he saw that it was already closing automatically. Once Dyson walked the length of the room to stand before the cardinal's desk, Goodfellowe, without rising from his seat, casually motioned to a chair next to Dyson without even deigning to look at his employee. "Sit down, Father."

Dyson sat as commanded, waiting nervously to discover what the cardinal could possibly want of him. For the first time in his life, he contemplated with quite some discomfort, he was keeping a secret from his Church. He felt like a schoolboy who had broken a window and was now sitting in the principal's office waiting to see if the principal knew it had been him, and what dread punishment would be doled out to him. As if Goodfellowe wanted to exacerbate the unaccustomed feeling of guilt already plaguing Dyson and causing him to feel extremely uneasy, he ignored Dyson for a while longer and continued mumbling at his workstation, dictating something inaudibly.

Despite his predicament, though, Dyson was not able to resist the urge to examine his astonishing surroundings more closely. At this end of the room, antique wooden cabinets covered much of the space along the walls. Then, after risking a glance in the direction of the cardinal, something caught Dyson's eye. On the wall behind and above Goodfellowe hung a digital 3D display measuring about two meters high by one meter fifty wide. In the center of the photo stood the Lamb of God, hands clasped before him, looking as serene as Dyson had seen him in hundreds of similar photographs documenting the Lamb's known visitations around the world. The only difference between them and this photograph was that this one also depicted a teenage boy standing proudly beside the Savior.

Dyson's studies had included sociology, art history, and anthropology, so it was with a trained eye that he studied the picture, completely forgetting for a moment the unpleasant situation he was in. The boy's arms were folded, posing for the picture. He was not actually smiling, but he looked extremely satisfied with himself: proud, confident. Something made Dyson believe that the youth had found confirmation in his beliefs. It was as if he was looking into the camera with the defiance of someone thinking: "Right, *now* let's see you deny what I told you!" The boy was tall but slightly built, about fourteen or fifteen years old. Dyson looked from the youth in the picture to the cardinal, then back to the youth again. Could it be?

"Yes," Goodfellowe said suddenly, as if he had read Dyson's mind. "I was fourteen when that picture was taken. It was 2026 in Egypt. I was on holiday with my parents and the Lamb suddenly appeared right there next to me. At the time my parents were startled, frightened even. But for me it was a sign. On that day, I decided that my life would take a new direction. That was the day I knew my life was to be devoted to serving the Lamb of God."

He sighed with what seemed to Dyson to be sorrow or regret, appearing to be lost in thought. For an instant, the Cardinal appeared to be more human, more vulnerable than usual. A moment later, however, Goodfellowe composed himself again, cleared his throat, and started the meeting in earnest. "Father Dyson," he said gruffly, his bony hands clasped on the desk before him, eyes raised to the ceiling, "it has come to my attention that you have been seeing a *woman*." The cardinal enunciated the word "woman" in such a way that it conveyed not only astonishment but also a not inconsiderable degree of distaste.

Dyson was shocked. *He must have eyes and ears everywhere*, he thought. *Oh Holy Lamb, what do I do now? What do I tell him?*

"Err, I, erm, but..." So many things were going through his mind all at once at this moment that Dyson feared he would not be able to articulate anything at all. His mind was spinning, reeling with anxiety. He had never felt such emotions before. Taking a deep breath to compose himself, he finally managed to pluck up the courage to stammer, "Err, I beg your forgiveness, Eminence, but that is not quite correct."

The cardinal looked at him skeptically for a brief moment, then returned his gaze to the ceiling, but otherwise he remained silent.

"I...if that's what you've heard, Eminence, then I'm afraid you've been misinformed."

"Oh?" Goodfellowe retorted finally, lowering his eyes from the ceiling and fixing Dyson with an icy stare. His level voice and expressionless face betrayed absolutely nothing of what might be going through his mind. "My sources are not usually wrong about such matters, as I am almost certain you have heard. Perhaps you would care to enlighten me by relating to me *your* version of events."

"Well, Eminence, as I only know one woman in New York personally, I suppose you mean her. But I've seen this woman I assume you are speaking of once and only once in my entire life. That was when she came here yesterday, in fact. So you, I mean, one, could really not call it actually 'seeing' her as such. I mean, it's, erm, it's not as if…"

"Is this woman perhaps a relative of yours, Father?" the cardinal interrupted, appearing to already know full well that she was no such thing.

"No, Eminence. She is a reporter with the *New York Gazette*."

"I see." Goodfellowe's cold gray eyes were drilling into him like icy daggers.

Oh Holy Lamb, he knows everything! He's playing with me! The DFP are probably waiting outside; waiting to take me away! I'm going to be tortured! My job. I'm going to lose everything!

Dyson felt like a frightened rodent hypnotized by a snake. Beads of sweat began to form on his forehead, and his white clerical collar suddenly felt very hot and tight around his neck. It was as if the collar were throttling him for betraying his Church by keeping secrets from it. "Thou shalt have no other God before me." *But I haven't betrayed God!*

"So then," the cardinal continued, "what might you have done, pray tell, to cause a representative of the Church-independent press to emerge from the slime of her gutter and defile this establishment by interviewing you at your place of work? *Sacred* work, I might add, for which you are not only recompensed with the promise of eternal heavenly rewards, but also with a not insignificant sum of money every month."

The slime of her gutter? Dyson balked at the cardinal's choice of vocabulary.

"Well, it wasn't actually about me, Eminence. It was about a friend of mine."

This was now getting too close to home for Dyson, who was also becoming irritated at the game of cat and mouse Goodfellowe was apparently playing with him. *If he knows everything anyway, why doesn't he just come out and say it?*

The cardinal continued relentlessly. "Couldn't the good lady have used the phone?"

Dyson squirmed nervously in his seat. *Exactly how much does he know?*

"I'm sure she could have done so, Eminence."

"So she came to see you personally to talk to you about a friend of yours?"

"Yes, Eminence." *For God's sake, either have me arrested or leave me alone, man! I've done nothing wrong! Please, please let me go...I'll never be unfaithful to the Church again!*

Now it was not only Dyson's heart that was pounding uncomfortably in his chest; his head had begun to throb as well. He felt dizzy, nauseous.

"And what did this friend of yours do to merit such a personal visit by the press? A personal visit that could have been rendered unnecessary by a simple phone call, I might add."

The voice was oily, sneering. Dyson reached breaking point and snapped in an outburst of fear, guilt and anger. Before he could stop himself, he yelled, "He died, dammit!" As soon as the words had left his mouth, he regretted them. He bit his teeth together to prevent the next part from coming out: *As if you bloody well didn't know, you bastard!* He closed his eyes and swallowed hard, waiting for the cardinal to blast him, and, in all probability, relieve him of his duties as Keeper of the Archives.

For a few seconds neither of the two men spoke. Dyson could not bear to make eye contact with the cardinal, preferring to stare blankly at the desk in front of him. However, far from being outraged or shocked by Dyson's insolence, the cardinal was now looking at him levelly. *Oh my God, man, you are one callous son of a bitch! At least react — show some human emotion! Fire me, yell at me, do something!* But the cardinal did not fulfill Dyson's wish: instead, he looked thoughtful, as if trying to make up his mind about something. Dyson finally broke the unbearable and highly embarrassing silence. His voice was repentant:

"I do beg your pardon most humbly, Eminence. I... I've been under quite a bit of a strain lately. My friend's death came as quite a shock."

The cardinal's reply came brutally fast: "Perhaps we should give you a few weeks' leave, Father. That is, until you are able to perform your duties again with the appropriate degree of concentration required in a position such as yours."

Dyson's heart sank. He needed access to the Archives. "Oh, no, please, Eminence. It is the Lamb's work and it is my duty to perform it. I humbly beg you to allow me to carry on with it. My work is all I have."

"Then I trust you will not be seeing this woman again?"

For the briefest instant Dyson's eyes looked down at his fingers resting on his lap. The breaking of eye contact to look down, however brief, Dyson knew from various seminars, was an indication of guilt. *Damn!* he thought as he looked up again, *I hope he didn't notice that.* Forcing himself to fix his own eyes on the cardinal's, he lied:

"I will not."

"Very well, Father." Goodfellowe nodded slowly in Dyson's direction. The cardinal reminded Dyson of an old, wise predator in the desert or the jungle whose prey had escaped for the sole reason that the predator had already eaten its fill. Yet the predator was so much more powerful than its prey, and it had the patience to stalk it mercilessly until hunger drove it to kill once more.

"You may go," the cardinal said, waving his right hand toward the doors at the far end of the room in a regal, dismissive gesture. "May the Lamb be with you."

Making a tremendous effort not to show emotion of any kind, Dyson stood up and bowed his head reverently toward the cardinal.

"I thank you for your concern for the welfare of my soul and for your wise words of guidance, Eminence. I shall take them to heart and I promise to learn from your wisdom," he said obediently. This was the standard clergy formula to be said to a superior after an official admonishment. Dyson took the traditional two steps backward from his superior and then turned to leave the palatial room, but when he reached the door, which swung open automatically when he was still two meters away from it, the cardinal called after him.

"Just one more thing." Goodfellowe's voice resonated across the length of the vast room.

"Yes, Eminence?" Dyson turned and waited obediently.

"Be careful. Be very careful, Father Dyson."

"Of course, Eminence. God be with you, Eminence."

Dyson shuddered involuntarily and left. *Oh Holy Lamb, what does he know? I'm glad it's over with at least.* When he returned to his office, however, he realized it was far from over.

— ⟨⟩ —

While he was holding up his arm so that the chip embedded in it would open his office door, Janet spoke to him from a pocket of his cassock.

"You have an incoming message, David. Audiovisual, real-time."

Fumbling Janet from the depths of his cassock, he opened the door and entered his office, simultaneously addressing his comPod.

"Who is it, Janet?"

"It's Rachel Watson, David."

Dyson's heart began to beat faster, although he could not tell whether this was because he was about to break his word to Cardinal Goodfellowe so soon after making a promise not to speak to the journalist again, or simply because he was about to talk to Rachel once more.

"Put her on, Janet,"

Rachel's face looked a little concerned as she appeared on the screen in his palm.

"Hi, David." Her tone was casual. "Listen, when I got home and opened my bag last night the document was there, but the mem-tab with Pete MacKenzie's interview wasn't. Did you put it somewhere safe?"

"Err, just a second," he said. "If I didn't give it back to you, it's still in the drive on my desk."

He walked over to the desk and let his hand hover over a particular spot. Nothing happened. He repeated the exercise with the other two spots. This would normally have ejected mem-tabs from their drives. Nothing happened. *Hardware malfunction?* he thought briefly. He flopped heavily into his leather armchair, leaned toward the monitor and called up the contents of the various drives, checking to see if there was a tab in any of them. All the folders on the virtual desktop were empty. There was no tab. Dyson's mouth opened to speak but he suddenly realized there was nothing to say. No words came out. Sweat formed on his brow, and he could feel the blood rising in his cheeks. He leaned back in the chair. *Oh my God, oh my God!*

"David? Did you find it? David, what is it?"

"Rachel, are you absolutely *sure* you haven't got it?"

"Yes, the only possible place it could have been was in my bag if you'd given it back to me. I turned it upside down and emptied it out completely. I definitely haven't got that tab. Don't tell me..."

"It's gone, Rachel. It's not in my computer."

On the display of his comPod Rachel closed her eyes and threw back her head in frustration, her usually full lips now pressed into a hard line as if trying desperately not to say something Dyson would regret.

"How many people have access to your office?" she asked, making a thinly disguised effort to remain calm. Although only her head and shoulders were visible on the screen, it was easy to imagine her arms crossed and her foot tapping impatiently.

Oh dear Lord, this is so embarrassing, Dyson thought. Victor had been in yesterday, and Artur only this morning. But in the end he decided to lay his cards on the table. "Ten or twelve," he admitted sheepishly, after a quick mental addition.

"Ten or twelve!" she shrieked. This came as a shock to Dyson, who had previously only experienced her being in total control. "So any one of a dozen people could have taken that tab? The tab on which your friend speaks of secret documents held under wraps by the Church. The tab on which Father MacKenzie, shortly before his mysterious death and the confiscation of his body by the DFP, talks about wanting to see a friend named David Dyson at the Church Archives department here in New York! The same David Dyson who was visited yesterday by a journalist called Rachel Watson, who can now be linked to a tab with possibly subversive material! Oh my God, I just don't believe this! I've tried for so many years..." The rant trailed off when Rachel ran momentarily out of breath. "You said you were new to the 'cloak and dagger stuff' but this.., this..." She was lost for words.

"Look, I know I've screwed up," he said, trying desperately to placate her. "But I think I know who it was."

Before she could cut him off with more harsh words, he continued, telling her about his meeting with Cardinal Goodfellowe.

"It was obvious to me at the time he knew more than he was letting on!"

When he had finished, Rachel's voice was calm but firm.

"If it really was him, why didn't he say anything? Why didn't he have you arrested by the DFP and tortured?"

"Steady on! I'm pretty sure the DFP don't actually *torture* people."

"Not what I've heard," she interrupted coolly.

The defense of a Church institution had been a knee-jerk reaction on Dyson's part; something which had been instilled in him through years of Church training. The way things stood at the moment, however, he had no problem whatsoever believing that the DFP could and would torture people.

"Well, anyway," he went on, "maybe he's waiting to see if anyone else knows about this. You know: find out who I'm working with. That sort of thing."

"Well, I think he already has a pretty good idea who that is by now," Rachel said sarcastically.

"Or perhaps he's waiting to see if I have any more of the documents."

"If I were him, I'd just torture it out of you," Rachel replied, with just a little too much feeling for Dyson's liking.

"All right, all right, let's try to stay positive here. You're the one with all the experience. What do *you* think? Why aren't I lying on a stone floor chained to a wall in a dungeon?"

"I'm not sure if it really is Goodfellowe. If it were, do you think we would be having this conversation now? Wouldn't you already be rotting in a DFP cell somewhere? On the other hand, he might just have you followed to see who else is involved. That's probably what I'd do first. The tab went missing sometime between you leaving the office yesterday and arriving there again this morning, you said."

"Well, I didn't actually check the drive till you called me."

"OK, OK, let me think. Of the *ten or twelve* people," she purposely stressed the "ten or twelve" to make it quite clear she hadn't forgiven his stupidity yet. "How many of them are at work today?"

Dyson looked miserable. "All of them, I'm afraid. It's rather unusual for them all to be here at the same time and not on some kind of fieldwork somewhere, but it's not unheard of."

"Great. Just great." She paused for a moment. "The way I see it now, there are two possibilities. The first scenario is that whoever took the tab — perhaps Goodfellowe — will turn it over to the DFP, in which case you will be unceremoniously hauled away to a cell within the next forty-eight hours, and I probably won't be far behind you. In the second scenario, the person who took the tab will blackmail you for something, if it's *not* Goodfellowe. If he doesn't get what he wants, *then* he'll turn you in to the DFP."

Dyson, who had never in his life been in trouble with the authorities before, felt nauseous. He couldn't believe that his whole existence could possibly be turned upside-down in a matter of days. Everything he knew and loved seemed to be floating inexorably away from him.

"Oh, Holy Lamb, what do you think I should do?"

"Wait and see," Rachel replied with calm in her voice, even though she didn't feel particularly calm right now. "If you go off accusing people or even asking them if they've seen anything, you might make things even worse. Anyone who isn't suspicious now might get suspicious if you start acting weird and asking stupid questions. Try to keep your wits about you and act as if nothing has happened. If we're lucky, whoever has the tab might just think Father MacKenzie was deranged, as I did myself before I saw the document."

"It's not going to be easy."

"Yeah, well," she said, treating him to one of her heart-melting smiles, "life's a bitch, ain't it?"

They agreed to keep their appointment on Friday. The only person who would be suspicious about Dyson sitting at a table near Rachel in a public reading gallery would be the person who had the tab, and that person already knew that there was a link between them.

CHAPTER 6

Residence of Cardinal Alberto di Galassini, US Representative of His Holiness the Arch-Cardinal New York City, 2077

"Come with me," the elderly woman muttered, scurrying along the wide corridors of the fortress-like mansion. It was late, but the cardinal had expressly told his housekeeper to admit this particular visitor at any time of the day or night, no matter what he himself might be doing at the time.

"Wait here," she curtly told the visitor. She then knocked respectfully on the white door, decorated elaborately in gold leaf. Without waiting for a response she entered and closed the door behind her. When it opened again after a minute or two, the cardinal's housekeeper beckoned the visitor to come in and then left without another word. The cardinal, a squat, bald man, looked as though he had been getting ready for bed, standing as he was by the fireplace in a richly embroidered dressing gown. Neither he nor the visitor seemed to mind, though.

"What news?" Cardinal di Galassini asked.

"We recovered another four pages."

"Excellent, excellent!" the cardinal replied, with deep satisfaction, even a trace of glee in his voice. He allowed his face, always completely under control, to form a rare smile. "How many does that make now in total?"

"Forty-five in all."

"Well done. Well done indeed. And the man who discovered them?

"He has been dealt with."

"Good, very good."

"I'm afraid there has been a complication, though," the visitor said.

The cardinal's face darkened immediately.

"Didn't I tell you I do not want to hear about the details? Didn't I tell you to report to me only when you have had a result?"

The visitor remained calm, his voice level: "Yes, but this time something went wrong. It looks as though someone working with the one who initially discovered the papers also received some of them. We are quite sure that there should have been more than the four sheets we recovered, but as yet we have been unable to find them."

"What makes you think there should have been more?" di Galassini growled, annoyed but curious.

"We suspect this because in the past, there were always a number of consecutive papers. The content was in a logical order," the visitor explained patiently. "In this particular case there is no continuity in the four papers we recovered. We tracked down the man we assumed may have taken the missing documents and wanted to take him in for questioning, but I'm afraid one of our agents was over-zealous. The suspect died," the visitor added, heeding di Galassini's admonishment that he did not want to hear about details.

"Not before you recovered the papers, I trust."

"I'm afraid we found nothing: neither on the man's body nor in his apartment."

"Are you telling me parts of the diary might be in the public domain? Just waiting for someone to pick them up off the street and sell them to the press!"

The U.S. representative of the Arch-Cardinal was gradually becoming very angry indeed, apoplectic even.

"Unfortunately that is not yet all," the visitor continued, his voice now clearly making an effort to remain calm. "New evidence has come to light to the effect that the suspect might have already passed the documents on to a journalist."

"*A journalist!*" the cardinal bellowed, now unable to contain his fury any longer. "And have you dealt with this journalist yet?"

"That is why this situation is so complicated. The journalist contacted a priest at the Department of Archives. And we don't know which of them has the missing documents; the journalist or the priest."

"Well, I hardly think that's *my* problem!" the cardinal hissed. "Why don't you just employ your usual methods to extract information from your suspects? I suppose you know who they are?"

"Of course we do. But we don't know if they made copies of the document or documents. We fear that the journalist might have passed them on to colleagues to be made public in the event of any, shall we say, 'unfortunate incidents' which might occur. We have made enquiries about this journalist and discovered that she is a force to be reckoned with."

"Wait a minute," the cardinal pondered. "If they really do have any of these papers, why haven't they made them public already? Do you think they want to blackmail the Church?"

"We wondered the same thing until we did some research into the journalist's biography. We feel that blackmail is almost certainly *not* one of her motives. She is one of those idealistic types. More likely she's a dissident."

"So why hasn't she published yet?"

The visitor looked thoughtful. "It's possible the papers they have don't constitute conclusive evidence. Depending on which page or pages they have, they may not know the full story. If we're lucky, they might not even suspect what's going on. Even if they know a little more, they may think the whole thing is a hoax or just the ravings of some ancient madman."

This placated the cardinal somewhat. "I do not need to remind you how important this is, I hope," he said, after some thought. "Listen, I am hereby granting you the authority to search anything and anyone in the United States of America under the Church Subversive Activities Amendment. Find those papers!"

"Of course. We have already dispatched plain-clothes officers to search the apartments of the priest and the journalist. But we must be careful not to arouse the suspicion of the press in general."

After some thought the cardinal decided there was nothing else to do but to hope and pray that his trusted ally would be able to sort out this whole messy business.

"You've never let me down before. Don't disappoint me now. You may leave."

"We have worked together for so long for the cause. I do not intend to start disappointing you now. Good evening."

Long after the visitor had been shown out by the housekeeper, Cardinal di Galassini remained sitting in his luxurious armchair before the open artificial fire which burned as hot and as brightly as he imagined sinners would burn in medieval hell. Swirling a particularly large glass of wickedly expensive brandy and inhaling its intoxicating vapors, he tried to soothe his troubled mind.

I am not a sinner, he attempted to console himself. *I am acting in good faith. I am acting to protect the Holy Church. The things I do, the decisions I make, are necessary to preserve not only the Church but our very way of life. Oh, God, make me strong,* he implored.

That night the representative of His Holiness the Arch-Cardinal did not sleep very well at all, despite the brandy.

CHAPTER 7

Carroll Gardens, Brooklyn
New York City, 2077

Dyson returned home uncharacteristically late. After leaving the office he had been exhausted and hungry because, as usual, he had been unable to tear himself away from work even to go to the canteen for one of their excellent lunches. He had been so tired today that instead of going to a supermarket and purchasing a 2-Min-InstaMeal to stick in the microwave, he decided to eat out for a change. Returning to Brooklyn on the subway, he exited in the leafy Carroll Gardens district and went to a diner on the way back to his apartment in Second Place.

For all that science and technology had achieved over the last decade or two, particularly in the field of producing enough cheap and very tasty nourishment to feed the world's hungry population, you still could not beat the occasional disgustingly greasy, heart attack-conducive, hand-made meal of burger and fries served in an old-fashioned diner. In spite of the health warnings he had to listen to from his comPod, which registered the carcinogenic compounds resulting from the burning fat on the meat, as well as the unusually large amounts of *sodium this* and *potassium that* which he was imbibing in his primitive feast of animal flesh, Dyson had enjoyed his brief minitrip into the hedonism of bygone eras very much indeed. Despite all the reasoning, all the pleading of late twenty-first-century thinkers, futurologists, animal rights activists, and miscellaneous philosophers and economists to ban the eating of meat, animals were still being slaughtered for food.

A similar campaign had been launched against the smoking of tobacco products at the beginning of the century, but it had taken almost forty more years to completely eradicate that particular unhealthy habit, so the meat-eaters of the world still felt pretty safe in the knowledge that their particular pleasure, or vice, depending on your point of view, would not be banned any time in the near future. One — some might say minor — concession to these protests was that all comPods and similar devices that constantly monitored the vital signs of their users were programmed to issue warnings about unhealthy food and drink. Much to the aggravation of some comPod users, these warnings could not be deactivated.

With a stomach full of dead animal products, all Dyson wanted to do now was to fall into bed and sleep until Janet woke him for work the next morning. His apartment was on the third floor of a mock-brownstone on Second Place in Carroll Gardens. Wearily he climbed the stone steps and entered the house through the two sets of front doors, then trudged up two flights of creaking wooden stairs to his floor. His apartment consisted of a bedroom/living-room, kitchen, and bathroom facing the back of the building, offering a wonderful view of the fire escapes on the back of the houses in the parallel street. On a clear day he could make out the top few floors of his workplace over in Manhattan. He was just about to hold his thumb to the print recognition lock of his apartment door when he thought he heard a noise from within. He listened for a second but nothing was discernible. Deciding he must be so tired he was imagining things, he opened the door. In his fatigued state he only realized after he had taken a step inside that the lights were already on.

Before he had a chance to take in his surroundings, something very hard suddenly smashed into his cheek. Dyson had never been hit in the face before, not even as a child at school, so it was not only the pain, but also the shock that caused him to drop to his knees. His vision was blurred and his ears were ringing as he scanned his living room, his head spinning. Two men wearing black clothes and black masks covering their faces were throwing his furniture about. Something out of the corner of his eye caught his attention and he turned just in time to see a black object shooting toward his head again. Seconds later he was lying unconscious on the floor, blood spurting from an ugly gash along his cheekbone.

— ‹› —

"David."

A woman's voice. Sweet. Soothing. Was it Rachel? Sweet Rachel.

"David, you are injured? Shall I call an ambulance?" When the voice spoke again, Dyson realized it was Janet.

Dyson's undershirt contained millions of microscopic sensors that registered all manner of biometric data. The data was wirelessly relayed to his comPod, which constantly monitored his well-being. Janet was programmed to react to certain data configurations, which meant if he'd had a heart attack or a stroke, for example, an ambulance would have been alerted immediately. However, the readings from Dyson's clothing were not yet serious enough to provoke such a measure, which is why Janet enquired once again:

"David, can you answer me, please? I am going to call an ambulance if you are unable to respond."

"No," he managed to gasp feebly. "Don't."

Several minutes passed, during which Dyson remained lying on the floor in a state of limbo somewhere between consciousness and unconsciousness. Janet spoke once again.

"David, you have an incoming message, audiovisual, real-time."

Rachel. Rachel?

"David, would you like to accept the call?"

Dyson sat up but his head began to spin so violently that he was unable to retain his balance and he fell to the floor again clutching his temples, which were throbbing excruciatingly.

"David, would you like to accept the call?" Janet repeated.

"Wait," he croaked hoarsely. He tried getting up again, slowly this time, and managed a sitting position.

Looking around the room, he realized that it had been completely ransacked. His furniture, which had not been particularly new in the first place, had been transformed into firewood. Cushions had been slit or torn open, their contents strewn over the floor and over the splintered remains of his furniture.

After first ensuring the intruders were no longer in his apartment, he managed to say, "Who is it?"

"Rachel Watson."

"Put... her... on."

Rachel appeared on the monitor looking panicked.

"David!" she yelled into her comPod. "My apartment! There were..." She suddenly noticed the blood trickling down his face.

"Oh, shit, David, what happened to you?"

"I — I came home. Men were here. They attacked me."

"Are you OK?"

"Think so. My apartment. They wrecked it."

She could see he was still dazed by his experience. "David, stay there, I'll be right over."

Even in his dazed state, Dyson knew it was dangerous for him to be seen with her again after he had told Cardinal Goodfellowe their meeting had been a one-off occurrence, but he simply did not have the strength to argue. Right now he desperately needed a friendly face and some sympathy.

"The caller has terminated the connection," Janet said.

— «» —

Rachel arrived about half an hour later. She did not need to ring the bell, as both the doors to the building and the door of the apartment were still ajar. Dyson was sitting on the shredded upholstery of his sofa holding a cold damp cloth to his devastated face. He looked up listlessly as she sat down next to him and tenderly pulled the hand holding the cloth away from his face so that she could assess the damage.

"Ouch!" she said sympathetically when she saw the bruising under his eye and the vicious gash on his cheek. "Looks pretty gruesome, but you'll live."

"Rachel, I..."

"Wait."

Holding a finger to her lips, she removed a glass ball the size of a child's marble from her pocket. Raising it to eye level, she seemed to scan the room with it, then stood up, walked to the television screen attached to the wall, and ran her fingers along the bottom edge. When she took her hand away, she showed Dyson a tiny black dot on her middle finger.

"But what...?"

Rachel once again silenced him by placing her finger to her lips. She walked to the bathroom, flushed the toilet and returned to the couch.

"OK, that was the only one they left."

"They bugged me?"

"Of course. What did you expect?"

Dyson was totally miserable.

"Want to tell me about it?"

"They were here when I came home," he told her. "Three of them. Wearing masks. They were obviously looking for something and I think they'd almost finished when I came in. Then they knocked me down and the next thing I remember was you calling me."

"Wait a minute," Rachel interjected, "They didn't question you?"

"No, why?"

"Well, if I were a thief — or a DFP agent for that matter — looking for something in your apartment and didn't find it, and I assume they didn't, I'm sure I'd ask you."

"Then why didn't they?"

"I think they wanted to frighten us."

Dyson's head was still spinning, but nevertheless something in what she had said alerted him to the fact that something was not right here. She'd said "us."

"Us?" he enquired.

"They were at my apartment, too."

"What? Are you all right?" he asked, looking at her properly for the first time, searching for signs of injury but finding none.

"They'd gone by the time I got there, but they left my place in pretty much the same state as yours. I think they just wanted to let us know they're onto us."

"The document."

"Yes," she sighed. "They found the document in my safe, which they broke open. But it's not as if I didn't have any copies."

"But why didn't they arrest us? Or at least take us in for questioning?"

"They're probably afraid we might have spilled the beans to other people."

"But we haven't."

"They don't know that, though, do they?"

Dyson groaned. This was all getting a bit too much for him. This cloak-and-dagger stuff was really not something he could ever get used to, he thought. "What about calling the police?"

"No point," she said simply. "What would you say?"

Rachel's voice dropped an octave and did a passable, if somewhat amusing, imitation of Dyson's English accent as she ran him through the scene.

"Well, officer, three men broke into my apartment, trashed my bloody furniture, beat the crap out of me and left without nicking anything. Oh, by the way, I think they might have been from the DFP. So, are you going to contact the Church and ask what the buggers wanted? Are you going to prosecute the DFP? What about starting by interrogating Cardinal Goodfellowe? I'm sure he's the bastard behind all this, you know. Evidence? Well, no, not really, officer. Actually I was hoping you might find some for me."

Despite the pain from his throbbing cheek and despite the fact that Rachel was mocking him, Dyson was unable to keep himself from smiling, which caused his injured face to hurt even more. Begrudgingly he had to admit that her impression of him had really been rather good. *She lights up my world.* Shocked at this uncontrolled thought in the aftermath of such dramatic events, Dyson tried to clear his head by shaking it briefly.

Rachel continued in her normal voice: "You're not cut out for this kind of shit, are you?" she said matter-of-factly. Their eyes made contact and for a second or two they just sat there, motionless and silent. Suddenly she leaned over toward him and hugged him tightly. The warmth of her body during that embrace and the sympathy in her voice soothed Dyson more than anything else he could ever have imagined. Nevertheless, his heart was beating at a most alarming rate. He was afraid someone would see their embrace. The consequences could be dire. But despite the vows he had made to his church, despite the duties inherent in his status as a priest of that church, he felt like a small child right now. *This must be what it feels like to have a wife; to be comforted by someone you love.*

CHAPTER 8

**Archives of the Holy Church of the Second Coming
New York City, 2077**

When Dyson arrived for work the next morning, he walked past the astonished staff at the reception, lowering his head in a futile attempt to hide his injuries. In this, he failed miserably; it was only natural that people would gawk at a priest with a bruised and beaten face. This was, after all, a sight you didn't see every day. Without asking at reception if he was there, Dyson went straight to O'Rourke's office, which, like his own, was also on the 175th floor. He knocked once and marched in without waiting for a reply. O'Rourke's office was smaller than Dyson's, but it nevertheless had a similarly impressive view of the city. As soon as O'Rourke saw the state of Dyson's face, he leaped to his feet much faster than Dyson would have thought possible for a man in his fifties and ran toward his colleague.

"Holy Lamb, David, what happened to you?" he asked, genuine concern in his voice. "Sit down. Tell me."

Dyson sat in the visitor's seat at O'Rourke's desk and told him all about his horrendous experience, carefully omitting any mention of Rachel from his story. O'Rourke had in the meantime become a trusted friend, but Dyson remembered Rachel's words nonetheless: *Trust nobody*, she had warned him. It truly pained him not to tell Tom everything, but he told himself it was also for Tom's benefit. For if Dyson was discovered investigating Church institutions, at least his friend Tom could not be implicated in any way.

"I'll send someone round to your apartment straight away," O'Rourke said. "By the time you go home this evening, everything will be fixed up again, I promise."

"Thanks, Tom, I really appreciate it."

He was just about to leave when O'Rourke said, "Oh, by the way, did you inform the police?"

"Err, no," he replied. "I thought the Church would settle it."

"Well done, David!" O'Rourke exclaimed, patting him on the shoulder and beaming. "I think you're really getting the hang of the way things work around here!"

—— «» ——

When Dyson reached his own office, he could hardly wait to get started with his private research. After being assaulted, it was now even more of a personal matter than it had been before. He searched his databases, looking for priests in the service of the Church who had died between thirty-five and forty-five years ago, probably aged between twenty-three and thirty-five at the time of their death. In Dyson's experience, this was the usual age of priests employed in the first stages of historical research: discovery/ recovery/ sorting. If he found nothing within this range, he could always expand it later, but he thought this would be a good start.

A total of eight names came up, which Dyson found surprisingly high. After all, he was examining a window of only ten years. All the subjects were priests, and all of them had been relatively young when they had died. Surely this mortality rate was higher than that of the population as a whole? Looking at the cause of the subjects' deaths he could almost certainly eliminate one unfortunate priest immediately. He had died of bone cancer in Ottawa, Canada, after spending two months in a hospital there, and was just thirty-four at the time of his death. It was quite unlikely that this man had been a victim of foul play, but David Dyson was nothing if not a thorough researcher. By virtue of his special status as Keeper of the Holy Archives, he was able to access almost any database in the entire Christian world, even medical records. He discovered that the priest had died in Ottawa's Church Hospital No. 2 in 2036. Logging on to the hospital's main computer, Dyson was able to ascertain that the records were all intact. He traced the unfortunate priest's medical history backward from the time of his death; through all the treatments that were tried and which had failed; back to the point at which he was first diagnosed with bone cancer. There was no doubt about it: the poor man had died of cancer far too young. There was no indication of any suspicious circumstances.

Dyson had never questioned the ethical problems inherent in such research methods. Until recently he had believed that he, as a key representative of the Church, responsible for historical research, was perfectly entitled to have access to such data, no matter how sensitive. After all, law-abiding, Church-going citizens had nothing to hide, did they? So why should they mind if an official from an important Church department such as the Archives looked at their data? Why should they protest if the Church monitored bank accounts at random to ensure that Church Tax was levied on all income? Why, indeed, should the man in the street not agree to his telecommunications being monitored by the DFP? After all, it was for the protection of society as a whole if subversive elements could be removed from that society before causing any serious harm. It was with these arguments, and many more, that Dyson had been indoctrinated during his years at Church schools, and this had continued — albeit at a more sophisticated level — at his Church-run university.

With a sudden pang, Dyson realized that these ethical problems were why his father had protested against the Church all those years ago. He had regarded his father as a reactionary, unwilling to accept the inevitable truth of the Church of the Second Coming; unwilling to open his mind to the tangible evidence that Jesus Christ had returned to earth to once again absolve Christian believers of their sins. But now Dyson was no longer so certain that the Church should really know everything about everybody. Should the Church really have access to the medical records of a priest who had died of a terrible disease? Was it so vitally important to the security of the Church that he, Dyson, be able to reconstruct the horrific details of a man's martyrdom to cancer? Particularly in light of recent developments, Dyson's opinion on this matter was rapidly beginning to change. He now knew from personal experience that there were some things he did not want his Church to know about him. He now understood what it was like to have something private that he wanted nobody else, particularly not some faceless bureaucrat from a Church department, to learn about him.

The second priest Dyson scrutinized had only appeared because the priest had initially been transferred to the historical research department to recover documents from archaeological sites and sort them. Before he had actually started work for this department, however, he had volunteered to take on a position as an aid worker in some God-forsaken village in central Africa. This was not actually what Dyson had been looking for, but he read on anyway. While in Africa the priest had apparently died of a heart attack. The database even contained electronic news articles about the priest, praising his selfless commitment to helping the poor, mentioning how ironic it was that a man who was doing so much good in the name of the Church should be cut down in his prime by a previously undetected heart problem. At this, Dyson's interest was piqued. Didn't his predecessor, Tim Nelson, die of a heart attack that was never confirmed by a Church-independent coroner?

A button flashed tantalizingly in the bottom right-hand corner of Dyson's monitor. The blue cube displayed the number four, to indicate the security clearance necessary to access further information. There were only five levels of Church security clearance. Level five was the highest: that was top secret rating, reserved solely for the Arch-Cardinal himself and a handful of supervising cardinals such as Cardinal di Galassini, head of the Church in the USA, as well as the heads of the Church administration in other countries. As head of the Central Church Archives, Cardinal Goodfellowe was also given level five clearance, whereas level four was normally reserved for bishops. Administrative workers assisting the upper echelons of the clergy were awarded level three, and ordinary priests received level two. Any document on the official Church servers that was given a level one status was available to the general public.

As the Keeper of the Archives, Dyson was in a privileged position and was able to access data with a level four security clearance, so he was now able to poke his finger into the flashing blue virtual button to have his fingerprint scanned and accepted. This enabled him to view data that would normally be hidden from anyone below the rank of bishop. According to the secret internal Church notes, Dyson now discovered to his amazement, there were rumors of the young priest in Africa having had some kind of relationship with one of the tribeswomen in the village where he had been residing, and he had apparently been killed by the woman's intended husband. Of course, the Church-controlled press reported simply, "Priest suffers fatal heart attack while doing missionary work." There was no mention whatsoever of any impropriety. Given the high security clearance of this information, and its content, Dyson was quite sure that the story of murder at the hands of a jealous lover was probably true. Thus the priest in question was no longer interesting for his research.

Candidate number three had died in a boating accident on the River Thames in London. This one had indeed been involved in historical research, but there was nothing in the files that pointed to any kind of amazing discovery. The priest had apparently been on an outing to London with a Boy Scout troop, and his boat had sunk after a collision with a boat full of drunken revelers. That was all there was on this case. Dyson could find nothing further in the Church files on the accident, or on the boat that had caused the accident. So, this was an untimely death of a young priest who had been a historical researcher with no corroborated details about the circumstances of his death. There was only a level one security clearance button for this page, which meant that it was generally accessible. That probably indicated that there would be independent, non-Church news reports about this somewhere. Dyson placed the priest on the shortlist anyway, at least until he could find out who had been responsible for the accident, if indeed it had been one.

With a start, Dyson realized that something was wrong. Was he really becoming a skeptic? A doubting Thomas? At any rate, he was no longer accepting things at face value, even if they came from Church sources, and this was worrying to him. Very worrying. He had always been faithful to his Church, but something now seemed to be happening to make him doubt things he had previously accepted without question. Why was he suddenly not sure of the veracity of Church records? Where was this going to end? He took a deep breath and shook his head as if to free it from such nonsense. *I am a man of the Church*, he told himself. *The Church is the one true faith. I believe in the Church.* Nevertheless, deep within him a voice nagged at the back of his mind: *Are you sure about that?*

The fourth candidate had been killed in a plane crash while travelling from Rome to Hong Kong on a MegaJet. A court given the task of investigating the crash, which killed all 1,950 passengers and crew, spent almost two years researching and debating before returning a verdict of death by misadventure after the huge aircraft had apparently been downed in a hurricane. Despite this verdict, Dyson's state of mind was now such that he even contemplated, although it was only for a second or two, whether or not the DFP might have murdered so many people just to cover up whatever it was they were trying to keep a secret. Once again, he shook his head in disbelief at his own audacity in actually accusing, if only in his own mind, an arm of the Church of the heinous crime of mass murder. However, when he dug a little deeper, he discovered contemporary Church-independent news articles in which it was proven that the plane really had been brought down by the storm. In this case, too, there was only a level one security clearance button at the bottom of the netpage, which meant that the information was available to anyone, even members of the public.

Candidate number five was another London contender. Also a historical researcher, this priest had been killed in a house fire. Consulting the independent, non-Church-related news of that period, Dyson found only reports of a tragic accident. It seemed there had been an electrical fault in the wiring of the old house the priest had been living in. Smoldering plastic in the antiquated insulation had released toxic gases, rendering the priest unconscious, which was why he had been unable to react to the smoke alarm. Scrolling down to the bottom of the article, Dyson then discovered a button for security clearance level three. *Oh-ho!* He thought. *Someone has something to hide! A secret house fire? I think not! Why isn't this accessible to the general public?* Inserting his finger into the button, he read that the man had apparently been suffering from psychotic delusions, and that his doctor had warned his employer, the Church, that the priest might have suicidal tendencies. According to this, it appeared that the priest had decided to commit suicide by burning down his house with him in it. *Hmm, a nut job*, Dyson thought, but shortlisted him anyway. It appeared the events of the last few weeks had shaken Dyson so badly that he was prepared to see demons almost anywhere. Pondering the level three clearance this information had been assigned, Dyson assumed that it would probably not be all that good for morale if ordinary priests could see that one of their number had committed suicide, so this information was reserved for cardinals, bishops, and upper administration only.

Although priest number six had also died a violent death, and had also worked for the Historical Research Division, Dyson was quite certain he could exclude him from his list. The man had been found guilty of sexually assaulting children. Normally, in the case of a layman convicted of the disgusting crime of pedophilia, the DFP would have publicly pressed for the death penalty, but as the man was a priest, they had protected him, arguing that the Church would punish its own staff in its own way. Unfortunately for the priest in question, he had lived and worked in a small village in Albania. Shortly after the county court had publicly acquitted the man, binding him over for subsequent Church-internal proceedings, the priest had been lynched by an angry mob of villagers, obviously out for vengeance, but also afraid that the priest would be released to continue with his sexual perversion, if not in their village, then in some other place. As this case was so well documented by the press, and as the Church had actually attempted to save this particular priest and not kill him, Dyson felt it was futile to follow up on this one.

The seventh candidate died in Mexico City. Cause of death: a bullet in the brain. The Church-controlled headline in the Mexican press called it "Mafia Execution of Beloved Priest." Apparently the priest had been an outspoken opponent of the drug barons who still controlled vast areas of Central America in the early twenty-first century. The Church press only ever mentioned this particular priest in a good light, treating him almost as a saint. Dyson's archives, however, told a different story. The priest had obviously been embezzling millions in laundered money from the Church and had established a private drug empire of his own. For Dyson it was obvious that the bullet in the brain had come from the high-powered rifle of a DFP officer, particularly after he had read the autopsy report. His suspicions seemed to be supported by the flashing blue rectangle in the bottom right-hand corner of his monitor, indicating that any further information on this case was available only to members of the clergy with security level five. Dyson knew that it would be no use at all to attempt opening a level five security button, but it was so tantalizing, he couldn't resist. Dyson stuck his finger into the display and, as expected, he was merely greeted with the standard message:

"You are currently registered in the system with level four status. The file you are attempting to access is available to level five users only. Any further attempts on your part to access this file without the proper authorization will result in your fingerprint data being submitted to the DFP for the purpose of instigating disciplinary measures."

As the dead priest had only been involved in historical research for a week at the very beginning of his career, though, Dyson was able to cross him off the list of possible candidates. For years afterward he had worked outside the historical department and had been left alone by the DFP until they had finally caught up with him for different reasons.

The eighth and final candidate was a priest in Australia. The man had been swimming in the ocean and was stung by a poisonous jellyfish. He had been a historical researcher and was of the age Dyson was looking for. Again Dyson considered all possible ways in which the DFP could possibly have made this priest's murder look like an accident, but there had been witnesses in this case. According to the press, lifeguards had pulled the priest from the ocean after he had called for help. Not only the Church-run press, but also independent news articles reported that the priest had been stung by a jellyfish while swimming. Thus, number eight also appeared to be a non-candidate.

The only really suspicious death seemed to be that of candidate number three, who had been killed in the boating accident on the Thames. There was still, however, a niggling feeling at the back of Dyson's mind. It was something about candidate number five, the house fire suicide. What was it? He went through the scenario again in his mind and then came up with a few questions: firstly, why would the doctor "warn" the priest's employer of anything? Surely the doctor-patient confidentiality rule should have been observed. But then again, the Church was so powerful that it could influence the doctor to spill the beans about anyone it was interested in. So far, so good. But why would the Church administration make this information available to a level three clearance? The doctor might have been compelled to inform the Church, but why would the Church inform level three admins? The Church never did anything without having a reason. So what did the Church stand to gain from letting the admins know that one of its own staff was a psychotic potential suicide? A cover up! thought Dyson. Discredit the man, make it obvious that he was responsible for his own death, then nobody will come asking whether anyone else might have been involved. This one was definitely staying on the shortlist.

So there were only two possible candidates who were of the right age, had worked in the right place at the right time, died of unnatural causes and therefore might have been involved with the secret documents, whatever they might be and for whatever reason. Dyson knew, of course, that all this was pure conjecture, and he was still like a blind man feeling his way through the darkness without a stick. There was absolutely no evidence whatsoever that there was any kind of conspiracy going on anyway. Perhaps Pete really had had some psychological issues.

But he was desperate to learn why his friend had to die, and once he had been presented with a problem, he would persist, leaving no stone unturned, until he had uncovered a solution.

The two names he had shortlisted were Father Paul Davies, who had been twenty-nine when he died in a boating accident on the Thames, and Father Christopher Crabtree, who had been twenty-four when his home burned down.

— «» —

Shortly before five o'clock, O'Rourke came to Dyson's office.

"I've just been to your apartment," he announced. "You know, making sure it's all in order for you."

"Oh, thanks again, Tom," Dyson replied, sincerely grateful for his friend and colleague's help.

"We had to have a new door fitted," O'Rourke continued, "but the print scanner was still OK so we didn't need to replace that. We tried to have the place decorated pretty much the same as it was before, but if there's anything you don't like, just let me know and I'll have it changed for you."

"Tom, I don't know how to thank you," Dyson said, clapping O'Rourke on the shoulder with heartfelt gratitude.

— «» —

When he returned home later that evening, he discovered that O'Rourke had been true to his word. The furniture was indeed very similar to that which had been destroyed by the intruders. The television screen covering one of the walls and the miniature ultra-hi-fi music system had also been replaced with similar, if not better, models. Somehow, though, it did not quite seem the same. Somehow, he could not shake off the feeling that his privacy had been violated. How could he be sure they hadn't planted bugs to spy on him? It made things even worse to think that this violation had not come from some moronic drug-addicted burglar looking for something with which to finance his next fix, but that his Church had ordered it. Dyson sat on his new sofa and took out his comPod.

"Janet, get me Rachel Watson, please. Audiovisual, real-time."

"Certainly, David."

Several seconds later the screen was filled with Rachel's pretty face, smiling at him.

"How's the wounded warrior today?" she asked.

"Better, thanks. Listen, I have two names. They might be candidates to fill the position we were discussing," he said, choosing his words carefully.

In the late twentieth and early twenty-first centuries, western governments and later the Church of the Second Coming had tried to ban encryption software that scrambled telecommunications to such an extent that not even the authorities could decipher them. The official line was that it would not be possible to combat terrorists and organized crime if the criminals could make it impossible for the authorities to monitor their communications. The ban had varying degrees of success and, for a time, there was almost no part of the private citizen's life the authorities, including the Church, did not have access to. Of course, the law-abiding Church-goers claimed, at least in public, that this was something society had to accept if the Church and the government were expected to apprehend atheists, anarchists, terrorists, and subversives and bring them to justice. However, there were still plenty of ordinary people who were courageous enough to defy the authorities. They made the code of their encryption algorithms free of charge so that anyone who wanted to was able to keep their telecommunications private. Still, many people could not believe that the Church would simply give up. In all probability, thought the doubters, the Church, particularly the DFP, had some kind of mega-code-breaking software they had not publicized. Whether this was just another conspiracy theory or if it was true, Dyson could not say, but he thought it prudent not to risk more than was necessary.

"Hmm," Rachel said, "I found something interesting, too. Someone who might know your candidates."

"Sounds good."

"So," she said, flashing her teeth at him. "Was there anything else, or did you just call to say hello?"

"Oh, I, err," Dyson stammered. Actually, he *had* just called to say hello and to see her, but that was not something he was prepared to admit right now. "Just wondered if we were still on for our meeting. No change of time or venue?"

"No; same time, same place as discussed," she replied.

"All right. See you then."

"See you then."

Dyson could have kicked himself. *Well, that was intelligent*, he thought. *Like a lovesick teenager!*

CHAPTER 9

**Library of the Church of the Second Coming, 4th
Avenue
New York City, 2077**

At two p.m. on Friday Dyson stood in front of the Church Library, which, like all the other modern Church buildings in New York City, was an awe-inspiring piece of architecture: a majestic sixty-story, steel-frame skyscraper clad with blue metallic mirror-glass with sprawling ten-story wings pointing east and west.

After waiting for a few minutes, Dyson realized it would be rather stupid to organize a clandestine meeting with someone and then enter the building together, so he decided to wait for Rachel inside. After allowing the armed guards at the doors to scan his ID chip, he strode into the building and took the elevator to the third floor: archaeology. Rachel, it seemed, had the same idea, and was already sitting at a table in the public reading gallery.

The Church Library had a branch in almost every town and city in the Christian world, and was the only officially sanctioned repository of data for the masses. As the Church banned any publications it considered to be subversive, private citizens were advised not to attempt to purchase reading material from any shady, unauthorized sources, so most people went to the Library when they wanted something to read. The Library did not contain literature in the old-style book form, as these antiquated and extremely fragile objects were no longer printed on a material for which precious trees had to be destroyed. Nowadays people could either sit at a table in the Library and call up the billions of Church-approved electronic books on the terminals there, or they could search for the data they wanted and have it transferred to their comPods. The advantage of this was that the Church guaranteed that everything a citizen downloaded from a Church Library was not only free of dangerous content, but also free of dangerous software.

There were actually subversive elements, though, not only in nations where other faiths were the dominant religion, but also within Christian societies, who claimed that the DFP actively uploaded ultra-viruses, micro-assassins, and spy-progs into the net. These programs would not only monitor users' movements through the net; some of them were actually capable of seriously damaging, even completely destroying, hardware. Supposedly the DFP mainly targeted sites that they believed undermined the tenets of the Second Coming, but the conspiracy theorists claimed the DFP's aim was also to spread general fear and uncertainty among net-users in Christian countries. The idea was that if you never knew if the DFP were monitoring your online movements or not, you would be more likely to use the Church-approved sources such as the Library. Of course the Church denied such machinations as "scurrilous rumors" and "baseless speculation" but, as always where the DFP might possibly be involved, people were wary, and the Church Libraries were therefore always buzzing hives of activity. At the Library, for a nominal fee, you could also print out any documents you might need. The material used for hardcopies was an extremely thin but very durable biodegradable plastic called eco-foil, but old traditions die hard and most people still called it paper.

There were four chairs at Rachel's table, two on each long side, but she had covered almost every square inch of the table with plastic photocopies to discourage anyone else from sitting there. To an outsider it looked as if she were doing some important, complex research; an idea that seemed to be working, as nobody had disturbed her since she had arrived half an hour earlier.

"May I sit here?" Dyson asked in a politely hushed voice, so as not to disturb the readers sitting at the other tables, but audible enough for people to hear and believe that he and Rachel were not acquainted with one another.

Rachel looked up and played along.

"Certainly, Father. Here, let me make some room for you."

She cleared away a few sheets of paper on the opposite side of the desk, so that when he sat down, he was facing her. Dyson took a few sheets of his own from his briefcase and spread them out. Then he pressed a few keys at random on his Library keyboard. Like the one in his office, the keys were projected from within the table onto a clear plastic plate embedded in the tabletop. The monitor was also like the one in his office: a virtual 3D cube appearing to hover over the desktop. The monitor was so transparent from the back that Rachel was able to read the title of the article, albeit backward, which Dyson had inadvertently called up from the Library database with his random typing.

"*Abhorrent Sexual Practices in Ancient Rome*," Rachel read in a whisper. "Nice choice!"

She was looking down at her own documents and smirking.

Dyson looked at his monitor in horror, and quickly stabbed at a key to clear the text before anybody else could read the title.

"Hi," she whispered.

"Hello," he whispered back, slowly regaining his dignity.

Dyson was determined not to look at her too much, in order to keep up the pretense of them not knowing each other, but he found this extremely difficult. He longed to gaze at her, to take in every contour of her face and body. He yearned to look deeply into her eyes, but this was impossible, particularly in their current surroundings. So Dyson made himself recall why they were there, forcing himself to concentrate on the task at hand. Separating one sheet of eco-foil from the rest, he was in the process of turning it around for Rachel to read, but she placed a hand on the sheet, as if by chance.

"It's OK," she whispered from the corner of her mouth. "Journalists can read upside down."

On the paper were printed the names and the dates and places of birth and death of the two priests he had shortlisted. He had also noted the cause of death.

"The two candidates," he whispered, barely audibly.

Rachel read the names, but neither meant anything to her. She then took a sheet from her own pile and slid it surreptitiously toward him.

"I found this," she whispered.

Dyson glanced casually at it, still distracted by the silky shine of her reddish brown hair cascading down to the table a mere meter away from him. He followed the hair with his gaze, ascending to her chin, then to those gorgeous full lips, the cute stubby nose, and her almond-shaped blue eyes.

Uh-oh, he thought. Her almond-shaped eyes were looking rather sternly into his own. Apparently he had been staring unashamedly at her, having totally forgotten why he was sitting there. Rachel's eyes darted down to the paper she had slid across the table, then back again to meet Dyson's eyes. At first Dyson noticed nothing spectacular, absorbed as he was by Rachel. Suddenly the sharp tip of a boot collided with his left shin. Stifling an indignant yell, Dyson glared accusingly at her. Rachel, for her part, glared once again, even more intensely than before, at the paper lying on the table before Dyson. The priest then glanced at the paper again and did a double take before reading the whole page.

Brian William Goodfellowe

Born: London, England, April 14, 2012

Occupation: Cardinal, Holy Church of the Second Coming of the Lamb

Education: Undergraduate student, De Montfort University Leicester, England, 2031-2035, Combined Bachelor's Degree in Theology/History

Postgraduate studies, University of the Lamb, London, England, 2035-2037;

Masters Degree in History, 2037;PhD, 2040.

Career: 2036; Ordained into the priesthood, Holy Church of the Second Coming of the Lamb.

2036-2038; field researcher, Historical Division of Holy Church of the Second Coming of the Lamb, London.

2038-2063; document surveyor, Historical Division of Holy Church of the Second Coming of the Lamb, London.

2063-2067; Bishop, Holy Church of the Second Coming of the Lamb, Liverpool.

2067; Cardinal, Holy Church of the Second Coming of the Lamb, Birmingham.

Career Related: After being appointed to the office of cardinal, became head of Historical Research Division Headquarters of the Holy Church of the Second Coming of the Lamb, New York.

Creative Works:

Author:

The Qumran Fallacy, 2052

The Scriptures of the Lamb, 2055

A Talisman for Christ, 2066

Awards:

Theocrat International Award for Historical Non-fiction 2053, *The Qumran Fallacy*

Order of the Lamb, 2nd Class, 2067, for services rendered to the Holy Church of the Second Coming.

Dyson looked from the eco-foil page about Cardinal Goodfellowe to the sheet he had slid across to Rachel. He looked back at the Goodfellowe sheet as if unable to believe his eyes.

"The dates!" he hissed. "They match!"

Rachel had been intrigued to discover that Cardinal Goodfellowe had been a Church field researcher for the Historical Division from 2036 until 2038, which fit perfectly with the time of the rumored discovery and subsequent disappearance of the mysterious papers. Now that she saw the priests' dates Dyson had presented her with, she was astounded. Father Paul Davies had died in 2036, Father Christopher Crabtree in 2037. Both in London!

For the first time that day she looked openly into Dyson's eyes for a little longer than usual. "It looks as though I might have been wrong about your Cardinal Goodfellowe," she whispered. "He was a field researcher when both of your candidates died."

Dyson closed his eyes and nodded. *I knew it*, he thought.

"What now?" he asked, addressing Rachel quietly.

"We need to find out more about the two priests. Did one of them really have any of the documents? Did they tell anyone else? Where are the papers now? Did they know Cardinal Goodfellowe? We'll have to go to England."

"We?" Dyson started in surprise. "You and who else?" he asked, although on second thought, he had a very good idea who she meant.

"Well, you, of course, who do you think?" she said. Exasperation had crept into her voice, causing it to become more of a mumble than a whisper. An elderly lady at the next table turned to glance at her disapprovingly, and Rachel took a deep breath before continuing in a whisper again. "Or do you think a female journalist from the States can just walk up to a Church organization in England and say 'Hi, I'd like to talk to you about some of your priests who died under mysterious circumstances forty years ago'?"

Dyson sighed a heavy sigh of inevitability. "And am I supposed to just drop everything at work and disappear for a while?"

"You're English, aren't you? Haven't you got family in England? Take some leave and visit them." A frown of uncertainty briefly crossed her face. "Priests *do* get leave, don't they?" she enquired.

Dyson smiled. People — even people as worldly and enlightened as investigative journalist Rachel Watson — sometimes had some very peculiar misconceptions about priests.

"Yes," he said, stifling a laugh, "of course priests get leave."

"Well, then, that's that sorted. Let's plan for a two-week stay. Let me know when you can make it."

"Hey, wait a minute! Is that it? I mean, just like that? What about you?" he wondered. "We can't exactly travel together. How would that look?"

"Oh, don't worry about me," she smiled. "I'll find some journalistic scoop in England. 'British Heretics Arrested by DFP'; something like that. My editor won't be able to get me on a plane fast enough. And don't panic: we'll take separate flights. Keep in touch."

With that she started gathering her papers and packing her bag. When she was ready to leave, she glanced down at the desk once more. "Enjoy your book, Father," she said, turned, and walked out of the Library without looking back.

Dyson remained seated for another ten minutes. His mind was reeling with so many emotions, it was difficult to think clearly. Was he really going to travel secretly to England with a *woman*? What was he *thinking*? This woman. This beautiful, enchanting woman... In a small part of his mind, alarm bells were sounding. The rest of it was falling in love.

CHAPTER 10

Archives of the Holy Church of the Second Coming
New York City, 2077

"Hi, Tom," Dyson said as he walked into O'Rourke's office on Monday morning.

"David, sit down," O'Rourke replied, buoyant as ever. "How's the apartment?"

Dyson took a seat. "It's fine. Thanks again."

"Don't mention it," O'Rourke said. "One of the many facets of my job is to make sure everything here runs smoothly, and that includes keeping everyone happy. So, is there anything else I can do for you?"

"Well, as a matter of fact, there is. As you know, I've been here for about two years now, and in all that time, I've only taken a week's leave each time my parents were over here for their annual visit. I really think I'd like to go back to England for a couple of weeks to see the rest of the family; you know, uncles, aunts, cousins and so on who I haven't seen since I've been here."

"David, that's completely understandable. And of course you are fully entitled to your leave. In fact, I don't know anyone more eligible to take it, especially in light of your recent experience. When would you like to go? For how long?"

"I was thinking of going for two weeks, starting next Monday. I've almost finished the latest project I've been working on and thought I'd like to take a little time off before starting the next one."

"Consider it done, my friend. All right, then," O'Rourke summed up, "one return ticket to Liverpool, England, departure next Monday, return two weeks from then. I'll get it sorted for you."

Although to all intents and purposes Dyson was officially O'Rourke's boss, it was O'Rourke who took care of the day-to-day administration of the department, including the coordination of leave and such matters. O'Rourke really was an excellent organizer and could probably even get Dyson a good deal on the plane tickets as well. Thanking him again, Dyson returned to his own office and began finishing off his projects so that he could make a fresh start with something new when he came back from England.

— «» —

That evening he called Rachel again from his apartment. "Alice in the park. Seven thirty tomorrow morning?"
"Yes."

— «» —

The next morning Dyson took the subway up to Central Park and walked to the Alice in Wonderland statue, a larger-than-life bronze sculpture featuring Alice, the March Hare, and the Mad Hatter. There he found Rachel waiting for him. She was sitting on a giant mushroom in front of the Mad Hatter, eating a bagel and sipping steaming coffee from a plastic cup.

"Want a bite?" she smiled pleasantly, waving the bagel at him.

"Err, no thanks." He looked around nervously, but apart from a few early-morning joggers in the distance, there was no one else around. "I think we should just exchange our information and get off to work."

Dyson then told her about his travel arrangements. They agreed that she would fly three days later and that he would spend the first few days with his parents in Liverpool, which would corroborate his story about visiting his family if anyone should ask.

Father Paul Davies had come from North Wales, not far from Dyson's hometown in the northwest of England, so it was decided that he would try to find some of Davies' living relatives. Dyson had initially groaned at the apparent impossibility of this task: in Wales the name Paul Davies was roughly as common as John Smith in England. From his database at the Archives, however, he had discovered that Davies had been born in the small seaside town of Llandudno, which at least gave him a starting point.

Rachel was going to try to find the family of Christopher Crabtree, who had come from Woking. As the name Crabtree seemed to be more common in northern England, and Woking was in the south, they felt she would be more likely to achieve a quick result than Dyson: theoretically there should be far fewer Crabtrees in Woking than in the north of England. After searching for, and hopefully finding, the relatives of their assigned priests, they decided to play it by ear and meet up somewhere in England.

— «» —

Ten days later Dyson had dutifully spent a few days with his surprised but very happy family. While he was there he had made a long list, an extremely long list in fact, of Davies families in Llandudno, hoping to eventually find someone who might in some way have been related to the deceased Paul Davies of forty years ago. Dyson phoned scores of people. Many of them knew or knew *of* a family member called Paul, but none of them had been a priest. After phoning more than half of the Llandudno Davies, he finally found a Kevin Davies who said he had an Uncle Paul, a priest, whom he had never met, as the uncle had died before his birth. Paul had been his mother's brother, but sadly, Kevin's mother Susanna had passed away two years ago. His Aunt Yvonne, though, was the sister of his mother Susanna and his Uncle Paul. She had married a Victor Fortescue and moved to Rotherham years ago. Dyson then found Victor and Yvonne Fortescue in the net phone index and called them on his comPod.

Yvonne took the call and seemed quite happy to talk about her brother, particularly when she spied Dyson's priest's collar on her monitor.

"Oh, he was such a lovely boy," she told Dyson in a sing-song Welsh accent. "A priest, you know, like yourself, Father."

Dyson had spent so much time finding her and was now so close to the information he wanted that he was quite restless. After several minutes of small talk he pressed her, gently but decidedly, to tell him all she could remember about her brother's death.

"Oh, Father," she told him, "it was such a tragedy. So very sad. Paul was on an outing with the Boy Scout troop he led on Thursday evenings. They'd gone down to London for a week. Stayed at a youth hostel down there, you know. Well, they were having such a nice time. Paul had organized everything for them. The hostel, outings to historical sites, and so on. Really, everything. Did I tell you Paul was interested in history, Father?"

"Yes, Mrs. Fortescue, as a matter of fact you did. Now, I'd really like to know what happened that day on the Thames. You know; the boating accident."

"Oh, that was such a tragedy, Father. Paul and the boys, about twenty of them I think, were on a small boat in the middle of the river. They'd stopped there to take some photos. Then this other boat appeared. It was going much too fast. It was only early evening, but the people on it were already having a party and no one seemed to be steering. Well, it was much bigger than Paul's boat. It crashed into his boat and sank it. They told me Paul drowned while he was trying to keep one of his unconscious Scouts afloat."

Dyson considered this for a moment. "So," he said eventually, "somebody was actually found guilty of causing the accident and was subsequently punished?"

"Oh, yes!" Yvonne Fortescue confirmed. "The man in charge of the other boat was sent to prison for five years." Her voice suddenly took on a more severe tone: "Not *nearly* long enough if you ask me. Our Paul and seven of his boys drowned that day, you know."

For Dyson it was now clear that Paul Davies was not the man they were looking for. If the DFP had been involved, it would have been a different kind of accident: perhaps one with no witnesses and certainly with no perpetrator. He thanked Mrs. Fortescue and contacted Rachel with the news.

She was not disappointed, as he had somehow expected she would be. "David, there's someone I'd like you to meet, but you'll have to come down to Woking."

"Is that really necessary?" he asked.

"It's worth it, believe me."

"All right. What have you found?"

"I'd rather tell you personally," she said, worried about their call being recorded. "Oh, and David. There's something else I wanted to say."

His heart fluttered momentarily. All sorts of emotions were suddenly coursing through his veins: hope, longing, desire. "Yes?"

"Don't wear your usual clothes when you come here." She was careful not to say the word cassock for fear of identifying him in any way over an unscrambled audio-only link and perhaps alerting anyone monitoring calls. "Put on something more civilian. I'll explain when you arrive. Meet you at Woking taxi station tomorrow. Let me know when you get in and I'll pick you up."

The next day Dyson's relatives drove him to Liverpool taxi station, which was actually an annex of the Holy Lamb Airport. The taxi station resembled a huge parking lot full of streamlined plastic cars. These cars had short, stubby wings containing large horizontal rotors encased in wire cages. Depending on the size of the vehicle, between one and four rotors stood upright at the rear. These were the taxis of the late twenty-first century. In vast countries like the USA, Canada, China, Australia, and Russia, huge numbers of such vehicles could be seen shooting across the skies at all times of the day and night. The combination of satellite navigation, advanced artificial intelligence, and national tracking networks made them an ideal means of transport in such large countries. Since they had now been on the market for so many years, the price had become so affordable that even private people on a middle class income were able to save up for one.

However, smaller, densely populated countries such as Britain and most other European nations did not enjoy such freedom. Despite modern guidance systems, the British government strictly regulated its airspace, banning almost all private flights with such machines and forcing commercial enterprises like taxi services to buy licenses. These flying taxis were fast, safe and reliable but they were only allowed to take off and land at official taxi stations and were only licensed for domestic flights. Dyson stood for a while in the short line for two-seater taxis. When his turn came, the pilot stored his suitcase in a small compartment in the nose of the vehicle and helped Dyson into his seat.

"Where to, Father?" the pilot asked, respectfully acknowledging Dyson's cassock, which he had kept on so that he didn't need to explain anything to his parents.

"Woking, please."

Pressing a button, the pilot closed the cockpit and let the air taxi roll along the tarmac, its wing tips just a few centimeters away from the other vehicles. Seconds later there was a mighty roar as the rotors in the wings began to spin and the jets beneath the vehicle fired up, and Dyson was pressed down into his seat as the taxi shot vertically into the air.

When the parked air taxis below them were reduced to mere colored specks, Dyson was thrust violently back in his seat as the taxi headed for its destination. Out of the corner of his eye, Dyson spied a malicious grin on the face of the pilot sitting next to him. For whatever reason, he seemed to enjoy giving his passenger a bone-jarring ride. A short while later Dyson's body relaxed as the acceleration phase ceased and they achieved cruise velocity. The flight was spent in complete silence. The pilot seemed to have other things on his mind and Dyson was not particularly keen on discussing his movements with a complete stranger.

Just under twenty-five minutes later Dyson felt his internal organs rise unpleasantly a few centimeters in his body as the taxi, without warning, suddenly dropped from the sky like a stone. His knuckles turned white as he clutched the armrests of his seat. A quick glance at the taxi pilot seemed to confirm that everything was apparently under control; the pilot was once again grinning like a maniac. Far too late, in Dyson's opinion, the maniac seated next to him reversed thrust, and pilot and passenger were pressed briefly down into their seats again before the taxi landed as gently as a feather on the tarmac of Woking taxi station. Staggering slightly, Dyson took his luggage from the pilot and paid him without offering a tip. He then did what he had promised

Rachel and went to the public toilets to change into casual civilian clothes: blue jeans, a white shirt, and a conservative blue rain jacket that he had taken from the wardrobe in his old room at his parents' house.

When he reached the exit doors of the terminal, Rachel was waiting to meet him.

"Well, don't you look handsome in your civilian duds?" she quipped.

He was so pleased to see her again, and so unused to anybody talking to him like that, especially an attractive young woman, that he could think of nothing to say, so he just smiled and said, "Hi." As they walked toward the parking lot and a car she had hired, courtesy of the *New York Gazette*, she told him what she had found.

"I've been talking to a Mrs. Jane McBride," she said enigmatically. Then she paused, as if for effect.

"OK, go on." He knew she was teasing him and was loving every minute of it.

"Mrs. McBride is eighty-nine years of age and she married Mr. McBride after her first husband died of a heart attack."

She paused again. Dyson, now on his home turf in England, far away from the stress of work and the events of the past few weeks, was in a buoyant mood, despite the recent trials of the taxi flight.

"Are you trying to wind me up?" he asked. "Get on with it, woman!" he added with humor, enjoying her company immensely.

She beamed at him.

"Well then. Mrs. McBride's first husband was one John Crabtree, and they were the parents of Christopher Crabtree, the priest we were looking for."

"Well done, Sherlock!" Dyson exclaimed happily. "But wait a minute. How old did you say she was now? Eighty-nine?"

She could see what was going through his mind.

"Ah," she said. "Now you're thinking Mrs. McBride might not have all her faculties any more. Lights are on but nobody's home? Uh-uh! This woman is not only in full possession of a complete set of marbles, she has a mind like the proverbial steel trap. She's amazing!"

"OK. And why did you tell me to dress in civilian clothes?"

"Well, apart from me wanting to see what you look like when you're dressed like a man for a change..."

"I beg your pardon!" he interjected, turning red.

"...cute butt, by the way..."

Dyson gasped.

"...Mrs. McBride is no friend of the Church," Rachel continued, smiling sweetly. "In fact, she has been in trouble with the DFP several times over the years for her outspoken statements. She even spent a few nights in DFP cells in her heyday. It seems she lost all faith when her boy died, and, get this: she blames the Church for his death! I talked to her on the phone for a while the other day and arranged to meet her today so she can tell us the details."

They were now walking across the parking lot and Rachel suddenly linked arms with him and looked up at him with playfully exaggerated adoration in her eyes, her head tilted to one side. She fluttered her eyelids at him coyly. Dyson cleared his throat nervously and looked around to see if anybody was watching. Then he looked at her questioningly.

"Oh, did I forget to mention?" she said. "We're married. You are David Jennings and I'm Rachel Jennings, your wife of six months. Practically newlyweds," she beamed happily.

Dyson almost choked. "We're what?!" He stopped, but she dragged him on, her arm still linked in his.

"That's our cover. We're journalists investigating Church conspiracies. Mrs. McBride was so pleased that someone finally had the guts to stand up to those — forgive me — 'hypocritical Church bastards'. She can't wait to meet me and my husband. I told her we always work as a team."

When they reached the rental car, Rachel got into the driver's seat and Dyson into the passenger side. On the one hand, he was secretly delighted even to *pretend* to be Rachel's husband. On the other hand, he was mortified. What if someone he knew caught him masquerading as a married man? If that happened, he thought, he needn't bother returning to the Archives. He would probably even be taken in for questioning by the DFP for breaking his holy vows!

But then again, he couldn't keep his eyes off his companion. *She's so beautiful. And intelligent. And vibrant!* And it really wasn't very likely at all that he would meet anyone he knew in this part of the country.

They drove for twenty minutes to the outskirts of the relatively quiet, very clean town of Woking, and Rachel parked outside a long three-story building with beautifully kept lawns all around it.

"Residential home for the elderly," she explained.

They walked up to the locked front door and Rachel rang the bell next to the name McBride.

A monitor over the bell flashed into life to display the face a grumpy octogenarian woman.

"Who are you?" she snapped. It was the voice of an old woman, but an old woman who still knew what she wanted, or, more to the point, what she did *not* want.

"Hello, Mrs. McBride, it's me, Rachel Jennings. And I've brought my husband, David."

Dyson flinched at the lie. A buzzer sounded and Rachel pushed the door open and walked in. Dyson followed and they went upstairs. The door to Mrs. McBride's apartment was open and the old lady was sitting in a comfortable-looking armchair, waiting for them.

"Get in here before all the warmth gets out!" she croaked at them impatiently. Admittedly, it was quite chilly outside the building, but even the corridors inside it were too warm for Dyson's liking.

He hurried inside after Rachel and closed the door gently behind them.

"Don't slam the door like that, dammit!" Mrs. McBride snapped.

"Err, what? Sorry..." Dyson began, but Rachel smoothed over the awkward situation.

"Hello again, Mrs. McBride. I'm Rachel Jennings, we spoke on the phone. And this is my husband, David."

Dyson took a step forward and offered Mrs. McBride a hand. She merely looked at it as if it were a piece of fish that had gone off.

"S'pose you've got some ID on you?" she said grumpily.

Dyson's eyes widened. *Oh, Holy Lamb, how did I ever think I'd get away with this subterfuge?* He began to stutter something about having left everything in the car when Rachel came to the rescue.

"It's all right, dear, I've got our press passes here," she said calmly, and, much to Dyson's surprise, pulled two authentic-looking ID cards from her bag. She held these up quite close to Mrs. McBride's face, saying, "Very wise, Mrs. McBride. You can't be too careful nowadays, can you?"

"Humph!" Mrs. McBride said. "No need to butter me up, girl." She looked at them suspiciously and added, "S'pose you'd better sit down, then."

Rachel sat on the sofa, pulling on Dyson's hand to indicate he should do the same.

"Now, Mrs. McBride, I'd like you to tell David what you told me. You remember I told you we work as a team, so it's important he hears everything firsthand from you, too."

"Listen girlie, I'm old; I'm not bloody stupid!"

"Oh, charming," Dyson muttered out of the corner of his mouth.

"What was that, boy?" the old woman demanded.

"Oh, excuse me, I said please carry on, Mrs. McBride."

After another few humphs and a couple of indecipherable words which may, or may not, have been obscene, the mother of Christopher Crabtree settled down and proved to Dyson and Rachel just how remarkable her memory still was.

"They sent us a letter when Christopher was just a lad. The Church, that is. Said how good he was at school. Top of his class! They wanted him to join the priesthood. Well, at first me and my husband said no. We didn't want no son of ours bein' a priest. Bunch o' hypocritical bastards!"

Rachel felt Dyson's hand, which she was holding next to her on the sofa, twitch, as if he were about to protest. Without turning to look at him, she clenched his hand a little tighter, which had the desired effect of calming him and preventing him from interrupting the old lady. Mrs. McBride continued.

"When they offered to pay for his schooling, though, we put Christopher's interests first. It was a once-in-a-lifetime opportunity for him. We didn't know anyone else who'd had a chance to go to private schools and university and whatnot, because no one we knew could afford it! So we put aside our personal feelings about the Church and let them take him. Oh, how he bloomed!"

Mrs. McBride smiled for the first time since their meeting had begun, obviously lost in fond memories of her son.

"He eventually joined the Historical Division. His plan was to do the obligatory field research in England for a few years before applying for a job abroad, perhaps in Israel or Turkey or Iraq. 'The world's my oyster, Mum!' he used to say to me. He loved being a part of the Church. In those days they'd just started with that new reformation stuff. Christopher wanted to help change it even more. He had such big ideas, did my Christopher. He really wanted to build a better world."

At this point Mrs. McBride closed her eyes as if reminiscing. Then she shook her head slowly, sadly.

"My Christopher was such a good boy," she said. Her voice started to falter and became softer as she vividly remembered every detail of the last contact she'd had with her son.

"He used to phone me every Friday evening, you know, to tell me if he was coming home for the weekend or not. Every Friday evening without fail. Such a good boy, he was."

Suddenly her voice became hard again; full of bitterness. She fixed Dyson and Rachel with an angry stare, almost as if they had personally been responsible for her son's eventual fate.

"He was far too naïve for his own good, though," she told them. "I warned him not to trust them but he wouldn't listen. One Friday he didn't call me. Of course, I was worried about him so I tried to call his place, but there was no answer. I didn't sleep that night. I knew something was wrong."

She took a deep breath, and Rachel and Dyson saw Mrs. McBride's shoulders tremble slightly when she exhaled, as she attempted to suppress the sobs caused by a pain that had never left her, even after all these years.

"The next morning he called me. He sounded so afraid, so very afraid. He said he wasn't really allowed to talk about it, but the DFP had taken him in for questioning the night before. It was something to do with his work, but he wouldn't tell me what it was. I warned him not to trust them, even though he always thought of them as his 'friends and colleagues'. That evening, that very same evening, someone from the Church came to my home. A priest, it was. He told me there had been a fire at Christopher's flat. The fire fighters had done all they could, but Christopher had died in the flames, he said."

She wiped away a tear with a tissue and her face became contorted with anger. "Those hypocritical Church bastards killed my son!" she shouted.

Despite her age and apparent physical frailty, Mrs. McBride managed quite a considerable volume. Rachel was worried a member of staff might come in and end the interview if the old lady became too agitated.

"Please, Mrs. McBride, try to remain calm," she said softly. "We want to find out exactly what happened. We want justice for Christopher, too. Believe me, if the Church is at fault here, we want to expose it for our readers."

Dyson then had a thought.

"Mrs. McBride," he said, as gently as he could, "what makes you think the Church had anything to do with Christopher's death?"

The old lady took a moment to compose herself and answered, "I know because I talked to Christopher's friend. They'd been working together with another man on the day they took Christopher away for questioning. His friend, Dmitri his name was, told me it was very dangerous for him to talk about it. The DFP had talked to him on that Friday, too, but Dmitri suspected something was wrong and told them he knew nothing. Clever boy, that one. Not as naïve as my Christopher. He told *me* about it, though. He said Christopher had found a diary, or part of one, anyway. The boys didn't take it very seriously at the time, but that's what the DFP wanted to talk to Dmitri about; the diary Christopher had found. They asked Dmitri if he'd seen it, too."

Rachel and Dyson were now on the edge of their seats, almost holding their breath in anticipation. The silence became oppressive. Rachel was the first to speak. "Mrs. McBride, I want you to think very, very carefully now. Take your time, because this is extremely important. Do you remember Dmitri's surname?"

"Of course I do! I'm not senile, girl! Not yet, anyway! It was Stanislous. Dmitri Stanislous."

Rachel noted it down.

"And what happened to Dmitri after Christopher died?"

"No idea," Mrs. McBride said. "Never heard from him again."

"And what about the third man?" Rachel asked. "Do you remember his name, too?"

"I remember the name, but I never had any contact with him at all. Christopher seemed to like him, though, from what he told me."

Again there was a momentary tense silence.

"And the name, Mrs. McBride? The name of the third man?" Dyson asked, the suspense in his voice unmistakable.

"Brian Goodfellowe," the old lady answered.

—— «» ——

Twenty minutes later, after a short car journey in almost complete silence as both of them were lost in their own thoughts, Dyson was sitting looking at Rachel across a small table in a café in Woking.

"We've got him," Dyson said.

"What do you mean?"

"Goodfellowe, of course. He's involved in the cover-up to do with these papers. He probably knows exactly what's going on. He was in it from the very beginning. He probably even had something to do with Pete's death."

"Hey, hang on! I know I said maybe I was wrong about Goodfellowe being involved, but we have absolutely no proof at all that he has anything to do with any deaths. I hate to pull rank on you, but I think I should remind you of my years of journalistic experience here."

Dyson looked downcast. "So, what do you think we should do now then?"

"Well, we know where to find Goodfellowe when we want him; he's not going anywhere soon. As we're already in England, let's find out what we can about Dmitri whatsisname. That's where your cassock will come in handy again."

They drove to London together that evening and found a hotel for Rachel. Dyson went to the local headquarters of the Church and found a room there, but not before Rachel had joked about getting married and divorced on the same day.

— «» —

The next morning Dyson had breakfast with some colleagues from the British branch of the Church's Historical Department. From them he found out where he could use a secure Church computer to access his database in New York, and he went to work trying to find out something about Dmitri Stanislous. At first it seemed all too simple. There was the name, date of birth, education, priesthood, time as field researcher, including sites he had worked at and then... nothing. Dyson performed the search again from scratch, thinking he had missed something, but the result was the same.

As Dyson's area of research was usually hundreds, if not thousands of years in the past, he was unfamiliar with the structure of this particular database. As an experiment, he entered the name Christopher Crabtree and was given similar information, but this time there was a date of death with the same remark he had seen at his own computer, to the effect that Crabtree had probably started the fire himself. So why did the data on Dmitri Stanislous simply cease after a certain point? There was another priest working at a computer station near his own, so Dyson casually asked him for advice on the Stanislous file. The young man came over to have a look.

"Oh," he said a moment later. "That means this person left the Church."

Dyson was puzzled. "Left, as in 'went voluntarily' or as in 'kicked out'?" he enquired, rather too flippantly, he thought, as soon as the words had left his mouth. The other priest looked around briefly to see if anybody else was listening, then he said in a hushed voice, "If you can't find any comment, or references to the DFP, he probably left of his own accord. If he'd been dishonorably discharged, so to speak, there would most likely be some kind of note in there to that effect. You know, so they can keep an eye on him; make sure he isn't plotting any subversive activities against the Church."

Dyson read through the file again, but found no such comments or notes, so it seemed likely that Dmitri Stanislous had indeed left the Church voluntarily, for whatever reason. The fact that there were no classified sections he could not access seemed to indicate that the Church did not believe him to be a threat to them. Dyson had never encountered such a phenomenon before. *So what happened to him then?* His date of birth was 2013, so he would be sixty-two now, if he were still alive.

"Hang on, though," he said as an afterthought to the priest who had helped him. "Surely if someone left the Church of his own accord, he must have had a very good reason. Wouldn't such a person be even *more* likely to be holding some kind of grudge? Wouldn't that make it more probable that he'd be placed under surveillance by the DFP?"

The other priest now began to look rather uncomfortable. *Holy Lamb*, he thought, *is this guy for real?* When he spoke to Dyson again, his voice was even more hushed than it had been before.

"Look, mate, I don't know what you're after, but I'll just say this: you must have known priests who wanted out. They find a nice girl, fall in love, want to start a family. Shit, we're only human, aren't we?" After a brief look at Dyson's quizzical expression, the priest suddenly realized that he was dealing either with someone with a cognitive disability or with one of those very rare creatures: a true, fanatical believer. Either way, the outcome could be dangerous for him, which is why the priest suddenly turned away, packed up his papers, and hastily left the room without another word.

This was certainly food for thought. *Is it really so common for priests to lose their faith? Are my feelings for Rachel not so unheard of, after all? Surely this can't be!* With a start, he realized he had for the first time admitted to himself in so many words that he actually had feelings for the American journalist.

While he was considering his next step, Dyson idly typed the name Dmitri Stanislous into a public — non-Church-controlled — search engine based in China. The Chinese maintained the largest free netbase in the world. About a thousand hits appeared in Greece and fifty or so in the United States. *No surprises there*, thought Dyson wryly. But then, right at the bottom of the list, he noticed a UK netsite: Dmitri Stanislous, Fishing Supplies. Dyson sat upright in his chair, his interest piqued. Calling up the netsite on his monitor, he discovered that the shop was in Cornwall. There was a postal address, email, and comPod. *A shot in the dark, but better than nothing*, Dyson thought. He noted the details and returned to his room. No need for anybody else to hear the conversation.

Dyson sat on the makeshift bed in his temporary, extremely Spartan, Church accommodation and got Janet to connect him to Dmitri Stanislous' comPod. A few seconds later a white-haired man in his early sixties with sun-tanned, weather-beaten, leathery skin and a full white beard appeared on Janet's screen.

"Hi there," he began jovially, "and welcome to…" but the broad, friendly smile suddenly collapsed when he caught sight of Dyson on his own monitor. "Oh," he went on in a much more subdued tone. "How can I help you, Father?"

Damn! thought Dyson. *Shouldn't have worn the collar! Damn, damn, damn!*

"Hello, Mr. Stanislous," he said, putting on a friendly tone and hoping the other man had not noticed his annoyance. "I'm sorry to trouble you, but I'm currently making some enquiries and I thought you might be able to help."

It was never wise to be rude to a priest; you never knew if they would go straight to the DFP and report you, so Stanislous made an obvious effort to be polite.

"Well, Father, of course I'll do anything to help the Church, but you know, I'm just a simple shopkeeper and part-time fisherman, so I don't know how much help I'll be to you."

Now that Stanislous had seen he was a priest, Dyson saw no point in beating about the bush.

"Well, let's start with your previous line of work, shall we. Could you tell me what you were doing for a living in 2037?"

Dyson saw an extremely brief look of wide-eyed shock cross the face on the monitor before his comPod screen went blank.

"I'm afraid the connection has been terminated without comment by the other party," Janet explained. "Would you like me to attempt to re-establish the connection, David?"

"Yes, please, Janet," Dyson replied. He was very doubtful, though, that Janet would be able to reconnect.

There was silence for a few seconds, after which Janet said, "I'm sorry David, but Dmitri Stanislous' apparatus is not granting me clearance to re-establish a connection."

Just as he had expected. "All right, thank you, Janet. Connect me to Rachel Watson, please."

Once his comPod had established the connection to Rachel, Dyson had to fight to keep his feelings under control. She was gorgeous. Struggling to maintain a business-like tone in his voice, he related his findings to her. Of course, once again, she wasn't at all thrilled about his lack of undercover skills, but was gradually coming to accept the fact that he hadn't been in this business as long as she had. They arranged that she would pick him up the next morning so that they could go together to the Cornwall address of Dmitri Stanislous. Of course, there was no reason at all why the former priest should talk to them, but Dyson felt he was now very close to some real answers, so he would not be put off by any doubts at this stage.

—— «» ——

Having made an early start with their rental car, Dyson and Rachel arrived at the small Cornish fishing village, which was home to Dmitri Stanislous, just before eleven in the morning. Janet had guided them to the shop, and Dyson had been careful this time not to wear his cassock.

When they entered the establishment, Dyson immediately recognized Stanislous from their communication the previous day, but it took a moment for Stanislous to recognize him. When it finally dawned on him, Stanislous took a step backward and shouted,

"We're closed. Go away!"

Rachel tried her soothing voice.

"Mr. Stanislous, if we could just have a brief word with you."

"Get out or I'll call the police!" he yelled.

"It's about Christopher Crabtree," Dyson said.

Suddenly all the fight seemed to have left Stanislous and he looked at the floor, sighing heavily.

"I knew someone would come around here one day," he said. "Poking around, asking nosy questions, looking for trouble. I don't want trouble. All that was a previous life. A life I left behind me a long time ago."

"Could you tell us about Christopher?" Rachel asked, her voice the quietest of murmurs.

"What do you want with Chris? He's dead. Let him rest in peace. I told you: I don't want any trouble. Especially not with the Church."

"Mr. Stanislous... Dmitri," Rachel said. "Nobody needs to know we were here."

"Ha!" Stanislous laughed sarcastically. "They know! They always know!"

"Dmitri, you know Chris can't rest in peace. Not until the truth about his death is told," Dyson said gently. "We want to find out what really happened. There are too many coincidences here. We don't believe Chris' death was an accident."

It looked as though Stanislous was struggling with something he had been keeping hidden for the last four decades. On the one hand, he needed to talk to somebody about it. He needed the truth to come out. On the other hand, if he talked now, he would not only be endangering his own life, but also the lives of these two people who had tracked him down. But worst of all, it would prove what a coward he had been for the last forty years. He had simply turned tail and run, letting those responsible literally get away with murder.

"All right," he said with an air of finality. He walked past them to the door of the shop and bolted it, turning round the quaint old sign to read 'closed.' "Follow me," he said, and led them to a small room at the back of the shop. Taking a seat on a rickety wooden chair, Dmitri motioned to an old leather sofa, inviting Dyson and Rachel to sit. "It's not much, but I'll tell you what I know."

Dyson and Rachel shared a glance at each other but remained silent.

"It was a Friday evening," Dmitri began. "I'll never forget that because I was looking forward to getting home for the weekend. When I got there, the DFP were waiting for me. They didn't even let me go in. They just grabbed me and threw me in the back of a van without a word. I don't mind telling you, I was bloody terrified. When we got to wherever it was they took me to, they blindfolded me and handcuffed me to a chair."

Rachel's sense of logic kicked in at this point. "They blindfolded you *after* they'd kidnapped you?"

"Yeah, I suppose it's just part of the intimidation. Or maybe it's so you can't see who's interrogating you. I was completely helpless. Anyway, at first they just asked me stuff about work: if I liked my job and if my colleagues were all right. Or if I'd like to be transferred somewhere else. And I remember thinking, *you've got to be kidding me!* You know, with the handcuffs and blindfold and all. They go to all that trouble and then ask such stupid questions. I told them everything was fine. My colleagues were great, and I loved my job. That was actually true, you know. But then they got down to business. They asked what we'd been working on that day, and I told them it was nothing out of the ordinary, just a bunch of old requisition orders. When they asked specifically what Chris had found, I lied to them. I lied to the bloody DFP! I said none of us, including Chris, had found anything out of the ordinary. That's when they broke all the fingers of my right hand."

Dyson almost choked. "They broke your fingers? But why?"

Dmitri smiled sadly. "Because they had the surveillance video of Chris. It was obvious from that he'd found something out of the ordinary. But I told them as far as I knew, Chris had found exactly the same as Brian and I: requisition orders from a government two hundred years ago which still wrote with pen and ink on paper made from trees."

"Chris found something out of the ordinary," Rachel said in an awed whisper. "What was it?"

"No idea, really. I think Chris said something about a diary," Dmitri replied. "That's why they eventually let me go. I admitted that Chris found something but I didn't know what it was. After they'd beaten the hell out of me for a couple of hours, they believed I was telling the truth and they let me go."

"Just like that?" Dyson said.

"Well, no. They said if I breathed a word of what had happened, then not only I, but also my parents, would suffer severe consequences."

"But you're talking to us about it now," Dyson said.

"My parents died years ago," Dmitri replied. "And now that I only have myself to look out for, I think it's about time people found out what happened to Chris."

His story finished, Dmitri sat back in the chair.

"After they let me go I decided to reverse what it says in the Bible," he told Dyson and Rachel.

They both looked at him in puzzlement until he smiled vaguely and explained: "I gave up being a fisher of men and became a fisher of fish!"

"You made contact with Chris' mother at some point, didn't you?" Rachel inquired.

"Well, she made contact with me, actually. When I heard about Chris' death, I knew it was no coincidence. It happened on the day after my interrogation. They killed him because he knew, or they thought he knew, something he shouldn't. Just before I left London, and the priesthood, Chris' mum phoned me. Naturally, she was beside herself with grief after just losing her boy. Well, I wasn't going to say anything but the poor woman pleaded with me, and I felt so sorry for her. All I could tell her was that Chris had found something but I didn't know anything more. I assumed my phone was bugged and at the time, of course, I was still afraid for my parents."

"Did you ever see Brian again?" Rachel asked.

"Never. I stayed in London for Chris' funeral and left the following day. I was so disgusted; I couldn't stay in the Church any longer. At the time, I thought Brian was still in DFP custody, because he wasn't at the funeral. But years later I found out he was a bloody cardinal! *How weird is that?* I thought. But then I wondered. Chris is dead, I'm all but forced to leave the Church, and Brian makes it to the top! He always was a high flyer, but I never expected that. I always reckoned he ratted us out somehow. But I could never really imagine him doing that."

— ⟨⟩ —

During the late evening drive back to London, Dyson felt somehow empty. For him there was still no tangible result. No evidence, no defendant to be brought to trial to answer for his friend's death.

"What have we actually achieved?" he asked miserably. "After traipsing all over Britain, what have we really got to show for it?"

"What do you mean?" Rachel said. "We've established that Christopher Crabtree was probably murdered by the Church because of what he knew. Dmitri Stanislous was interrogated by the DFP and was beaten and threatened because the DFP suspected he might know something as well. We know that Stanislous and Crabtree worked with your Cardinal Goodfellowe when he was a young man. And we know that Goodfellowe not only got off scot-free, he also rose in the Church hierarchy to a level not far below the Arch-Cardinal himself."

"So what do we do now?"

"Well, I for one would like to find out what Cardinal Goodfellowe really knows."

Dyson raised an eyebrow and looked at Rachel.

"Oh, right, that's a good idea. I'll make an appointment with him when I get back to the office. 'Excuse me, Eminence', I'll say, 'did you have your colleague killed forty years ago because he read someone's diary?'"

Rachel looked at him. She was a little hurt by his tone, but she understood that this had been a wholly new experience for him. His safe little world had practically collapsed around him like a house of cards and now he was afraid and cranky.

"Well, that's not exactly what I had in mind," she told him, "but we really need to find out more about this diary and what the good cardinal knows about it. Now that we're sure he was involved in the original incident, I was thinking more of having a look in his office. You know, when he's not there."

"My God, Rachel!" Several emotions ran through Dyson's mind simultaneously: outrage, shock, fear. "You're talking of breaking and entering now! I sometimes think you forget that I'm a priest of the Holy Church!"

Rachel could not contain her frustration any longer. She took the next motorway exit, just a few hundred meters ahead of them, pulled the car over at the side of the deserted road, and switched off the electric motor. Then she turned in her seat to look him squarely in the eyes.

"It's either that or we just forget the whole thing, David," she said tersely. "You go back to your Archives, I go back to covering stories about corruption in local politics. I would really, *very* much like to nail the story of the two-hundred-year-old diary which people at the top of the Church hierarchy are willing to murder for, but I suppose I could settle for Congresswoman Mary Wyman's trip to Walt Disney Universe with her family; a trip which was financed by the taxpayer. And you, you can go back to work knowing at the back of your mind for the rest of your life that the people at the top of your organization are murderers. So, just tell me what you want, David. Let me know at your convenience. God dammit, David, to put it in words you will understand: give me a sign!"

Dyson did not need to think about what he wanted. His mind was full of her, it was like an obsession. It went against everything he had believed in for the past twenty years, but he knew it was right. He had known for some time now that he would eventually have to choose one path over the other. That time had now come. But it was still so difficult that he hesitated for a moment. The saying, old habits die hard, was just a meaningless phrase when one was faced with the reality of imminently making a major, life-changing decision such as the one Dyson was about to make. Once committed, there would be no turning back. But he *knew* what he wanted.

He turned to look at Rachel and paused. They gazed at each other in silence for a moment. *Oh, Holy Lamb, she is so beautiful!* Then, plucking up all the courage he could muster, he reached over to her and let his right hand slide as gently as he could up the back of her neck into her hair. At this point he was terrified she would push him away or yell at him angrily, but Rachel's eyes widened, seemingly in surprise, as she let out a tiny, almost inaudible whimper of pleasure. Encouraged, he slid his hand further up to the back of her head and let his fingers play slowly and gently with her hair. His heart was pounding, but the surprise on Rachel's face quickly gave way to lust and longing. Her pupils were dilated as she looked up at him. She seemed just as excited as he was, and for once she was allowing *him* to take the lead.

He stretched out the palm of his left hand and placed it softly on her right cheek. His hand felt hot on her face as he stroked it so gently that he was barely touching her soft, smooth skin. It was softer and smoother than he could ever have imagined. Her eyes closed briefly and her lips parted slightly as she gasped at his touch. Dyson let his hand slide down the side of her neck and under her blouse to first caress her shoulder and then explore the shape of her collarbone with the tips of his fingers. She tilted her head back and to the side, obviously relishing his gentle caresses, inviting him to continue stroking her neck. He drew her head gently toward his. He almost seemed to feel the touch of her lips even before they met his.

The anticipation of that first kiss was like a physical ache. As soon as they made contact, the effect was electrifying. Dyson had so often imagined what it would feel like to kiss that beautiful mouth, but his imagination had been too feeble to prepare him for the actual sensation of her lips pressed against his. He felt light-headed. Her tongue suddenly pushed hungrily into his mouth, causing a wave of pleasure to course through Dyson's body. Rachel grasped the back of his neck and pressed her lips even harder against his. He felt her fingers tugging the shirt out of his trousers, then her small, warm hand was stroking and scratching his bare back. He had never been so aroused in all his life. When she slowly removed his hand from her neck and placed it firmly on her breast, the last vestiges of doubt in Dyson's mind dissipated like morning mist in the first rays of the sun. This was where he belonged. He belonged to her.

CHAPTER 11

**Archives of the Holy Church of the Second Coming
New York City, 2077**

It was the beginning of December, two months after Dyson's return from England. He and Rachel had been meeting in secret: a situation with which neither of them was completely happy, but it was vital for their mission, and probably their safety, that both of them remain in their jobs without their clandestine relationship being discovered. Over these two months their love had truly blossomed. It seemed that both of them had found something that had previously been missing in their lives. They now felt complete.

Rachel had asked Dyson about Cardinal Goodfellowe's movements; any regular appointments when he was not in his office and the like. Dyson had replied, half-jokingly, half seriously, that Goodfellowe was like the Lord: he moved in mysterious ways. There seemed to be no pattern in the Cardinal's movements. For two months now they had been biding their time, immensely enjoying being together in their secret, intimate relationship, but making no headway whatsoever in the mystery of the documents.

One day, though, Dyson had an idea. Christmas was approaching. That meant almost every member of staff in his whole building would be away for the holidays. Most of them went to join their families, either in the States or in their various countries of origin. The point was, apart from a skeleton maintenance staff, the Department of Archives would be deserted. It would be no problem for him to gain access to the building; he had a chip for that. Cardinal

Goodfellowe's office would not be so easy to enter, though. He imagined it would be secured with all manner of safety mechanisms and alarms, but he could think of no better opportunity to make an attempt to search it. He discussed it with Rachel, admitting his plan was still incomplete, but not knowing what else to do.

"Leave that to me," Rachel said confidently. "I'll get the Wizard onto it," she added mysteriously.

— «» —

Dyson went to the Archives on the morning of Christmas Eve.

"Forgot something in the office," he explained to the reception staff with an apologetic smile.

At eleven thirty, Dyson called reception from his office. "I'm afraid I have a network problem," he told them.

"OK, Father Dyson, shall I call the network administrator for you?" the desk clerk asked.

"No, thanks," he answered. "Klaus Anders is already at home with his family in California and I really don't want to disturb him at Christmas, so I've called a Church-approved external company called NetWerx. I just wanted to let you know so you'll show them to my office when they get here."

"No problem, Father Dyson," the clerk said.

— «» —

At noon precisely the clerk appeared on Dyson's monitor.

"Your technicians from NetWerx are here, Father Dyson," he said.

"Oh, thank you, Carlos. Would you show them up, please?"

— «» —

A few minutes later there was a knock at Dyson's door and Rachel and a young man of barely twenty, both of them wearing navy blue overalls, were ushered into his office by Carlos from reception.

"The NetWerx people, Father Dyson," the clerk announced.

Dyson thanked him and sent him away. Once the clerk had left, Dyson closed his office door and nodded curtly to Rachel and the young man. Rachel, however, ran up to Dyson, flung her arms around his shoulders and hugged him until he could hardly breathe.

Dyson looked speechlessly from Rachel to the twenty-year-old, his eyes wide.

"It's all right, David," Rachel explained. "He knows!"

"And just *what* does he know exactly?"

"Everything," Rachel said. "This is Mike, aka the Wizard. Mike, this is David, my, err, friend."

Mike nodded briefly, looking Dyson up and down.

The Wizard sat at Dyson's computer terminal typing, muttering and poking his fingers into the display for about five minutes. He then opened his huge black briefcase and proceeded to attach a multitude of wires from it to various connections underneath Dyson's desk, the existence of which Dyson had previously been unaware.

"And just what is your wizard friend doing?"

"Well," Rachel replied, "if you want details, forget it. I understand about as much of the technical stuff as you do. But I told him we need to open a door and that's what he's working on at the moment."

Dyson raised a skeptical eyebrow.

"You did tell him we don't want anyone to know we opened the door, I hope?"

Rachel stroked his cheek as if he were a small child.

"Yes, my dear," she said playfully. "He knows what he's doing."

"You want to tell me just who he is?" Dyson whispered.

"He does freelance work for the *Gazette*," Rachel whispered back. "When we need to, ehm, access certain data, you know, background information for a story."

After what seemed like an eternity, Rachel's friend threw himself back in Dyson's chair, exhaled loudly, and announced he had managed to crack the code.

"It wasn't easy," he said. "This guy had some serious programming behind him. Looks like a DFP coding signature to me."

Dyson's heart skipped a beat at the mention of the DFP. "OK, so what now?" he enquired.

"Wait a sec," the Wizard replied, pulling a small black box from his oversized briefcase. He attached this to yet another connection underneath Dyson's desk and said, "I need your chip."

Dyson was doubtful, but Rachel nodded confidently so he extended his arm. Mike the Wizard then scanned the embedded chip with his small black box, typed something into the computer and returned the box to the briefcase.

"There you go," he said with a self-satisfied smile. "Your chip should now open the door."

"Should?" Dyson asked. "You mean this isn't certain?"

"Hey," Mike said nonchalantly, "is anything ever certain in life? I'm pretty sure that chip will now get you into the room you want to get into undetected, but there's no such thing as a one hundred per cent guarantee."

Once again, as so often in the past few months, Dyson could almost feel the icy hand of the DFP on his shoulder, inviting him to a little tête-à-tête in some dark underground cell to discuss his views on Church policy.

They thanked the Wizard and sent him on his way. Rachel and Dyson then hugged, as if it were their last opportunity in this life, and left Dyson's office. When they exited the elevator on the 192nd floor, they encountered a building caretaker in the corridor who looked quite surprised to see two people walking around on Christmas Eve. Luckily Rachel had purposely retained her blue-overalled guise as a computer technician for just such a situation.

"Server technician," Dyson explained, pointing at Rachel, and the caretaker walked past them without further comment.

When they arrived at Cardinal Goodfellowe's door, Dyson realized with an air of apprehension that this was really it. Up until now he had not actually broken the law. He had been dishonest toward his employer, and he was involved in a relationship with a woman, thus breaking his holy vows. One of the features of the old Roman Catholic religion that had been adopted by the Church of the Second Coming was celibacy among the clergy. In the early days, the Arch-Cardinal of the New Christian Church, as it was initially called, met with senior cardinals from around the world to agree on doctrine and policy. This resulted in the birth of the Church of the Second Coming. At this congress, the Arch-Cardinal of Rome declared that anyone wishing to remain or to subsequently become a member of the New Clergy must swear a Holy Oath to remain celibate. For Dyson, this was bad enough, since his church had given him everything; it had nurtured his talents as if he was its child. It had made him the man he was now. At the beginning of his relationship with Rachel, he had actually felt as if he were betraying a wife by cheating on his marriage vows. However, this was before he discovered what was really going on within the Church. All this being said, he had not yet done anything that could actually be considered criminal by a non-Church court of law.

This was the point of no return for him. If he really went through with this *insane* plan and gained access to the cardinal's office through illegal means, things could never be the same. He would never feel secure in his job, or his life, ever again. Even if they got away from the scene of the burglary unrecognized at the time of the crime, he would live the rest of his life in a state of nervous panic, wondering when they were going to come for him. There was no going back now, though. He drew himself up to his full height and attempted to make his voice sound more confident than he was actually feeling.

"All right," he said, "here we go."

He held out a trembling hand toward Rachel, who gently held it for a second before guiding his forearm toward the small white box on the wall. The doors of Cardinal Goodfellowe's office swung silently open. The chip worked! There were no alarms; no obvious ones, anyway.

Dyson fumbled with the light switches on the wall next to the door, experimenting with the settings until he finally illuminated the room just enough for them to see, but not enough for them to draw attention to the room from the corridor or from outside the building. He was utterly miserable. Not only had he just illegally entered his superior's office in league with a female journalist; his very presence in this room bore witness to the fact that he had turned his back on his employer, the Church, and also on his faith. For who else but a heretic would dare to do what he was now attempting? If he really believed in the Second Coming of the Holy Lamb, then there would be absolutely no reason at all for him to be doing this. He would believe, as priests were supposed to do, that the Church and the Arch-Cardinal were infallible. The DFP, as an extension of the Church, would therefore also be infallible.

Dyson was aware that his life as he had known it was in tatters. Only two brief years ago he was a respected priest at the pinnacle of his working life who had just been awarded his doctorate by the organization that had nurtured him. He had been promoted to an exalted position within the Holy Church and could look forward to a long and illustrious career. But now.... Now he felt like a criminal. He had consistently lied to his colleagues and his superior and now he had broken into his boss's office with a view to stealing property. *How deep have I sunk?*

He was jolted from these morbid reveries by Rachel, who grabbed his hand and pulled him further into the room.

"Are you coming?" she whispered urgently.

Dyson followed her with trepidation, and they began searching the huge room for any signs of a safe. The obvious, if cliché, place to look was behind the paintings, but they were disappointed. Most of the paintings were on the glass outer walls of the building anyway, and those that weren't had nothing behind them. Goodfellowe's computer was also a dead end. It required a password, which neither Dyson nor Rachel nor the manipulated chip in Dyson's arm could supply. The filing cabinets contained nothing of any interest to them, nor did the drawers of the cardinal's desk.

Dyson felt thoroughly frustrated and was just about to vent his feelings to Rachel when the door from the corridor was violently flung, or more likely kicked, open. Two men dressed from head to foot in tight-fitting black uniforms with black scarves covering their faces stood in the shattered doorway pointing vicious-looking weapons at him and Rachel, who let out a yelp of surprise.

It took Dyson a second longer to react. "Hey, wait a minute!"

But there was no point. Before he could continue, two sharp pops issued from the men's weapons, whereupon Dyson and Rachel fell heavily to the floor. With his remaining strength, Dyson tried in vain to touch Rachel one last time. Her eyes were wide open and glazed. *She's dead*, Dyson thought as blackness took his consciousness away from her motionless body.

CHAPTER 12

When Dyson awoke, his head was pounding wickedly and his throat and mouth were bone dry. He was lying on a thin, hard mattress in a tiny, windowless room. He had been lying on his left arm for so long that he was unable to move it. On a little metal shelf attached to the frame of the bed stood a small plastic bottle of water. Struggling into a half-sitting position, he rubbed his dead arm vigorously until the circulation began to return, then made a clumsy grab for the bottle, managing to catch it just before it toppled to the floor. Despite his groggy condition, including his blurred vision, Dyson checked that the seal of the lid was still intact before he opened it. He then greedily gulped down the lukewarm liquid. After he had finished half the bottle, he let himself fall back heavily onto the bed and breathed deeply for a while, taking in his surroundings.

The floor space of the room was tiny, but the walls were so high that he would have been unable to reach the single light fixture set into the ceiling, even if he had stood on the bed. The sturdy-looking metal door, white like the walls, contained an aperture at eye-level, which looked as though it was covered from the outside. There was also a rectangular indentation at the bottom of the door. The only other features of the room were the lid-less toilet and a washbasin with a single tap, both made of stainless steel. The room was obviously a prison cell. Dyson was now resigned to the fact that he had been caught red-handed and that he could expect no mercy whatsoever from his captors. It was almost a relief somehow. Now all he had to fear were the consequences of his defiance. A chill suddenly ran down his spine. *Rachel!*

Dyson sat up as quickly as he dared in his weakened state and staggered painfully toward the door.

"Hey!" he shouted. "Hey, open up! I'll talk! Open up! Whatever it is you want from me, you can have it!"

He waited a few seconds and listened intently at the cold metal door, but nobody responded. He tried again, this time banging and kicking at the door, but the metal was so thick that his efforts were futile: no matter how hard he kicked and banged, nobody would hear anything on the other side. Frustrated, he threw himself dejectedly back onto the bed and waited. They would come for him soon enough, he thought.

While he was lying there, hands clasped behind his head, he noticed a small black circle on the high ceiling next to the light fixture. *A camera*, he assumed. Looking straight into the black spot, he raised both his hands, palms upward, as if to say, *OK, I'm here. Now what?* This did not have the desired effect of causing someone to come for him, though. All he wanted was to find out about Rachel. Where was she? Was she all right?

After what seemed like hours — Dyson had no way of telling, as they had taken his watch and his comPod — he perceived the faint sound of a bunch of keys rattling on the other side of the thick door of his cell. He sat upright, bracing himself to be either manhandled out of the room to be taken somewhere else, or maybe beaten to a pulp in his cell. Remembering the beating he had received at the hands of the DFP thugs in his apartment, his apprehension was gradually turning into terror. All that happened when the keys stopped rattling, however, was that the small hatch at the bottom of the cell door slid open just long enough for a plastic tray to be thrust through by a black-gloved hand. At first Dyson was too stunned to react, and by the time he had finally jumped toward the door, the hatch had already been slammed shut again. The keys rattled faintly on the other side of the door and the guard was gone.

"Hey! Come back!" he yelled. This time he was even more desperate. So many hours seemed to have passed since he had seen Rachel. But he could see they were still not ready to interrogate him, or to perform whatever horrific acts they might have in store.

All he could do now was to wait, so he inspected the tray they had given him. It contained a plastic bowl filled with what looked like vegetable soup. There were also two slices of white bread, a plastic spoon, and another bottle of water. Much of the soup had splashed over the side of the bowl when the tray had been shoved through the hatch so carelessly. Dyson was by now so famished that he no longer cared whether they had drugged the food or not. Leaving the spoon lying on the tray, he drank the almost cold soup straight out of the bowl and mopped up the spillage on the tray with the bread, stuffing this into his mouth ravenously. Not long after he had finished his meager meal, the light in his room was extinguished without warning. It was only in the ensuing total darkness that he realized how exhausted he was, and he flopped down on the bed once more and slept a dreamless sleep.

— «» —

The clanking of someone unlocking the cell door woke him abruptly. The light had been switched on again and two men dressed in black sweaters and black trousers stood in the doorway. One of them walked over to Dyson and shook him, making sure he was awake. When he looked up at them, the one who had shaken him addressed him:

"Come with us, Father Dyson."

The man's voice sounded neither brutal nor angry, as Dyson had somehow expected it would. Still, it would have been pointless trying to argue with them. There were two of them, after all, and Dyson did not even know where he was. He thought it was better to play along, at least until he could find out what had happened to Rachel, so he got up and let the guards lead him down the corridor. On each side of them they passed doors identical to the one behind which he had been incarcerated. The only difference was the consecutive number painted in black over each door.

"What is this place?" Dyson enquired, addressing neither of his guards in particular. The two burly men, one on either side of him, looked straight ahead and did not respond.

"Where are we? Where are you taking me?" he tried again, but again his guards ignored him completely.

Moments later one of the men placed a hand on Dyson's shoulder to indicate that they had arrived at their destination. The door resembled all the others they had passed, but on the wall next to this one Dyson read "Interrogation Room 6". Suddenly all the horrendous rumors he had ever heard about DFP interrogation methods ran through his mind and an involuntary shudder ran through his body. He would never have believed it, but he now discovered that it was indeed possible to go weak at the knees. A guard pushed the door open and indicated with a brief nod of his head that Dyson should enter.

The room contained very little in the way of furnishings. An extremely robust-looking metal chair with plastic straps for wrists and ankles was bolted to the floor in the center of the room. Facing it was a metal table behind which stood two simple plastic chairs. A long mirror set into the wall behind the table was probably a two-way mirror behind which his captors could observe the proceedings. His guards pulled him down into a sitting position and began fastening the plastic straps tightly around his wrists and ankles, effectively immobilizing him. His heart began to beat faster as he imagined all kinds of horrors they were most likely about to perform on him. Sharp knives and needles played a major role in his imagination.

"Hey, look," he said to his jailors in what he hoped sounded like a reasonable tone of voice, "there's really no need for all this. The woman I was with; let her go and I'll play along. Just tell me what you want to know and I'll talk. Honest. Just let the woman go. I'll cooperate fully!"

His guards remained impassive. They had an almost bored air about them, as if they had been witness to this scene so many times they simply didn't pay attention any longer, which was probably true. Once Dyson was firmly strapped to the chair, the guards left the room without a word.

A few minutes later, another man arrived. He was small and thin, his long pointed nose and large front teeth reminding

Dyson for all the world of a rat. He sauntered casually into the room, hands behind his back. The man wore round, black-rimmed glasses. Through these, his glistening, black eyes peered curiously at the seated Dyson. The fact that the man was wearing glasses at all was unusual. In the last quarter of the twenty-first century, virtually any ocular ailment could be medically remedied for the same price as a good pair of glasses, so anyone still wearing corrective lenses was almost always considered rather eccentric. When the man spoke, it was in an unpleasantly high voice that immediately grated on Dyson's already jarred nerves.

"So, Father Dyson, we've fallen quite some distance from our prestigious position as Keeper of the Archives, haven't we?"

One of Dyson's pet peeves was people who used the first person plural instead of the second person singular when addressing someone directly. It was bad enough when medical personnel asked "And how are *we* feeling today?" but in his current situation it sounded absolutely ludicrous. Nevertheless, Dyson held his tongue and waited to see what would happen next.

"Thought we were safe, did we?" rat-man continued. "Well, we thought wrong, didn't we?"

A strange, high-pitched hacking sound emanated from the man's mouth, and it was a second or two before Dyson realized his tormentor was laughing.

"Listen," he said to rat-man, hoping he sounded unafraid. "Could you just tell me what you've done with the woman I was with? Just tell me she's all right and I'll tell you anything you want to know." Despite the condition Rachel had been in the last time he had seen her on the floor of Goodfellowe's office, Dyson was desperately fishing for some indication that she was still alive.

"Oh, worried about the woman are we? Pretty little thing, isn't she? Well, you don't need to worry about her. It'll be her turn soon enough!" rat-man grinned. "And I'm sure you won't find her quite so pretty once I've finished with her," he added, and cackled horribly once again.

Dyson's feelings were mixed. On the one hand, he now felt relief wash over him, as he knew that Rachel was safe, at least for the moment. But the thought of her being left at the mercy of this lunatic made him feel sick.

"Right then, let's get started, shall we?" With that, rat-man withdrew the object he had been holding behind his back. It was a strip of silver-colored plastic about five centimeters wide, studded all over with tiny silver semi-spheres.

Dyson was confused. The thing rat-man was now placing around his victim's forehead looked remarkably like a BrainBox band! When Dyson was a teenager he had occasionally played computer games, and the year he turned fifteen had seen the advent of a gaming revolution: the BrainBox, a small silver box that established a wireless connection between the user's brain and a computer. The device stimulated areas of the brain to make the player believe that all kinds of things were physically happening to him.

The surprised look of recognition which momentarily crossed Dyson's face apparently did not escape his captor.

"I see we recognize the band," rat-man said. "Or at least we *think* we do. Maybe we had one of these in our youth, hmm? Maybe we remember the sweet and pleasant sensations of smelling perfume and tasting fresh fruit? Well, Father Dyson, let me clarify something. This is certainly no game. This instrument can cause pain; serious pain. Without actually inflicting physical damage on the victim's skin, it can cause agony so excruciating that it can lead to madness. I'm told it can be like having large shards of broken glass passing through your intestines. Just imagine the beauty of it, Father Dyson. No mess, no fuss. Without the physical injuries caused by other methods of interrogation there is no reason why it should not be possible for the detainee to suffer for days, weeks even, before the heart gives up or the mind simply switches off altogether. Permanently."

Despite the visions of horror currently battling for priority in his mind, Dyson attempted to reason with his adversary.

"Look," he said, "There's absolutely no need at all for any of this. Let the woman go and I promise you I'll tell you anything you want to know. Anything! Just leave her out of this. She knows nothing anyway. Just tell me what you want and I'll cooperate fully."

Rat-man's grin became wider; something that Dyson had not believed possible. It was obvious that here was a man who was an expert at his job, and therefore relished it. He placed the plastic band around Dyson's head and clicked it shut.

"Oh, no, Father Dyson. You won't get off that easily," he hissed. "Once they've sent you to me, you're mine!" he added triumphantly. "How many people do you think know you are here? I'll tell you, shall I? Five or six. That includes me and the men who brought you to this room. And how many of them do you think would care if I simply snuffed out your life? The answer to that one, Father Dyson, is *none at all*! You are a traitor to the faith! You have betrayed your holy vows, and you are a common burglar! Your life is already over, you miserable worm! You just haven't realized it yet. If I manage to get some answers from you, then so be it. If I don't…well, that doesn't really matter. Either way, you will be either dead or a vegetable when you're taken away from here."

Dyson was about to attempt to reason with his captor once again. He was formulating an argument in his head, something along the lines of 'forgiveness' and 'turning the other cheek,' when his vision suddenly failed and something that felt like a red hot knife was plunged into his intestines. Someone was screaming like an animal in pain. Agony. Helplessness. Burning in the fires of Hell. Spots of brilliant white light. Screaming. A million suns exploding in his head. His stomach was clutched in a giant fist. The fist squeezed until his stomach burst, its acid contents burning into his other organs, dissolving them.

Several seconds later Dyson's brain had recovered enough from the shock to realize that the bestial screaming had come from his own throat, which was now raw and sore. He gasped for breath, eyes open wide, searching in vain for the source of such hellish punishment. But there was none.

"Well, well. I see the machine has made quite an impression," rat-man crooned, with an air of extreme satisfaction.

"Please," Dyson gasped quietly. But he had no strength to continue.

"Oh, we're nowhere near ready to interrogate you yet, Father. We have to be quite certain that you won't tell us any lies. And we can only be certain of that when you have been acquainted with all the possibilities of the machine. You can tell me whatever you want when your spirit has been well and truly broken."

With that, the room winked briefly out of existence once more. Blunt knives were hacking at his belly, tearing out huge chunks of flesh. He was deaf and blind from the needles being slowly, excruciatingly inserted into his eyes and ears. There was no body, no soul. There was only pain: searing, burning torment in the deepest pits of hell.

Once more it stopped. Once more rat-man materialized before him. He said something, but this time his words were incoherent to Dyson. On it went. Incorporeal agony, then a moment's respite before the pain returned. Each time it stopped, it was more and more difficult for Dyson to focus. It seemed to him as if the torture continued for hours. Rat-man was indeed an expert at his foul art. He knew precisely when to stop and when he could continue without any danger of his victim inadvertently dying. Dyson realized in the dim recesses of his mind that he could not stand much more of this torture and was on the verge of giving up all hope. He began to make his peace with God in silent prayer when the next assault came. This time it was his head that was being filled with liquid. Hot liquid. Pressure building up in his skull. The rest of his body was as numb as if it no longer existed. Why didn't his head explode? The pressure increased. The screaming became ever more distant. Then there was nothing. Dyson's mind had switched off. Oblivion. That was what he craved. Nothingness. His body was motionless, without feeling. His mind was no longer in his body. His mind sought escape; peace. *Let me go. Let me die. Jesus on the cross. Why hast thou forsaken me? Holy Lamb of God. Take me.*

Suddenly there was a sound of a door opening. It was in another world, far, far away from this place. A voice. Dyson could not make his brain understand the words. A voice in the wilderness. In the void. Salvation. Holy Lamb. *Have you come for me at last, Lord?*

A loud, piercing howl of frustration issued forth from rat-man.

"How am I supposed to do my job when people just burst in here when they damn well feel like it?" he yelled. "This is not a fucking taxi station!"

The young priest who had opened the door was wearing a black cassock like Dyson's. He now walked hesitantly up to rat-man, clutching a single piece of eco-foil. In his semi-conscious state, Dyson did not know if what he was seeing was real. Whatever the priest whispered into the torturer's ear, it echoed through Dyson's head like a rifle shot in the mountains. It was loud, violating his sensibilities, and yet it was incomprehensible. Dyson's brain had been subjected to such an onslaught that it threatened to close down completely, permanently, as rat-man had forewarned.

Oh, my God, what's happening to me? he managed to think before the thought itself betrayed him and refused to remain coherent. He felt like screaming, but could produce no sound. He could not remember how. His screaming had been done. Now nothing was left. Nothing but death. *So, you've come for me, God. I'm ready.*

The young priest then raised the foil he was carrying and displayed it demonstratively before the jailor's face.

"I don't fucking believe it!" rat-man screeched.

He was absolutely livid. He raised both hands, palms outstretched, to the ceiling, rolling his eyes behind his round, black-rimmed glasses as if beseeching some higher power to intervene. The priest who had brought the news was obviously somewhat intimidated by the display of emotion on the part of the torturer, but he nevertheless managed to concentrate on the job at hand.

"I am extremely sorry," he said, his words rattling around incomprehensibly in Dyson's mind. "But those are my orders. And yours. I must insist."

With that, rat-man pushed past the priest and stormed wordlessly out of the room, slamming the door behind him like a petulant child. The priest began rapidly to loosen Dyson's bonds. While he was doing so, he whispered conspiratorially into the prisoner's ear.

"Listen to me carefully, Father Dyson. I am here to help you. A friend sent me to get you out of here. You are safe for the moment, as long as we hurry. I realize you must still be in shock after what you have just been through. I'm afraid I didn't manage to get here before they started. But I need you to focus. You must come with me now. I will take you to safety."

Dyson's mind slipped into and out of consciousness. He was unable to focus, as the man had requested, but the word "safety" registered vaguely in his foggy brain. He wanted to nod his assent, but his mind was unable to control the neck muscles. He attempted to stand, but his knees wobbled precariously and must have buckled, for the next thing Dyson felt was the cold floor on his cheek, but he had no memory of falling. The other man somehow managed to grapple him back into the chair and made a fresh attempt to get him to stand. This time he managed to rise from the chair and let the young priest lead him, half carrying him from the torture chamber with one of Dyson's arms slung over his shoulder.

Dyson vaguely registered that he was being led down winding corridors. At some point he was guided into an elevator and was dropped unceremoniously to the floor when the young priest could no longer support his weight. The elevator descended for several seconds before the doors opened again and he was steered into a dimly lit parking lot. After being ushered into the back seat of a dark limousine, the last reserves of Dyson's strength were depleted and he blacked out completely.

CHAPTER 13

Dyson awoke with a start and was thoroughly confused by his surroundings. His vision was still a little blurry but, lying on his back, he made out a wood-paneled ceiling. Further examination revealed he was lying in a soft bed with clean white sheets in a room furnished with antique wooden furniture. Brilliant sunlight was streaming in through large windows on the other side of the room. It was so comfortable, so tranquil, that, despite his curiosity, he fell into a deep, peaceful sleep.

Hours later he awoke once again, to find a middle-aged woman standing next to his bed holding a tray.

"How are you, Father?" she asked softly. "Do you feel like eating something?"

A loud rumbling sound emanating from his stomach answered the question for him. He was famished.

"Oh, yes, please," he managed to reply weakly. His throat was very dry and very sore. Suddenly Rachel once again appeared in his mind.

"Where is Rachel? The woman I was with. Where is she?"

The woman deposited the tray gently onto the small table next to his bed and spoke to him in a soothing voice.

"Father, I'm afraid I don't know anything at all about a woman called Rachel. I have been instructed to look after you. I am to offer you food and drink, to spoon-feed you if necessary. I have been told that you have been through a terrible ordeal and need to recover here. Otherwise, Father, I know nothing about what has happened or what will happen. Now, please, let me do my job. Can you manage to feed yourself, or would you like me to help you?"

Dyson thought for a second before answering.

"Thank you, I can eat by myself."

In trembling, weak hands, he gratefully accepted the bowl of thick, steaming vegetable broth she had brought him. He managed very slowly to bring the spoon up to his mouth, and there was an explosion of taste as his tongue experienced the first decent food it had come into contact with in days.

"Who are you? And where am I?" he asked.

"My name is Maria. I am the housekeeper of His Eminence, Cardinal Goodfellowe. And you are a guest in His Eminence's home."

Dyson dropped the spoon he had barely been able to balance in his weakened hand. *Oh, Holy Lamb! Out of the frying pan into the fire*, he thought.

"What am I doing here?" he asked.

"I've already told you all I know, Father. You are safe here and I am to look after you until you regain your strength. His Eminence has given strict instructions that you are to be left in peace until you feel you are ready to talk to him."

"Talk to him?" Dyson asked sarcastically, his sore throat making the tone of his voice sound even harsher than he intended it to. But when he noticed the woman's shocked look, he decided to hold his tongue until he knew a little more about what was going on. He had to admit this place was warm, comfortable, and seemed safe enough. And if it was Goodfellowe who had him rescued from the torturer, he reasoned, then it was unlikely that anything worse than that appalling fate would befall him here.

"I'm very sorry," he said as gently as he could manage. "I'm not quite myself yet. I'll be all right again when I've eaten something and freshened up a little. What time is it, by the way?"

The cardinal's housekeeper smiled softly. "It's about eleven a.m., Father. You slept for almost twenty-four hours. As soon as you feel up to it, there's a bathroom with a shower through that door, and I've laid out some fresh clothes for you."

In a motherly tone, she added, "But don't you be trying to get up till you feel strong enough, do you hear? Cardinal's orders!"

"Thank you very much, you are most kind, Maria." Dyson replied.

As soon as the housekeeper had left the room, he began hungrily devouring the broth. After finishing it and the hot herbal tea that had also been on the tray, he felt drowsy again and drifted off to sleep.

After another few hours he felt strong enough to go to the bathroom, where he showered away the gruesome memories of his recent captivity. Half an hour later he was again standing in the bedroom, revived by the shower and, wearing the fresh dark blue shirt and black trousers the housekeeper had provided, feeling almost completely like his old self again. *Now what?* he thought. If he just walked out, they might think he was trying to escape. On the other hand, they had gone to the trouble of rescuing him, so it was unlikely that he was a prisoner here. Then again, he couldn't just go wandering around the cardinal's house as if he owned the place.

As quietly as possible, he tried the door through which the housekeeper had left. To his relief, he found it was unlocked, proving that he was not being held captive. He tentatively poked his head out into a long corridor lined with identical ornate wooden doors on both sides. There was no one in sight, so Dyson chose a direction at random and began walking slowly and silently away from his room. At the end of the corridor he turned a corner and almost collided with the housekeeper, who was coming to clear away his dishes.

"Oh, my Lord!" she exclaimed. "You gave me such a fright, Father!"

Otherwise, the housekeeper did not seem upset, or in any way inclined to raise the alarm, so Dyson also remained calm.

"I'm so sorry. I didn't mean to scare you like that. It's just that I felt OK again, so I thought I'd, err ..."

"That's quite all right, Father. I'm glad to see you're out and about," she replied with a smile. "Well, then," she added after looking him up and down, as if she wanted to make sure he was presentable, "you'd better come with me."

With that, she turned and led him back the way she had come. Dyson followed without speaking until they arrived at a pair of double doors. The housekeeper knocked politely before opening them both simultaneously and looking inside.

"Nobody here," she informed Dyson. "You take a seat over there by the fire, Father, and I'll go and let his Eminence know you're up."

Ten minutes later Dyson, who had been meditating and almost falling into a drowsy sleep in a comfortable armchair near the fireplace, was startled by the double doors being thrust open. He jumped to his feet, heart pounding, half expecting to be arrested by DFP guards.

"Good afternoon, Father Dyson." It was Cardinal Goodfellowe.

Dyson was at a loss. If this really was the man who had saved him, he should be eternally grateful to him, but old habits die hard, and it was difficult to dispel the suspicion he felt.

"Your Eminence," he replied curtly, playing it by ear until he knew why he had been brought here. He did not even approach the cardinal to kiss the older man's ring, wary of any movements that might be construed to be threatening; there might be DFP guards in the corridor behind the cardinal.

The situation was awkward in the extreme, but unlike their previous encounters, Cardinal Goodfellowe now appeared willing to talk.

"Sit down, my son," he said gently. Dyson obeyed but said nothing. "I trust you have come to no serious harm?" the cardinal enquired, taking a seat in an armchair identical to Dyson's, facing him.

"I'm fine, Eminence." he said. "Thank you."

"Father Dyson. David, I can tell by your tone that you feel I have done you an injustice."

When Dyson wordlessly, albeit involuntarily, raised his eyebrows as if to say *You must be bloody joking!* the cardinal went on.

"I promise you that there is nothing you can say to me that will offend me or put you in any kind of danger whatsoever. Look beyond the color of my robes and treat me merely as a man and not a Church official. Please, David, speak freely."

Not for the first time during his meetings with Cardinal Goodfellowe, Dyson's mind reeled in confusion. *Where do I begin?* he thought. Suddenly he blurted out the first thing that came to mind, no longer caring about how much the cardinal knew about his affair. After all, this man was a master of the art of surveillance, and probably knew more about Dyson and Rachel's affair that Dyson would ever have suspected.

"Where is Rachel Watson?"

"She is safe," the cardinal replied simply.

Aha, thought Dyson. *So you're not going to tell me where she is.*

But the cardinal continued.

"At present, I am not aware of her precise whereabouts, but she is being brought here as we speak. And she is unharmed. I know that for a fact. I have merely been waiting for you to make a full recovery from your ordeal before, shall we say, *overtaxing* your emotions."

His voice was calm, gentle even. There was no trace of admonishment, no recrimination. For a few seconds, the only sound in the room was the crackle of the open fireplace. It did not burn precious wood, of course, but the holographic illusion and the sound effects were perfect, and the warmth radiated by the hidden heating elements was soothing. Dyson relaxed a little. For some reason, he believed the cardinal, perhaps mainly because he only wanted to hear that Rachel was safe, but he also found himself beginning to trust Goodfellowe. Making the effort to look beyond the robes, as the cardinal had suggested, Dyson saw an elderly gentleman who seemed concerned, so he made up his mind to test this new freedom of speech he had been unexpectedly granted.

"Err, if you don't mind my saying so, Eminence, your behavior toward me, and toward my colleagues at the

Archives, was never, please forgive me, marked by Christian charity and brotherly love."

Dyson himself almost flinched as the words were spoken. He could scarcely believe they had left *his* mouth. The cardinal smiled at Dyson's careful choice of phrasing.

"When one lives among wolves, it is usually wise to not dress as a sheep," he responded enigmatically.

Dyson's expression conveyed his puzzlement. "Would you mind expanding on that a little?"

"Well, on the one hand my behavior, which might have seemed strange or hostile to you, can be put down to the fact that I did not know whom I could trust. And on the other hand, I knew *precisely* whom I could *not* trust. Let's say my behavior was a shield to protect myself and my interests."

"Fair enough."

Dyson decided to go one step further.

"Did you have my friend, Pete Mackenzie, killed?"

Once again, he regretted saying it so directly as soon as the question had left his mouth; not merely because it was so tactless, but mainly because he now had no desire to offend the man who had apparently saved his life. He embarked upon an awkward apology, but the cardinal cut him off with a smile and two upraised palms.

"David, I want you to believe what I am about to say. The only people who have ever died through any fault of mine were those who were killed before I had an opportunity to help them. I have spent many hours praying for forgiveness for my human failings. Sometimes I did not act quickly enough because I received vital information too late. But other times — may God have mercy on me — I procrastinated because I was afraid of giving myself away. It is the latter action, or rather non-action, of which I am deeply ashamed."

"But you had Pete's body confiscated by the DFP!"

"No, my son. I attempted to have the body *secured* so that it might be examined by a state coroner, but the DFP intercepted the vehicle in which your friend was being transported. There was nothing I could do after that."

"But you're a cardinal! Surely you have authority over the DFP!"

"There is something you should understand about the DFP, David. I may be able to put the fear of God into individual DFP members and perhaps influence them a little when they are alone and vulnerable, but as an institution, I have no power over them whatsoever. Once an order has been issued to a DFP unit by their commanding officers, even *my* hands are tied. These men are loyal to their institution to the point of arresting bishops and disobeying cardinals."

"Well, who controls them then?"

"Here in the United States they are under the direct command of Cardinal di Galassini."

Dyson was astonished. "The Arch-Cardinal's right-hand man controls the secret police? The secret police who torture and kill people?"

"That is correct." *He didn't deny that the DFP kill people!*

"What about Christopher Crabtree? What do you know about his death?"

A sad expression came over the cardinal's face, and he nodded slowly as if acknowledging that Dyson had done his research well.

"I am quite sure that he was murdered by the DFP."

"Are you saying you didn't know anything about it at the time? Why weren't you at his funeral?"

The cardinal sighed, remembering his days as a young priest working on historical excavations.

"I am assuming you located and talked to Dmitri?"

Dyson nodded silently.

"Well, at the time of Chris's funeral, I had just been questioned by the DFP for several days. Needless to say, I was in no fit state to attend a funeral after they had finished with me. Back then, the interrogation methods were not as subtle as they are these days. They broke my leg in two places and shattered the kneecap. Afterward they denied me treatment. I walk with a limp to this day, as you may have noticed."

Dyson was amazed. "But they didn't keep Dmitri so long. And they didn't hurt him. Well, not seriously, anyway."

"Ah, but Dmitri wasn't the team leader. I was. And as such, I was expected to write a report at the end of each working day to sum up the findings of my team. As I failed to do that, I was suspected of hiding something."

"So you must have seen the papers Christopher Crabtree had seen!" Dyson exclaimed. He felt that the secret of the mysterious papers was now — finally — within his grasp.

"At the time, alas, I did not. I am now what one might term exceedingly conscientious in my work. What I do, I do well, and I do thoroughly. In those days, however, I had not yet fully developed these character traits. I remember that it was a Friday when Chris discovered the documents. As team leader, I decided that we had done enough work for the week and we left everything just lying around. After all, who would know? Who would care? I was expecting to get back to it again on the following Monday, at which time I intended to write the report. It never came to that, of course. Many times I've wondered what might have happened if I had performed my job properly. If I had written my daily summary on that Friday, I might have realized that Chris had found something dangerous. Perhaps he would still be alive today. Then again, perhaps Dmitri and I would be dead, too."

"And my predecessor, Father Tim Nelson? Did the DFP have him killed, too?"

"Tim Nelson was a close personal friend of mine, David. As far as I know, his death had nothing to do with the DFP. Although I cannot be sure, of course, I do believe his heart attack was brought on by the knowledge I shared with him. I knew I could trust Tim with my life, so I told him about my past and the papers. With hindsight, I see this was a mistake. The burden was simply too much for the poor fellow. As far as Tim is concerned, I think you are displaying a certain degree of paranoia regarding the DFP."

"So at the time of his death, you had discovered something about these documents, and you discussed it with him?"

"That is correct, David."

"Then in a way, his death *did* have something to do with the papers that killed Pete and Christopher Crabtree."

"Papers and knowledge do not kill people, my son. Evil men kill people to conceal their own evil deeds. It seems that Tim could not handle the truth."

A new question suddenly demanded an answer. "How were you able to follow my movements twenty-four/seven? You knew exactly where I was and what I was up to in the Archives building."

The cardinal smiled ever so slightly. "Many people believe that life as a disembodied entity only has disadvantages."

"So it was Bjørn! In theory, I suppose he could access every computer and camera anywhere and no one would notice."

The cardinal merely raised an eyebrow.

"So you had Bjørn monitor my movements all over the building."

"Not only at the Archives, David. I think you're forgetting what Tom O'Rourke told you on the day you met Bjørn Svensson for the first time: Deploy your staff with their particular skills in mind, and you'll be maximizing their usefulness."

Holy Lamb, he sees and hears everything! thought Dyson. Changing the subject, he asked, "And are you going to tell me about these documents?"

Before the cardinal could reply, there was a brief knock on the double doors, which were opened seconds later by the cardinal's housekeeper. She just about managed to say "She's here, your Eminence," before Rachel rushed into the room, ignored Goodfellowe completely, and flung her arms around Dyson's neck.

An incredible range of emotions ran through the priest: joy at seeing his beloved Rachel again, holding her close, smelling her perfume; embarrassment that his superior and his superior's housekeeper were witnesses to his illicit relationship with a woman; an underlying fear, despite everything that had happened over the last half hour, that there would be serious repercussions for breaking his holy vows. This last thought was unfounded, though, as the housekeeper had quietly left the room, closing the doors behind her, and Cardinal Goodfellowe had discreetly turned away to regard the open fireplace. Neither the cardinal nor his housekeeper seemed even remotely interested in their relationship.

After exchanging a few brief kisses, and after they had each quietly assured themselves that the other was unharmed, Dyson cleared his throat to indicate to the cardinal that he was ready to continue their conversation.

"Ahem. Please forgive us, Eminence."

"That's quite all right, my son. I understand."

And judging by the sincerity in the Cardinal's voice when he said it, Dyson actually believed him.

"Eminence, may I introduce Rachel Watson, my err, friend."

"Delighted to make your acquaintance, Ms. Watson," the cardinal replied. "I've heard so much about you."

"Cardinal Goodfellowe." Being Rachel, she refused to address him properly as Your Eminence, kiss his ring, or curtsy before him, but she shook the hand he offered her as an equal. She then raised a quizzical eyebrow in Dyson's direction, as if to say, *what have you been telling him about me?* Dyson, for his part, shrugged and raised his eyebrows in surprise to indicate, *I've told him nothing about you!*

"Please take a seat," the cardinal said, indicating a plush sofa near the fire.

Dyson and Rachel sat down, and Goodfellowe took a seat in an armchair opposite them. He then addressed Rachel, his voice calm and level.

"Ms. Watson, I have been explaining to David that many things are not what they seem to be at first sight. As time is pressing, I will not go through it all again for your benefit; David can do that later." Addressing them both together, he said, "For now I would be interested to learn how much you two actually know."

Rachel turned to Dyson with doubt clearly written across her face.

"It's all right," Dyson replied gently. "The cardinal is the one who saved our lives. He knows all about us and probably a lot more about the documents than we've been able to find out."

Over the next few minutes, they told Cardinal Goodfellowe their story: what they had found, whom they had talked to, what they suspected. They still did not know exactly what was going on or why anybody had to die for becoming involved with the mysterious documents or diary or whatever it was they were dealing with.

"It's obviously something damaging to the Church," Rachel ventured when they had finished. "But what could possibly be so damaging that the Church would be prepared to have people murdered for it?"

The cardinal observed them gravely. Then he stood up and walked to a corner of the room to a piece of furniture about a meter high that had been completely covered with an ornate cloth hanging down almost to the floor, upon which had been placed a vase of flowers. He removed the flowers and the cloth to reveal a featureless metal cube. When he pressed his hand against the front of the cube, however, a rectangular outline appeared in green light and the door of the thick-walled safe swung open soundlessly. The cardinal reached into the safe and took out a clear plastic folder that contained some eco-foil copies. Returning to his chair, he looked at Dyson and Rachel once again.

"Have you ever wondered," he said, his voice almost a whisper, "why the re-appearance of the Lamb of God did not herald the beginning of Armageddon, as it is foretold in the scriptures?"

Dyson's knee-jerk reaction did credit to the constant indoctrination he had received from the Church from primary school to the seminary.

"Because He has pleaded on our behalf with the Father to spare us one more time, proving to mankind the divine mercy of the Lord."

Rachel cast him a sideways glance. *Yeah, right*, she thought, but held her tongue. Fortunately, Dyson was waiting for Goodfellowe's reaction, and did not notice her silent cynicism.

"Very well," went on Goodfellowe in the same gentle tone. "Let us suppose you are correct in your assessment of the situation. Why, then, does the Lamb of God continue to return to some point around the globe? Surely He must look down upon us from heaven, from His Father's right hand, and see that we have recognized Him and have restructured the Holy Church to honor Him. Why does He feel the need to keep coming back?"

There was a nagging feeling at the back of Dyson's mind. It was a familiar sensation, one that had over the years endeavored time and time again to push itself forward into the forefront of his thoughts. It was like the Biblical temptation of Jesus in the desert: an oily-tongued voice, perfectly reasonable in its argumentation, filling him with doubt. Over time Dyson had learned to keep the voice at bay, banishing it to the dark recesses of his unconscious mind, from where it would occasionally manifest itself as a horrible nightmare. But if he were honest with himself, he had to admit: this voice had always been with him, no matter how hard and how often he had tried to suppress it. And now, faced with the blunt question from a cardinal of his Church, Dyson did not trust himself to reply. Rachel, though, had no such qualms. She had not been indoctrinated — or brainwashed, as she called it — as Dyson had.

"Are you saying, Cardinal Goodfellowe, that there is something wrong with these appearances of Jesus all over the place?"

Goodfellowe turned to Rachel with a kindly smile.

"That, Ms. Watson, is exactly what I am saying."

"But your entire church...most of Western society...is built on those appearances."

Goodfellowe walked over to where they were sitting and offered them the plastic folder from the safe. Dyson looked from the folder to the cardinal, whose eyes displayed almost pitying understanding, then back to the folder. He was unable to take it. Even without knowing what was in it, he realized it was something earth-shattering, and he felt his own secure, private little world begin to crumble even more rapidly than it had been doing over the past few months. Up to now he had still been able to deny the nagging doubts because nothing had been certain. Now, though, certainty was being handed to him on a silver platter, so to speak. Rachel's journalistic curiosity made it difficult for her not to snatch the folder unceremoniously from Goodfellowe's hand. With a surprising display of supreme willpower, she managed to take it with at least a degree of decorum.

"I'll fetch us some brandy," the cardinal said. "I think you will find it most welcome once you have read what is in that file."

CHAPTER 14

**Residence of Cardinal Alberto di Galassini, US
Representative of His Holiness the Arch-Cardinal of
the Church of the Second Coming of the Lamb of God
New York City, 2078**

The bright sunshine reflecting from the crisp, fresh snow on such a fine January afternoon was in sharp contrast to the dark despondency the visitor felt as he waited in Cardinal di Galassini's parlor. He had believed he had everything under control. The pathetic little worm who had helped Dyson and his girlfriend to break into Goodfellowe's office had been apprehended as soon as he had descended into the lobby of the Archives building after the crime had been committed. There was no need to interrogate him: they knew all they needed to know about him and his movements. Instead, they had carted him off to a secure DFP facility to undergo "correctional treatment." If the little bastard ever saw the light of day again, it would be in a much more "acceptable" frame of mind.

Dyson and the woman had been trapped like rats in a cage and taken for interrogation to find out exactly what they knew and whom they had informed. With the help of the DFP transmitter in Dyson's watch, it had been no problem at all to follow his every move. The visitor had wanted to leave it a little longer and continue to observe and listen in on his quarry, but di Galassini had understandably become impatient with the waiting game. He had ordered measures to be taken immediately when they realized that Dyson had broken into Goodfellowe's office. Things were getting out of hand. This nosey priest's snooping was going decidedly too far: burgling the office of a cardinal of the Holy Church was the last straw.

The parlor door opened and Cardinal Alberto di Galassini strode in. Initially he was looking rather pleased with himself, but then he noticed the downcast expression on the visitor's face.

"What is it?" he enquired. "Has the priest died at the hands of your interrogator?"

"I beg your forgiveness, but I am afraid the situation is far worse than that." The visitor swallowed hard before continuing. "Dyson and the woman have been released from the DFP facility."

He closed his eyes, waiting for the tirade of fury to pass over him like a tempest over a secluded beach. Di Galassini did not disappoint him. Minutes later the still heavily-breathing and red-faced cardinal had seemingly run out of steam. Now he merely hissed dangerously: "How could this happen?"

"It appears that two priests walked into the facility brandishing release orders signed by a high Church official, Eminence. They left the building separately with the prisoners and took them to an as yet unknown location or locations."

"But Dyson's tracking device...?"

"It was removed when he was taken to the facility. Standard procedure."

"Who were the priests?" the cardinal growled.

"I'm afraid nobody bothered to record their names, Eminence. After all, they had official release forms."

It seemed the cardinal was about to embark upon a second bout of shouting, but he checked himself when another question occurred to him.

"Whose signature and stamp were on those release orders?"

The visitor glanced briefly into the cardinal's eyes before looking down at his own shoes. This was the question he knew would eventually be asked, and which he had been dreading.

"They were yours," Father Simon Evans said in abject misery.

The cardinal was apoplectic.

CHAPTER 15

November 13, 1877

I despair of ever making this damned contraption work! Should I cast away my grand ideals, the impossible-seeming goals I have been setting myself for what seems like an eternity, or should I persevere in my lonely quest, despite my ever-growing isolation, despite not having had a coherent conversation with another human being for the past two weeks at least?

After years of arduous labor, both by day and during my all but sleepless nights; after neglecting both family and friends; after almost losing my position as a scientific researcher at the institute due to the frequency of days on which I am physically incapable of dragging my badly fatigued body to the laboratory, or because I simply forget what day of the week it is, I am no longer certain how I should proceed.

I am so tired, so uncertain. God, if you really do exist, give me guidance, for I cannot live the life of a ghost for very much longer.

November 14, 1877

Theoretically my machine (which I have in the meantime christened "Temporal Projector") should enable me to visit any time period of my choosing, allowing me to appear as a casual observer, dressed suitably for the occasion, of course, so as not to arouse suspicions of my modern-day origins in the nineteenth century nor startle the living daylights out of any unwitting bystander.

Whether past, present, or future; my projector should actually allow me to appear as a solid entity at any place, at any time. Although I would not actually be physically present at the site of the projection, I should be able to perceive my surroundings as if I were there, and anyone close to the projection should be able to perceive me visually. If only I could make the damned thing function as it should do, that is. Something is wrong with my calculations, however. I have checked and double-checked my equations, but there has still been no noticeable effect on the cursed machine. I experience a slight tingling feeling in my limbs and become somewhat light-headed after a trial run, but otherwise my experiments are a total failure. I feel I am so close that success is almost tangible. What am I doing wrong?!

November 19, 1877

The most incredible event has come to pass this evening! As usual I was contemplating my calculations in an attempt to eliminate an error, the nature of which I was, and indeed at present still am, completely unaware, when suddenly I had that peculiar feeling one sometimes has when one is being secretly observed. Upon turning, I was so startled that I dropped the sheaf of papers I was holding, for I found myself gazing at a man standing in a corner of the room in a dense cloud of vapor! If I had ever had an identical twin, then surely he would have resembled me no less than this man! Realizing just who he was and what he represented, I struggled to prevent tears of pure joy from rolling down my cheeks!

The image of myself was smiling the sublime smile of success. He (I, we), had perfected the technology of the Temporal Projector! My identical likeness was standing there as large as life; as solid as if I myself had walked into that particular corner, the sole difference between us being that he was wearing his (my, our) dark blue suit, whereas I was wearing a brown suit.

Apart from this, he looked even more fatigued than I myself did, but the remarkable sense of triumph etched into his weary features more than compensated for his otherwise disheveled outward appearance.

I attempted to communicate with my temporal brother, but he raised one hand, pointed to his ear, and then shook his head. Apparently, due to the nature of the Temporal Projector, my counterpart was unable to hear me; nor was he able to communicate with me verbally. However, his very presence in the room was enough to give me the encouragement I was so desperately in need of. My future-self would, of course, have known the exact point in time at which to effect his enigmatic appearance, namely on the very day on which I was about to give up my hitherto seemingly pointless experiments and return to the life of the living.

After about five minutes, which seemed to me, in my almost catatonic state of shock, to pass in the wink of an eye, my temporal counterpart grinned broadly, raised one cheery hand in farewell, and vanished into thin air without a sound.

It was only after his disappearance that several rather disturbing questions occurred to me. First and foremost: if he had found the error in my calculations, which for me had been so evasive, why had he not informed me of this error by means of a written message which he could have shown to me on a piece of paper? Secondly, why had he left me completely ignorant of the date upon which he had perfected the Projector? For all I know, I may have to continue my labors in a state of total frustration for another year or more before ultimately discovering the solution to this wretched conundrum. Why did he not appear to me four years ago when I had initially stumbled upon the power source to build the Temporal Projector? That way, I would have been spared many sleepless nights and moments of anguish.

November 26, 1877

I have discovered it at last!!!

After a week of fits of rage and despair, I have finally found the error in my calculations. It turned out to be such a relatively simple adjustment that I can only ascribe it to fatigue that I did not realize it earlier. My Temporal Projector will now enable me to visit other time periods as fancy takes me: not physically as such, but as a projection of my physical self into the chosen zone in time and space. By setting the geographical coordinates as well as the temporal, I shall be able to project my image not only into different times, but also into different locations around the globe.

The first projection I shall attempt will be rather unambitious, however. As with any manner of scientific experiment in which very large variables are involved, an almost insignificant error in the calculations can lead to disastrous results when the error is multiplied by the very large variable. For a simple explanation of this effect, one need only consider a cannonball in flight. A miscalculation of a mere few degrees in the firing angle of the cannon will become a targeting error of several yards at the point of impact of the cannonball.

Apart from this particular detail, there is an additional reason for my choosing a very small leap in time and space as my first experiment with the functioning machine: one week ago, I appeared to myself in what is now my subjective past. I began pondering what could possibly happen if, after discovering the error in my calculations, I failed to return to this past to prove to myself that my machine works. Would my counterpart in that time give up the search and destroy the projector in a fit of rage as I was actually on the verge of doing one week ago? Would I now find in my own present that I no longer have a Temporal Projector and/or could no longer remember how I had finally rectified the fault in its design?

Then I remembered the questions I had asked myself one week ago after seeing myself appear and disappear in my laboratory. Why should I not return to a time four years in my past when the idea of the Temporal Projector had initially occurred to me, and present myself with all the plans and calculations for the machine? Surely that way I would spare myself the mental anguish I have suffered! The simple fact of the matter is: this did not happen. I have spent the last four years working on the projector. The only help or encouragement I received in all that time was seeing my own image appear a week ago. Somehow I have a very ominous feeling that if I should endeavor to alter my own past, my present might be altered in such a way that I no longer recognize it.

Bearing this uncomfortable, disquieting notion in mind, I have today been pondering the unusual circumstances surrounding the time of my temporal counterpart's appearance. Why indeed did he appear when he did and not earlier? Could it be that the nature, even the very structure, of time itself is far more delicate and/or complicated than I had hitherto believed? Was my counterpart treading extremely carefully in order not to destroy something of which I am as yet fully unaware?

My course of action is now clear to me: I must appear to myself as I was one week ago. I must wear my dark blue suit and wave farewell after five minutes. I must not supply my counterpart in what is now my past with any information whatsoever pertaining to the Temporal Projector.

But this poses some very serious questions: am I controlling the Projector, or is the Projector controlling me? Is there a rigid course of events in time and space that cannot or must not be altered? What if someone came along and attempted to alter or even succeeded in altering the course of events that would have unfolded if nobody had interfered with them? As a scientist I do not, cannot, believe that some deity has preordained all mankind's actions from Creation to Armageddon; but I do have a healthy respect for the laws of nature, and I realize the importance of the continuation of events in a structured pattern. Despite my natural scientific curiosity, I am wary of disrupting the balance of something I do not yet fully understand, in much the same way as I would be wary of tampering with the delicate mechanism of my pocket watch. After all, I am not a watchmaker. If my tampering resulted in damage to my pocket watch, I would be unable to rectify that damage.

Currently my machine does not allow me to make physical contact with the people and things I might encounter on my travels. This is because the machine is at present merely a prototype, which will serve as the basis for future, more sophisticated models. These, I am confident, will one day be so advanced that I shall be able to appear in the flesh at any place and time of my choosing. The possibilities that would then be open to me are mind numbing! Theoretically I could travel through time and space altering anything I chose to, simply on a whim.

Apart from moral issues, however, there is the practical question of what would happen to the world as I know it if I, a mere mortal with all my human failings, were able to alter the course of history by changing people's destinies. What if I accidentally prevented the birth of a future statesman by sneezing near his great-great-grandmother, thus infecting her with a virus which was, at that time, incurable, and she died? This future statesman might have fought a war which prevented a terrible dictator from ruling the world and causing the deaths of thousands, even millions, of innocent people. However, what if the future statesman had himself become a terrible dictator who was responsible for the deaths of millions of people and I had the means to prevent his rise to power, yet had not done so? Would I then be responsible for the deaths of the innocent millions because I had failed to act?

Would it indeed be my moral obligation to travel through time and space to seek out tyranny and eradicate it in its early stages? But who am I to say what is tyranny and what is a legitimate desire to achieve freedom at any cost?

The more I contemplate the intricacies and implications of my machine, the more I am drawn to the conclusion that what I am doing is fundamentally wrong. Doubt stalks me like a dark shadow, nagging tenaciously at my conscience, bidding me to forego any further research, to forget all I have hitherto achieved.

But I am ashamed to admit that in this matter, I resemble one of those unfortunates who have become addicted to those awful oriental drugs. I cannot purge the notion from my mind that I must continue along the path of my own destruction. In my heart of hearts I know this path to be fundamentally wrong, but I can do no other.

I have always believed myself an atheist, or at least an agnostic, but over the past few days I have found myself increasingly imploring God for guidance, for who else could understand my predicament? Some of my contemporaries call this era the Age of Doubt, and I am beginning to experience first-hand the reason why.

December 5, 1877

The initial euphoria of my discovery and my apprehensions about the consequences of using my machine have now dissipated somewhat, although I am still in a state of incredulity as far as my Temporal Projector is concerned.

My first expedition was, as previously reported in these journals, a visit one week into my own past. I was very cautious to attire myself in my dark blue suit and to make only those gestures that I remember my future self making when he visited me. It was such an uncanny experience to see my former innocent self standing in the laboratory, not knowing what was happening to him, the poor fellow!

Next I desired to attempt a jaunt into the not-too-distant future. For the purposes of verification of the success of this visitation, I defined the exact coordinates of the tiny but well-frequented newsstand on the other side of the road from my house. I then set my instruments for December 10, 1877, and projected my image to those coordinates for two minutes. I pulled back the brass lever of the Temporal Projector and found myself standing almost immediately before Alf, the newspaper salesman, in his newsstand. Luckily he was not looking in my direction as I appeared; otherwise he might have died of shock. Unfortunately, this morbid consideration only occurred to me after I had already materialized near poor, unwitting Alf, and is a matter which I shall have to address in earnest once I have made more progress toward understanding the practical, as opposed to the theoretical, physics of my device. Indeed, I quite often have the impression that I am wandering in a desert of ignorance, and occasionally stumble upon a small oasis which prevents me, albeit temporarily, from dying of thirst.

Needless to say, as soon as Alf saw me, I was addressed with his usual words of greeting in his unmistakable London accent, "Ev'nin', guv", and treated to the broad, friendly grin which always spreads across the newspaper vendor's ruddy face when one of his regular customers turns up to peruse his wares. Apart from not permitting the traveler to communicate verbally with the people he meets on his travels, it is also impossible to hear what others in a past or future projection say. This is yet another one of the things I shall have to work on with regard to future models of the projector. Suffice to say here that Alf always greets me with the same salutation every evening when I purchase a newspaper from him, so it was not unduly difficult for me to lip-read his words. I waved a genial hand in greeting and hoped with all my heart that this would satisfy the man. Upon inspecting the dates on the newspapers Alf was purveying, I was able to ascertain with quite some self-felicitation that my experiment had been a complete success. The current edition of The Times bore the date December 10, 1877. My experiment had worked!

Something else which I shall have to endeavor to rectify with some expediency is the development of dense clouds of condensation which occurred when my projected form materialized. It would appear that for some reason (which I am currently at a loss to explain), my projected image causes a sudden and dramatic drop in temperature at the point of its materialization. This then leads to the relatively warm air condensing around the projection, causing a noticeable cloud of steam. Fortunately, this seems to have gone unnoticed in the typical thick London pea-souper which prevailed at the time of my materialization at Alf's newspaper stand.

December 7, 1877

A most curious thing has come to pass. I was fairly certain that my calculations were correct and that I could set my instruments for any time period and any geographical location I cared to choose, and then project my image to that place and time and record the events there. Apparently this is not the case, and there is still more work to be done before I can truly claim with any degree of veracity that I have perfected my machine.

Although I have considered myself to be an atheist since the age of nineteen or twenty, on the odd occasion I nevertheless find myself questioning my doubts about the reliability of religion. Could it really be that millions and millions of people with their thousands of different, but in some way similar, religions are wrong? Is it really so simple? For this reason I had a sudden inclination to observe for myself one of the pivotal moments of Western religion: the crucifixion of Jesus Christ. For was it not this event, and those which are purported to have followed just three days later, namely the resurrection, which constituted the spark of Christianity? With this in mind, I had my machine calculate the coordinates of the hill of Golgotha, reputedly the site of the crucifixion, in April of the year AD 33 and expected to find myself on a green hill in the Middle East.

What actually came to pass, however, was an event so unexpected that I was initially dumbstruck, for I materialized in some great hall in an unknown part of the world. Expecting to witness the crucifixion of Christ, I had foolishly set the Projector for a full two hours, which meant that I was powerless to interrupt the projection until the timer had ceased its infernal countdown.

Those two hours in that great hall were the most fascinating and at the same time the most disturbing two hours of my life. When I materialized, I was looking out from some kind of podium into a sea of faces which appeared to be representative of every creed, race, and religion of the entire Earth.

My narrow-minded contemporaries in the nineteenth century would have been deeply shocked by the fact that all these mixed races were apparently sitting together as equals in the great hall. I must admit that I myself do not share their abhorrence of such racial mingling. Indeed, how could I? For I am the product of an English father and a Tunisian mother. As such, I have inherited the piercing blue eyes of my father and the olive skin and black hair of my mother, lending me a most unusual appearance in my own time and location in nineteenth-century London, but in this great hall, I was one of the less remarkable figures present. Due to the racial mixture present in that hall, and the fact that I was unable to perceive any sound, it is impossible for me to say in what country or even on what continent this odd meeting was taking place.

I had only a few seconds to take in my extraordinary surroundings before a number of heavy-set men wearing some kind of dark uniform proceeded to approach me, apparently in an attempt to apprehend me or remove me from the podium upon which I was standing. As soon as they realized that my form was intangible, there was a space of approximately thirty minutes in which I was left alone and the great hall was cleared, presumably because it was believed that I posed some kind of unpredictable threat to those gathered there.

While the people were leaving and I was left temporarily to my own devices, I had the unprecedented opportunity to observe my curious surroundings more closely without distraction of any kind. I noted that most of the men currently exiting the hall were wearing suits quite similar to the ones I myself normally wear in my everyday life, that is, when I am not disguised as an inhabitant of the Middle East two thousand years ago. The main difference was that these men's suits were cut shorter and were tighter-fitting than the ones of my own time period. The collars of their shirts were turned down, disappearing beneath the lapels of their jackets, unlike the upright, starched collars of my own era.

Many of the women, however, were clad in an extremely bizarre fashion indeed! While some of the dark-skinned women wore colorful African dresses, as they do in our nineteenth-century Imperial British colonies, many white women were clothed like men. A number of them even had cropped hair, apparently in an effort to resemble their male counterparts! As a scientist I must at all times make an effort to keep as open a mind as possible concerning what I experience, attempting to filter the facts objectively from mere initial impressions of a subjective nature. Nevertheless, I must admit that I was most perturbed by the sight of these people.

Some time later, a group of armed guards returned to the podium upon which I was displayed like a fish at the market. They were escorting a number of men, and even some women(!), attired in white lab coats, apparently scientists. They brought with them all manner of apparatus with which they proceeded to measure, examine, and probe me. Very few of their instruments were even remotely recognizable to me, most of them being so futuristic that their possible use was thoroughly beyond the scope of my understanding.

I will purposely not go into too much detail about the instruments these people used, nor even speculate about their application, and I shall do this for two reasons: firstly, if these notes should happen to fall into the wrong hands — although I have taken precautions to store my calculations and technical notes separately from the journals which merely describe the results of my experiments — reality as we know it might be altered in such a fundamental way that it could bring about the destruction of all we hold dear. Secondly, I am still undecided as to whether I should continue with my experiments or not. My appearance in the great hall was an unforeseen accident, and I somehow feel that it did not have much of an impact upon the people who witnessed my projected image. There were scientists on hand, after all, and presumably they would have recognized my projection as what it was: a scientific experiment.

However, this does not detract from the fact that it was an accident, and although in this case it most likely did not alter much in the course of historical events, I find myself wondering what would have happened if I had made a deep impact on some section of a less advanced society, perhaps one which was more susceptible to religious mania.

December 21, 1877

The Temporal Projector, the calibration of which I am in the meantime able to adjust with an error factor of less than two percent spatially and less than one percent temporally, is now perfected to such an extent that it enables me to project an image of my physical form accurately to any place around the globe and at any time; past, present, or future.

As I have already mentioned, I am, as a scientist, by nature an atheist and a skeptic. I do not believe that a deity created the universe, and I require unequivocal proof of any claim or event before I will believe it, and so it was with a pounding heart that I had my machine once again calculate the spatial and temporal coordinates for the hill of Golgotha in April of AD 33. After the days spent calibrating my instruments I am now almost certain of achieving my goal of witnessing the crucifixion of Christ. However, as I am uncertain as to which day the event took place, I have set my machine to project me to that location from 3:00 p.m. to 3:10 p.m. on each of the thirty days of April in the year AD 33. Once I have narrowed down the search to find any part of the crucifixion, I will be able to set my machine with the proper times to witness the full event.

Anyone who finds and reads these journals in the distant future — for I have taken precautions to ensure that they will not be found for many years after my death — may wonder why I did not choose to follow Christ's life and teachings instead of morbidly seeking the moment of his barbaric demise at the hands of the brutal and heathen Romans. There are several very simple reasons for this: firstly, the nature of my still experimental machine does not (yet) permit the projected image of the traveler to perceive sound, so I would be unable to hear Christ's voice. Secondly, even if I were able to hear his voice, I would not understand what he was saying, as I do not speak his language, Aramaic. Another reason is that, as a skeptic, I would first like to see the resurrection to be sure of Jesus' divinity before embarking upon following him and his teachings.

December 30, 1877

I have spent the last several days repeatedly projecting my suitably dressed white-robed image to the month of April in the year AD 33 with no success whatsoever. Whereas I did indeed witness the inhumane slaughter of numerous miserable creatures on the hill of Golgotha in that month of that year, all dying - on makeshift wooden crosses - of thirst or loss of blood from various wounds, or shock after having one or more of their limbs shattered by their mocking tormentors, or slowly suffocating as their legs could no longer support their bodies, and they slumped forward, unable to breathe, none of them appeared to me to be in the least remarkable. Nor did any of the wretched men who were condemned to die appear to have anything remotely similar to a crown of thorns upon his head.

To me as a scientist, this would seem to suggest one of two things: either the timeframe of the crucifixion, which has been passed down from generation to generation for the past two thousand years, is erroneous, or the entire story of Christ is a myth and never occurred in the way depicted in the Bible and accepted to this very day.

Looking at the problem as a scientist, there is only one option open to me. If the story is merely a myth, then there is absolutely nothing I can do to change that, and I will never find what I am looking for, because it simply does not exist. However, if the date has been passed down erroneously, I can consult books and experts in the hope of eventually discovering the true date of the event. I now plan to seek out some experts in this field at the local university, which is a mere fifteen-minute carriage ride from my home.

March 2, 1878

I believe I have found what I have been searching for! Learned men who have studied the scriptures in far more detail than I could ever hope to accomplish in my lifetime are in agreement that the dates of the birth and the crucifixion of Christ, which we in the nineteenth century have come to accept as being factual, are, in fact, erroneous!

During the course of my recent trip to the theological department of the local university, I interviewed several respectable and noteworthy professors of history and theology who were only too pleased to assist me with my research into the facts relating to the life and death of Jesus Christ. Not wishing to startle the venerable gentlemen, or to convey to them the impression that I am some crackpot, (for who would believe in the existence of a machine such as mine?), I did not reveal to them my true intentions. I must admit, I was startled in the extreme when my ignorant eyes were opened to the fallacies that we have come to accept as truth. However, as is often the case with scholars, the gentlemen in question were apt to disagree bitterly with one another and proved themselves prone to vanity when their version of events was challenged.

The first popular belief that one of the learned gentlemen corrected was that December 25 was the day of Jesus' birth. Actually, the Gospels of Matthew and Luke do not state a date or even a time of year of his birth. I learned that the pagans had always celebrated the winter solstice on December 21 or thereabouts, and that this date was adopted by Roman Christians around the year AD 330 to celebrate the birth of Christ. Later, as more Europeans became Christians, the date was moved to December 25, presumably to replace the birthday of the Roman god, Sol Invictus. A second professor, on the other hand, informed me that, in his learned opinion, Jesus' birth was linked according to Jewish tradition to his conception. This means that if he was conceived on March 25, his birth must be exactly nine months later on December 25. As a scientist, I am disinclined to believe that either of these explanations can provide the slightest proof whatsoever of Christ's actual date of birth.

Another fact of which I was previously completely ignorant is that our modern Anno Domini calculation goes back to Dionysius Exiguus, who attempted to place an accurate date on the birth of Christ, and calculated a figure of 753 years after the founding of Rome. Dionysius set Jesus' date of birth at December 25 and designated the following year as AD 1. According to this system, the current year for Dionysius was at that time 532. Almost two centuries later it became accepted as the established calendar in Western civilization.

This, however, is also inaccurate. A short time before the death of Herod the Great, who is an important figure in the Gospel according to St. Matthew, a lunar eclipse was reported by the contemporary historian Josephus. This would mean that Jesus was born sometime in the year we have come to call 4 BC, due to the errors described above. Although not all of the learned gentlemen agreed on this point, the majority of them concurred.

The scholars at the university also assisted me in learning a more or less accurate date for the death of Jesus. Some of them believe that the Gospel of John depicts the crucifixion just before the Passover festival on Friday, 14 Nisan. However, two of the synoptic gospels, Matthew and Luke (but not the third, Mark 14:2), describe the Last Supper, immediately before Jesus' arrest, as the Passover meal on Friday, 15 Nisan. Nisan is the first month of the ecclesiastical year and the seventh month (eighth, in leap year) of the civil year on the Hebrew calendar. Nisan corresponds to March — April in our modern calendar. On the other hand, some of the learned men informed me that the synoptic account tallies with the account in John. Allowing for the period of Pontius Pilate's time as procurator and the dates of the Passover at that time, Jesus' death is most likely to have been on April 7, 30 AD, they believe.

As surprising as all this new information appears to be, it has nonetheless given me a starting point at least, from which I shall be in a position to embark upon more accurate research with a view to pinpointing the exact date.

Based on this information, I now intend to set my projector once again to visit every day in April, but this time proceeding from the year AD 30. However, the recalibration work I shall have to undertake will be such a time-consuming exercise that I have decided to rest for a few days before beginning.

June 8, 1878

I resumed the painstakingly intricate recalibration work on the projector today, and undertook an experimental jaunt to the year AD 30, aiming for the ancient city of Jerusalem. When my image materialized, however, something appeared to be amiss, for I was unable to see clearly. As usual, my projection had caused clouds of steam, but this did not explain the fact that my vision was impaired to such an extent that I was practically blind. Seconds later, the mystery was solved when two women, both clothed in the flowing garments typical of the era, which indicated to me that my calibration had succeeded in sending me into the past, dropped a large sheet or blanket they had apparently been hanging up to dry, and fled hysterically from the site of my materialization, presumably screaming in fear, although I was, thankfully, unable to hear them.

I realized at that moment that my image must have appeared within or extremely close to their blanket, which they had dropped on the ground before me in their haste to flee as quickly as they could from what they must have perceived as some sort of demon appearing to them in a cloud of smoke. Looking down, I made a most interesting observation, for imprinted on the cloth was an image of myself as I stood in the box of my Temporal Projector. The image was not as clear as the modern photographs produced in my own era, but my features were distinctly recognizable: eyes, nose, mouth, beard, long hair. Even the positions of my limbs in the box of my Temporal Projector were clearly visible. As I always attempt to remain as immobile as possible when I initiate a projection, for reasons that need not be reproduced in detail in these journals, but saved for the technical manual, I have acquired the habit of folding my hands before me in the box.

Surprisingly, and as yet inexplicably, the image, which seemed to leave a colored impression upon the cloth in the same way as a dye might, displayed all the contours of my body, but had not been extended to the reproduction of my clothing, namely the long white robe I have been wearing to inconspicuously blend in. Fortunately, for the sake of modesty, my hands were clasped before my genitals. I can only hope that the women would have burned the offending blanket when they finally returned to it, so that it would never be seen in public again!

June 12, 1878

During the continuing calibration work on my machine I have covered a span of two thousand years, spending only several minutes at each location to record the temporal and spatial coordinates.

One strange phenomenon worth mentioning was that, as I progressed further and further into the twenty-first century, two hundred years into my own future, crowds of people rushed toward the places in which I materialized. Although I find it difficult to believe that this is actually the case, on occasion it seemed as though they were actually waiting for me! But how could that be? On more than one instance I believe I glimpsed, either from the corner of my eye or somewhere in the distance, borne by the crowd, a photographic image of myself dressed in my white robe. I sincerely hope that this is not the case. As I have stated before in these, my private, non-technical journals, I have no desire whatsoever to interfere in the course of history.

July, 3, 1878

Even as I put this journal entry to paper, twenty-four hours after returning from the last projection into the distant past of civilization, my mind is reeling.

But I will start again at the beginning. After several days of searching through different dates at different times of the day, I was standing, so to speak, at the foot of the relatively gentle slope known as Golgotha or "the Skull". Suddenly a crowd of people came into view, slowly climbing the hill.

The first thing I noticed was that five men were carrying heavy-looking wooden crosses on their shoulders, their heads and backs bent with the strain. Four of these men were stripped naked, which appalled me terribly. Not only were they goaded with wickedly pointed spears and thick leather whips wielded by Roman soldiers, they also had not a scrap of clothing with which to cover their modesty. The fifth man carrying a cross was wearing relatively clean and tidy robes and was ignored by the soldiers. "Could this be Him?" was my first thought. Strange.

But then I glimpsed something which made my heart skip a beat: two Roman soldiers were dragging another unfortunate captive up the hill. This man was so covered in blood that it seemed to me a miracle that he was still alive. He was also completely naked so that I could see the blood still pouring freely from the open wounds all over his back. His head was bent forward and, as he was being supported by the two soldiers, one on either side of him, I was unable to see his face, but on his head he wore some manner of wreath woven out of a species of dried plant with what looked like extremely long and viciously pointed thorns. The thorns had cut so deeply into his flesh that his long black hair was matted with blood. There was no doubt about it: it was Him! I knew that I was now bearing witness to the crucifixion of Jesus Christ. I stood helplessly in the cramped confines of my projector box, an innocent bystander; the only man alive in my own time to witness to the birth of a world religion.

My eyes burned as they nailed him to the cross. Tears flowed unchecked down my cheeks as I watched him cry out — for my ears without sound, however — in agony as the cross was raised with ropes into its erect position. I stood there impotently as Jesus of Nazareth suffered on the cross. This wretched creature suffered almost as the gospels had described. His wrists — not the palms of his hands — and his ankles — not his feet — were pierced. Ropes around the wrists provided more support to hold him to the cross. A Roman centurion actually did thrust a spear into his side. There was, however, no storm. No clouds darkened the skies. It was a singularly normal day as far as the weather was concerned. But still, the plight of this man, this historical figure, touched me deeply.

Infuriatingly, the timer on my projector chose just this moment to terminate its countdown, and I was returned to my modern-day laboratory, but I had seen enough of the suffering. Now I desired to bear witness to the resurrection, so I returned to the same geographical location three days later.

Upon my arrival on the following Sunday, I searched my field of vision for a tomb of some fashion, perhaps with women standing outside it rejoicing, and perhaps, if I was lucky, actually witnessing the resurrected Christ, but I saw nothing. Apart from some new victims dying on crosses, the area was deserted. This was almost to be expected, I thought. After all, when dealing with a two-thousand-year-old myth that does not provide accurate dates and times, one cannot expect to have everything fall into place so easily.

CHAPTER 16

When Dyson had finished reading, the papers he was holding were shaking in his trembling hands like leaves in the wind. Beads of cold perspiration trickled liberally from his forehead, and his shirt was sticking uncomfortably to his back. Despite the profusion of moisture on his skin, his mouth was bone dry. He felt a burning sensation in his eyes and had to struggle to hold back the tears of anger, fear, disappointment, and a host of other emotions he was as yet unable or perhaps unwilling to identify. He was devastated; a broken man. Looking up, he saw that Cardinal Goodfellowe was fixing him with an expressionless stare.

"What does this mean?" Dyson asked in a hushed voice.

"You know very well what it means," the older man replied, not unkindly.

"But I… Don't you…?"

"David, listen to me. You hold in your hands the proof that the Church of the Second Coming is founded on a lie."

"You believe this?" Dyson said hoarsely. He still had not found his normal speaking voice.

"Don't you?" Goodfellowe replied. He gave Dyson and Rachel each a rather full glass of brandy before he continued.

"I have been living with this lie for more years than I care to remember. Some men have died trying to uncover the secret. Others have discovered it and died trying to reveal it to the world at large. In the meantime, I have done everything in my power to prevent as many of these unnecessary deaths as possible. Sometimes this has meant protecting the secret, even though it was against my better judgment to do so."

"But you've held the proof for so long! You could have gone public with it. Why didn't you?" Dyson wondered. "If you'd said something, all this could have been over years ago!"

"There were several contributing factors to my silence." The cardinal's eyes were downcast, his voice low. "At first, of course, I was skeptical. For years I simply refused to believe it, despite all the evidence to the contrary. At first there were only a few pages of the diary. It could have been anything from a novel to a malicious hoax. But then more and more papers were discovered in different places and the evidence began to mount up. In the end I had no other choice but to believe what was unbelievable but at the same time undeniable."

For the first time since Dyson had known Rachel, she seemed to be at a loss for words. Her mouth was open slightly, and she was staring at the last page, slowly shaking her head. Although she had never been a churchgoer, she had been brought up in the faith of the Second Coming. The Church had been established before she was born, so she had never known anything else. Its symbols and rites had accompanied her all her life. The crosses with the two at the center were everywhere: in schools, universities, public buildings, on official letters, passports; simply everywhere. When she finally spoke, her voice conveyed a sense of helplessness.

"Are you saying that all this is meaningless?" She gestured around the room, indicating the cardinal's house and the cardinal himself in his Church garments.

"Well, I would not quite say 'meaningless,' Ms. Watson," the cardinal replied rather indignantly. "After all, there are many good people working for the Church who pursue the noblest of motives, who have brought aid and succor to millions."

"And oppressed millions of others," Rachel cut in abrasively. Dyson laid a calming hand on her arm, even though he himself seemed shell-shocked.

The cardinal sighed and bowed his head.

"Yes, I know," he said quietly. "You are quite right, of course. This is no longer the Church I joined as a young man. It is riddled with corruption and fear. The house of

God should be filled with the joy of life, not with the threat of death."

"I don't mean to be impolite, Cardinal Goodfellowe, but you still haven't answered David's question. Why didn't you put an end to all this years ago, before the Church could become as powerful as it is today?"

"As I said, at the beginning I was a believer, too. As a boy I actually stood next to the 'Lamb.' I was most fervent in my beliefs in those days; well into my thirties, in fact. Then, when the truth began to emerge.... Well, I am ashamed to admit it even now, but I was afraid.

"As under any totalitarian regime — for if we are honest, that is what the Church has become — there are four groups of people, as in the case of the Church of the Second Coming. First there are those who rule, and their helpers. Whether they actually believe their own propaganda or not is neither here nor there, because they can rule their domains with the absolute authority of people who are willing to murder an innocent population in order to protect their own privileges. These are the power-mongers and their parasitic thugs who protect them from the masses.

"Secondly, there are those who are outside the regime but who accept it willingly because they have something to gain. Under communist rule, for example, the peasants often supported the fledgling revolutionary government because of the promise of the upper and middle classes being eradicated. This did not actually free the peasants from oppression by the regime itself, but there was at least the promise of fewer middlemen supposedly oppressing them. And, under fascist dictatorships, the rich often become even richer at the expense of minorities.

"Thirdly, there are those who resent and even hate the regime, but are afraid to do anything about it. They put on a brave face and try to make the best of it. If they hear rumors of state murder, indeed of any crime at all committed by the state, they will, publicly anyway, refuse to believe it. And in private they may talk of it in hushed tones to their spouse or some other confidant, afraid of being overheard. It is to this group, I must admit to my eternal disgrace and shame, that I belonged for many years.

"Finally, there is the fourth group. These are people who not only oppose the totalitarian regime, but have also made it their cause to overthrow it, by any means available to them. These people are not usually in a strong enough position to wage open warfare against the regime because they are in such a small minority, so they are compelled to employ other methods, such as infiltration, manipulation, and, if there is no other way to prevent innocent people from being harmed by the state and to liberate that state, the occasional political assassination."

"But you could be describing the religious terrorists at the beginning of this century," Rachel said.

"Of course I could, my dear. Which is another reason why it took me so long to join the opposition. As a man of the cloth — and I do not mean a Cardinal of the Church of the Second Coming, I mean a believer in God Almighty — I abhor such methods. For many years, I could not bring myself even to contemplate being tarred with the same brush as the people who wanted to overthrow the Holy Church, precisely because they were willing to take such violent steps."

Rachel was curious: "But you don't hear of violent attacks against the Church. I'm a reporter, and I know how quickly the wrong words to the wrong people can get you into some serious sh... err, trouble," she corrected herself. "You don't hear of bishops being assassinated or attempts to overthrow the Church."

Goodfellowe smiled. "No, of course not. Who do you think controls the media, though? You hear of house fires, road accidents, plane crashes and the occasional gas explosion. These are caused by both factions: the Church in the form of DFP agents, as well as the opposition. It is merely not in their interest to wage open war against each other. Why do you think it is necessary to have armed guards posted outside Church establishments?"

Dyson had never thought about that before, but now that the cardinal mentioned it...

"No, it has always been this way," Goodfellowe continued. "The Church will not admit it is under attack, for that might at best encourage people to contemplate the reasons for it, and at worst to join the armed opposition. And the opposition is afraid to act openly for fear of revealing themselves and being eradicated."

"So now you've joined the terrorists?" Rachel enquired, a little too bluntly for Dyson's taste, but he remained silent and listened.

"Well, it really does depend which side of the fence you are on."

"What do you mean?" Rachel asked.

"Let us suppose a soldier is nineteen years old, and he has been drafted into the armed forces of your country, against his will. If he does not march into a neighboring country with his regiment, he will be shot as a coward and a traitor. Does he deserve to die, either at the hands of his compatriots or at the hands of those whose country he is being forced to invade?"

"No, of course not," Rachel replied, her ethical radar kicking in immediately.

"Now let us suppose that our soldier had joined his regiment, but saw no combat whatsoever during the advance on the other country. All the fighting was over by the time he got there. He is now stationed in the capital of the foreign country. The people there are not happy to have an occupying force on their territory, of course, but in time, perhaps after a few years, most of the population have come to terms with it and are now going about their business as normally as possible under the circumstances. Does he deserve to die yet?"

Rachel looked nonplussed for a second. "No, why should he?"

"Perhaps," Goodfellowe went on, "our soldier has even found a girlfriend among the local population. Now picture this: the young man is sitting in a café with his girlfriend when terrorists calling themselves 'freedom fighters' throw a bomb into the place, killing everyone in there, including the innocent soldier and his girlfriend. My question to you is: are they justified in apparently committing murder because the young man was a member of the army occupying their country?"

Rachel thought for a second and said, "No, of course not. The soldier hadn't harmed them personally. He was there keeping the peace, making sure anarchy didn't break out. The people who killed him are cold-blooded murderers."

"And what if I told you that our soldier was killed in 1942 while he was sitting in a café in Paris? He was a member of the Nazi army that invaded France, deported Jews to concentration camps, and jailed and murdered anyone else who openly opposed them. The young man in question, although personally innocent of any crime, perhaps, was 'liquidated' as an enemy soldier by the French *Résistance.* I am not a gambling man, Ms. Watson, but I am willing to bet that things do not look quite so black and white to you now."

Rachel contemplated and murmured, "Hmmm."

Goodfellowe could see that she had understood his point.

"That is precisely the predicament I was in," he told her. "When there is no black and white, when they blend into gray, the finest shades or nuances are not so easy to distinguish. What is goose-wing gray; what is silver gray? What is right and what is wrong when there is no clear delineation? There can be no absolutes, only discretion and eventually a decision. And the determination of a particular shade of gray might take quite some time, depending on the nuances we are dealing with, and on the brightness of the light illuminating those nuances.

"It took me years to decide because I always saw the good things the Church was doing: the charity work, education, the fight against crime, the contribution to world peace. All these things influenced me. But all the time, the evidence was growing that the Church of the Second Coming had no right to exist. Once I had accepted that this Church is not founded on divine inspiration and the return of our Lord, it became easier for me to rebel against the corruption and terror instigated by the institution itself." The cardinal's voice had become bitter and hard.

For a short time, thoughtful silence prevailed in the room. Rachel and Dyson were now beginning to understand the cardinal's motives, but they were still no closer to resolving the problem. Dyson took a sip of his brandy and reflected.

"So what happens now?" he asked shakily. His life was in tatters, but he was putting on a brave face, struggling to accept the incredible, awful facts. "Should Rachel take these copies and use them as evidence to back up the article she's bound to write for the *New York Gazette*?"

"Think about it, David. Who would believe it?" Goodfellowe asked.

"But we have proof!"

"Do you really believe that?" the cardinal replied gently. "All we have here is a handful of eco-foil copies. Anybody could have made those copies. They might well be copies of documents that were written two hundred years ago. On the other hand, my son, they could be copies of fake documents that we prepared ourselves only last week!"

"So we get our hands on the originals!" Dyson was becoming agitated. His initial denial was gradually turning into anger: anger that he had been betrayed. Not only him, but billions of people all over the world. It would have been different if it had been an honest mistake, a misunderstanding. That would have been shocking enough, but as things stood, it was clear that the Church had deceived the world intentionally, knowingly, in order to protect its own interests and its power. That was the worst thing for Dyson: the hypocrisy. The Church's leaders knew what was going on but they kept their flock in ignorance, preaching to them in all walks of life that their only salvation was the Apparition that appeared at irregular intervals in some part of the world. If it had not been so tragic, Dyson would have laughed aloud. "If you have copies, you must have had the originals at some point."

"The originals that have been found here in the U.S.," Goodfellowe informed him levelly, "are locked away very safely somewhere in Cardinal di Galassini's residence. I have people working as field researchers, and when anything like this is discovered, they are sometimes able to secretly make a copy before the original is delivered to di Galassini. As it is, these men risk their lives. But they would surely be killed if they attempted to divert such a document. As you know, the researchers always work in teams, and you never know whom you can trust. And before you get any ideas, consider this: if you were not able to gain access to *my* office at the Archives without being detected, what chance do you think you would have of trying to recover something from the U.S. representative of the Arch-Cardinal?"

Dyson had no answer to this, and when he looked at Rachel, hoping for advice, she raised her palms to indicate that she, too, had no idea what to do next. Seeing that both his guests now understood the gravity of the situation, Cardinal Goodfellowe nodded to them and took a sip of brandy. "I have another plan."

CHAPTER 17

**Residence of Cardinal Alberto di Galassini, US
Representative of His Holiness the Arch-Cardinal of
the Church of the Second Coming of the Lamb of God
New York City, 2078**

The yellow electric cab pulled up silently in front of the palace on the outskirts of the city. Of course, it would have been easier for Dyson to take a flying vehicle, but the prohibited airspace in force within a ten-kilometer radius of the residence made that impossible. Cardinal di Galassini's residence was built on a small hill with a single perfectly straight road leading to it. The road ended at a pair of enormous metal gates set into a high wall that surrounded the hill. Armed guards with vicious-looking dogs constantly patrolled the perimeter.

"This is it, Father," the driver said, in an accent Dyson believed might have been Dutch. The Dutch had spread all over the world after the demise of their own country, which had been consumed by the rising sea levels caused by climate change. *Yes*, Dyson thought miserably, *it certainly is*. He felt like the Biblical Daniel about to enter the lion's den. For a moment he hung his head in prayer to the Lamb through force of habit, but raised it again almost immediately when he realized what he was doing. He had spent his whole life praying to the Lamb of God, the physical entity that had been appearing to mankind over the last six decades. For the first time in his life, he actually felt a little foolish for doing this. It had been a hard, an extremely difficult, transition. He had believed with all his heart and soul in Jesus Christ, the

Savior; he had also believed with all his heart and soul that Jesus Christ had been returning to Earth with a silent but clear message of peace and love for all mankind. But over the past few days this situation had changed. He now knew that he had been wrong about the Second Coming. The cardinals had been wrong. His whole beloved Church had been wrong. Even the Holy Father the Arch-Cardinal had been wrong. And after reading the last sentence of those damned papers, he was not even sure about the First Coming!

The driver leaped enthusiastically from the cab and rushed to the rear door, which he proceeded to open politely for his passenger. He almost certainly would not have dreamed of doing such a thing if Dyson had not been a priest and if his destination had not been di Galassini's private residence. Dyson let out a heavy sigh of resignation and stepped out. He paid the driver and then, with ponderously slow steps, trudged toward the heavily guarded gate in the fortified wall around the Cardinal's palace. He did not relish the idea of directly confronting such a senior member of the established Church like this, but what was he to do? This was their last-ditch effort to get the Church to admit to the deception they had been propagating all these years.

An armed guard stepped forward to scan Dyson's ID chip.

"Do you have an appointment, Father?" he asked brusquely.

"I do not, but I'm sure his Eminence will be more than happy to see me even without an appointment," Dyson replied.

The guard looked very doubtful indeed.

"I'll ask, Father," he said. He turned away from Dyson and walked back to the closed metal gate, where he pressed a button on the wall. The face of an efficient-looking woman in her early forties appeared as a holographic image on a flat panel.

"There's a Father David Dyson here who would like to speak to his Eminence the Cardinal," the guard said.

The woman's image looked down for a moment, presumably looking for a name on some kind of list.

"Tell Father Dyson his Eminence does not see visitors without an appointment. You should know that."

Dyson, who was nervous enough as it was, had no time for this. After taking a deep breath to steady himself, he marched resolutely up to the monitor and spoke to the woman directly.

"Might I have your name, madam?" he enquired politely.

"My name is Giulia Vincetti, the cardinal's scheduling assistant," she replied, obviously a little taken aback by a stranger who dared to question her authority.

"Well, then, Ms. Giulia Vincetti, the cardinal's scheduling assistant, listen to me very carefully," Dyson said slowly, calculatingly, trying to make his voice sound stronger and more confident than the turmoil he actually felt inside. "Because I am only going to say this once. If I leave now, then tomorrow morning, at the latest, the cardinal will find out that Father David Dyson was here wishing to speak to him. He will also find out that you, his scheduling assistant, were the reason I was not admitted to him. When that happens, my dear lady, I for one would certainly not like to be in your shoes."

"With all due respect, Father, I object to being threatened for doing my job!"

"With all due respect to you, madam, I am sure you are very good at your job, but these are exceptional circumstances. If I am not admitted to Cardinal di Galassini on the spot, heads will roll, and none of them, I assure you, will be mine!"

The woman now looked unsure. She was used to being obeyed without question. She was, after all, responsible for organizing the schedule of the most powerful man in the USA. *Damned if I do, damned if I don't,* she thought.

"Just a minute, Father. I'll ask if his Eminence would be willing to make an exception to his rule."

Dyson noticed the doubt in her voice and forced a tight-lipped smile in order to underline his thinly veiled threat. "Now that's a very good idea, Ms. Vincetti. Thank you."

Several minutes later a uniformed guard came scurrying out of the building and bowed hurriedly and apologetically to Dyson.

"If you would like to follow me, Father, I've been instructed to take you to the cardinal," he blurted breathlessly. "Without delay."

The guard led Dyson through the gate at a brisk pace that was almost a run. He was then confronted in the flesh by Giulia Vincetti when she opened the front door for him.

"Please forgive me, Father. His Eminence said I am to let you in immediately." *This guy must be damned important*, she thought. *I can only pray he doesn't drop me in it with the boss.* She took his coat and led him to a white door decorated with gold ornamentation, just like the doors in Cardinal Goodfellowe's house. The cardinal's scheduling assistant then thrust open the door, pointed the way into the enormous, high-ceilinged room, and left. Dyson entered and stood in the center of the room waiting for the cardinal to arrive, too nervous to sit.

A short while later, an extremely flustered Cardinal Alberto di Galassini burst, panting, into the room, with two black-uniformed men, armed with machine pistols, flanking him. The cardinal looked just like the pictures Dyson had seen of him: a short, chubby man with white hair that was thinning to non-existent. The pronounced Roman nose and thick lips combined with the ornate purple silk lounging robe he was wearing certainly did not give this man the appearance of being the decider over life and death for an entire continent. Surveying the situation, the cardinal decided he was safe and ordered the armed guards to stand down, but one of them bent down and whispered something in the cardinal's ear, inaudible to Dyson.

"Very well," di Galassini said in a bored tone, "if you must." It sounded as if he were indulging small children. Then he added to Dyson, with regret in his voice, "I'm afraid my bodyguards feel it is necessary to search you for weapons — ones that didn't show up in the metal detectors you passed through at the gates — before they will leave us in peace to talk."

Dyson merely shrugged, and one of the guards approached him while the other looked on attentively.

"Raise your arms and spread your legs, please, Father," the guard said gruffly. Dyson obeyed and was patted down by expert hands searching his person for concealed weapons, recording devices, and the like. The guard reached into one of Dyson's jacket pockets and removed his comPod. After examining it with a SmartScanner, and subsequently switching it off, he placed it on a table and bowed toward the cardinal.

"Situation under control, your Eminence!" he barked.

"Very well, you may stand down now," the cardinal said, with a flourishing wave toward the double white doors.

The guards turned and began to leave, but the one who had searched Dyson leaned over and whispered something into the cardinal's ear. The cardinal nodded silently, his expression giving absolutely nothing away. Once the guards had retreated to the corridor and closed the doors behind them, the cardinal addressed Dyson in a fawning voice, indicating the priest's comPod.

"I'm ever so sorry about that, Father Dyson, but we wouldn't want your machine there accidentally recording everything we say now, would we? It is such a pleasure to finally meet you in person, my son! I am sure we shall be able to clear up this horrible misunderstanding very soon. Would you like a drink?

"No, thank you, Eminence."

"Please, my son, be seated."

The two men sat down on opposite sides of the wooden conference table the cardinal had indicated, and eyed each other warily. Both knew exactly what was at stake, but for the moment neither was prepared to admit it openly.

"So," di Galassini said after the brief, uncomfortable silence, "is there something you want to tell me, Father?"

"Just one thing, Eminence," Dyson answered, trying to take a deep, calming breath without the cardinal noticing. "We have two choices here: either *you* announce the truth to the world, or *we* do."

"And just what 'truth' would that be, then, my son?" the cardinal replied, friendliness and innocence practically dripping from his voice. Di Galassini was unaware that

Dyson had been briefed by Goodfellowe. Nor could he be sure which, or how many, of the secret documents Dyson had seen, so he was holding his cards close to his chest.

"Eminence, please don't take me for a fool," Dyson responded, equally unwilling to lay his cards on the table, thus perhaps disclosing information di Galassini might not yet possess. Goodfellowe had instructed him well. "We both know about the documents. We both know that our whole organization has no right to exist; that the Church of the Second Coming is founded on a lie."

Di Galassini ruminated for a moment before replying. Raising his head a little to look at Dyson down the length of his aquiline nose, the mask suddenly dropped. Although the cardinal's voice still sounded calm and under control, it had definitely taken on a more dangerous tone.

"I do not like ultimatums, Father Dyson. I particularly object to them rather strongly when they come from pathetic idealistic priests who understand nothing about the larger scale of world events and who have betrayed their holy oath by indulging in sordid affairs with women of doubtful repute."

Dyson struggled to stay calm. If truth be told, he would have liked to reach across the table and punch the cardinal in the face, but that would have to remain on his mental to-do list. Once again he thought of Goodfellowe's training: they had played the situation through many times over in many different constellations of possible outcomes. Dyson realized that di Galassini was deliberately trying to provoke him into losing control. If the older man succeeded in doing that, Dyson knew, all would be lost.

"Eminence, I repeat: either *you* go public with this, or *we* do."

"And just who, pray, might be behind your enigmatic 'we'? Why aren't these mysterious others here to back you up with your ridiculous claims? Or do you mean that Watson woman and yourself, perhaps? Or could it be that you are actually working alone, Father Dyson?"

He doesn't know about Cardinal Goodfellowe. "As you must surely be aware by now, I am not working alone, but I think it would be foolish of me to let myself be side-tracked by this petty nonsense. Could we stick to the matter at hand, Eminence?"

The cardinal involuntarily raised an eyebrow, which Dyson did not fail to notice. The older man was beginning to realize that his opponent was not the greenhorn he had previously thought.

"I simply cannot believe that you would walk into my home and threaten me like this!" the cardinal snapped. "Don't you realize with whom and with what you are dealing?"

Dyson felt his heart beginning to pound uncomfortably in his chest. He could see that his apparent calmness in the face of such overwhelming odds was starting to unnerve the cardinal, who was gradually showing signs of extreme irritation. But Dyson carried on regardless.

"I realize exactly what I am doing and I'm afraid I must insist on an answer. Will you tell the world the truth or shall we do it?"

The older man's tone changed so abruptly that it caught Dyson off guard for a second.

"You realize that if this gets out, we're finished!" the cardinal hissed, his face turning crimson. As his anger became apparent, so did the remnants of an almost-forgotten Italian accent. The cardinal was losing control.

Looks like I hit a nerve, Dyson thought, closely observing his adversary's body language. The cardinal's fingers were steepled on the table before him, and he was unable to make eye contact with Dyson.

"But we're talking about the *truth* here, Eminence!" Dyson was exasperated. "What more can I say? There *was* no Second Coming. Our Church, our whole way of life, has been based on the experiments of a nineteenth-century scientist. It's amazing, yes; it sounds completely bizarre, impossible, even! But it is by no means miraculous or even remotely religious."

The cardinal shot a hate-filled glance at the priest.

"Are you telling me you would be willing to give up everything? Our order, our position in society, our... our..." He was lost for words, breathing heavily and sweating profusely.

"Our dictatorship? Our power to murder innocent people for the heinous crime of not agreeing with us?" Dyson offered.

Again, the glare of hatred.

"You may mock all you want, Father Dyson, but just you remember exactly how much power our order has." His eyes were blazing, as if to emphasize the point.

Was that an open threat to have me killed?

"Eminence, the Second Coming is a fallacy. It never happened! We can keep the Church as such. We can go back to the way things were before the Second Coming. Our position in society might change a little when this gets out, but..."

"*If* this gets out!" spat the cardinal. "And what would you have us name our new organization, Father? The Church of the Almighty Fallacy, perhaps?" The cardinal's voice was dripping with sarcasm and hatred.

Dyson continued undeterred, attempting to remain calm and focused. "With all due respect, Eminence, I'll stick with 'when this gets out.' There is absolutely no way we can keep a lid on this thing. Too many people already know about it! It's bigger than..." He thought for a moment, trying to come up with a suitably powerful comparison. All he could think of, though, was "...than the Second Coming itself! Just think of the scientific, the ethical repercussions! Someone has discovered how to travel through time. Just think of the possibilities...the dangers!"

The cardinal detected the passion in the younger man's voice. *So that's where he's coming from.* Taking a deep breath, the cardinal checked the emotion that had been causing his voice to tremble. He suddenly changed his tactics and smiled, almost pleasantly, at Dyson.

"Father Dyson," he crooned, his tone offering the proverbial olive branch. He paused for reflection, apparently attempting to slow down the pace, giving them both time to settle down a little before things got completely out of hand. "You are to be commended on your research, your concern for the Holy Church, for the fate of everything we stand for. Your ethics are indeed truly admirable, David. But just think of the changes and the dangers that you yourself speak of. Just think of what might happen if we were to lose our credibility. We currently sustain a higher level of support, financial and otherwise, to developing countries than any other religious or secular organization worldwide, past or present.

"What would become of that aid if our believers, our 'supporters' if you will, were to lose faith in us? Millions would suffer the painful death of starvation. Innocent children would be sacrificed on your altar of righteousness. And for what? David, I ask you as a Christian, as a servant of the Holy Church: are you willing to destroy the work of over two thousand years? Will you be the man named in the history books for all eternity as the one who destroyed a charitable organization and brought so much suffering to so many innocent people? Will you be the one who brings about the downfall of all we believe in? Will you kiss our cheek and deliver us unto our enemies?"

Feeling that the cardinal was becoming overly melodramatic, Dyson raised his right index finger and opened his mouth to reply but before he could utter a single word, the cardinal had another epiphany: "Quite apart from the damage to our faith, my son, I would remind you of the complicated science. I know you are a scientist at heart; that is one reason why you were chosen for the position of Keeper of the Archives. So just think, David, what is at stake. We know that someone in the nineteenth century discovered a means to travel through time, or at the very least to project his image through time. This in itself is absolutely incredible, of course! But that is not all: he was apparently also able to travel through space simultaneously! This would appear completely impossible. But all the evidence would seem to indicate that this is indeed the case. So what if there was no Second Coming! We can still carry on the good work of the Savior."

Dyson's heart leaped. *Gotcha!* Outwardly, however, he remained utterly impassive, just as Goodfellowe had trained him.

"So just imagine, David, what would happen if we were to make this discovery public. Imagine the misery that would engulf the entire civilized world in a matter of weeks. There would be wars when the common religion the nations now adhere to disappeared, leaving them to fall back into their petty squabbles. There would be famine when, once again, no one nation or organization could do enough to feed the starving billions across the globe. Crime would once again skyrocket when the man in the street felt there was no need to fear for his immortal soul. And then, my son, imagine that your name would be synonymous with that misery. For the next thousand years, people will remember David Dyson as the man who brought about the end of the longest period of peace and prosperity the world had ever known. Your name will be dragged through the mud for generations. Do you really want that?"

The cardinal was now cajoling Dyson, lulling him into acquiescence with the calm voice of reason. His arguments were indeed sound, but Dyson had been over this in his own mind and with Cardinal Goodfellowe so many times that there was no chance whatsoever of him changing his point of view now. He did not reply, so di Galassini went on.

"Science fiction novels, Hollywood blockbusters, and television have already introduced the concept of time travel to an otherwise scientifically ignorant public. Just imagine, though, what would happen if we, the Church, were to admit openly and officially that we know time travel is a reality. This is not Hollywood, this is real life! We know that the inventor lived in the nineteenth century and that he travelled to times in his own future, and probably will travel even to times in *our* future. Perhaps our announcement that we know time travel is possible would cause someone in our own time to work on and eventually develop a time machine.

"What if this inventor, sometime in our own not-too-distant future, travelled back in time to his nineteenth-century colleague and decided, for purposes completely unknown to us, to prevent him from continuing his travels, or even killed him? That would mean the Lamb never appeared to us. Our Church would never exist! Just imagine what dangers are inherent in such possibilities, David. Imagine what might happen if mankind could tamper with the course of history!

What if someone went back in time and gave Julius Caesar a steam engine? The world today might still be ruled by the heathen Roman Empire before Constantine introduced Christianity. They might have persecuted Christians to the point that our religion became extinct! Perhaps we would all be speaking Latin today and worshipping false Roman gods!

"Or imagine if Hitler were given the atom bomb in 1944! Maybe German would now be the world language. Perhaps the Nazi party would still be in power in many European nations today, even here in America. Think of the millions the Nazis murdered in their twelve-year reign of terror in our own history. Think of all the billions of innocent people they might murder if they had a way of actually realizing their goal of a thousand-year Reich! These things would not only change our past but also our present and our future.

"You and I might suddenly cease to exist! Of course, in the larger scale of things, this might not matter all that much, but just think of the state of the world if there were no set rules and regulations for its existence; if there were nothing there to keep the stream of events on a constant course. What would happen if the course of events, of world history, were so dynamic and fluid that they could be altered by one single time traveler, a man whose moral standing may be absolutely faultless, but on the other hand — which is actually more likely to be the case — may be driven by greed and egocentricity."

The cardinal's arguments were indeed extremely persuasive, but they failed to sway Dyson in the slightest: his faith in God and in humanity was stronger. Although he now knew that there had been no Second Coming, he still fervently believed in a benevolent God who had mankind's best interests in mind. Nothing and nobody could ever take that away from him.

"Before we conclude our business here, Eminence, I would be grateful if you would just indulge me for a second by answering one very simple question for me."

"And what would that be, my son?" the cardinal enquired warily.

"Do you believe in God, Eminence?"

"I beg your pardon! I am a cardinal of the Holy Church! Have you taken leave of your senses?"

"Please, Eminence, indulge me. Just say yes or no. Do you believe in God?"

"Well, of course I do! What kind of question is that to ask a man in my position?"

"Then you also presumably believe in a kind and merciful God who has the best interests of mankind at heart?"

"Father Dyson, I do not know what you are driving at, but I am starting to find this conversation not only pointless but also tiresome in the extreme."

"Please, Eminence, just a minute or two more of your valuable time. Do you or do you not believe that a loving and merciful God would ensure that the existence of man, the jewel of his creation, would continue?"

"Father Dyson, I believe that the Lord our God has put power into the hands of the leaders of our Church to guide sinners back to the path of righteousness and to keep the righteous firmly on that path. If an iron fist is required to achieve this, then so be it. I believe that the Arch-Cardinal of the Church and his cardinals as his deputies, including my humble self, have been appointed by God to do His bidding here on Earth. I believe that the appearance of this Lamb of God, *no matter what its origin*, was sent to us in order that we might be able to fulfill our holy mission. It is an instrument with which to rule. Like the scepter of a monarch, it is also a symbol of power.

"I will admit, if you really insist upon hearing it from my lips, that the vision of the man who repeatedly appears somewhere in the world on June 12 is a scientist. He is a mere man who has discovered a scientific means of travelling through space and time. All the evidence we have managed to gather over the years points to this fact. But just stop to think for a minute, Father Dyson. What effect has this man had on the world? He has ignited the beginnings of a new world order! The world is actually a better place than it was seventy years ago. We have saved the Earth from ecological disaster. We have eradicated most forms of crime. We have put mankind firmly back on the path of righteousness!"

Dyson had been prepared for this argument. "Eminence, what you say is true. But for me and for millions of people like me, there is one thing missing from your equation. The Lord our God placed mankind above all other creatures in His creation. And He did this by giving us free will. Each and every individual has the God-given ability — no, it is more than that, it is a *right* — to express himself or herself freely without fear of reprisal. This Church of ours has not only denied the individual the right of free expression; it has also committed — and regularly commits — the ultimate sin of murder for the base goal of protecting its own interests. This Church, Eminence, has played into the hands of the Antichrist."

The cardinal goggled at the priest and spluttered a little before he was able to speak coherently.

"Father Dyson," he managed to choke out after a while, "this time you have really overstepped the mark. How... how *dare* you!" he yelled apoplectically.

Dyson knew the meeting was over and that he could not expect the leaders of the Church to change or admit anything at all in public, so he decided to play his trump card at last. "Eminence, I must inform you that my comPod has been fitted with a micro-transmitter powerful enough to transmit a coded signal over a distance of eight kilometers. The transmitter has its own built-in power source that means the comPod itself need not be switched on. There is a vehicle parked somewhere within the eight-kilometer range of the transmitter picking up everything we say."

Dyson paused to gauge what effect his words were having on his adversary, but the cardinal remained calm, as if waiting for him to finish. So Dyson continued: "I have not been told where it is, so it would be pointless to try to torture this information out of me. Digital analysis will prove beyond a shadow of a doubt that the voices on the recording are yours and mine. A time signature embedded in the recording has been received from an atomic clock. The exact time and date of this conversation have been stored together with our voices in such a way that they cannot be edited without the alterations being detected. Eminence, we now have in our possession a recording of you, the Arch-Cardinal's representative in the USA, admitting that the figure we call the Lamb of God is a time traveler, and that there was no Second Coming of Jesus Christ on Earth."

Dyson had been preparing for this meeting in his mind for the past few days, but his voice had nevertheless been shaking during his monologue. He was now expecting, and prepared for, all kinds of reactions from Cardinal di Galassini: fury to the point of having him shot on the spot; despair leading to tears or a heart attack; pleading accompanied by attempts at bribery or promises that the Church would reform. What happened next, however, had not occurred to Dyson in his wildest dreams. The cardinal threw back his head and laughed. He actually laughed like a maniac! Eyes closed, mouth wide open, he was a man who knew he held all the cards. Nothing could touch him.

"Do you take me for a *fool*, man?" he yelled, still grinning and wiping away the tears with a sleeve of his robe. "Men of God might once have been regarded as being behind the times, but you are dealing with a Cardinal of the Church of the Second Coming! How in God's holy name do you think we could have maintained our position all these years without investing the time and effort in learning everything there is to know about modern technology?"

Dyson's eyes widened.

"Yes, Father, you might well look surprised! My guard scanned your comPod when he searched you earlier. The miserable little transmitter chip it contains might well have a range of eight-kilometer, but it is completely useless here! The walls of this room are electromagnetically sealed — no signal gets in, no signal gets out. This room is a desert island in an ocean of communications, Father Dyson! You have *nothing*!" The cardinal began to laugh once more, then, after taking a deep breath, he continued to humiliate Dyson's failed attempt to trap him. His voice was dripping with sarcasm. "Let's sum up, shall we? A priest and his journalist girlfriend.... Oh, wait, let us be clear on this point before we go on, shall we? A priest who has broken his holy vows to the Church by having an illicit affair with a woman has some photocopies of documents purportedly written two hundred years ago. Perhaps the priest and his girlfriend, who may both have an impeccable reputation right now, but certainly will not have one tomorrow morning after the Church press release, have one or two originals to which even I have not yet been privy.

"If these documents had really been proof of anything, the priest would never have dared to enter the home of the representative of the Arch-Cardinal in the USA and threaten him. The priest would have published whatever he knew without informing the Church of his intentions beforehand. So far, so good. The priest and his journalist girlfriend claim that these papers prove their theory that the Second Coming never happened and that the global appearances of the Lamb of God are actually those of a time traveler who, by coincidence, just happens to resemble Jesus Christ. Hmmm. Now supposing that the priest and his girlfriend ever manage to transmit this so-called 'evidence' to the media — that is if they manage to survive long enough — which media could they possibly transmit it to? Which media would be foolhardy enough to publish such a thing? Which media would be *fast* enough to publish such a thing before the very long arm and the extremely hard iron fist of the Church descended upon them and ensured that there was nothing left to publish; indeed, no offices left to publish it in?"

Dyson could not reply. The cardinal had known about the concealed bug; their conversation had not been transmitted to any vehicle.

"I think you'd better leave now, don't you?" the cardinal grinned. "And take your comPod with you," he added, waggling an impatient index finger at the offending but impotent device.

Dyson still had no words. What was there to say, after all? He stood up and began to leave.

"Oh, and Father Dyson?"

"Yes, Eminence?"

"It would be easy for me to have you dragged out of here and tortured for days, even weeks, until you told me whatever I wanted to know. However, I believe you to be astute enough firstly to have ensured that you would not be able to betray your comrades even under torture, and secondly, I believe I have a far better punishment for your betrayal. Don't bother turning up for work after the holidays. Your presence is, of course, no longer required by the Church."

Naturally, Dyson had not expected to be able to return to the Archives ever again, but nevertheless he felt a sickening, sinking feeling in his stomach when he was actually officially fired from the job he loved so much.

"Apart from losing your position with the Church," the cardinal smiled smugly, "you will also find that, as of tomorrow, your name will appear as a persona non grata in Church files all over this country. That means, for one thing, you will never be able to leave the USA, as your passport will be revoked, nor will you be able to find work here, nor will you be eligible for any kind of social security benefits. Anyone who takes you in will be guilty of aiding and abetting an enemy of the Church, and will be dealt with accordingly. So, *Mister* Dyson, I wish you good luck finding a bridge to sleep under and enough waste in the dumpsters of New York City to survive on."

The two armed guards who had been waiting outside the doors looked briefly into the room as Dyson left.

"Escort this gentleman outside," di Galassini called. "Our business here is done."

The guards bowed to the cardinal, replying in unison, "Yes, Your Eminence." They then proceeded to guide Dyson wordlessly to the front door and down to the huge gates through which he had entered earlier. Once these had clanged shut behind him, Dyson used his comPod to call a taxi.

CHAPTER 18

**Rachel Watson's Apartment
New York City, 2078**

Dyson looked over his shoulder several times before ringing the doorbell. A futile exercise in the days of satellite observation that could pick out a pin on the ground, but it gave him a feeling of relative safety to think there was nobody actually breathing down his neck, waiting to kick in the front door as soon as he had entered. Rachel let him in and hugged him tightly.

"Well, how did it go then, my hero?" she asked.

Due to the nature of their precarious situation and secret affair, their relationship had been marked by an all-consuming passion. Every moment they spent together had been lived and loved to the full. Despite this, Dyson sometimes even now failed to understand when Rachel was being facetious and when she was being serious. There sometimes seemed to be a kind of transatlantic communications breakdown between them.

They walked into Rachel's living room, and Dyson was just about to tell her all about the meeting, when he realized they were not alone. A young priest was sitting on the sofa sipping a cup of coffee. As Dyson did not recognize the priest, his first concern was that they had been betrayed; that Cardinal di Galassini had second thoughts about letting him go and sent people to arrest them. His immediate reaction was to take a step backward and scan the room for armed DFP thugs, but Rachel held on firmly.

"David, wait, it's all right," she said softly. "You remember Giacomo, don't you?"

The look of extreme puzzlement on Dyson's face told both Rachel and the visitor that he did not remember Giacomo at all. The young priest stood up and smiled warmly, offering Dyson a hand.

"Giacomo Fiorello," he said simply.

Dyson shook his hand, but was none the wiser for it.

"David," Rachel said, "Giacomo was the one who saved you. Cardinal Goodfellowe sent him to get you out of the DFP cells."

Vague memories stirred. Torture, pain, a young priest, waking up in Goodfellowe's house. Then it dawned on him.

"Of course," he said. "I'm so sorry, but I wasn't quite myself when we first met."

Fiorello smiled. "That's perfectly all right. I understand completely."

"I must say I am deeply in your debt," Dyson said with feeling. "It's a great pleasure to meet you. I mean, with a clear head this time."

"The pleasure is all mine," Fiorello said, nodding graciously.

"So, what's going on?" Dyson enquired.

"Well, we felt it was too dangerous for Cardinal Goodfellowe to go wandering around the streets. Even if he were disguised, too many people know him from photos and interviews, and so on. So Giacomo here is acting as his envoy. Cardinal Goodfellowe had Giacomo flown in from Nicaragua to get you out, as he's never been to New York before, so nobody knows him here. He'll report everything you tell us about your visit to di Galassini to Cardinal Goodfellowe. So, how did it go then? Did he fall for it?"

Dyson sighed heavily and dropped his head, looking dejectedly at his shoes.

"I'm afraid his guards saw through the comPod ruse straight away," he said sadly. Fiorello looked crestfallen, but Rachel punched Dyson playfully on the arm.

"You know damn well what I mean!" she said. "Now, out with it!" She hugged him tightly, and for Dyson all was well with the world for a brief moment.

CHAPTER 19

Residence of Cardinal Alberto di Galassini, US Representative of His Holiness the Arch-Cardinal of the Church of the Second Coming of the Lamb of God New York City, 2078

"I have a job for you, Father Evans," the cardinal said.

"Anything I can do to preserve the Holy Church," the visitor replied, having been fully apprised of the events that had transpired the previous evening.

"Your colleague Dyson and his whore are becoming most troublesome. I thought I would simply forget about them, but now I'm having second thoughts. It is about time they were removed from the equation."

Evans was anything but naïve; he had known for quite some time now that it would eventually come to this. Nevertheless, he was still extremely reluctant to even contemplate doing what the cardinal was now suggesting.

"If I might speak freely?"

"Very well," the cardinal said, with a dismissive wave of his right hand. There was a distinct air of boredom in his voice, but Evans had served him well over the years and was allowed, on occasions, to speak his mind. Neither was Evans forced to constantly address him as Eminence as other priests and even bishops had to do. "But keep it brief, if you please," the cardinal added. He turned to warm his hands at the artificial fire. Evans considered for a moment before replying.

"I would like to plead for the life of David Dyson."

"I beg your pardon!" the cardinal interrupted, turning abruptly from the warm glow of the fire to cast an icy glare at Evans.

"I mean, is Dyson really worth killing?"

Cardinal di Galassini looked as though he were about to explode.

"Worth killing?" he squealed. "Worth killing? Do you realize what you are saying, man? Do you know that he has already almost destroyed all that we hold dear? Are you perhaps not aware of the fact that Father David Dyson is a loose cannon that could go off at any minute?! Father Evans, I am sick of these constant games! I am sick of waiting for the next challenge this man will come up with to jeopardize us. He is tenacious, Evans. He will not simply forget about it and go away. He is a man with a mission, and I do not intend to sit back and watch him complete his mission and bring about our destruction." After a moment's thought, the cardinal added in more subdued tones, "But if you feel you're not up to the job, I'll find someone else. Needless to say, your own services will then no longer be required by this office."

Evans knew that tone. Indeed, he had heard it often enough over the years he had been in the cardinal's pay, and had grown used to it. He was therefore completely calm when he replied.

"I have served you and the Church for many years. You must know by now that I am not a man to turn tail and run when the going gets rough. As unpleasant as this particular task may be for me personally, I will carry out your orders. I will not fail you again."

CHAPTER 20

Rachel Watson's Apartment
New York City, 2078

"Oh! You mean Cardinal Goodfellowe's *other* plan?" Dyson laughed innocently. "That worked fine!"

Rachel growled at him playfully. Giacomo Fiorello, who was not in on what seemed like a private joke, merely looked mystified but remained silent and waited to learn what Dyson meant. Rachel opened a small metal box and removed a thin sliver of plastic with a tiny suction pad on one end.

"Here," she said, handing it to Dyson. "Out with it."

Dyson took the strange-looking instrument, sat down, and looked up at the ceiling. Opening his left eye wide with the thumb and index finger of his left hand, he placed the suction pad onto his eyeball. When he removed the implement again, there was a clear contact lens stuck to it.

"It looks as if Cardinal di Galassini isn't quite as up-to-date as he likes to think," he grinned.

Toward the end of the twentieth century, scientists had begun to experiment with metal alloys and plastics that could 'remember' the shape they had been given when they were manufactured. If they were then subsequently deformed, heat could be applied and the alloy would bend itself back into its original shape. Almost a hundred years later, this technology had been developed to such an extent that individual molecules could be made to react not only to temperature changes, but also to light and vibration. If the molecules were then reset to their original state, they could actually be made to remember the changes in light and the vibrations they had been subjected to, and to reproduce these memories on a monitor in the form of video and audio signals.

By the year 2076, bio-molecular memory chips were already being used extensively by many government and Church organizations, and were just beginning to appear on the commercial entertainment market. State of the art solar-powered video cameras capable of recording for days resembled credit cards that could be worn on clothing like a badge. The contact lens that Dyson had worn during his meeting with Cardinal di Galassini was something very special, though. This was cutting-edge technology designed by some of the most brilliant minds in the world. *Luckily*, thought Dyson, *these minds — belonging to people like Mike the Wizard — were working for the underground, and not for the Church.*

"Right then," Rachel said, holding up the metal box. "I'll get this to my editor straight away. Giacomo, you report to Cardinal Goodfellowe that David made it back safely and that we have the lens."

"And what shall *I* do?" Dyson asked.

"You stay here and pray that this thing actually recorded something," Rachel replied. When she saw that he was about to protest about letting her go alone, she added, "David, they'll be watching the streets. They know us. If we travel together, we'll be easier to spot. Stay here, my love. You've done your bit for today. I'll get this off to Eddie and I'll see you tonight."

With that she kissed him, pulled on her coat, and left the apartment with her collar pulled high around her face. Giacomo Fiorello waited for five minutes; then he left to inform Cardinal Goodfellowe about the latest developments. The plan now was for Rachel to take the recording, along with the photocopied documents from Cardinal Goodfellowe, to a secret meeting she had arranged with the editor of her newspaper, Edward Griswald.

Griswald was one of those strange characters who lived on a knife-edge, courting danger but never falling victim to it. Although he hated the Church and everything it stood for, he was on friendly terms with the Church leadership, printing flattering articles about them, extolling the virtues of the clean, safe society the Church had made possible. This made him a figure of contempt among the grassroots underground members, who knew nothing of his true loyalties. On the other hand, the top echelon of leaders of the underground movement knew Griswald to be a committed opponent of the Church. His unique position as a journalist and, seemingly, a friend of the Church, meant that he received a lot of information from religious leaders, which he was able to pass on to the underground. The double life Griswald led enabled him to organize a meeting at a moment's notice with almost anybody he wished to talk to, and it was this ability that made him a key player in Goodfellowe's plan.

Over the years Cardinal Goodfellowe had adopted a healthy degree of paranoia as far as disclosing his real feelings was concerned: a survival instinct. He was known throughout the United States as a staunch Church man with unshakable principles. For this reason he could not possibly have approached Griswald in person. For although Griswald would have been only too happy to interview him, pretending fervor for the Church, in all likelihood it would have been impossible for Goodfellowe to convince him that he, the cardinal, was anything but a defender of the Church.

Neither would Dyson have been a suitable candidate to send to Griswald. Even with the incriminating evidence against the Church in the form of the recording, Griswald would have been suspicious if an unknown priest had come to him. He probably would have assumed they had finally rumbled him and now intended to set a trap.

No, it had to be Rachel who took the recording to the editor of the *New York Gazette*. She had worked for, and with, Griswald for the last eight years. Although he was old enough to be her father, Rachel thought their relationship was more like one shared by equals. There was a certain degree of mock rivalry, but there was also a great deal of mutual respect and amiability.

Griswald, on the other hand, felt a great affection for Rachel. He always thought of her as the daughter who had been taken from him. Like Rachel, Griswald's own little girl also had reddish brown hair, and she had been so very inquisitive. "My little star reporter," he had always called her. His daughter had been killed in an explosion when she was just seven years old. All the evidence pointed to a domestic gas explosion. The little girl had chanced to be walking past a house when an explosion reduced it to a pile of rubble. His daughter's name had been Rachel, too. On that fateful day, Edward Griswald lost not only his little girl, but also his faith in God and in the Church. This loss of faith had developed into outright hatred toward the Church when his own private research revealed that the "gas explosion" had in all probability been an assassination — or rather an execution — of dissidents by the DFP. His daughter had simply been in the wrong place at the wrong time and been caught in the crossfire. Over the following years he became a hard, bitter man, outwardly courting the Church, but inwardly biding his time until he could find a way of contributing to its downfall. His wait had been a long one, though, and the power and popularity of the Church had grown with each passing year, which had made it even more difficult to attack.

The Church of the Second Coming had made a major contribution to what had once been thought an impossible dream. In the countries that had embraced the new faith, there was peace. Law-abiding, Church-going citizens were able to walk the streets at night — before curfew, of course — and not only felt, but actually *were*, safe. Towns and cities worldwide were virtually crime-free. Since about 2035, countries whose official state religion was the Church of the Second Coming of the Lamb had been spotlessly clean. Muggings were practically unheard of; graffiti was almost non-existent; the occasional murder, which shocked society to its core, was more often than not a domestic affair that had nothing whatsoever to do with crimes based on greed or drug abuse. Only the rising suicide rate still blemished the progress these societies had made.

Once it had gained a foothold in societies with a major economic influence, the Church of the Second Coming revived a medieval-style fear of God as a mighty, omnipotent and omniscient deity; vengeful when disobeyed, yet merciful if people lived according to His laws. Anyone found guilty of a crime against the Church was taken in shackles to a public place and punished for all to see, either by beating or, in more serious cases, by death. The Church justified this with Job 34:26-27, "He punishes them with their wickedness where everyone can see them, because they turned from following him and had no regard for any of his ways." Such was the power and influence of the Church of the Second Coming of the Lamb.

As a peace-loving man, Edward Griswald knew that on the one hand he was fortunate that he suffered neither hunger, nor fear of war, nor the threat of violent crime. On the other hand, his sense of democracy, of justice, was affronted by the reality that the Church was the de facto ruling body of his country rather than the elected politicians. He was outraged that a religious dictatorship was able to liquidate its opponents with no fear of reprisal either by the elected representatives of the people or by the populace as a whole. The elected secular representatives of the people were not even able to overturn a decision made by Church leaders. If innocent lives had to be sacrificed to achieve the goals of the Church, well, then that was just too bad, or so it seemed. And for years Edward Griswald nursed a cold and concealed hatred of his daughter's murderers.

Then, one day, Rachel Watson had walked into his office and into his life, looking for a job as a reporter. It was as if he had never lost his beloved daughter to the bomb on that cold autumn day. It seemed as if his little girl had just gone away for a few years and had then returned, all grown up, as his young star reporter. Griswald had nurtured her inquisitive instincts, training her, preparing her for the day when she would assist him in carrying out his plans. Edward Griswald had no idea about the scam the cardinals — perhaps even the Arch-Cardinal himself — had been a party to, but, like David Dyson, he was a man with a mission. Although he had no idea about the true identity of the "Lamb of God," he could not rest until he found something which destroyed the Church, as the Church had destroyed his family.

Rachel knew that Edward Griswald hated the Church and all it stood for. She also knew why. And, although he had never openly talked to her of his contacts to the underground movement, she knew about these, too. He had never wanted to endanger Rachel's life by making her a part of his personal vendetta against the Church, and she had never wanted to compromise him by asking. Both of them seemed happy with this state of affairs, neither of them wishing to upset the balance of things by speaking of the matter openly.

CHAPTER 21

New York Gazette **Building**
New York City, 2078

Rachel Watson hurried furtively into the brightly lit foyer of the *New York Gazette*. Not slowing down to say hello to the staff at the front desk, not even acknowledging their existence, she almost jogged toward the elevators. Reaching the top floor of the building, she pushed open the doors of Edward Griswald's office without knocking.

"Eddie, I've got something here that needs your attention. Right now."

Griswald looked up from his monitor, a mock grimace crossing his face.

"Rachel, if anybody else had burst in here like that, I would've kicked their ass by now." He suddenly broke into a broad grin. "What you got, babe?"

"Eddie, I need you to trust me."

"I'd trust you to the ends of the Earth, sweetheart."

"You need to get a group together," Rachel said simply. "A group of people who will appreciate what I have here. This could finish the Church."

Griswald's eyes widened, shining wickedly. Then he smiled at his protégée.

"Let's see what you've got, then, my little star reporter," he said.

For the next few minutes, Rachel told her boss and mentor what she had been concealing from him over the last few months. She finally took out the little silver box containing the contact lens, and placed it next to Griswald's computer monitor. Rachel pressed her thumb onto a Perspex inlay in the box, and two seconds later, Griswald's computer said "signal acquired."

— «» —

Outside, thirty floors below, a black limousine was parked on the opposite side of the road. Father Simon Evans was sitting in the back seat wearing a wireless earpiece. He had waited and listened to Dyson's girlfriend, Rachel Watson, and her boss, Edward Griswald, the editor of the *New York Gazette*. The DFP officer now sitting in the driver's seat had returned to the vehicle after releasing a tiny, spider-like mechanical bug at the foot of the building. It had scaled the office block in a matter of seconds, until it reached the window of Griswald's office. It had then attached itself to the glass and relayed a multi-coded audio-visual signal to Evans' comPod, which he listened to through the earpiece to prevent his uninitiated driver from hearing or seeing anything that was going on in the editor's office.

— «» —

Neither Rachel nor Griswald had ever before seen the results of an eye camera, and they were both extremely impressed. The video image was crisp and clear, and the audio was so digitally enhanced one might have thought the protagonists were in the room with them. The meeting between Dyson and Cardinal di Galassini had been recorded in its entirety. The software enhancements programmed into the silver box containing the recording lens had efficiently removed any jerking movements of Dyson's head. The blinking of his eyelids had also been compensated for with no loss of quality whatsoever.

When they had watched the full meeting in silence, but for a few gasps of astonishment, Griswald's mouth hung open incredulously.

"You gotta be shittin' me!" he exclaimed.

Rachel, who was also quite stunned by the recording, shook her head slowly, and pulled copies of the documents from Cardinal Goodfellowe from her bag. Griswald inspected them briefly and slammed them down onto his desk, a look of utter triumph crossing his usually sullen face.

"I got people to call!" he said, and lunged for his comPod.

The video signal in Evans' car was relatively good, despite the fact that the bug was looking through a tinted window and was trained on the rear of Griswald's 3D monitor, which meant that the images of Cardinal di Galassini, as seen from Dyson's perspective, were somewhat blurry. The audio transmission, however, was excellent. Evans was shocked. He had been witness to the meeting as if he had actually been there listening in person. But now he had heard enough. Now it had become an urgent exercise in damage containment. He had to act before Griswald managed to contact the outside world. Leaning forward, he murmured almost inaudibly into the driver's ear, "Do it."

A moment later there was a bright flash high above them, then, a split second after that, an ear-shattering boom followed by a low rumble. Before the debris from Griswald's office reached street level, the black car had pulled silently away. It had already turned a corner when the glass and metal began to rain down onto the sidewalk. The electronic bug had been vaporized when it exploded, ensuring that nothing could trace the blast back to the Church.

CHAPTER 22

Home of Cardinal Brian Goodfellowe

For days Dyson had shut himself away in his room at Goodfellowe's residence. He had hardly slept, hardly eaten. Much to the housekeeper's dismay, he had also neglected to shower. Rachel's death had induced an almost catatonic state in him. She had been his first, indeed his *only* true love, and she had been taken from him so unexpectedly, so suddenly, that he had not even had time to say a proper goodbye.

Of course, the Church-controlled press had explained the deadly explosion in the middle of Manhattan as an attack by subversives against the person of Ed Griswald: "Cowardly Attack Kills Newspaper Editor"; "Sad Day for the Church"; "Murder of Church Supporter." In public, Edward Griswald had been seen as a staunch ally of the Church, and the Church had used this common belief and milked it for all it was worth. But the people who had really known him believed Griswald was probably turning in his grave over these headlines.

For many weeks, Cardinal Goodfellowe had been exceptionally understanding and had come to see Dyson regularly, but nothing the cardinal could say had been able to comfort Dyson. Then, one day, Goodfellowe decided the time had come for the mourning to cease.

"Listen to me, David," he said gently. "I can only guess what you must be going through, and believe me, I truly feel for you. Over the past few months you have become like a son to me. But there is a time for grief and there is a time to return to the life of the living."

"What have I got left, Eminence?" Dyson replied miserably. "They've taken everything from me: Rachel, my faith, my job."

"My son, you could simply lie down and die if you wanted to, but do you know what that would mean? It would mean they'd won. Rachel's death would mean nothing. All this pain you have suffered would have been for nothing. And it is not just *your* pain; not just *my* pain. I'm talking of all the people who have ever suffered at the hands of this so-called church. And I'm talking about all the thousands of people who will suffer at its hands in future if we now sit back and admit defeat. And that, I'm afraid to say, David, is just what you are doing. You are cowering in here like a wounded animal. But even wounded animals recover, become strong again, and live to fight another day."

"But what's the alternative? I have no way to make a living. Sure, it's unlikely now that the Church will bother having me killed, but that's because we have no evidence against them anymore. Without the evidence of the recording, all we have are a few eco-foil copies that might just as well be forgeries, as you yourself said not so long ago. Unless I find some way to get a new identity, it's unlikely I'll ever find another job again. And I needn't even bother trying here in the States. I'm probably on every Church blacklist there is! And I can't leave the country since my passport has been invalidated."

"Listen to me, David. There is another solution." Goodfellowe paused and looked at the floor. When he looked up into Dyson's eyes again, he added solemnly, "It is drastic, though."

Seeing the cardinal for the first time in a mood as dark as his own, Dyson's interest was piqued. Now that he believed he had nothing more to lose, he no longer cared about his own safety. However, it seemed that Goodfellowe's words had struck a chord, and Dyson felt it would do him good to concentrate on something other than his loss for a while. Taking a deliberately deep breath and releasing it slowly, Dyson attempted to clear his head and concentrate on emerging from his shadowy existence.

"All right," he said. "What are you thinking of?"

The cardinal smiled, his eyes kind. At least Dyson was responding now.

"What do you know about the Second Coming; about the beginnings of our Church?" he asked.

"Are you serious?" Dyson asked. "I'm a priest!"

"Very well then, *Father*. Share with me your expert knowledge," the cardinal said, folding his arms and looking at Dyson expectantly, one eyebrow raised in mock challenge. "Where was the first appearance of the Lamb?"

Puzzled by the question, the answer to which any child would have been able to supply without a moment's hesitation, Dyson answered automatically, parrot-fashion.

"The first appearance of the Lamb of God was at the United Nations general assembly in New York City."

"When?"

"December 17, 2010."

"And the second appearance?"

"Greenwich, London, January 1, 2011." Again, the reply came to Dyson without thinking. These were dates and places any elementary school child could have recited.

"What about the third appearance?"

"Err," Dyson began. "Just a minute. Hmm. I don't quite remember that one."

"And the fourth appearance?" Goodfellowe enquired.

"Erm." There was a moment's silence. "Oh, I think I see what you mean," Dyson said, his brow furrowed in consternation.

"But I'm sure you could tell me on what *date* the Lamb has always appeared to the world since 2015, couldn't you?"

"Well, yes, it's always been June 12."

"Why?"

"I beg your pardon?"

"Why, David? The question is simple enough. Why does the Lamb of God always appear on June 12?"

"Well," Dyson replied, wondering what the cardinal was getting at, "people have been debating that for over sixty years now. Nobody knows. So how should I know?"

"All right then, a different question: how often does he appear?"

"There is no real pattern. He just sort of turns up somewhere at random. Sometimes he appears three or four years in a row, sometimes he isn't seen at all for a few years."

"Don't you think that is rather odd?" Goodfellowe asked.

"Actually, I'd never really thought about it before. But then again, until recently I had always believed the Lamb of God was, well, just that: the Lamb of God! So it wasn't really my place to question his divine purpose, of course. But now that I know more about him, yes, come to think of it, it *is* odd. Why would he appear at irregular intervals all over the world for over sixty years? Why not regularly, every year in a different major city of the world? It reminds me of those scurrilous stories one reads of the face of the Lord Jesus or Mary the mother of God appearing on tortillas in Mexico in the twentieth century. Why didn't he seem to have a plan? Why not stop after five or ten years? After all, we got the message, didn't we? Or at least we thought we did," he added grimly.

"David, I have a job for you. I'd like you to find the answers to these questions. If the Church ever looked into this thoroughly, I, for one, have never heard about it. I have a suspicion, but I do not wish to influence your research by disclosing it to you just yet. I will pay you as a research assistant doing a full time job."

"But, Eminence," Dyson objected, "your hospitality alone..."

He certainly did not want alms from the cardinal. After all, the man had already rescued him from certain death and had taken him, a fugitive from the Church, into his home, probably risking his own life in doing so.

Goodfellowe raised his hand. "You of all people have earned the right to be given an opportunity to discover the truth."

"But you're practically, no, *actually*, harboring a criminal! How can you employ me and let me stay under your roof? If they ever found me here..."

The cardinal merely smiled. "David, there are several things I would like to tell you if it will put your mind at rest. Firstly, I am quite confident that my reputation within the Church is such that no suspicion will be cast upon me. As you yourself once put it, I believe: my behavior toward you and your colleagues was never particularly marked by 'Christian charity and brotherly love'."

Dyson blushed at the memory of his words. In light of the events since then, he felt very embarrassed indeed about being reminded of the harsh and wholly unjustified things he had said about the cardinal in his unenlightened past.

"And secondly, you *were* caught attempting to break into my office, after all. Why would you need to undertake such a risky business if we were collaborating? Thirdly, my home is at least as well protected as that of Cardinal di Galassini. In fact, this place is probably as secure, both structurally and electronically, as the Arch-Cardinal's offices in Rome. I do have a certain number of useful connections, you know. Finally, neither the tunnel leading to the locked door in the alley at the South Street Seaport, nor the door itself, are marked on any map. To a passerby the door merely looks like the rear entrance to a run-down house in an area where nobody asks any questions about their neighbors. It is also so far away from my house that it is utterly impossible to assume, for an outsider, that they are in any way connected. So you see, David, I am quite sure that I am safe in keeping you here. The only other living souls who know of your presence here are my housekeeper and Giacomo, and I trust both of them with my life.

"So I repeat my offer to you, David: I will pay you to use your extraordinary research talents in my employ. You will live here under my roof while doing so, and of course, you are free to use the tunnel and the door whenever you like. All I ask is that you use them discreetly. Once you have made some progress in your research, we will discuss the results and I will disclose my thoughts on the matter."

Dyson was overwhelmed by the offer and more than a little daunted by the task that lay before him, and the expectations the cardinal had of him. Nevertheless, he felt better than he had for many days. Thoroughly invigorated by the sense of purpose he had unexpectedly been offered by his equally unexpected benefactor, Dyson figuratively awoke that afternoon from what seemed like a deep sleep. Symbolically casting off his mantle of abject misery, he took a very long, very hot shower. After shaving off the stubble he had acquired over the past few days and dressing in clean, fresh-smelling civilian clothes, he felt as if he had been reborn. The housekeeper had laid out a number of garments for him to choose from, including a priest's cassock, but Dyson was quite certain he would never be able to don one of those again.

— «» —

Over the next few weeks Dyson immersed himself in his research. The cardinal had already demonstrated how little he actually knew about the beginnings of the Church, so this is where he started. It seemed as if the Church had purposely skimmed over its origins in its canonical literature. It was not as though they had actively tried to *conceal* information as such — for there was already too much information generally available to do that — but the Church's founders did not seem to attach any great importance to the reformation of the Roman Catholic and Protestant churches into the Church of the Second Coming. It was also a direction of research that had never really been encouraged by the Church administration: a fact that Dyson had, until now, simply accepted without question.

He went back almost a hundred years and examined the condition of the world at the time the "Lamb" first appeared.

The destruction of the twin towers of the World Trade Center in New York City in 2001 had merely been the premiere of a string of terrorist atrocities. London, Madrid and Paris followed soon after, although not to such a devastating extent as 9/11. In 2021, New York City was again the focus of a terrorist attack. This time the perpetrators employed a "dirty bomb" which exploded in a van in Times Square. Although no real atomic detonation in the form of nuclear fission was involved in the blast, the bomb released radioactive particles into the air, contaminating a wide area. More than fifty people were killed by the non-nuclear blast from the car bomb itself, but the radioactivity was so dispersed that nobody actually died of radiation poisoning immediately after the explosion. However, decontamination of the area took over a year to complete, in which time a large part of mid-town Manhattan was uninhabitable. There was also a marked increase in the number of cancer cases diagnosed in the area.

And the terror continued. In 2025 it was Paris. Extreme right wing politicians had, for several years, been curtailing the rights of immigrants to France, even expelling them from the country for misdemeanors. A terrorist group claimed responsibility for an attack calculated to humiliate the French by directly targeting their national pride. On July 14, the most important holiday in France, Bastille Day, a guided missile, previously stolen from the French military and loaded with high explosives, struck the Eiffel Tower, killing thousands of tourists in and around one of the world's most famous monuments, and reducing the tower itself to 7,300 tons of partly melted scrap metal. Once again the terrorists had succeeded in disrupting life in a western capital, simultaneously striking fear into the hearts of its citizens.

However, the terrorist threat was not the only factor causing worldwide misery. Scientists first noticed the gigantic hole in the ozone layer over the South Pole in the early 1980s. It was mainly caused by the industrial gases that could be found, and indeed were being increasingly produced, in almost every household in the "civilized," i.e. the western, world. By the late 1980s the hole had increased to such dimensions that it seasonally affected Australia and New Zealand.

The next phenomenon to be scientifically confirmed was the warming of the Earth's atmosphere known as the "greenhouse effect." This was mainly caused by the burning of fossil fuels and all the combustion engines on the planet, whose vast numbers increased almost as rapidly as the human population. The carbon dioxide given off as a waste product was responsible for preventing the warmth of the sun's rays from leaving the Earth's atmosphere. The gradual warming of the Earth's surface led to the direst consequences imaginable.

In 2004, parts of the South Pacific and India were devastated by a tsunami. Hundreds of thousands of people were killed in what was at the time the most unimaginable and devastating natural disaster in living memory. In 2005, three huge hurricanes, Katrina, Rita, and Wilma, caused major damage. The devastation caused by Katrina in New Orleans was unprecedented.

In 2023, thousands of lost their lives during the hurricane season, and hundreds of thousands more lost their homes. A combination of the hurricanes and the greenhouse effect, which had begun to melt the polar ice caps, thus causing a rise in sea level, meant that the floods not only came with the winds, but they remained after the hurricanes had ebbed in mid-March. This brought disaster to the European Low Countries and vast areas of southern Asia.

The Great Benelux Seawall had been built between 2020 and 2023. For all the ingenuity, for all the astronomical amounts of money that people had expended on this project, the forces of nature nevertheless defeated it. In 2025 the Great Wall, which had been built to defend the low-lying countries of Belgium, the Netherlands, and Luxembourg against the encroaching tempest, finally succumbed to a power far greater than any form of defense man had to offer. Gradually people began moving away from the coastal areas to higher ground, finally realizing that they had lost the battle against the violent elements. They left everything behind them and set out to start a new life in another country. This soon escalated to a mass migration of entire cultures into areas where they were, for the most part, not at all welcome. Social tension reached epic proportions. There were race riots, class riots, and culture riots. Cultural Displacement Imbalance Syndrome became the subject of numerous volumes of sociological, political, and psychological theses.

And in the aftermath of such geographical and sociological upheavals, Earth had become noticeably weary. Somehow the people not immediately affected by the worst of the environmental changes still managed to cling on to the vestiges of an almost normal life, but even these lucky ones realized that their days of normality were numbered. People were desperate for even the slightest glimpse of hope; anything that would once again bring order to their miserable, uncertain lives in a world that had become so threatening and precarious that they were no longer able to predict what the following month would bring. As a historian, Dyson of course knew the facts and figures involved in what he was currently reading. But once he started on the contemporary eyewitness reports of what had happened to real individuals his heart went out to them, even though they were now, for the most part at least, long dead.

Whatever reasons people might have had for believing or not believing in the Second Coming of the Lamb, for believers there was no denying that the Holy Scriptures were sending a very clear message to humanity. Signs mentioned cryptically in the Bible thousands of years earlier were being interpreted on a daily basis in news broadcasts. Everything seemed to fit. It was time. The Savior, the Lamb, was coming to end the world, and nobody could deny it. In the Biblical Book of Revelation written by Saint John, the "end of days" is described in great detail. In his vision, he sees seven scrolls predicting the end of the world. These scrolls bear seven seals, each one being opened by the Lamb upon His return to Earth.

Revelation 6:2; "And I saw and beheld a white horse and he that sat down on him had a bow, and a crown was given to him, and he went forth conquering and to conquer."

For Christians this was clearly a reference to the Lamb of God returning to Earth wearing the crown of the Son of God, the Prince of Heaven, and carrying the bow with which to judge mankind for his sins. Doubters had pointed out that the Apparition neither wore a crown nor carried a bow, but believers merely stated that these references were only symbols, figuratively representing the power of the Savior.

Revelation 6:3-4; "And when he had opened the second seal... And there went out another horse that was red: and power was given to him that sat thereon to take peace from the earth, and that they should slay one another, and a great sword was given to him."

Obviously this describes war and terror. In the years before the Second Coming of the Lamb, the whole world was in a constant state of alert, waiting for the next terrorist atrocity. People lived in permanent fear, wondering if it would be them or their loved ones who would be next on the growing list of casualties.

Revelation 6:5-6; "And when he opened the third seal I heard the third living creature saying, come and see. And I saw and beheld a black horse, and he that sat on it had a balance in his hand and I heard a voice…saying, a pint of wheat for a denarius and 3 pints of barley for a denarius; and do not harm the oil and the wine."

The climate changes over the past two hundred years had meant that more and more of the earth's surface was being turned gradually into desert. The black horse of famine would destroy wheat and barley, which would become so rare that only the rich would be able to afford them: a denarius represented a whole day's pay in Biblical times, so the poor would starve. The oil and the wine refer to olives and grapes, which can survive droughts because they have deep roots.

Revelation 6:7; "And when he opened the fourth seal I heard the voice of the fourth living creature saying, come and see…"

Revelation 6:8; "And I saw, and behold, a yellow-green horse, and the name of the one sitting on it was Death and Hades followed after him. And authority was given to them to kill over the fourth of the earth with sword, with famine, with death, and by the wild beasts of the earth."

In the twentieth century, two world wars devastated the earth, but there was a definite beginning and end to each of these catastrophes. In the twenty-first century, however, ethnic wars continued unabated for years. Famines and disease decimated the human population in the poorer regions of the world, and the "wild beasts of the earth," not actually animals as such, but anything from ruthless state dictators to thugs who roamed the streets at night before the Second Coming, were responsible for much of the misery.

Revelation 6:9-11; "And when he opened the fifth seal, I saw under the altar the souls of those having been slain for the word of God, and for the witness which they had. And they cried with a great voice, saying, until when, holy and true master, do you not judge and take vengeance for our blood, from those dwelling on the earth. And there was given to every one a white robe, and they were ordered to take their rest for a little while, till the number was complete of the fellow slaves, and their brothers, who would be put to death, even as they had been."

The fifth seal represents a persecution of believers, the people who believed in the word of God and were prepared to die for their faith. This had been happening all through history and, in certain parts of the world, still was at the time of the Second Coming.

Revelation 6: 12; "And I saw when he opened the sixth seal. And behold, a great earthquake occurred. And the sun became black as sackcloth made of hair, and the moon became as blood."

This prophecy had appeared to be coming true at the beginning of 2026. A huge earthquake decimated San Francisco, killing thousands of people. Several weeks after this tragic event, it was announced that a meteor had been discovered at the edge of the solar system and it was heading toward the Earth. Of course, no government actually went as far as admitting that it would hit the Earth, but worldwide panic ensued. Experts said the impact, if it came, would black out the sun and moon for months, causing the death of almost every living thing, plant or animal, on the surface of the planet. Of course, this tragedy never happened, because the meteor eventually failed to hit the Earth, but experts said it was only a matter of time until it really occurred. Believers claimed the Lamb of God had averted the disaster, of course, but as yet there was no Church of the Second Coming, and the handful of people who believed this were ridiculed.

Revelation 6:13; "And the stars of heaven fell to the earth, as a fig tree being shaken by a great wind casts its unripe figs."

Another theory of scientists and the popular press in 2026 was that the meteor would hit the moon, shattering it and causing vast chunks of rock to be hurled at the Earth, causing even more devastation, and much sooner, than the impact of the meteor with Earth.

Revelation 6:14; "And the heaven was separated as a scroll being rolled up, and every mountain and island were moved out of their places."

Only the catastrophic impact with another heavenly body would be enough to bring about the destruction described in this verse.

Luke 21:25; "And there shall be signs in the sun, and in the moon, and in the stars..."

Matthew 24:29; "The sun will be darkened, and the moon will not give its light, the stars will fall from the sky, and the heavenly bodies will be shaken."

The Gospels corroborate the prophecies in Revelation.

Revelation 6:15; "And the kings of the earth, and the great men, and the rich men, and the chief captains, and the mighty men, and every bondman, and every free man, hid themselves in the dens and in the rocks of the mountains."

Indeed, the rich and the powerful began to excavate huge caverns in which to hide from the disaster, stocking these places for themselves and their families, expecting to emerge when it was all over and most of the less fortunate population had been wiped out.

But everything changed with the appearance of the Savior, the Lamb of God. The Roman Catholic Church, which had remained practically unchanged for almost fifteen hundred years, underwent an unprecedented reform. This reform made it possible for believers from other Christian faiths to join the former Roman Catholics, while many ultra conservatives in the Roman Catholic Church left it for precisely the same reasons.

Twenty years later the reformed Catholic Church had begun calling itself The Holy Church of the Second Coming of the Lamb. In an attempt to attract as many believers as possible from other faiths, the importance of the Virgin Mary was gradually reduced to be honored on only one special day of the year, and even then on a purely voluntary basis. So successful was this reform that the Church of the Second Coming indeed became the major Western religion; all others were reduced to the status of insignificant sects.

With this religious power also came political influence, as senior politicians, having now seen irrefutable evidence of a higher power in the universe, were eager to accommodate the Church wherever possible, while simultaneously asking forgiveness for their sins. This eventually led to a merging of state and church in most western societies, which in turn led to the introduction of a ten percent Church Tax in all countries in which the Church was established. As this was based on the idea of tithing from the Bible, nobody could really object; at least not officially or openly. With the fabulous wealth the Church acquired in this manner over the years, all kinds of charitable organizations, hospitals, and schools were funded. Nobody went hungry in western society. Everybody had accommodation; if not private, then at least in a Church hostel.

Of course, as in any society, there were always malcontents and misfits who believed that they should have more than others. They even had the audacity to allege that the Church was in fact only using a fraction of its earnings for charitable purposes, and that without regulation of any kind extremely large sums of money were disappearing into Church coffers. Such miscreants, however, were rooted out by the Doctrine of the Faith Police before they could disrupt the new life the people had built for themselves in the light of God, through the grace of the Lamb.

Dyson had been aware of all these facts from his school and seminary education, but it was nevertheless a strange experience to actually read about them first hand, and from sources outside the Church. He found three digitized copies of old newspaper clippings reporting the very first documented sightings of "the Apparition," as the Lamb had been dubbed.

Uproar at UN General Assembly

The New York Times
December 18, 2010

A meeting of the UN General Assembly in New York City was disrupted yesterday when the figure of a man dressed in garb traditionally attributed to Jesus Christ appeared on the podium behind the speaker, accompanied by what witnesses described as "a cloud of smoke."

Security staff were quick to act. Fearing an attack on the delegate, they stormed the podium in an attempt to apprehend the supposed intruder, only to discover that the figure appeared to be some kind of holographic image and had no solid substance. The hologram was so realistic that even when in its immediate vicinity, security believed they were dealing with a very real threat.

As the extent of the danger could not be established with any degree of certainty, the assembly hall was cleared while experts with scientific equipment moved in to examine the apparition. After exactly two hours, the incident came to an end when the figure suddenly disappeared again without warning as if, as one witness phrased it, "someone turned off a light."

Scientists who examined the apparition at the scene say they as yet have no idea how such a realistic three-dimensional image could have been produced on the UN podium with no ascertainable local source. It is assumed, however, that the whole incident was some kind of elaborate hoax.

Oh my God?!?

The Sun
December 18, 2010

UN delegates were stunned yesterday after sharing a mass religious experience when a vision of Jesus Christ appeared on the speaker's podium in a puff of smoke.

Security staff zoomed into action immediately, attempting to pounce on the apparition. Their efforts were in vain, though, as the apparition was just that: a 3D image; some kind of hologram.

Scientists called to the scene were quick to deny any link with religion. Dr. Larry Dexter, a spokesman for the team of experts said, "This is some kind of scientific phenomenon. There must be an explanation for it; we just haven't found it yet. Personally, I believe it's a hoax by physics majors from the local university, but I must say I'm impressed by their technology."

Now it's over to you. Do you believe that the Son of God has appeared again? Is the end of the world nigh? Or do you think it's just a student stunt? Email us at The Sun and tell us what you think!

Unusual Sighting at Royal Observatory

The Guardian
January 2, 2011

Scores of people, Londoners and tourists alike, witnessed a remarkable event at the Royal Observatory in Greenwich yesterday.

At exactly 12:00 noon local time, Mrs. Doris Hearne, 58, of Fort Lauderdale, Florida, was having her photo taken straddling the Time Line (the so-called Prime Meridian, where east and west meet at 0° longitude) at the Royal Observatory when the figure of a man suddenly appeared in front of her. Eyewitness Mr. Herman Hearne, Mrs. Hearne's husband, who was taking the photo, says the man appeared out of thin air amid a thick cloud of smoke or steam.

The figure had shoulder-length dark hair and was dressed in a white robe and brown leather sandals. Although he appeared solid, even at close quarters, any attempt to touch him met with failure, as objects simply passed through him. This has led to speculation among scientists that the figure was some kind of hologram, particularly as it vanished without trace as suddenly as it had materialized. However, no apparatus for producing holographic images was found on or near the scene.

There has already been talk among Christian groups of the Second Coming of Jesus Christ. According to the Biblical Book of Revelation, this will herald the end of the world, which, according to some sources, is already long overdue.

The event is reminiscent of an occurrence on December 17 last year when the image of a similarly dressed figure appeared at a meeting of the UN General Assembly in New York City. Scientists have been unable to explain that incident.

— «» —

As he read these old reports, Dyson felt the hair on his arms stand up, and a shiver ran down his spine. *The doubters were right! It was just a projection.* And he wondered what the world would be like now if the doubters had been able to find evidence to support their theory all those years ago.

Now, almost seventy years after the first documented appearance of the Apparition, it was no easy task to catalogue the projections. In the early years, nobody had bothered to record the sightings of the Lamb officially, for the simple fact was that they did not know what they were looking for, or indeed that they were looking for anything at all. Therefore, it was highly likely that the majority, or at the very least many, of the weird and wonderful experiences people of the time had ascribed to close encounters with extra-terrestrials, substance abuse, schizophrenia, etcetera, had in reality been a sighting of what Dyson now knew to be the traveler. Other such sightings in all probability had gone unrecorded, as the witnesses did not want to be saddled with the stigma of being a substance abuser or mentally unstable. In later years, after the Church had managed to establish itself, any research that may have cast even a shadow of a doubt upon the divinity of the traveler, or rather the Lamb of God, was considered to be heresy, and as such was punishable by death. It was therefore very rare indeed that anybody possessed the courage and motivation necessary to pursue any research along these lines.

Thus, Dyson's progress was exceedingly slow. Very gradually he began to build up a database of sightings, ordering them chronologically, geographically, and according to the probability of the sighting actually being the traveler. The work was extremely tedious and, he had to admit, the meager results were anything but encouraging. Despite the power of late twenty-first-century computers, they were still only able to process data that was available to them after being entered by human researchers. No data input meant no processing. No processing meant no answer.

The next chronologically reported sightings, numbers three and four, were in Mali in 2022 and Sudan in 2023. Cotton farmers working their fields in Mali were convinced that the prophet Mohammed had appeared to them in a flowing white gown for about two minutes. *Presumably*, Dyson thought, *this is why the Church had never been big on making these sightings generally known: it wasn't Christ the people had reported, but Mohammed.* A handful of reporters had been motivated enough to actually travel across the country from Mali's capital city of Bamako and had possessed the commendable foresight to take along a photo of the apparition that had appeared at the United Nations in 2010. Without knowing that the photo they were being shown was twelve years old, the farmers agreed unanimously that it was, indeed, the same figure.

The story of the fourth sighting, in Sudan, was almost identical. Muslim farmers in the north of the country witnessed an apparition matching the description of the one that had appeared at the UN. They too had identified it as a vision of Mohammed, their prophet, who had appeared to them for approximately two minutes.

Dyson began asking himself why both sightings were on June 12 and one year apart. Why that particular date? Both countries were in Africa and both were predominantly Muslim. In both cases the Apparition appeared to poor farmers. Why?

The next reported sighting was in Mexico in 2027. Again, the witnesses were farmers, but this time they were Spanish-speaking Catholics who identified the Apparition as Jesus Christ. The date was also June 12, though. Dyson was frustrated. Religion and language seemed unimportant to the traveler. Again, why the date, and why farmers? And this time, why a gap of four years between appearances where the gap had previously only been one year?

There was another sighting in Algeria on June 12, 2028. This time it was a group of western tourists — a mixed bunch of Christians, atheists, and assorted others — who witnessed the appearance. All of them, however, were willing to confirm that the apparition they had seen looked like one of the typical paintings or representations they normally associated with Jesus Christ.

The next June 12 appearance, however, was the most sensational since the Apparition had appeared at the UN. Dyson was by this time absolutely furious with himself for his inability to understand why the date was apparently so significant to the traveler. The so-called Lamb of God appeared in the city of New Orleans between Almonaster Avenue and the Inner Harbor Navigation Canal. Although the Lamb appeared for a mere two minutes, hundreds of citizens were able to record the event for posterity on their mobile phones. Huge sums of money exchanged hands between the witnesses and television stations for the rights to broadcast the evidence of the Second Coming of Christ.

A year later, in 2031, and once again on June 12, a house in Castellon de la Plana, Spain, was visited by the Apparition in a street called Camino de la Fileta. Terrified residents called attention to the sighting, which was then witnessed by scores of neighbors, many of them photographing and recording the sighting on their mobile phones.

After a five-year absence, the Apparition appeared again in front of a residential home in East County Line Road, Petersburg, Illinois. Again on June 12; again for two minutes.

Dyson could see no pattern at all in the sightings. He would often lie awake in bed, sometimes angry, sometimes feeling sorry for himself. On more than one occasion he stared at the ceiling in the semi-darkness of his room, tears streaming freely from his eyes and wishing that Rachel were lying beside him.

Oh, God, why did you take her from me? You'd know what to do, wouldn't you, my love? You'd find the pattern.

After weeks of noting an abundance of information, but making no headway at all as far as answering Cardinal Goodfellowe's questions was concerned, Dyson decided to turn to his benefactor for advice over dinner one evening.

"Eminence, when you set me this task, you said you suspected something but you didn't want to influence me or my research. Well, I regret to tell you I haven't really discovered any pattern at all, apart from the fact that he always seems to appear on June 12. Otherwise the whole thing seems so random as far as geography and the year of the appearances are concerned! I was thinking maybe now would be a good time for you to take me into your confidence."

The cardinal smiled at his guest.

"Well, tell me what you have so far, David."

Dyson told Goodfellowe about his research to date, after which the cardinal merely nodded. Then he closed his eyes for a few seconds in contemplation.

"Very well, then," he said at length. He opened his eyes and narrowed them to fix Dyson with an intent stare. "You presume there are gaps in the traveler's visits, don't you?"

"Well, yes. Sometimes there are annual appearances; sometimes there are gaps of four years or more. But it's not only my presumption. There is no data whatsoever on any visitations during these gaps. I checked and double-checked that. Surely there would have been newspaper and net reports if the traveler had actually appeared somewhere."

"Do you remember the rather large photo in my office?" the cardinal enquired. "The one of me as a boy standing next to the Lamb of God?"

"Err, yes, Eminence," Dyson replied quietly, already suspecting what the cardinal was going to say next.

"Have you found any reference to that particular encounter on any net page or in any news broadcast?"

"No," Dyson had to admit, his suspicion confirmed.

"And do you nevertheless believe that it actually happened?"

"Emm, yes, of course. I've seen the photo. Naturally I know photos can be forged, but I also have your word, and I consider you to be a reliable source."

The cardinal bowed his head graciously in Dyson's direction before he replied. "Well then, I think we would both acknowledge, as men of science, that things which are reported do not necessarily have to have happened. And we have now established that things that happened do not necessarily have to have been reported."

After a moment's thought, Dyson believed he knew what the cardinal was getting at.

"So then remind me, Eminence: when and where was your personal encounter with the 'Lamb'?"

"It was in Egypt in 2026."

"Any idea where? I mean a little more precisely."

"I'm afraid my recollection of the exact circumstances is rather vague, David. It was a very long time ago, after all. I do remember that it was a desert trip, though. We were about a hundred kilometers from the town of Al Qahirah, where we were staying at a hotel."

Dyson pulled Janet from his jacket pocket. He had lost his original comPod when he had been arrested, but had given his new instrument the same female voice and the same name. Not wanting to be traced to Cardinal Goodfellowe's house, though, he had refrained from downloading his contact lists from the net. He called up his table of all the appearances he had found.

"Ah," he said a moment later. "So now we have an un-reported sighting which fills one of the gaps; one of the missing years. Do you think the traveler might have appeared every year, and the appearance simply wasn't reported?"

"Well, yes, either seen and not reported, or not seen at all. After all, why would the traveler *want* to be seen if he is not the Second Coming of Jesus Christ? I believe he wanted exactly the opposite, in fact: he wanted to see but not necessarily be seen."

Dyson considered this for a moment. "But why then did he appear in the middle of an institution as important as the UN and in built up areas in towns?"

"Well, I'm only guessing, but perhaps in the nineteenth century, these places were insignificant, and the traveler could not possibly have known that he would materialize in the midst of a crowd of people."

On the one hand it did indeed seem logical that the traveler would not particularly want to attract attention if he were not the Second Coming, but on the other hand, it made Dyson's task even more difficult: now he was looking for undocumented appearances of the traveler.

— «» —

A few days later Dyson discovered something on the net that made him sit back and take a deep breath. He had an epiphany. It was a reported sighting of the Lamb on June 12, 2037. This one was different from all the others, however, in that it occurred on the English Channel. Not on a ship, but floating steadily about a meter above the choppy sea. Hundreds of ferry passengers on the world's busiest waterway had witnessed the sudden appearance and, two minutes later, the disappearance, of a mysterious figure dressed in a white robe, seemingly walking — or perhaps more precisely in this case, standing — on water, as he had been purported to have done more than two thousand years earlier.

Of course! Dyson thought, feeling that the proverbial scales had at last fallen from his eyes. It was like taking a step back and seeing the complete picture for the first time. The traveler had written that he was calibrating his machine. Dyson had previously imagined the scientist working away in his nineteenth-century laboratory adjusting a simple mechanical device and then checking the readings against some sort of handwritten table.

But now he realized that this genius from the past had not merely been performing theoretical calculations; he had actually been projecting his image in a series of experiments so sophisticated that nobody, not even two hundred years later, had been able to repeat them. In order to compile a useful database of coordinates he had carefully selected points all over the globe and had gone about his task with the meticulous precision of a good scientist, methodically charting his progress. Dyson became increasingly excited as he gradually began to understand the full, astounding picture.

He was now relatively certain he had at last discovered the solution that had been eluding him. He now believed he could answer the cardinal's questions.

— «» —

That same evening, at his regular dinner with the cardinal in the luxurious dining room, Dyson triumphantly revealed his findings and his assumptions to Goodfellowe.

"There *is* a pattern," he said, unable to keep his eyes from gleaming.

Cardinal Goodfellowe looked pleased. "Go on," he encouraged.

"The traveler calibrated his machine by plotting a course around the globe. He almost always used coordinates containing a round number of degrees, but no minutes or seconds. For example, the exact coordinates of his appearance in New Orleans in 2030 were 30° 0' 0" N, 90° 0' 0" W. I've just discovered a sighting in the English Channel in 2037: the instruments on the ships that witnessed the appearance put the traveler at 50° 0' 0" N, 0° 0' 0" W. When he appeared on Highway 1 in Western Australia last year, the coordinates were 20° 0' 0" S, 120° 0' 0" E. That explains the gaps in his appearances: around seventy-one per cent of the Earth's surface is covered in water! It doesn't matter to him where he appears, as long as the coordinates are correct. That's why he sometimes appeared for several consecutive years, when he materialized on land, and sometimes remained unseen for years, when he appeared somewhere on the ocean or in remote unpopulated areas of the world. As we have seen, he materializes in an ethereal form, so he's not actually there himself, just as a projection. That's why he seems to float on water, if anyone sees him at all, that is."

"Why, then," the cardinal enquired, intrigued by Dyson's findings, "did he not fine-tune his calibrations by calculating with degrees, minutes, and seconds?"

"I'm pretty sure he did!" Dyson beamed. "But he did it so cleverly that almost nobody noticed! I found a report of a sighting in China at 40° 0' 0" N, 90° 0' 0" E in 2033. There was another sighting in 2069 that didn't fit in at all with the general round-the-world pattern. At first I thought I'd have to go back to the drawing board with my theory, but then I realized what was going on. This was an additional visit using finer, more accurate coordinates. The traveler was homing in on a spot he thought was uninhabited, but on both occasions that I know of, he was observed. This is only a theory of mine; I don't have any evidence of other sightings, but the coordinates of this second visit to the same region were 40° 10' 0" N, 90° 0' 0" E, which means he had altered one of the coordinates by exactly 10'."

"Just a minute," the cardinal interrupted. "How can you be so accurate about coordinates of the second visit if it was only casually perceived by presumably unskilled observers?"

"Well, Eminence, they might have been unskilled, but they were certainly religious. They built a shrine on the exact spot of the appearance. The shrine is still there to this day at those very coordinates."

Satisfied by the explanation, Goodfellowe nodded to indicate that Dyson should continue.

"I'm quite confident that there were other sightings in the same area, but in very diverse years. As the region is still practically uninhabited today, it would be almost impossible to prove my theory if there were no eyewitnesses who had recorded any sightings."

"Excellent work, my son. I suspected something like this myself, but without concrete data there was no way of proving it. One thing, though, which has evaded me completely, is the date. What about the date, David? As you have already mentioned, people have been debating its significance for nearly seventy years now. Have you discovered why the traveler always appears on June 12?"

Not wanting to appear smug, Dyson nevertheless allowed a self-satisfied smile to cross his lips.

"Yes, Eminence. I do believe I have."

The cardinal raised his eyebrows in surprise. "Please, enlighten me, if you would be so kind!"

"Once religion is eliminated from the equation, things become quite simple, really, Eminence. I began thinking of the nature of the traveler and his machine. He can travel through time and space at will. So, if he were working in his laboratory at the end of the nineteenth century, he could travel to January 1, 2100, and remain there for two minutes. In reality, though, he would not have left his actual position: London in the nineteenth century, at his own subjective time of day. He could then travel to December 31, 2099, or to January 2, 2100. He could, in theory, even travel once again to January 1, 2100, perhaps even changing events that happened the first time he was there, merely by appearing there. The point is; he spent perhaps one day of his own subjective time projecting his image across a time span of maybe two thousand years or more.

"He was initially looking for Jerusalem two thousand years ago, and was dressed for the occasion. When his experiment didn't work, he didn't bother to change his clothes, he merely set his instruments for a round the world trip along the lines of longitude. Naturally I cannot even guess at the science involved in accomplishing this, but it would appear he programmed his machine to do just that. Then he needed to perform some fine tuning exercises. I believe by that time he might have realized that people were becoming aware of him. As he didn't want to attract any more attention, he chose some deserted area in China for that purpose, for example.

"And the day on which he actually did this just happened to be June 12. Eminence, I believe there is nothing remotely mystical in this date at all. It could have been March 3 or September 21. The fact is, the traveler just happened to calibrate his instruments on June 12 and set the date to send him backward or forward in time, covering points all around the globe, starting in the morning and finishing that very same afternoon, perhaps in time for tea!"

Believing he had now completed his task, Dyson allowed himself to recline a little in his chair and waited for the cardinal's response. When it finally came, however, it was not the whole-hearted, congratulatory speech Dyson had been expecting.

"So when and where is he going to appear again?" Goodfellowe asked.

Dyson was startled, and sat upright once more.

"I beg your pardon, Eminence?"

"Well, let us for a moment assume that everything you have just told me is correct: that the traveler was indeed calibrating his instruments by projecting his image to precise geographical locations. Do you have information that would lead us to believe that his calibrations suddenly ceased last year with his appearance in Australia? Had he by then completed his calibrations?"

Dyson realized instantly what Goodfellowe meant. *Dammit! Why didn't I think of that?* He could have kicked himself for being so negligent.

"I'm sorry, Eminence, I'm afraid I didn't think of that at all. I have no such information."

"Then I think it might be a good idea for you to find out just when and where he might appear again so we may be ready for him."

"Ready for him?" Dyson was puzzled.

"Well, wouldn't you like to meet the Savior, the Lamb of God, in person, David?"

It was an extremely strange idea for Dyson that he might have an encounter with a man who had probably been dead for two hundred years. For if the traveler had not developed his machine to physically carry his body through time — and nothing in Dyson's research indicated that he had — then his subjective timeline would not have altered, and he would have died some time at the beginning of the twentieth century at the latest. But the cardinal's logic was faultless. With a time machine, even with one which merely projected images and not physical entities through time, this brilliant scientist who had lived two hundred years in Dyson's past could well make (or, from the traveler's perspective, have already made) an appearance in what was now Dyson's future. The whole idea was mind-boggling to Dyson, who still struggled with the notion of two completely different timelines suddenly diverging at one point. He had always imagined timelines, when he gave the matter any thought at all, to be like railway tracks; never the twain shall meet sort of thing. But now he was pondering an event as strange as two railway tracks crisscrossing.

CHAPTER 23

Paraguay, June, 2078

The past few weeks and months had taken their toll on Dyson. There had been the sheer ecstasy he had felt during his brief time with Rachel; the excruciating pain he had suffered in the DFP prison; the joy at being reunited with the woman he had loved more than life itself; and then the complete and utter devastation which had overcome him when she had been taken from him so unexpectedly. It had all been like a rollercoaster of intense emotions, at the end of which he was left feeling nothing but numb emptiness.

He no longer felt as angry as he had done a few weeks ago. He knew that the desire for revenge was a singularly unproductive, futile emotion, but that is what his anger had turned into. They, the Church that is, had robbed him of his faith, his love, and his livelihood. And they had done this while being fully aware of the cold-blooded deception they were employing; a deception affecting more than half the population of the world. Dyson could now see the Church through the eyes of one of those insipid dissidents he had for so many years decried as vile heretics. Once the sense of awe had been removed — the mysticism surrounding his beliefs — he could see the Church of the Second Coming for what it really was: nothing more than a brutal dictatorship that oppressed its opponents with imprisonment, torture, and murder. Gone were his oh-so-noble notions of piecing together the complete historical truth behind the development of civilization and of one day presenting this, his life's work, to the world. For David Dyson had discovered a more sinister, a more urgent truth, which needed to be told, and told quickly if more innocent people were to be saved from this brutal regime, this troop of bullies and liars.

Only one slight chance remained. If his calculations were wrong, then he had wasted a lot of time and money — not his own money, but money taken, actually stolen, from the Church — on a pointless journey that would not bring him any closer to a solution and would certainly result in his death if the Church caught him again. If he was right, however, he would soon meet a genuine time traveler; not only that, but a man who had altered the course of history in a more fundamental and longer-lasting fashion than Julius Caesar or Napoleon or Hitler could ever have dreamed of doing, albeit in this case involuntarily.

And if he managed to meet this time traveler, Dyson would attempt to alter the course of history once again. Or should he say, preserve the course of history as it should have developed if the time traveler had not interfered? Or should he say...? Well, *what* should he say? Who is to say what will, would, might happen if the time traveler were stopped or if the lie were allowed to continue? How could he stop something that had already happened? What about those who had become victims of the Church's brutal system? Would they miraculously come back to life? What about Rachel? But if it hadn't been for the Church, he would never have met Rachel in the first place. Or would he? Dyson's head started to spin, as it had done more and more frequently over the last few weeks. *Probably best not to spend too much time thinking about it*, he told himself, yet again.

The money taken from the Church had been transferred to a special credit card by Cardinal Goodfellowe, who was the only member of the team of conspirators who had the authority to create such an account without its registration with, and without receiving permission from, the CFA (Church Financial Administration). It was a gamble that could cost him his life if anyone outside the circle of conspirators ever found out about it, but Goodfellowe said, "I have spent the greater part of my adult life searching for the truth behind this matter. I refuse to let one insignificant misdemeanor stand in my way when I am so close to finding it, no matter what the cost may be to myself."

Dyson had used the special credit card to book a plane ticket from New York City to Mexico City. From there he had booked a seat with a small local airline to fly him to Paraguay. The card was programmed in such a way that the service providers would indeed be paid for their services, but their bank statements would show that the money had been credited to their accounts in twenty small payments on twenty different days and had come from at least twenty different sources purchasing anything from stationery to spare parts for machines. Of course, it played havoc with the accounting systems of the companies involved, but at least they didn't actually lose any money in the transactions: they just found it impossible to tally their accounts electronically and had to revert to the age-old method of manual accounting to rectify the errors. Such was the influence of the Church that payments, if necessary, could be made completely anonymously; truly a miracle in this day and age.

After landing at an inconspicuous airfield in Paraguay that morning, Dyson had hired a small electric car and driven to a cheap hotel off the beaten track where he could hide from anyone who might have been tailing him, although he was quite certain he hadn't been followed. Parking the rental car in a courtyard behind the shabby-looking brick building, Dyson pressed a button to open the door of the vehicle, and was left gasping for breath when he was hit by a wave of hot air. Grabbing his small backpack, he hurried around the outside of the hotel to the front entrance, expecting to enter a cool, air-conditioned lobby. The front door of the hotel, however, stood wide open; a sure sign that there was no air conditioning.

Disappointed, but so weary it did not matter anymore, Dyson walked up to the reception desk, already sweating profusely from the humidity, his soaking wet shirt clinging uncomfortably to his back. A small 3D monitor perched on the desk was showing what looked like a corny soap opera in Spanish. A scruffy-looking man who could have been anywhere between seventy and ninety, sitting on a simple plastic chair, was so engrossed in this mind-numbing distraction that he did not even bother to look up when Dyson entered. The old man, dressed in a pair of boxer shorts and a grubby t-shirt that might once have been white, was basking in the relatively cool air provided by a small electric fan that looked even older than he did. Dyson assumed he was the owner of the hotel, but the man just muttered, "Si?" in a bored, gravelly voice, obviously irritated by the disturbance.

Dyson was half expecting to have to show some form of identification and fingered the false passport in the pocket of his jeans, which identified him as Dennis Quent, a university professor of archaeology from Manchester.

"I'd like a room please. For one night. Single."

Not taking his eyes away from the screen, which was blaring away at an incredibly loud volume in rapid Spanish, the owner shoved a tatty, old-fashioned book with pages made of real dead-tree paper across the desk.

"Sign," he croaked. "Hondred feefty dollar."

"Credit card?" Dyson asked, hopefully.

"Hondred feefty dollar," the owner replied tersely, his eyes still glued to the monitor.

The three words were simple enough, but the tone of his voice managed to clarify the fact that he would only accept cash, that he was not used to "welcoming" gringos to his establishment, and that this particular time of day was not an ideal moment to disturb him. Looking up for the briefest of moments, he eyed his new guest for the first time before turning back to his soap. To Dyson's relief there was no indication of suspicion or alarm in the man's dull old eyes.

With a resigned shrug, Dyson scribbled his false name in the book and with some difficulty peeled three fifty-dollar notes from the wad he had stuffed into his pocket. Having used a credit card to pay for everything from a carton of milk to a three-piece suit for almost all his adult life, using cash was totally alien to him. He was thus forced to examine each bill individually to ensure that it was indeed the denomination he needed. He had also been concerned that someone might recognize his passport as a forgery, but it seemed as though the old man probably couldn't have cared less what name

Dyson used as long as he paid "hondred feefty dollar" for his room in advance and in cash.

After Dyson had dutifully laid the money on the stained, cracked plastic counter, the owner made no move to get up to give Dyson a key or show him to his room, so Dyson cleared his throat meaningfully. A grunt ensued from the old man and, grudgingly, he rose laboriously from his chair. His movements were so agonizingly slow that Dyson could have sworn he actually heard the man's bones creaking. Eyeing Dyson accusingly, presumably for making him move, he grunted and pointed a disgustingly dirty fingernail at the stairs across the lobby.

"You come, meester," he croaked.

At a painfully slow pace, the sweaty, malodorous owner then led Dyson up two flights of stairs to his room. Dyson almost gagged when the man opened the door. The stench was so overpowering that he turned his head to the corridor to grab a deep breath. The room was a cockroach-infested box, also with no air-conditioning. It was appalling, truly filthy, but it was the only hotel which was anywhere near his destination, and it was so obscure that there was practically no chance at all of him being detected here. If his calculations were right, his rendezvous would take place at precisely 8:00 p.m. in the middle of nowhere, so he simply had to bide his time as best he could until then.

In the hotel room, Dyson began to work out roughly where he had to go. He had Janet display a map of the area, on which he could see that his destination was a relatively flat grassy plain. At around two o'clock he was lying, exhausted from the heat, on his creaky old bed, dozing, when he heard a loud altercation coming from outside. Peering cautiously out the open second-story window he saw two men in black t-shirts and black trousers arguing loudly with the owner of the hotel in the courtyard. All three were speaking Spanish; a language Dyson didn't understand. Nevertheless, something told him the sudden appearance of these two men could not be a mere coincidence. Judging by their attire, they were obviously non-locals, and they had appeared in this god-forsaken area when he himself had only just arrived.

Although Dyson could not make out who the strangers were, as they had their backs to him, one of them did seem somehow familiar, even from so far away. Dyson craned his neck out of the window in an attempt to get a closer look at the men and suddenly felt a sickening, sinking feeling in the pit of his stomach.

This sinking feeling turned to panic when he clearly heard one of the strangers say "Dyson." Not only that, he recognized the voice. He had never heard it speaking Spanish before, but it was definitely the voice of Simon Evans. Dyson's mind reeled. No, not Simon. Anyone else, but not Simon. Surely Simon would — could — never betray him. They had been *friends,* for heaven's sake!

The hotel owner was becoming agitated. Dyson had given a false name, but how many other gringos turned up at his hotel unexpectedly? Obviously not wanting any trouble from the two newcomers, one of whom looked like he could, and probably would, cause him some serious damage if he wanted to, the owner suddenly pointed toward the window of Dyson's room. The two strangers turned to look where the man's grubby finger was pointing. There was a brief moment of eye contact between Simon Evans and David Dyson, whose face turned suddenly pale as he realized he had been spotted. Grabbing his backpack, he bolted, stumbling, from the room. Charging down one flight of stairs, he heard shouting from below. His pursuers were now speaking English.

"Stay there!" Evans called to the other man. "I'll go up!"

Knowing he had no chance against two of them, unarmed as he was, Dyson was desperate. Footsteps came trampling up the bare wooden staircase from the ground floor. Just before they reached the landing, Dyson crashed through a second-story door he had chosen at random, assuming the room behind it looked out onto the courtyard at the rear of the hotel. Luckily for him, the building was so old and in such a state of disrepair that the ancient wooden doorframe splintered easily, as he had suspected it would. Dyson lurched into the room, off balance, and landed heavily on top of the door. The impact echoed along the corridor. The room was empty, but he could now hear the footsteps of his pursuer running swiftly and purposefully along the corridor in his direction.

Dyson knew he was playing his last card. If they caught him now, he was finished anyway. No time to check if he could work the foreign mechanism to open it, or even if it would open at all. He hurled his backpack at the window. The pane of glass exploded and a thousand pieces of shattered window tinkled onto the courtyard outside. Peering out briefly, he remembered all the vids he had ever seen in which someone had to jump from a height and was told to roll on landing. Even so, the distance to the ground looked much more perilous in real life than it did in those cheesy vids. Having no other choice, he swung himself through the opening, tearing a trouser leg on a shard of glass, but fortunately not cutting himself. He bent his knees and prepared for the roll, but the impact was much harder than he had anticipated. He fell badly on his left side, which knocked the wind out of him, then rolled onto his back, gasping. For the briefest of moments he lay there, dazed. Seconds later a surprised Evans stared down at him from the window he had leaped through.

"David," he called. "It's me, Simon. Let's talk. We don't want to hurt you, but we can't let you do this. Look at it from our point of view, David. Just stop and we'll figure something out."

Seeing that Dyson remained unimpressed, and was now starting to get his breath back, Evans tried a different tack.

"David, listen to me! Cardinal Goodfellowe has been arrested. It's all over. We know everything. We've been monitoring you since you went to Cardinal di Galassini's house. Please, David, I'm begging you. I don't want to see you get hurt! Let's figure something out together! Surely we can come to some arrangement. We could even help Cardinal Goodfellowe if you give yourself up and talk to us! Please, David, listen to me!"

Dyson was deeply shocked to learn that they had been watching him for so long. Apparently they had just been biding their time, waiting for him to betray his intentions and his compatriots before springing the trap. He had actually been at their mercy for months, and they had just played along, allowing him to reveal to them the identities of his friends and allies. Dyson was now extremely worried about what they might do to his benefactor, Goodfellowe. He had always believed the cardinal was far too powerful a figure for them to attack, but it was obvious now that they would stop at nothing to protect their secret. They would probably murder the cardinal and say he had died peacefully in his sleep, then give him a state funeral with full Church honors, just to keep up appearances. What was it Mrs. McBride had called them? "Hypocritical Church bastards!"

Dyson didn't even bother to reply to Evans' insincere pleas and scrabbled painfully to his feet, clutching his injured side as he did so.

"Round the back!" Evans screamed to his companion. His motivation, however, did not appear to be so great that he felt the need to follow his now absconding prey through the broken window.

Dyson snatched his backpack from the hot, round cobblestones and limped toward his rental car as fast as his injuries and the uneven surface would permit. Fumbling clumsily with the infra-red key, he managed to get the vehicle open and threw himself inside. His whole body was shaking like a leaf, his heart pounding, sweat dripping from every pore. On the section of the windshield display that showed the scene behind his vehicle, he noticed another car parked several meters behind his own. It was too new to belong here in this godforsaken wilderness, he reasoned. He was right. Evans' muscular companion came hurtling round one corner of the building. He scanned the courtyard behind the hotel, looking for a man running away. At first he was disappointed, then he spotted Dyson in his car. Grinning maliciously, the DFP man began to run in Dyson's direction.

Without really thinking about it, Dyson put his car into reverse and slammed his foot hard on the accelerator. The vehicle lurched violently backward and crashed loudly into the other, pushing it into the brick wall of the hotel. With any luck he would have damaged the battery of the other car's electric motor, thus immobilizing his enemies. It was a long shot but it comforted him somewhat that they might not be able to follow him now. Throwing his own car into drive, Dyson sped away from his now cursing pursuer.

— «» —

After driving at high speed for almost half an hour, constantly glancing nervously at the monitor displaying the view behind his vehicle, Dyson allowed himself a brief respite. He got out of the car to take stock of the situation, the heat outside the controlled environment once again hitting him with a powerful blast when he opened the door. A cursory check revealed that nothing seemed to be broken, but his entire body ached horribly. There was a nasty bump on the back of his head that hadn't registered until now, and his left arm was badly bruised in several places. Also, his hands were still shaking, but other than that he seemed to be all right.

A glance at his comPod screen told him it was now 2:45 p.m., so he still had a lot of time to kill. He wasn't going to risk going to another town, though. He'd had the foresight to pack a few bottles of water and some cookies in his backpack, so he returned to the car to snack on these, quickly closing the door to keep the air inside cool. The heat outside was sweltering. Despite the invisible coating of microscopic solar cells covering the entire body of the car, using the air-conditioning at full blast still meant a severe drain on the battery, so Dyson was wary of letting it run continually.

As he had fled blindly from his pursuers, he now had no idea where he was or where he had to go from here, so he inserted his comPod into a standardized holder provided on the car's dashboard. The interface gave his personal device full control over all features of the car.

"Janet, I'd like to go to the following global coordinates: 20°0'0"S and 60°0'0"W."

"Certainly, David," his electronic assistant replied, sounding as calm and chirpy as ever. "We are currently 126 kilometers from the target and need to go northwest from here. Would you like me to show you?"

Damn, Dyson thought, realizing he had fled in the wrong direction, moving him further away from his target.

On second thought, he mused, *that might have wrong-footed Simon, assuming, of course, that Simon didn't already know where he was heading.* "Yes, please, Janet."

Instantly the view through the windshield was overlaid with a semi-transparent 3D map of the immediate vicinity, indicating in green the route he should take.

"Would you like me to drive, David?"

"Oh, yes please, Janet," Dyson answered, who realized now that the encounter with his would-be assailants had taken more out of him than he would have liked to admit.

"Do you have any special wishes for the journey?" the pleasant female voice of his electronic companion enquired.

"Not really… Oh, wait, yes. Could you play me something by Bach? Organ concerto. Low volume. And dim the windows, please."

"Of course, David."

With that, his comPod searched the global net and found a number of Bach organ concertos timed to roughly coincide with the duration of their journey. Simultaneously Janet caused the microscopic photosensitive cells embedded in the DuraGlas windows of the car to become opaque, thus blocking out the blinding sunlight, and proceeded to steer the car toward their destination, ensuring that it did not exceed the local speed limits, which would have drawn unwanted attention to them.

Dyson pressed a button on the dashboard and reclined the driver's seat into sleep mode, and for the next hour and a half he was dead to the world.

He was awakened by Janet, who had realized that he was asleep when he didn't respond to her. She switched on the car's interior lighting.

"David, wake up… David…. Wake up, David."

"Huh? Janet?"

"David, we have arrived at our destination. You were sleeping. It is now 4:18 p.m. The outside temperature is thirty-eight degrees Celsius."

Dyson rubbed his eyes and drew his seat back to a sitting position.

"Could you clear the windshield, please, Janet?"

Immediately, the car's windshield became transparent and Dyson was temporarily blinded by the bright sunlight that flooded into the car. He was looking out onto an empty, relatively flat, grassy plain.

"Where are we?"

"We are at 20°0'0"S and 60°0'0"W, as you requested, David," his electronic assistant replied pleasantly.

There was an almost four-hour wait ahead of him. The car was in the middle of flat, scrubby land strewn with thin trees. The sparse foliage offered practically no protection from the sun beating mercilessly down on it. Despite the solar cells covering the vehicle, without the additional cooling provided by air intakes while the vehicle was in motion, if he kept the air-conditioning on, the battery would be dead in…he looked at the display on the dashboard…two hours.

"Janet, we need to find shade," he said.

— «» —

Dyson's request, "We need to find shade," would have been an impossible problem for a computer of an earlier age to solve. Janet, however, was far more sophisticated than her primitive ancestors. She was programmed to understand that "we" meant machine and owner, i.e. the comPod currently called Janet and the human owner currently called David Dyson. Janet also understood the verbs "need" and "find" and processed them appropriately, in a matter of milliseconds running through all the meanings and contexts which could be found in her own onboard database as well as on the global net, testing them and adapting them to the situation. The problem for computers in the past would have been the word "shade." But Janet ran through all available global web dictionaries, thesauri, wikis, blogs, splogs, theses, encyclopedias, dictopedias, netpedias, etcetera. There were dozens of definitions and nuances of the word "shade", which Janet also interpreted in a matter of milliseconds. *What kind of shade, what degree of shade, for what purpose should shade be found?*

"We need to find shade as shelter from the sun," the comPod said, to confirm Dyson's request. "David, there is a group of trees 2.4 kilometers east of here. Shall I take us there and use the shade to protect us from the sun?"

"Yes, Janet," Dyson replied with relief. "Please do that."

When they arrived at the small grove of trees a few minutes later, Dyson took control of the car and parked it strategically to give them shade for the next few hours without having to move it.

"Janet, we have a long wait ahead of us. While the outside temperature is still over thirty degrees Celsius, I'd like you to keep the temperature inside the car at twenty-two degrees."

"Yes, David."

"And would you read to me?"

"Of course, David. What would you like to hear?"

A wry smile formed on Dyson's lips. Despite the fact that most people considered it hardly in keeping with his position as a man of the cloth, he had always been somewhat of a science fiction fan.

"What about *The Time Machine* by H. G. Wells?" he said.

"Ah, one of the classics," Janet replied, and downloaded the book from the ether.

"Just one thing, though, Janet. Make sure I'm awake at 7:30 p.m."

"All right, David." And she began to read: "'The Time Traveler (for so it will be convenient to speak of him) was expounding a recondite matter to us...'"

After Janet had been reading for ten minutes, Dyson found his eyelids were becoming heavier and heavier, and he soon fell into the deep sleep of exhaustion.

He woke just after six o'clock. Janet had long since stopped reading after registering his heavy, even breathing.

"What time is it?" he enquired in a thick, croaky voice.

"It is 6:08 p.m.," his electronic companion replied.

Dyson was now famished, but all he had was the bottled water and a few packets of cookies left from the stash in his backpack. He had not been planning on leaving the hotel until just before it was time to rendezvous with the traveler, expecting either to eat there or at some place a little more appetizing in the same village. Having to make do with these meager provisions, he had Janet display news programs on the windshield of the car, hoping to hear any news of Cardinal Goodfellowe. He did not have to wait very long before America's CNN, the Church National Network, made an announcement:

"After rescue services were called to a huge explosion at a large residence in downtown Manhattan this morning, the United States was shocked and saddened to learn that it was at the home of Cardinal Brian Goodfellowe."

The piece was accompanied by footage of Goodfellowe's home in flames, ineffectual fire trucks obviously powerless to prevent the building from being burned to the ground.

"NYPD detectives and DFP agents at the scene say that three bodies have so far been recovered from the blaze, which was thought to have been caused by a gas explosion. The deceased are thought to be Cardinal Goodfellowe, his housekeeper Maria Cervantes, and a visiting priest of the Church of the Second Coming, Father Giacomo Fiorello. Cardinal Goodfellowe, originally from England, had been the head of the important Church Archives department in New York City for many years. Church officials have already said that a memorial service will be held next Tuesday, after which the cardinal will be interred with full honors befitting such a stalwart of the Church."

Dyson felt numb. He realized with an air of finality that he was now quite alone in the world. He knew he would never be able to return to the USA: even his fake identity was now probably compromised, as was his Church credit card. He had nowhere to go. Furiously he slammed his fist onto the center of the steering wheel. Taking a deep breath to calm himself a little, he forced himself to think clearly. He had been watching Church-doctored international news, so he asked Janet to find an English-language news channel from a country not in the grip of his former employer.

"I'm very sorry, David: there are seventy-six television channels in Paraguay, but they are all affiliated with the Church of the Second Coming. I am currently unable to receive any satellite signals from other channels."

Bastards, Dyson thought. *They're blocking everything else.*

The only other alternative for entertainment in English was for Janet to read to him again. They passed the time like this until 7:05 p.m., when Janet suddenly stopped reading and mentioned, quite casually, "David, I'm picking up a comPod signal 2.2 kilometers from our current location." Dyson's heart sank.

"Is it moving? Which way?"

"If the device broadcasting the signal continues to follow the dirt tracks through the scrubland, it will reach us in approximately nine minutes."

"Can the other comPod see you, Janet?"

"At my current settings, yes, David."

Oh crap! Dyson hadn't thought of that. "Janet, conceal your signal now!"

"Signal concealed, David."

He waited a few seconds. "What is the status of the other comPod now?"

"The speed of the vehicle in which the other comPod is travelling has been reduced."

"And the direction?"

"The direction is the same."

Of course, Dyson contemplated. *Out here in the wilderness there's only one dirt track.* "Janet, calculate a random course for us to reach the target coordinates at 7:50 p.m. Do not use the dirt track, do not drive in one direction for more than one hundred and fifty meters, and make sure we do not come into direct contact with the other comPod."

He had hardly finished his last sentence when Janet replied, "I will do my best, David, but the other comPod has switched off its tracking signal. I am now unaware of its position."

Dyson's comPod steered his vehicle through thickets of scrub and stumpy trees that scraped savagely along the sides of the car. As per his orders, the vehicle suddenly changed direction frequently in an effort to confuse his pursuers, but even though the car lurched this way and that in an apparently random path, Dyson somehow knew the game was up. If they were already this close, there was no way he could realistically shake them off now. They would probably have satellites guiding them to him, as he was, after all, the only other vehicle in this entire area at the moment.

"The target is one hundred and twenty meters to the west, David."

Dyson stopped the car and walked the rest of the way, as he wasn't sure what would happen if the time traveler were to materialize in the middle of his vehicle. Taking his backpack from the car and fastening the jacket he'd had the foresight to bring along against the now chilly wind, he proceeded in the indicated direction. Janet's display showed him that the local time was 7:35 p.m. The pale moonlight on the now colorless grassy plain made the terrain look like an alien planet; it was indeed a far cry from the hustle and bustle of New York City to which he had gradually become accustomed.

Well, Rachel, here I am, he thought. *I'd give anything if you could only be here with me now, my love. I have no idea what I'm doing here, or even if anything is going to happen at all, but I'm sure you'd have some common sense advice for me.* Dyson became lost in his reveries for a while, but before he could become too melancholy, he glanced at his watch and realized it was almost time.

At precisely 8:00 p.m., the air about five meters in front of him began to shimmer vaguely. He could still see the grassy plain through it, but the plain was distorted. At first the mysterious effect was about the size of a football and seemed to hover about a meter off the ground. A few seconds later the random shimmering that surrounded the core of the object began to pulsate rhythmically. It became solid and grew to the size and shape of a man. When the traveler was fully materialized, Dyson lowered his arm, which he had instinctively raised to protect his eyes, unsure as to how the traveler would materialize or if there would be any danger to bystanders such as a blinding light or some kind of explosion. Although there had been no reports of such dangers in the accounts he had read, Dyson worked on the tried and trusted principle of better safe than sorry.

After the accompanying cloud of steam had dissipated, Dyson's first impulse was to drop to his knees and weep, for there, standing before him, was Jesus Christ, the Lamb of God! All the paintings, all the photos he had ever seen were representations of the man now standing a matter of meters away from him.

No! he told himself. *This is just a man!* It was a truly incredible experience, though. The figure before him was instantly recognizable as the Jesus from the Bible. He had seen this figure his whole life; nailed to crosses in churches, depicted in thousands of paintings all over the world, even recorded live on television. Dyson knew this person. He had prayed to him all his life. Dyson knew him by his shoulder-length black hair, his straggly beard, the white gown and the simple sandals. It was him! Dyson made a fresh effort to pull himself together and walked a few paces closer to the Apparition. Even upon closer inspection there was absolutely no difference between the serene figure standing before him and the one Dyson had seen in hundreds of pictures, including the one depicting a youthful Brian Goodfellowe. As Dyson had predicted, the Apparition had not aged as much as a day, despite his appearances stretching over so many years.

For his part, the traveler seemed surprised to see anyone out here in the wilds. It was not too unusual for him to be seen, but the gentleman now standing before him appeared to have been waiting there for the very purpose of meeting him. A quizzical expression crossed the traveler's face: a fellow scientist, perhaps?

Opening his backpack, Dyson removed a sheet of paper and held it up to the figure before him. "I KNOW YOU ARE A TIME TRAVELER."

The traveler smiled kindly and blinked his eyes to acknowledge that he had read and understood Dyson's message. His theory had been correct: a fellow scientist. A colleague from the future.

Dyson let the paper fall silently to the ground, revealing the next sheet, on which was written in the same bold capital letters: "YOUR APPEARANCE HAS CHANGED EVERYTHING." At this, the smile on the face of the ethereal figure faded. He looked very surprised indeed; upset, even. With his elbows still tucked in at his sides, he lifted his palms so that they faced Dyson, and raised his eyebrows.

Suddenly two bright lights illuminated the scene around Dyson and the traveler. At first Dyson believed it had something to do with the traveler; that he was about to dematerialize already. But no, it was the artificial glow of car headlights targeted at the place where Dyson was standing. Turning to look over his shoulder, Dyson saw the silhouetted shapes of Evans and his companion from the hotel. They had apparently waited for a new car and had then followed him here. But how? *They must have known about the coordinates.*

"Don't move, David, I'm begging you. *Please* don't move."

"What do you want, Simon?"

"You know what I want. We can't let you interfere. We don't know what will happen if you interfere. Just drop whatever you're holding and stand still. For the love of God, David, please do what I ask. Please, I really don't want you to get hurt. I couldn't forgive myself if we had to harm you. But the Holy Church is at stake here. Our whole way of life! Don't you see that?"

There was a pause that seemed to last an eternity while Evans waited for some kind of response from Dyson. When none was forthcoming, Evans continued: "Look, David, we really can't risk everything just for one individual. You know I could never personally harm you. You're my friend, for God's sake! But my companion here has no such scruples, David. He doesn't know you. He doesn't care about you like I do. He is under strict orders not to allow you to communicate with the Lamb."

Dyson had intended to ignore Evans and simply carry on pleading with the traveler, but he just couldn't leave Evans in the belief that the Church was founded on anything but a lie.

"Simon, you must know as well as I do that this man standing here in front of me is NOT the Lamb of God! He is a time traveler. As impossible as that might seem, that is what he is. Nothing more, nothing less. Surely they've told you the truth!"

After a brief pause, Evans replied. His voice seemed to have lost all urgency; he was now calm and calculating: "Yes, David, I know what's going on. Did you really think I was so naïve that I could still believe in the myth after all your research?"

He knows everything I've discovered, Dyson thought. "But how can you possibly defend this sham? People are being murdered just because they know the truth!"

"Truth is a dangerous commodity, David. Too much of it can be fatal."

Dyson could hardly believe what he was hearing. His friend, the gentle Simon Evans, was telling him in so many words that the Church would murder anyone who found out that the "Lamb of God" was merely a human time traveler.

"But how can *you*, a man of the cloth, possibly condone murder?"

"Oh, David, you really *do* think I'm naïve, don't you? A man of the 'cloth'? What cloth would that be, then? Really now!"

"So you're saying you don't even believe in the priesthood now?"

"Of course I believe in the priesthood! As long as it serves my interests, as it has been doing all these years now, I don't see any reason to disband the goddamn priesthood!"

Dyson knew that if he stopped now, nothing would change. They would kill him for certain; maybe not here, not today, but they would kill him sooner or later. And the Church would carry on. Innocent people would be conned into believing a lie so that the Church could hold onto its absolute power in so many regions around the world. If anyone refused to accept the lie, they would be tortured. If they then still refused to accept Church dogma after being subjected to "corrective social measures", they would be murdered. This was his last chance. It was now or never. And he had nothing more to live for: this was something he had realized quite some time ago. In an attempt to buy a little more time and hopefully distract Evans, he called over his shoulder once again to his former colleague.

"How did you find me out here, Simon?"

"This is a Church-run country, David. All the cars here are fitted with tracking devices. I would have thought you knew that."

Dyson was not interested in the answer. Time was running out. Based on previous reports of the traveler's appearances, he never stayed very long in any one place during the calibration phase of his travels. While Evans was talking, he raised another sign to the traveler's face.

"PEOPLE HAVE DIED BECAUSE OF YOU."

A loud bang tore violently through the silence on the grassy plain. Something pushed Dyson from behind, causing him to take a step forward. Confused, he looked up into the face of the time traveler, which was suddenly frozen in horror, staring at Dyson's chest. Dyson looked down and saw blood pouring from a gaping wound. He sank to his knees, then collapsed sideways onto the cold earth. As Dyson's consciousness slipped very quickly into oblivion, the wind blew away the sheet of paper he had shown to the traveler. There was one last sheet still clutched in David Dyson's dead hand.

"PLEASE STOP!"

If Dyson had been able to see, he would have observed the time traveler raising his eyes to the night sky as if imploring the heavens to rectify the tragedy unfolding before him. The time traveler's body, unable to move very much in the confines of his machine, and therefore unable to move as a projection, was wracked with violent, silent sobs. Tears streamed down his cheeks as he looked down at the man at his feet and the sheets of paper the man had shown him.

In the distance, two men in black coats had appeared out of the gloom, becoming clearly visible only when they reached the light of the flashlight still held by the man now lying dead on the ground. One of the men carried some sort of weapon, still recognizable to the time traveler as a rifle as they had in his day, but far sleeker, far more deadly.

"Murderers!" he screamed, but his projection made no sound. The time traveler willed himself to disappear from this place. Overcome with grief and guilt for the death he had obviously caused this evening and the untold number of deaths he had apparently caused at other times, in other places, he wished, not for the first time, that he had never continued with his experiments when he'd had his first doubts.

The two men in black coats had now stopped in their tracks about ten meters from the projection. The larger of the two men, the one holding the weapon, seemed dumbstruck, his mouth open, but not daring or able to speak. He was, after all — so he believed — gazing upon the Savior of the human race, the Son of God. He had just committed the ultimate sin of murder before the eyes of Jesus Christ himself. The smaller, fitter-looking man looked alternately at the traveler and at the dead man lying prone on the ground. He shook his head slowly, sadly.

"I really didn't want it to end like this, David."

Seconds later, the Savior, the Lamb of God, the Apparition, vanished into thin air. The only sound which broke the ensuing eerie silence was the clatter of the rifle as it slipped out of the awed gunman's hand and fell unceremoniously to the ground.

CHAPTER 24

Liverpool
England, 2075

David Dyson's whole life had been leading up to this moment. He felt a warm glow inside, remembering the faces of his proud, aging parents watching him being awarded his doctorate certificate by the Vice Chancellor of the University of Liverpool.

He had always been somewhat of a prodigy, never having to actually sit down and learn; simply soaking up knowledge and storing it as his teachers had imparted it to him, excelling at every subject at school. Whenever anyone had asked him, even at a very early age, what he wanted to do when he grew up, he would invariably reply, "I want to learn all about the history of the world!" This passion had led him to eventually study history and archaeology at his hometown university in Liverpool, culminating most recently in his doctorate in history.

Yes, he had been a high flyer. His parents, who had never been particularly wealthy, had leaped at the opportunity for their only child to be educated at a local private school after winning a scholarship at the tender age of ten. They had been delighted when letters from the headmaster, full of praise for their son's academic abilities and strength of character, had arrived at their small flat. And when their son had graduated from that school as the student of the year, the pride felt by Mr. and Mrs. Dyson had known no bounds.

And now he had returned to his alma mater as a senior lecturer. Although it was Saturday, and he was not officially meant to start work until the following Monday, Dyson had not been able to wait to see his new workplace. He had shown his pass at reception, taken the elevator, and now stood before the door of his new office, secretly thrilled to see the nameplate already attached to the wall, announcing that this was the office of *Doctor* David Dyson.

Taking a deep breath and pulling the plastic disc from a pocket of his pale blue jacket, he held it up to the small white box on the wall. A discreet beep issued from the box and a small orange light turned green for a second. Almost simultaneously there was a click from the locking mechanism of the door, which Dyson pushed gently open to reveal the interior of his new office.

After briefly surveying his new domain, a three by four meter room on the second floor, with a view of Liverpool's round Catholic cathedral, Dyson sat down on the simple artificial leather swivel chair behind the gray plastic-coated desk. Placing his clasped hands behind his head, he leaned back and swung his feet up onto the desk. He closed his eyes and thought, *Does it get any better than this?*

The last six months had been the best in his life. He'd had a few girlfriends up to now, but none of them had turned out to be anything really serious. Six months ago, however, he had met his soul mate, Rachel, an American journalist who had been in England researching a story about the Anglican Church for a magazine article. After what they call a whirlwind romance, they had flown to New York, Rachel's hometown, and married there after a courtship of just four months. Of course, his best friend Pete had come all the way from an archaeological dig in Israel to be his best man.

Returning to England after their honeymoon, Dyson continued working as a lecturer at the University of Leicester. Then, shortly after he had been awarded his doctorate, the position of senior lecturer in History had become vacant at Liverpool University. Rachel had received job offers from several news broadcasting companies she had applied to, and had eventually accepted a position at the BBC. *How did that old saying go? 'Today is the first day of the rest of your life.'* He had never really thought much about this saying in the past, but for Doctor David Dyson, it looked like the rest of his life was going to be very good indeed.

Over the years Dyson was able to pursue his research to his heart's content, always finding students willing to assist him, partly for the extra credit and partly because they wanted to share in his dream of unraveling the mysteries of the past and piecing together the great puzzle. And apart from anything else, Dr. Dyson was a pretty cool guy.

CHAPTER 25

Liverpool University
England, 2107

The door scanner of Dyson's office indicated that there was a student wishing to enter. A brief look at the monitor revealed it was Jana Mutlu, a half-Egyptian, half-English student who was doing some post-graduate field research for him in nineteenth-century British government requisition orders. The subject was horribly dull, but one of Dyson's latest projects was to fill small holes wherever he could find them and Jana was a keen student.

"Come in, Jana," he called.

The door opened and a pretty, brown-skinned young woman in her mid-twenties clutching a plastic folder entered Dyson's office.

"Take a seat," Dyson offered. "What can I do for you today, Jana?"

The young woman smiled and sat down. Dyson was a popular lecturer. Despite his seniority in both age and academic achievement, he always treated his students with respect, and was looked upon as a guru of history, as well as a wise and kindly grandfather figure by his students. Jana offered him the folder.

"Something weird has turned up, Professor, and we don't know what to do with it. I made a copy for you."

Dyson took the folder, which contained one sheet of extremely thin but sturdy biodegradable plastic; an eco-foil. It was a copy of a yellowed piece of real paper, ragged at two of its corners and hand-written. Dyson dated the writing as being typical of the late nineteenth century, so it was in keeping with the period Jana and her fellow field workers were supposed to be researching. The handwriting was unusually neat, as if the author had carefully considered every word before writing it. Dyson read:

I am standing at what one would most likely refer to as a watershed. Indeed, were one to be of a more dramatic nature, one might also go so far as to designate it as the proverbial knife-edge. Science, technology, intelligence, wisdom: no matter by what name it is known to mankind, it is a God-given force which puts great power into the hands of imperfect men; a power with which they are, with their base emotions such as greed and vanity, most ill-equipped to deal. For with great power also comes choice; the choice to do good, or the choice to do evil.

Although I now realize that the experiments on which I have been working over the past few months have been tantamount to blasphemy — meddling in God's natural universe — I know in my heart that I am not an evil man. I have indeed been privy to certain divine insights that have altered not only my beliefs in God Almighty and the afterlife, but also my entire outlook on this mortal sojourn on the Lord's earth.

I have seen great good, and, I fear, great evil. I have seen things of a bizarre and frightening nature; things which would send a man of lesser substance directly into a state of madness. Some things I have understood, many things I have not, and the latter has become the reason for what I do now. For surely it is a fool who continues to pursue a pastime which he knows to be unsafe, blasphemous even.

Until only recently, I now realize, I had been untrue to myself. I pretended to have no conception of the dire consequences of my actions; not only to myself but also to my fellow men. However, a singularly ghastly event in my recent past has shown me what I did not wish to see and made it clear to me that I had no right to engage in God's domain.

The events I have seen, instigated blindly in my overwhelming ignorance and arrogance, shall go with me to my grave. The means with which I affected my experiments I have utterly and completely eradicated. I am determined that my acts of godlessness, which I perpetrated due to the inadequacies of my own character, shall not be the cause of any other man losing his soul to the demons of science.

Now I put my faith in the Lord God and pray that He will right the wrongs I have committed, for they are legion and they are sins most deadly. With the humility of a repentant sinner I beg forgiveness for the lives I have ruined. With my infernal meddling in the affairs of God, I have inadvertently destroyed not only innocent human lives but — I am certain of this — even history itself. I pray that this confession and the measures I have taken to right the wrongs which I, in my monumental arrogance, committed in the name of the false god, science, will be enough to save my own soul when my time comes.

If this paper is found and read in some distant future, know this, my dear reader: you will not understand, but not understanding is far better than the alternative that I almost brought about. So, despite not knowing who I am, I beg a favor of you, kind sir, gentle lady: pray for my soul. Pray to God Almighty that I may be forgiven for what I have done. Pray that the Lord may have mercy on me, and intervene to turn back the clock and eradicate my deeds.

For the briefest of moments Professor David Dyson's hand trembled. It was an extremely strange feeling, as if someone just walked over his grave. After a second, though, the feeling passed and Dyson had no idea why he had felt such a sensation. Shaking his head a little to clear it of such strange thoughts, Dyson turned his attention to the waiting student.

"Well, Jana," he said with a smile, "it looks like you've stumped me on this one!"

Jana looked pleased with herself. It wasn't very often that a student found something Professor Dyson was not able to explain.

"You really have no idea, Professor?" she asked, rather surprised.

"Well, I can tell you it appears to be an original nineteenth-century handwritten document, and it certainly doesn't belong in a box of requisition orders for pens and ink," he replied with a kindly smile. "Other than that I know just as much about this as you do!"

— «» —

In due course the original yellowed piece of paper was registered under a long and complicated research filename and consigned to the historical archives, and nobody took the trouble to read this particular sheet again.

If you enjoyed this read

Please leave a review on Amazon, Facebook, Good Reads or Instagram.

It takes less than five minutes and it really does make a difference.

If you're not sure how to leave a review on Amazon:

1. *Go to amazon.com.*

2. *Type in Yesterday's Savior by Keith Bliss and when you see it, click on it.*

3. *Scroll down to Customer Reviews. Nearby you'll see a box labeled Write a Review. Click it.*

4. *Now, if you've never written a review before on Amazon, they might ask you to create a name for yourself.*

5. *Reviews can be as simple as, "Loved the book! Can't wait for the Next!" (Please don't give the story away.)*

And that's it!

Brian Hades, publisher

About the Author

After emigrating from England to Australia, Keith lived there for five years as a child before his family moved back to England. He received a bachelor's degree in German from Leicester University and moved to Germany in 1983 where he worked as a self-employed translator for over 20 years before becoming a lecturer at the University of Siegen in 2005. From there he received a master's degree in English literature and is currently working on a Ph.D. about the effects of Darwinism on early science fiction between 1818 and 1918. He is still teaching English at the University of Siegen, and claims it is the "best job in the world".